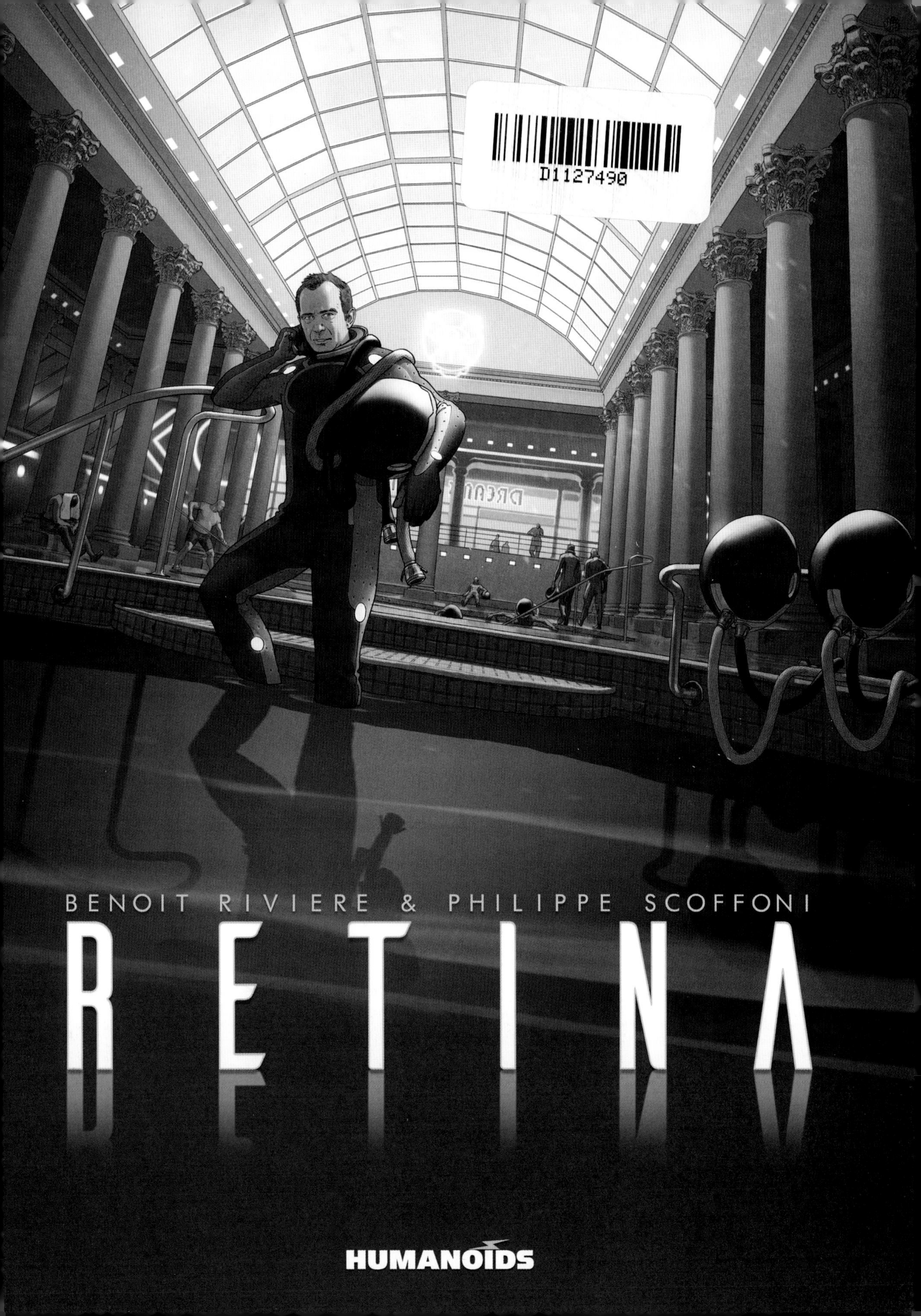
BENOIT RIVIERE & PHILIPPE SCOFFONI
RETINA
HUMANOIDS

BENOÎT RIVIÈRE
Writer

PHILIPPE SCOFFONI
Artist

•

MARK BENCE
Translator

•

ROB LEVIN
US Edition Editor

AMANDA LUCIDO
Assistant Editor

ÉLISABETH HAROCHE
Original Edition Editor

JERRY FRISSEN
Senior Art Director

FABRICE GIGER
Publisher

Rights and Licensing - licensing@humanoids.com
Press and Social Media - pr@humanoids.com

RETINA. This title is a publication of Humanoids, Inc. 8033 Sunset Blvd. #628, Los Angeles, CA 90046.

Library of Congress Control Number: 2019914903

Originally published by Delcourt under the title *Milo* (2008-2011).

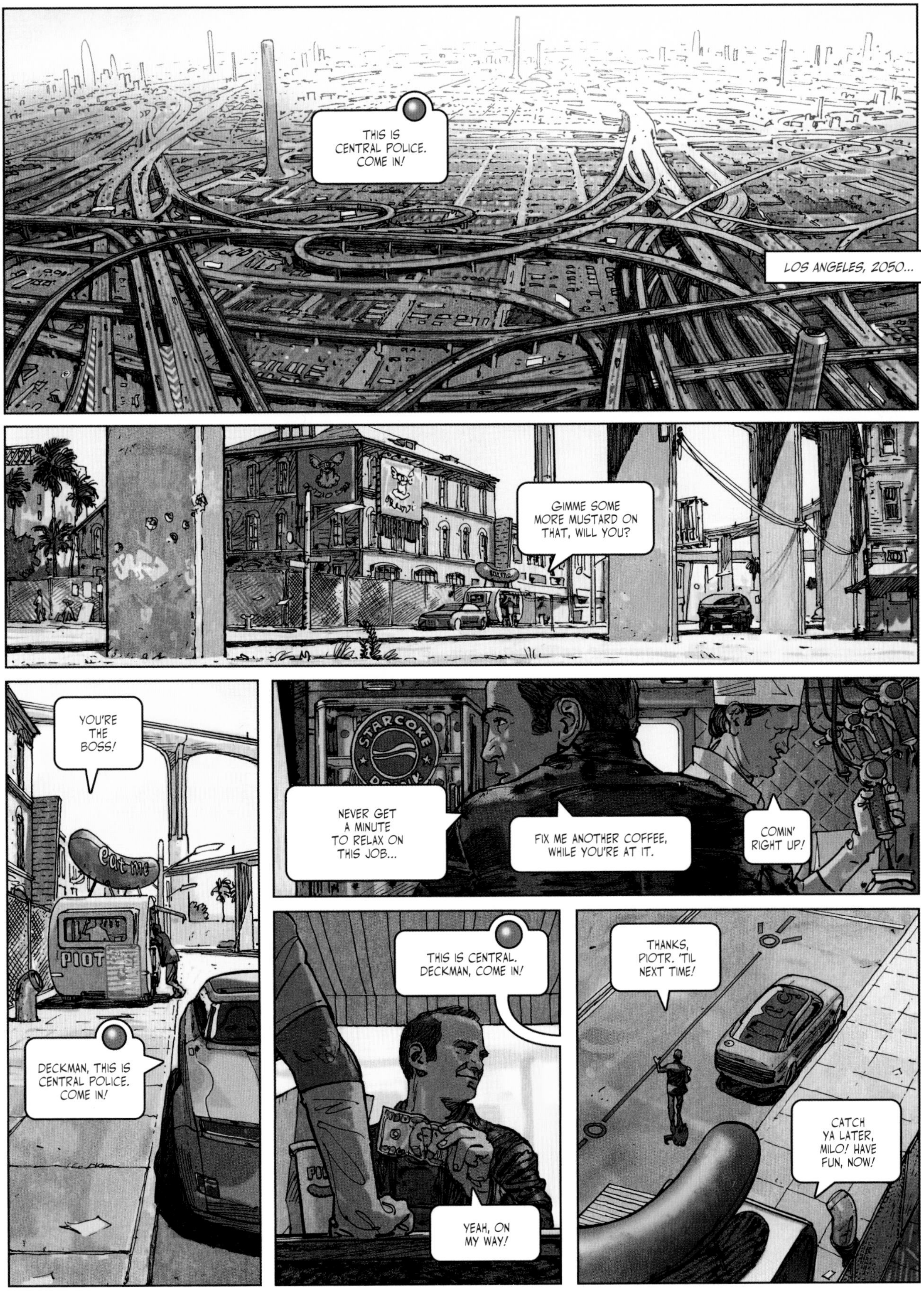
THIS IS CENTRAL POLICE. COME IN!
LOS ANGELES, 2050...
GIMME SOME MORE MUSTARD ON THAT, WILL YOU?
YOU'RE THE BOSS!
DECKMAN, THIS IS CENTRAL POLICE. COME IN!
NEVER GET A MINUTE TO RELAX ON THIS JOB...
FIX ME ANOTHER COFFEE, WHILE YOU'RE AT IT.
COMIN' RIGHT UP!
THIS IS CENTRAL. DECKMAN, COME IN!
YEAH, ON MY WAY!
THANKS, PIOTR. 'TIL NEXT TIME!
CATCH YA LATER, MILO! HAVE FUN, NOW!

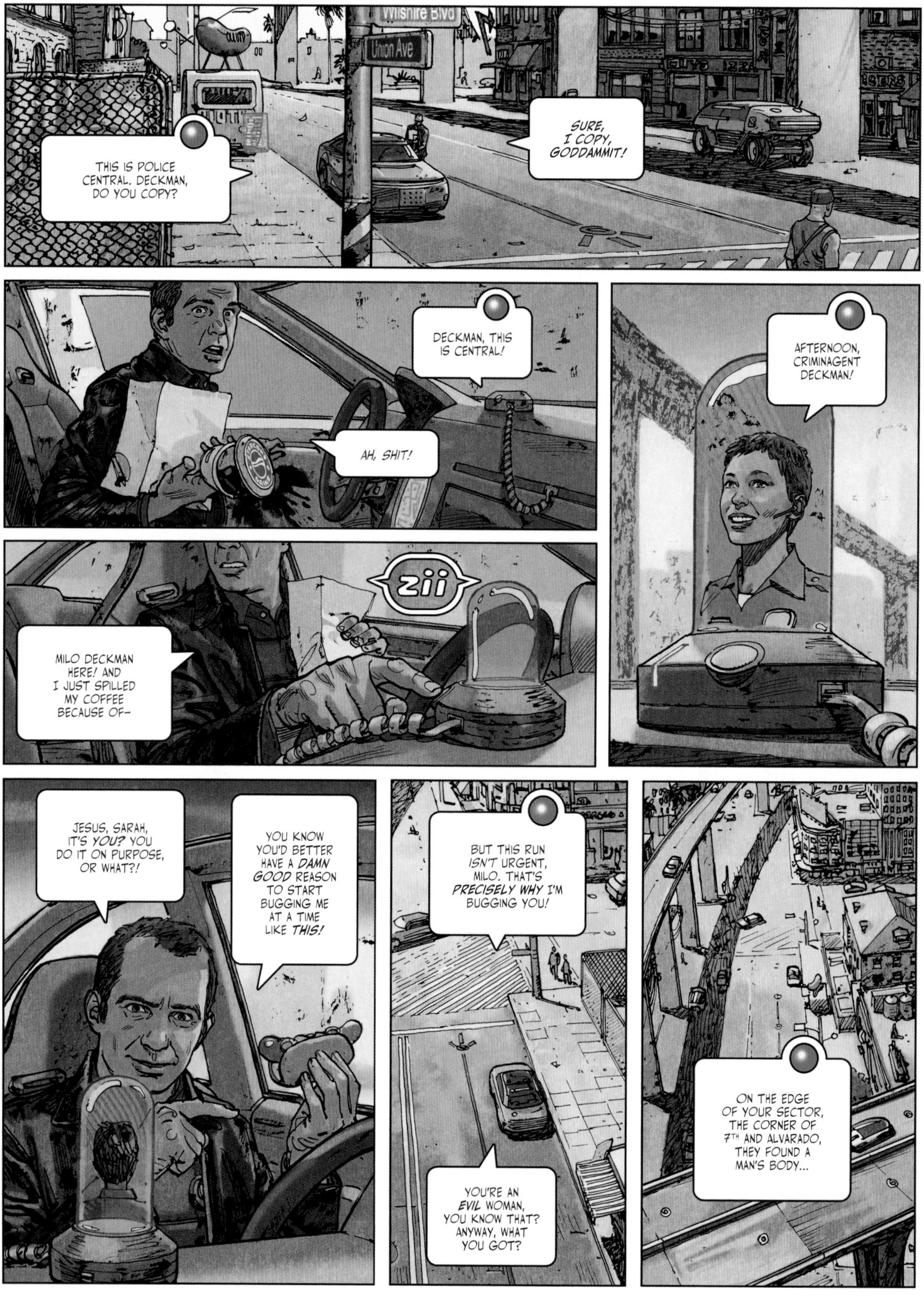
Wilshire Blvd
Union Ave
THIS IS POLICE CENTRAL. DECKMAN, DO YOU COPY?
SURE, I COPY, GODDAMMIT!
DECKMAN, THIS IS CENTRAL!
AH, SHIT!
AFTERNOON, CRIMINAGENT DECKMAN!
zii
MILO DECKMAN HERE! AND I JUST SPILLED MY COFFEE BECAUSE OF–
JESUS, SARAH, IT'S *YOU?* YOU DO IT ON PURPOSE, OR WHAT?!
YOU KNOW YOU'D BETTER HAVE A *DAMN GOOD* REASON TO START BUGGING ME AT A TIME LIKE *THIS!*
BUT THIS RUN *ISN'T* URGENT, MILO. THAT'S *PRECISELY WHY* I'M BUGGING YOU!
YOU'RE AN *EVIL* WOMAN, YOU KNOW THAT? ANYWAY, WHAT YOU GOT?
ON THE EDGE OF YOUR SECTOR, THE CORNER OF 7TH AND ALVARADO, THEY FOUND A MAN'S BODY...

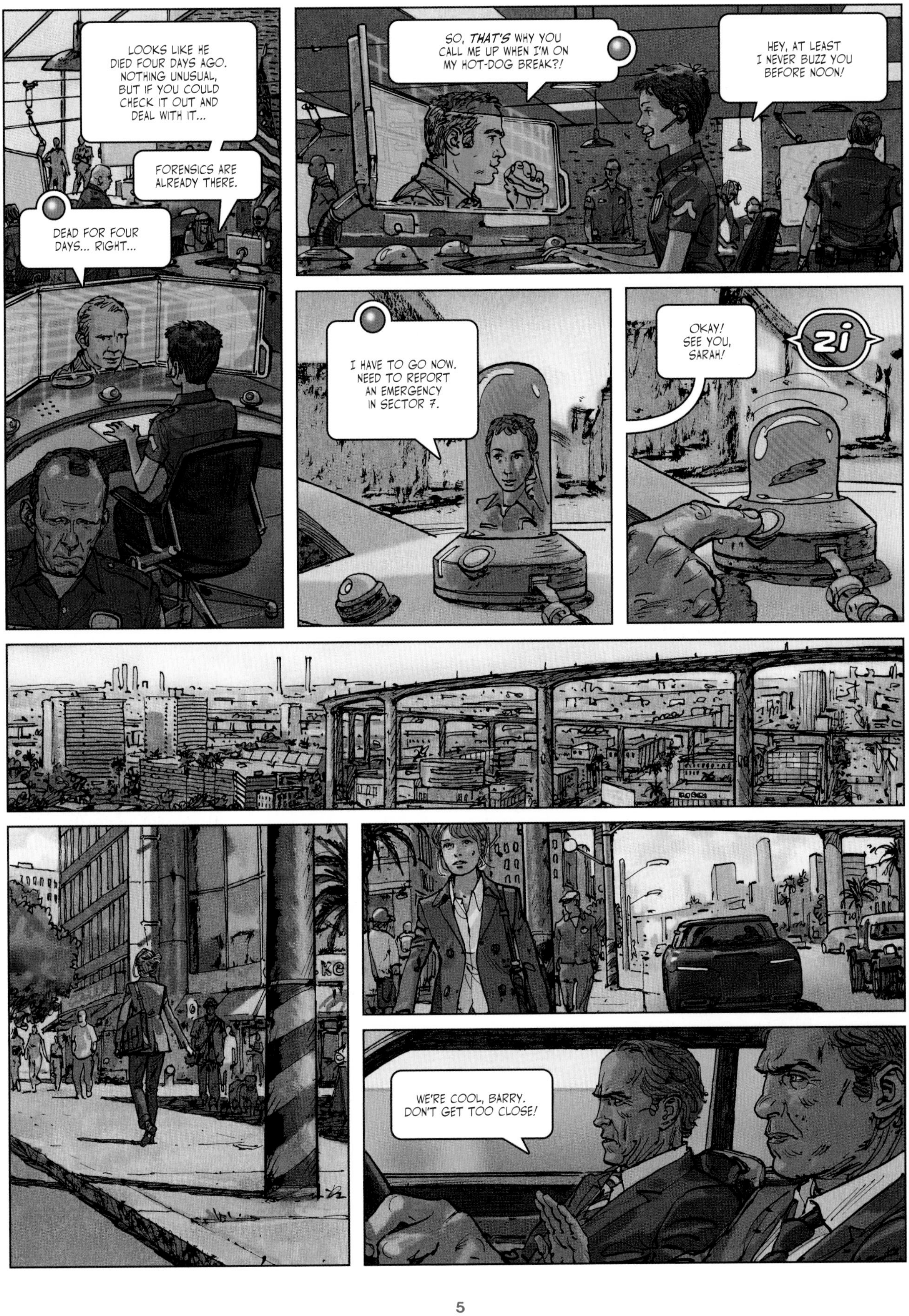
LOOKS LIKE HE DIED FOUR DAYS AGO. NOTHING UNUSUAL, BUT IF YOU COULD CHECK IT OUT AND DEAL WITH IT...
FORENSICS ARE ALREADY THERE.
DEAD FOR FOUR DAYS... RIGHT...
SO, THAT'S WHY YOU CALL ME UP WHEN I'M ON MY HOT-DOG BREAK?!
HEY, AT LEAST I NEVER BUZZ YOU BEFORE NOON!
I HAVE TO GO NOW. NEED TO REPORT AN EMERGENCY IN SECTOR 7.
OKAY! SEE YOU, SARAH!
ZI
WE'RE COOL, BARRY. DON'T GET TOO CLOSE!

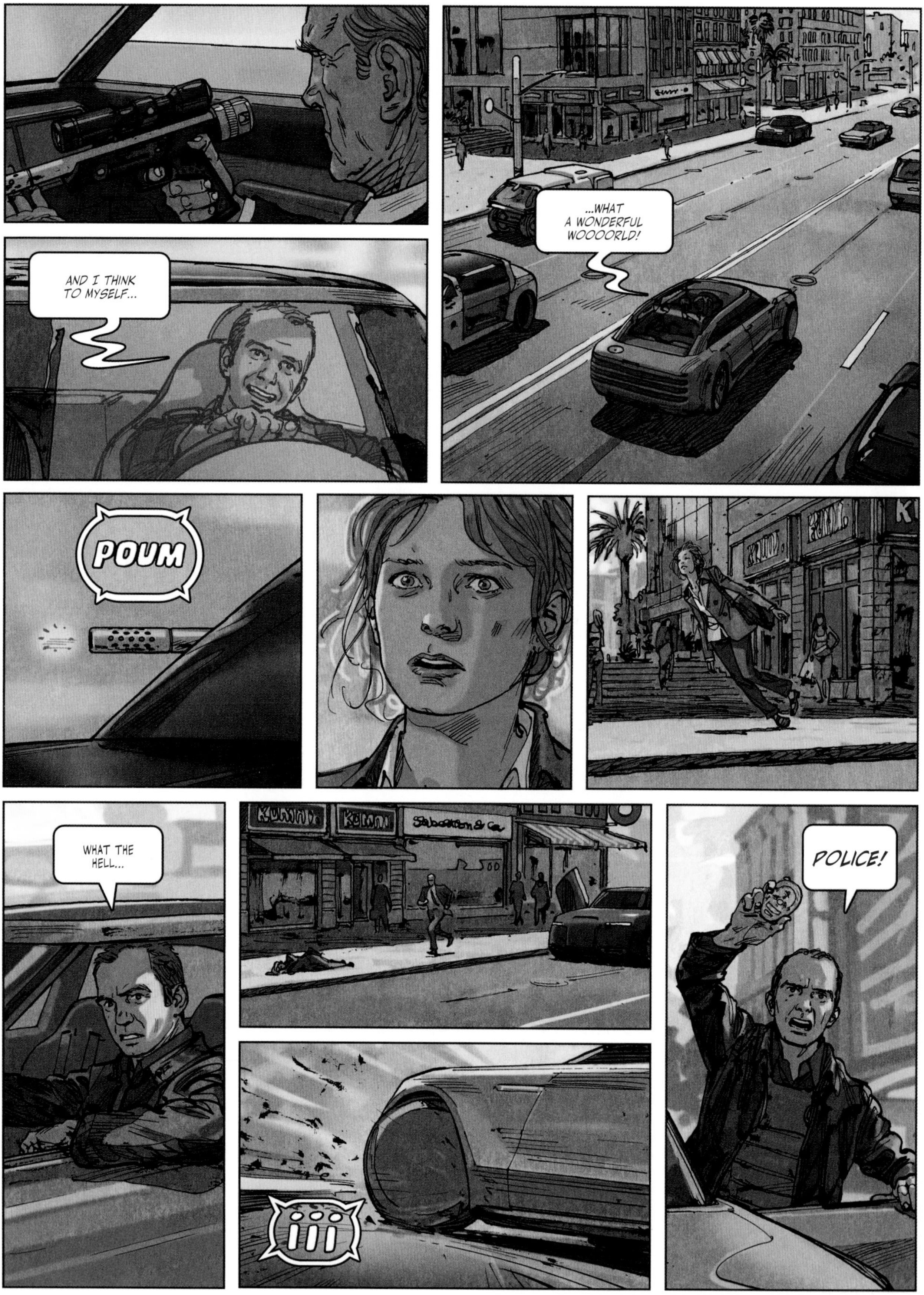
AND I THINK TO MYSELF...
...WHAT A WONDERFUL WOOOORLD!
POUM
WHAT THE HELL...
POLICE!

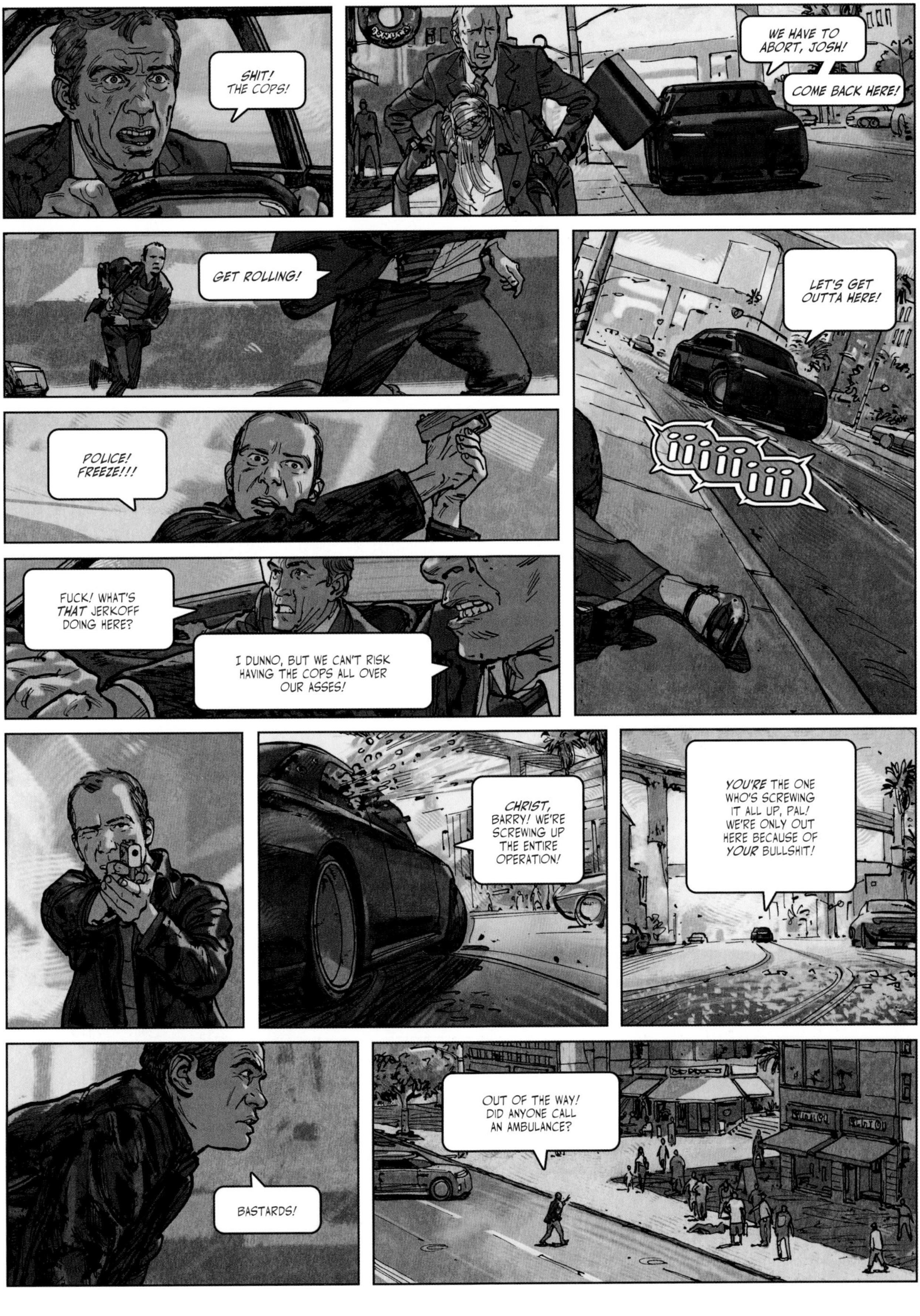
SHIT! THE COPS!
WE HAVE TO ABORT, JOSH!
COME BACK HERE!
GET ROLLING!
LET'S GET OUTTA HERE!
iiiiiii
POLICE! FREEZE!!!
FUCK! WHAT'S THAT JERKOFF DOING HERE?
I DUNNO, BUT WE CAN'T RISK HAVING THE COPS ALL OVER OUR ASSES!
CHRIST, BARRY! WE'RE SCREWING UP THE ENTIRE OPERATION!
YOU'RE THE ONE WHO'S SCREWING IT ALL UP, PAL! WE'RE ONLY OUT HERE BECAUSE OF YOUR BULLSHIT!
BASTARDS!
OUT OF THE WAY! DID ANYONE CALL AN AMBULANCE?

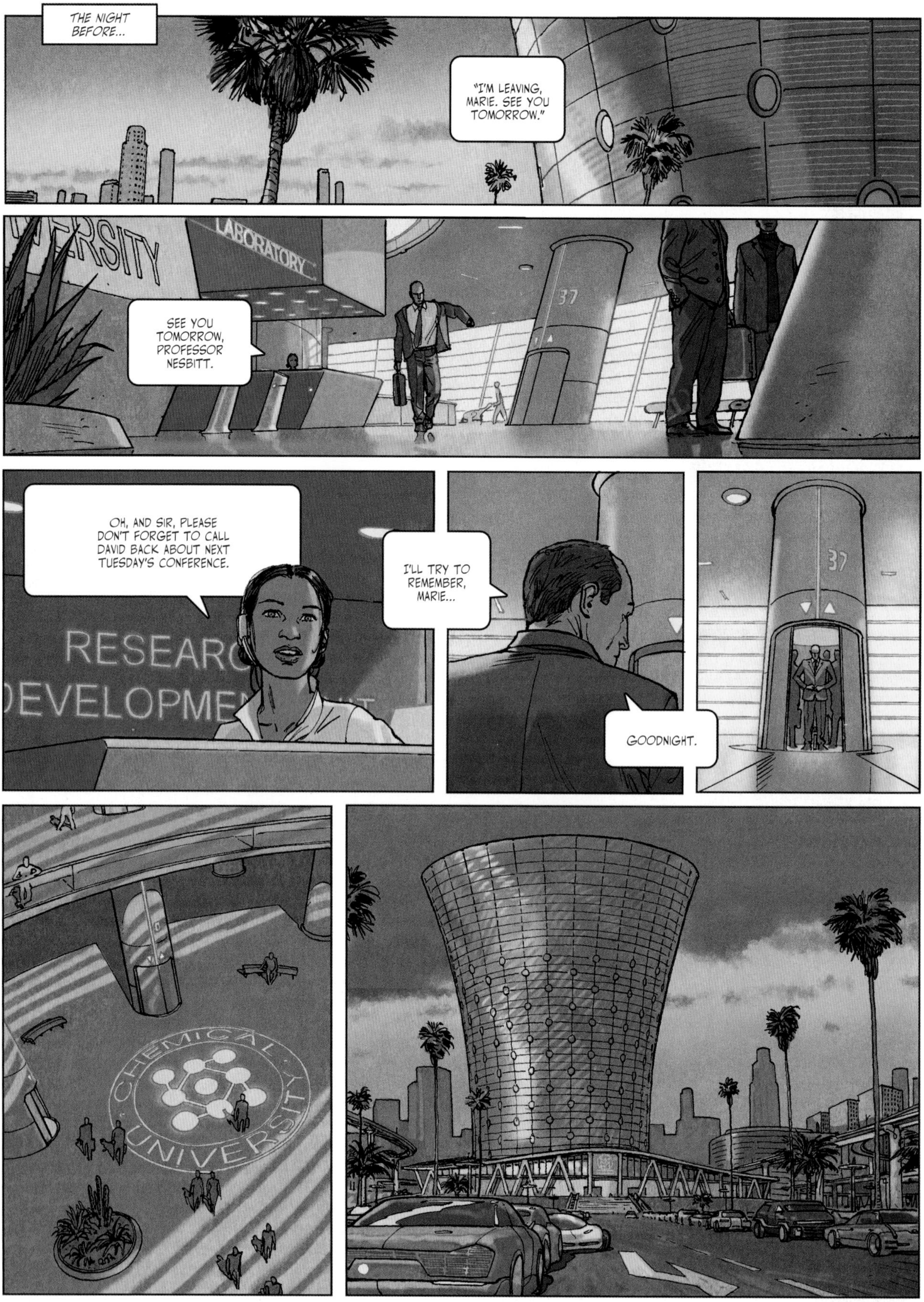
THE NIGHT BEFORE...
"I'M LEAVING, MARIE. SEE YOU TOMORROW."
LABORATORY
SEE YOU TOMORROW, PROFESSOR NESBITT.
OH, AND SIR, PLEASE DON'T FORGET TO CALL DAVID BACK ABOUT NEXT TUESDAY'S CONFERENCE.
I'LL TRY TO REMEMBER, MARIE...
GOODNIGHT.
CHEMICAL UNIVERSITY

BIP

BIP BIP

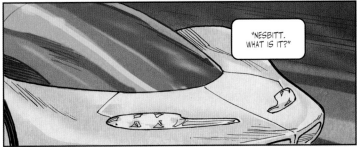

"NESBITT. WHAT IS IT?"

THERE'S BEEN A CHANGE OF PLAN.

THE MEETING WON'T BE HAPPENING ON THE DATE WE SET.

WHAT DO YOU *MEAN* "THE MEETING WON'T BE HAPPENING"?!

ARE YOU BEING *FUNNY?*

MR. NESBITT, DO YOU REALLY BELIEVE WE'RE IN THE MOOD TO MAKE *JOKES?*

THE SECURITY ARRANGEMENTS ARE INADEQUATE. WE'LL BE IN TOUCH LATER.

BUT YOU CAN'T *DO* THIS TO ME! I JUST CAN'T *WAIT* ANY—

HELLO? HELLO?!

"FUCKING HELL*!!!*"

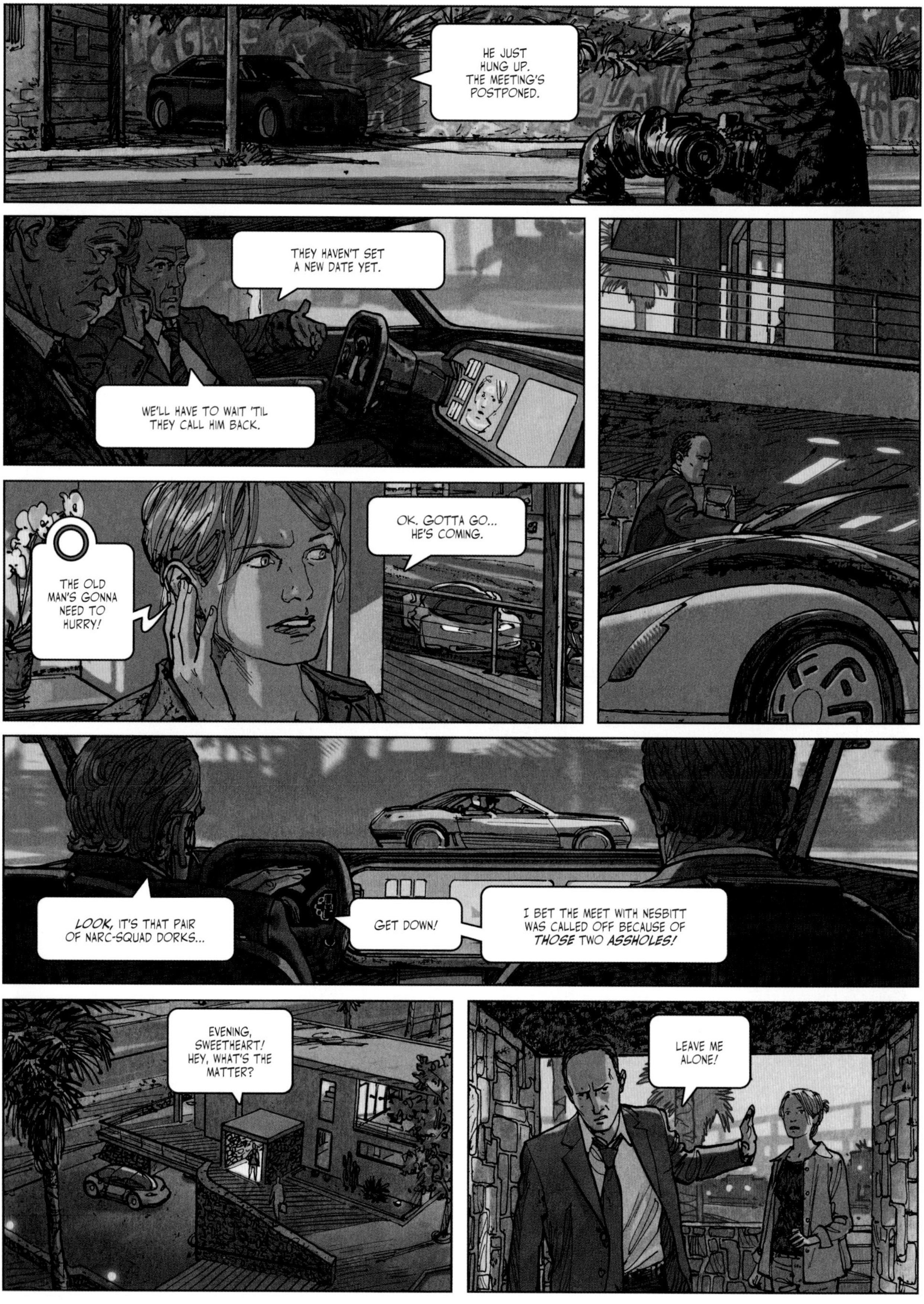
HE JUST HUNG UP. THE MEETING'S POSTPONED.
THEY HAVEN'T SET A NEW DATE YET.
WE'LL HAVE TO WAIT 'TIL THEY CALL HIM BACK.
THE OLD MAN'S GONNA NEED TO HURRY!
OK. GOTTA GO... HE'S COMING.
LOOK, IT'S THAT PAIR OF NARC-SQUAD DORKS...
GET DOWN!
I BET THE MEET WITH NESBITT WAS CALLED OFF BECAUSE OF *THOSE* TWO *ASSHOLES!*
EVENING, SWEETHEART! HEY, WHAT'S THE MATTER?
LEAVE ME ALONE!

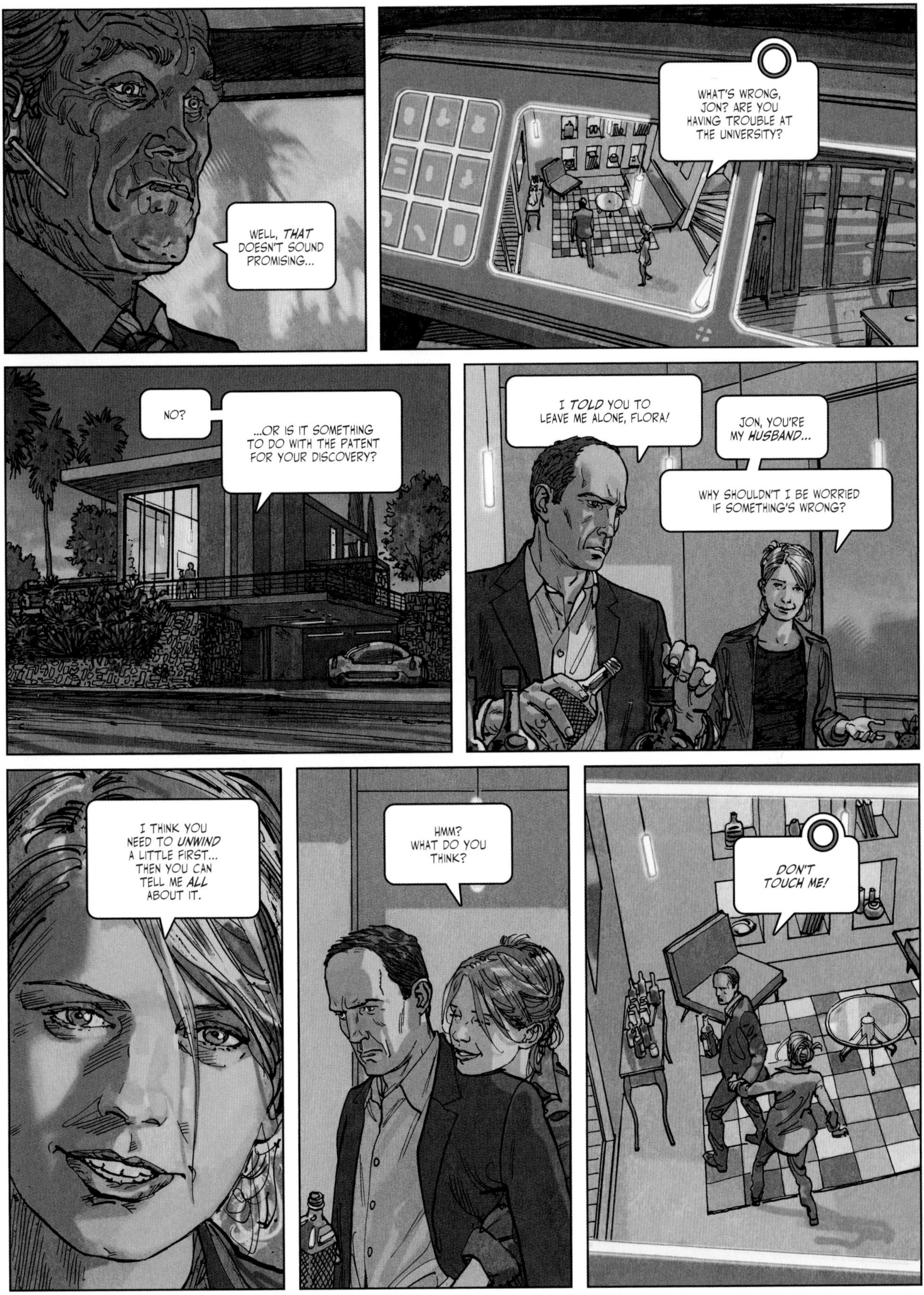
WELL, *THAT* DOESN'T SOUND PROMISING...
WHAT'S WRONG, JON? ARE YOU HAVING TROUBLE AT THE UNIVERSITY?
NO?
...OR IS IT SOMETHING TO DO WITH THE PATENT FOR YOUR DISCOVERY?
I *TOLD* YOU TO LEAVE ME ALONE, FLORA!
JON, YOU'RE MY *HUSBAND*...
WHY SHOULDN'T I BE WORRIED IF SOMETHING'S WRONG?
I THINK YOU NEED TO *UNWIND* A LITTLE FIRST... THEN YOU CAN TELL ME *ALL* ABOUT IT.
HMM? WHAT DO YOU THINK?
DON'T TOUCH ME!

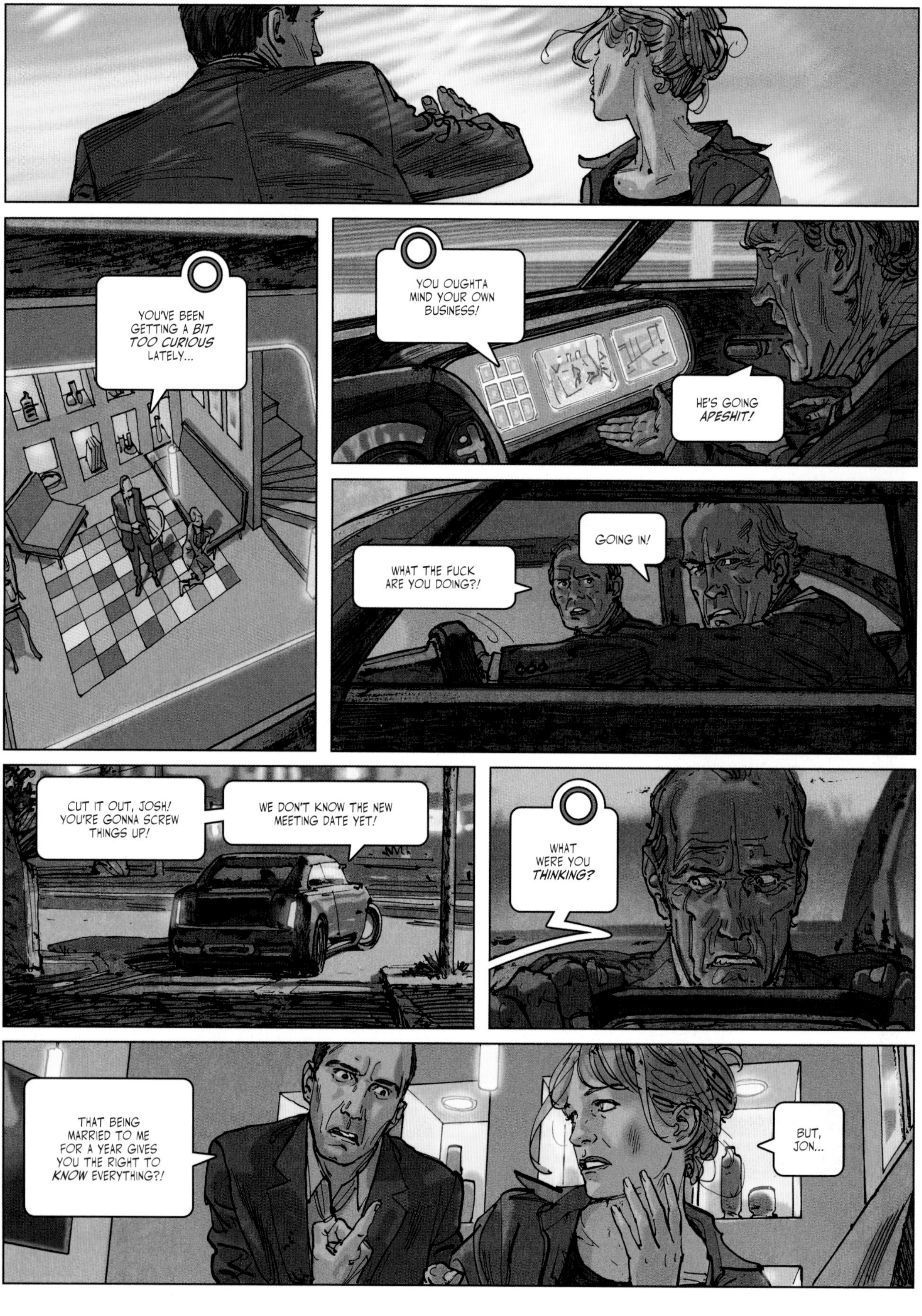

YOU'VE BEEN GETTING A BIT TOO CURIOUS LATELY...
YOU OUGHTA MIND YOUR OWN BUSINESS!
HE'S GOING APESHIT!
GOING IN!
WHAT THE FUCK ARE YOU DOING?!
CUT IT OUT, JOSH! YOU'RE GONNA SCREW THINGS UP!
WE DON'T KNOW THE NEW MEETING DATE YET!
WHAT WERE YOU THINKING?
THAT BEING MARRIED TO ME FOR A YEAR GIVES YOU THE RIGHT TO KNOW EVERYTHING?!
BUT, JON...

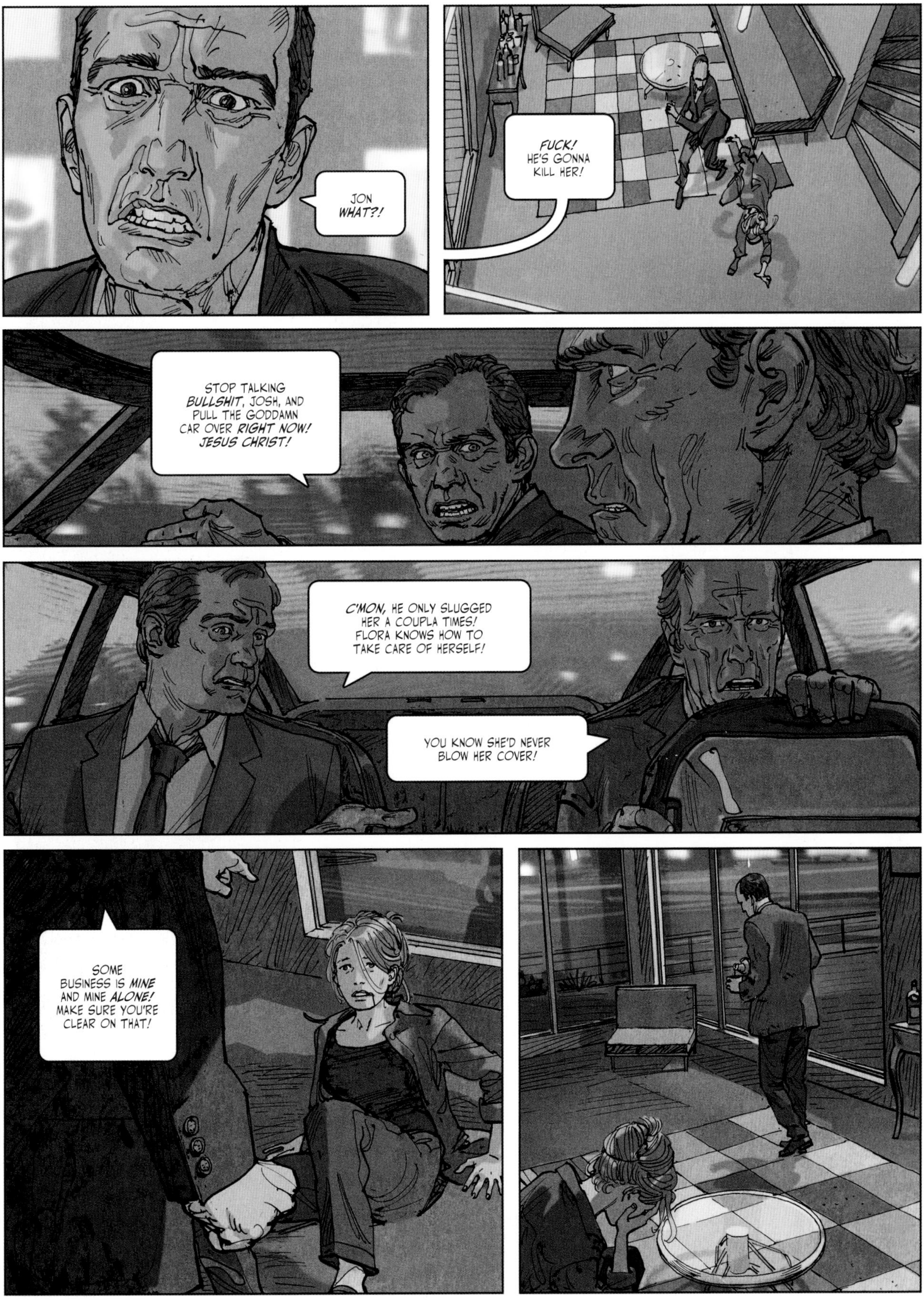
JON WHAT?!
FUCK! HE'S GONNA KILL HER!
STOP TALKING BULLSHIT, JOSH, AND PULL THE GODDAMN CAR OVER RIGHT NOW! JESUS CHRIST!
C'MON, HE ONLY SLUGGED HER A COUPLA TIMES! FLORA KNOWS HOW TO TAKE CARE OF HERSELF!
YOU KNOW SHE'D NEVER BLOW HER COVER!
SOME BUSINESS IS MINE AND MINE ALONE! MAKE SURE YOU'RE CLEAR ON THAT!

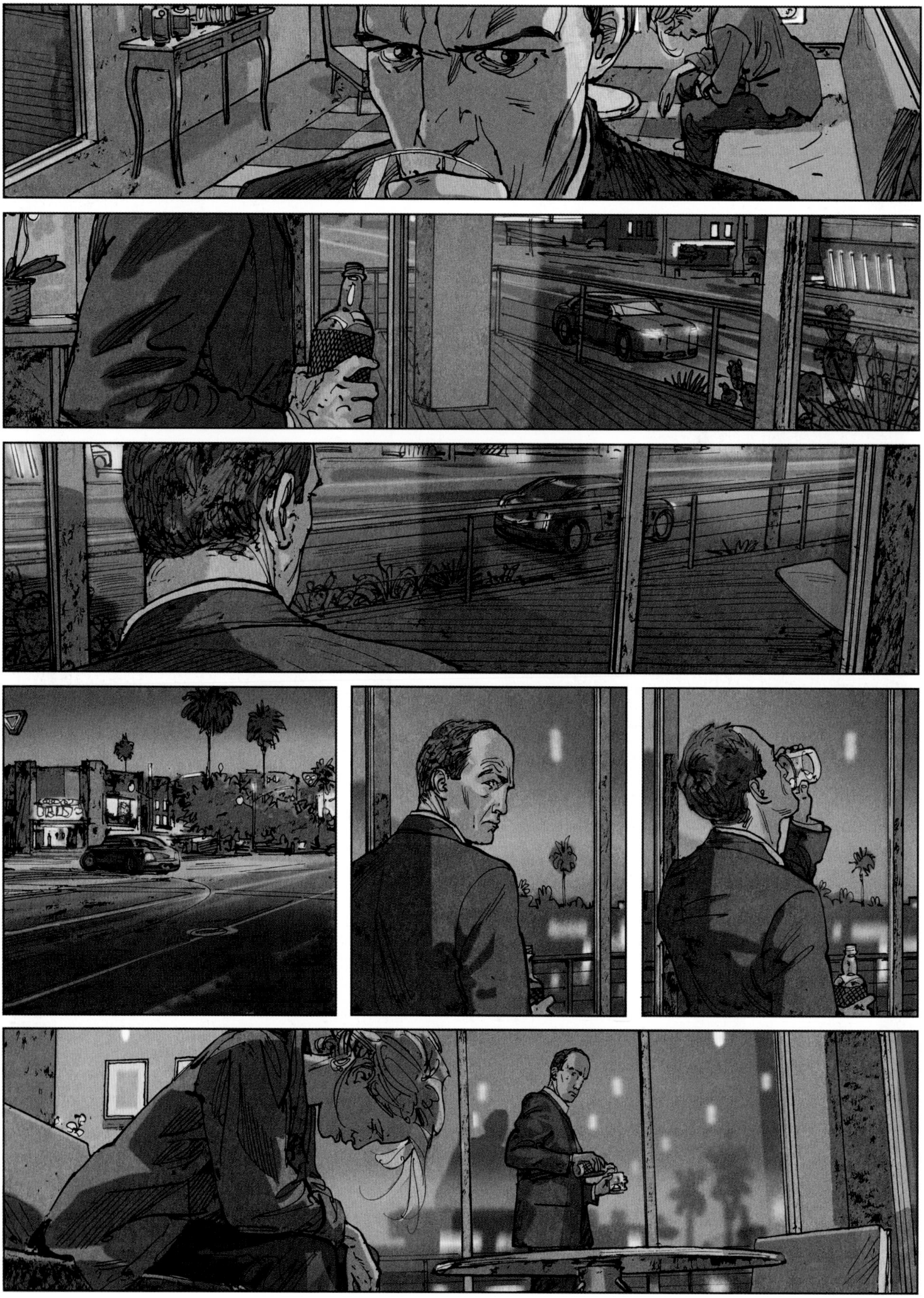

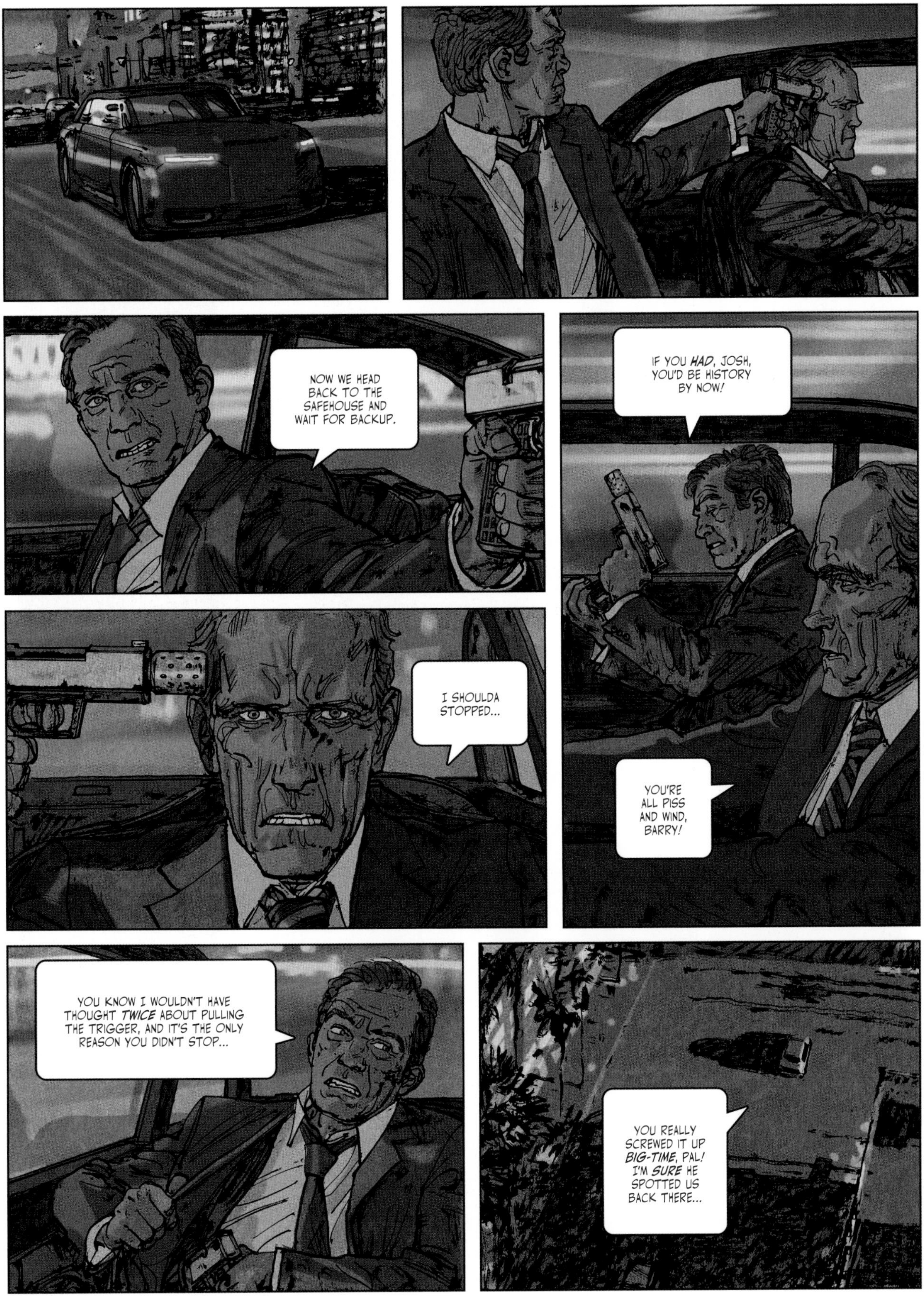
NOW WE HEAD BACK TO THE SAFEHOUSE AND WAIT FOR BACKUP.
IF YOU HAD, JOSH, YOU'D BE HISTORY BY NOW!
I SHOULDA STOPPED...
YOU'RE ALL PISS AND WIND, BARRY!
YOU KNOW I WOULDN'T HAVE THOUGHT TWICE ABOUT PULLING THE TRIGGER, AND IT'S THE ONLY REASON YOU DIDN'T STOP...
YOU REALLY SCREWED IT UP BIG-TIME, PAL! I'M SURE HE SPOTTED US BACK THERE...

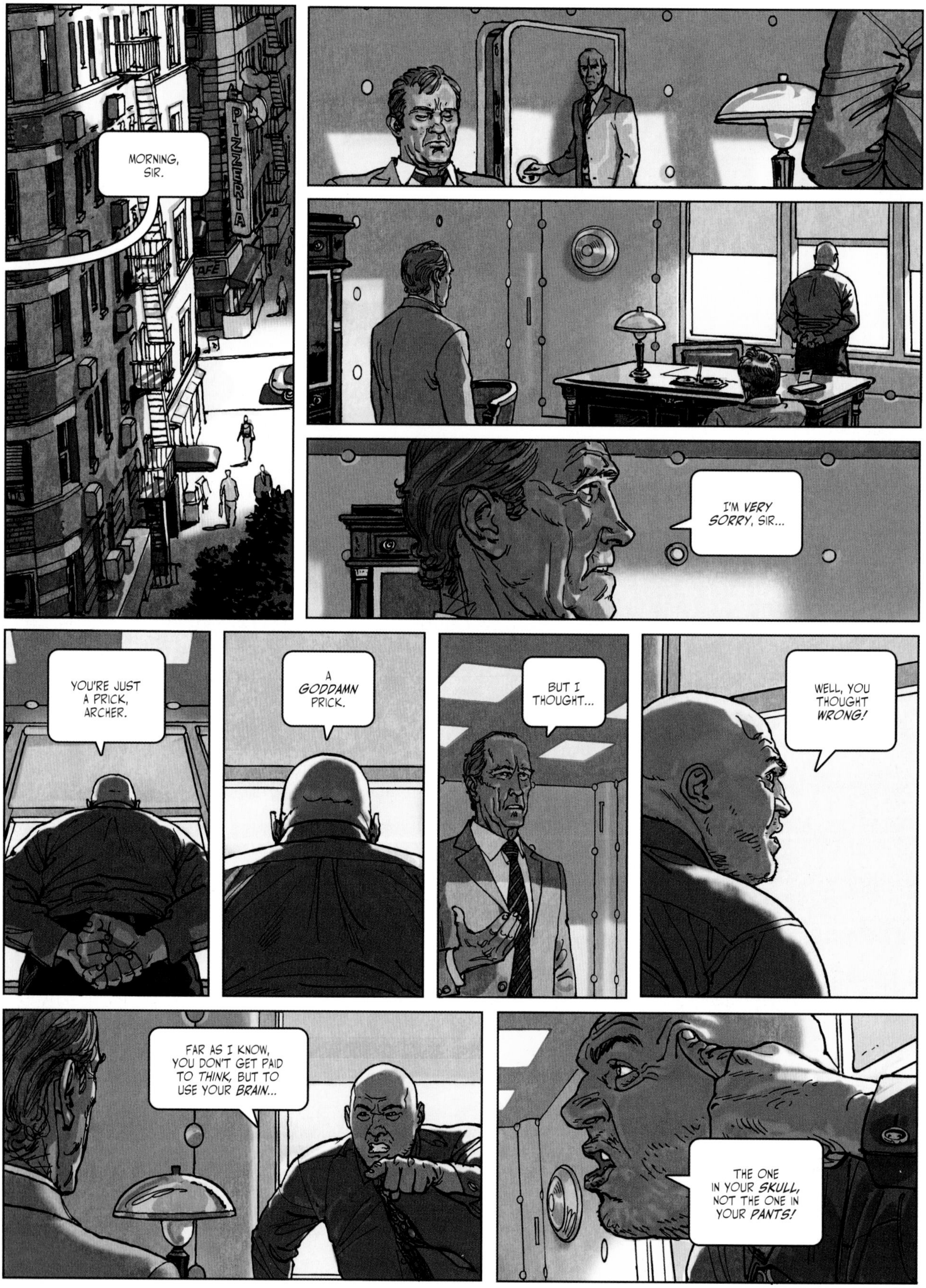
MORNING, SIR.
PIZZERIA
CAFÉ
I'M VERY SORRY, SIR...
YOU'RE JUST A PRICK, ARCHER.
A GODDAMN PRICK.
BUT I THOUGHT...
WELL, YOU THOUGHT WRONG!
FAR AS I KNOW, YOU DON'T GET PAID TO THINK, BUT TO USE YOUR BRAIN...
THE ONE IN YOUR SKULL, NOT THE ONE IN YOUR PANTS!

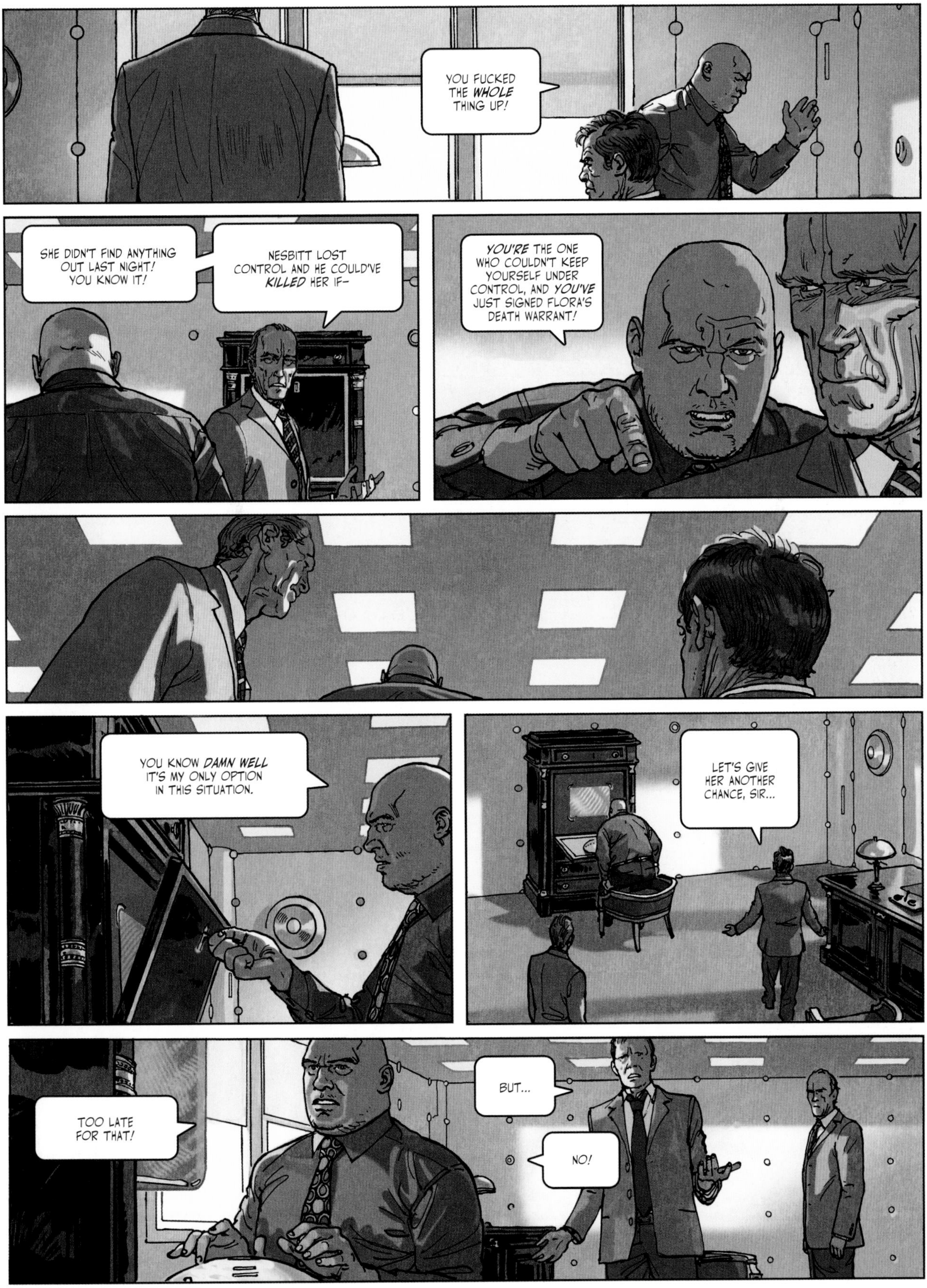
YOU FUCKED THE WHOLE THING UP!
SHE DIDN'T FIND ANYTHING OUT LAST NIGHT! YOU KNOW IT!
NESBITT LOST CONTROL AND HE COULD'VE KILLED HER IF–
YOU'RE THE ONE WHO COULDN'T KEEP YOURSELF UNDER CONTROL, AND YOU'VE JUST SIGNED FLORA'S DEATH WARRANT!
YOU KNOW DAMN WELL IT'S MY ONLY OPTION IN THIS SITUATION.
LET'S GIVE HER ANOTHER CHANCE, SIR...
TOO LATE FOR THAT!
BUT...
NO!

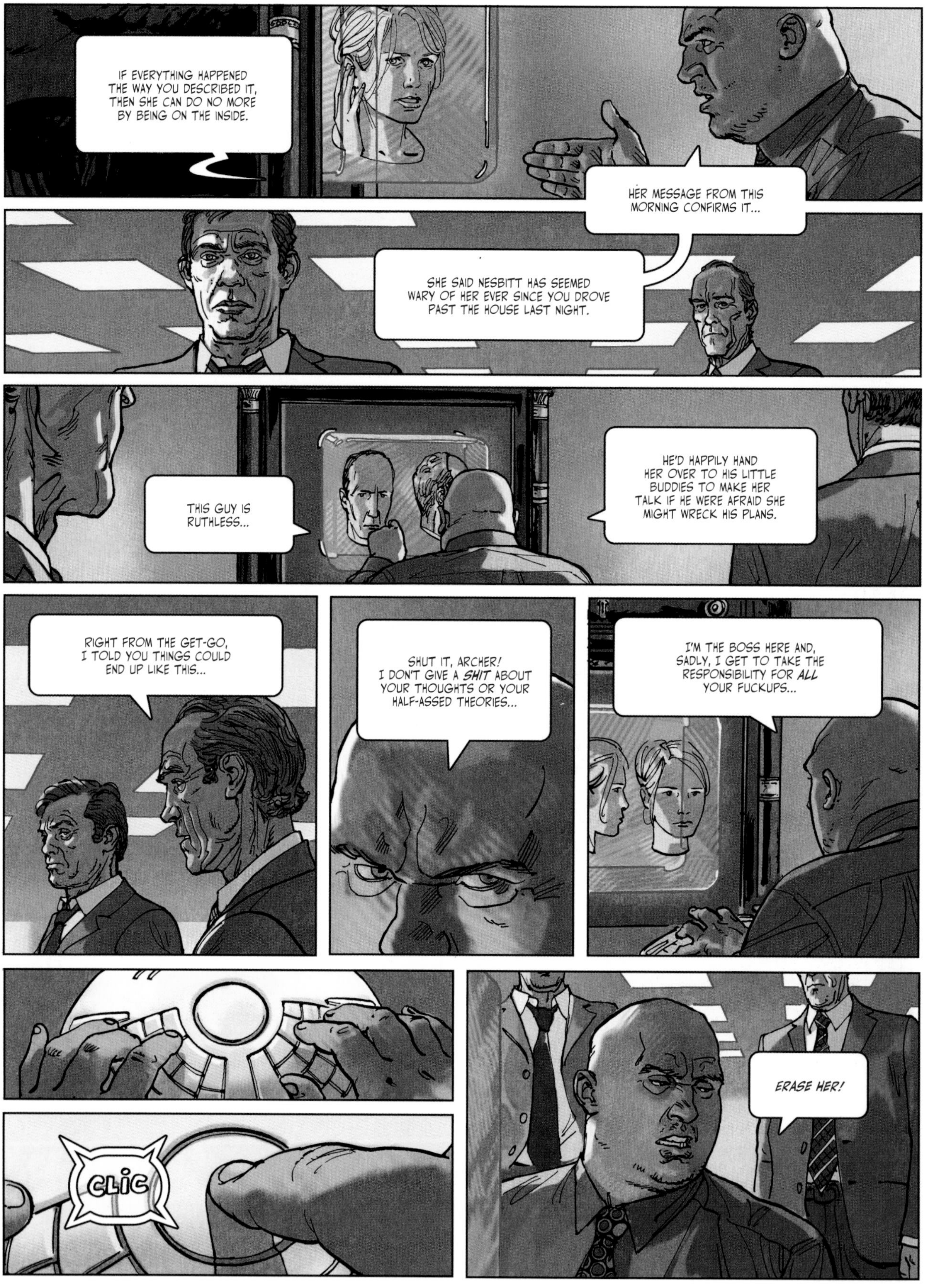

IF EVERYTHING HAPPENED THE WAY YOU DESCRIBED IT, THEN SHE CAN DO NO MORE BY BEING ON THE INSIDE.
HER MESSAGE FROM THIS MORNING CONFIRMS IT...
SHE SAID NESBITT HAS SEEMED WARY OF HER EVER SINCE YOU DROVE PAST THE HOUSE LAST NIGHT.
THIS GUY IS RUTHLESS...
HE'D HAPPILY HAND HER OVER TO HIS LITTLE BUDDIES TO MAKE HER TALK IF HE WERE AFRAID SHE MIGHT WRECK HIS PLANS.
RIGHT FROM THE GET-GO, I TOLD YOU THINGS COULD END UP LIKE THIS...
SHUT IT, ARCHER! I DON'T GIVE A *SHIT* ABOUT YOUR THOUGHTS OR YOUR HALF-ASSED THEORIES...
I'M THE BOSS HERE AND, SADLY, I GET TO TAKE THE RESPONSIBILITY FOR *ALL* YOUR FUCKUPS...
CLIC
ERASE HER!

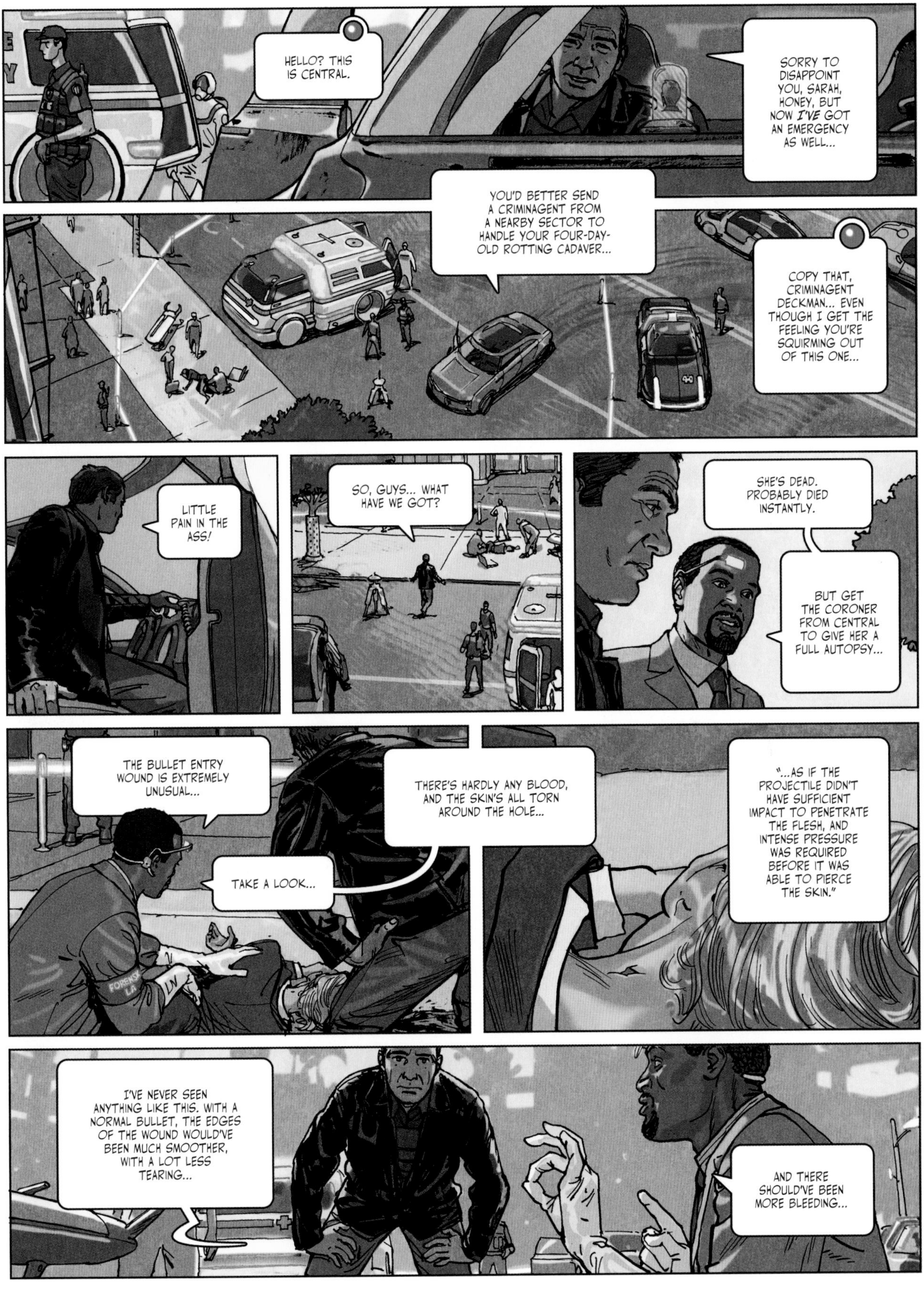
HELLO? THIS IS CENTRAL.
SORRY TO DISAPPOINT YOU, SARAH, HONEY, BUT NOW *I'VE* GOT AN EMERGENCY AS WELL...
YOU'D BETTER SEND A CRIMINAGENT FROM A NEARBY SECTOR TO HANDLE YOUR FOUR-DAY-OLD ROTTING CADAVER...
COPY THAT, CRIMINAGENT DECKMAN... EVEN THOUGH I GET THE FEELING YOU'RE SQUIRMING OUT OF THIS ONE...
LITTLE PAIN IN THE ASS!
SO, GUYS... WHAT HAVE WE GOT?
SHE'S DEAD. PROBABLY DIED INSTANTLY.
BUT GET THE CORONER FROM CENTRAL TO GIVE HER A FULL AUTOPSY...
THE BULLET ENTRY WOUND IS EXTREMELY UNUSUAL...
TAKE A LOOK...
THERE'S HARDLY ANY BLOOD, AND THE SKIN'S ALL TORN AROUND THE HOLE...
"...AS IF THE PROJECTILE DIDN'T HAVE SUFFICIENT IMPACT TO PENETRATE THE FLESH, AND INTENSE PRESSURE WAS REQUIRED BEFORE IT WAS ABLE TO PIERCE THE SKIN."
I'VE NEVER SEEN ANYTHING LIKE THIS. WITH A NORMAL BULLET, THE EDGES OF THE WOUND WOULD'VE BEEN MUCH SMOOTHER, WITH A LOT LESS TEARING...
AND THERE SHOULD'VE BEEN MORE BLEEDING...

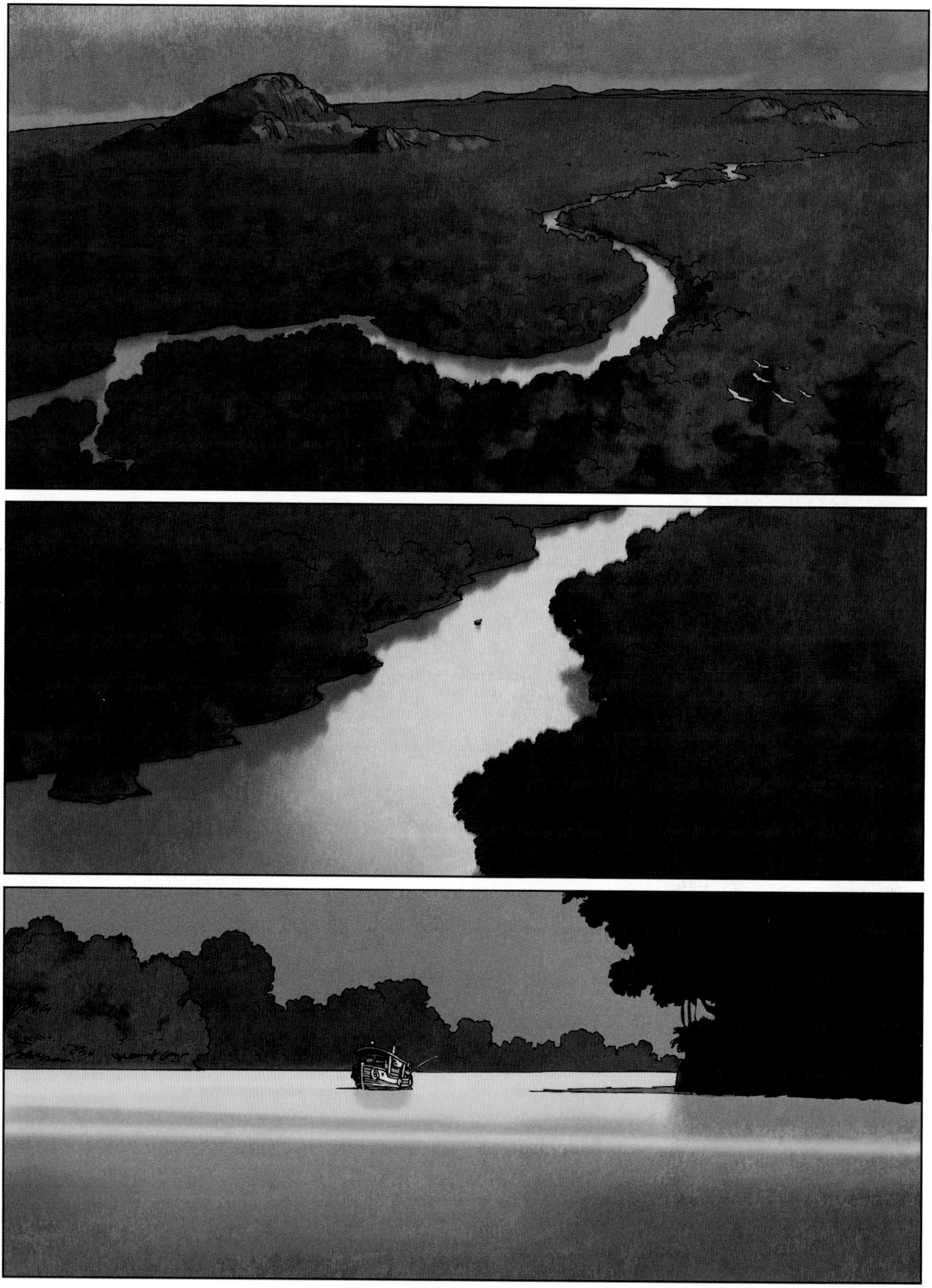

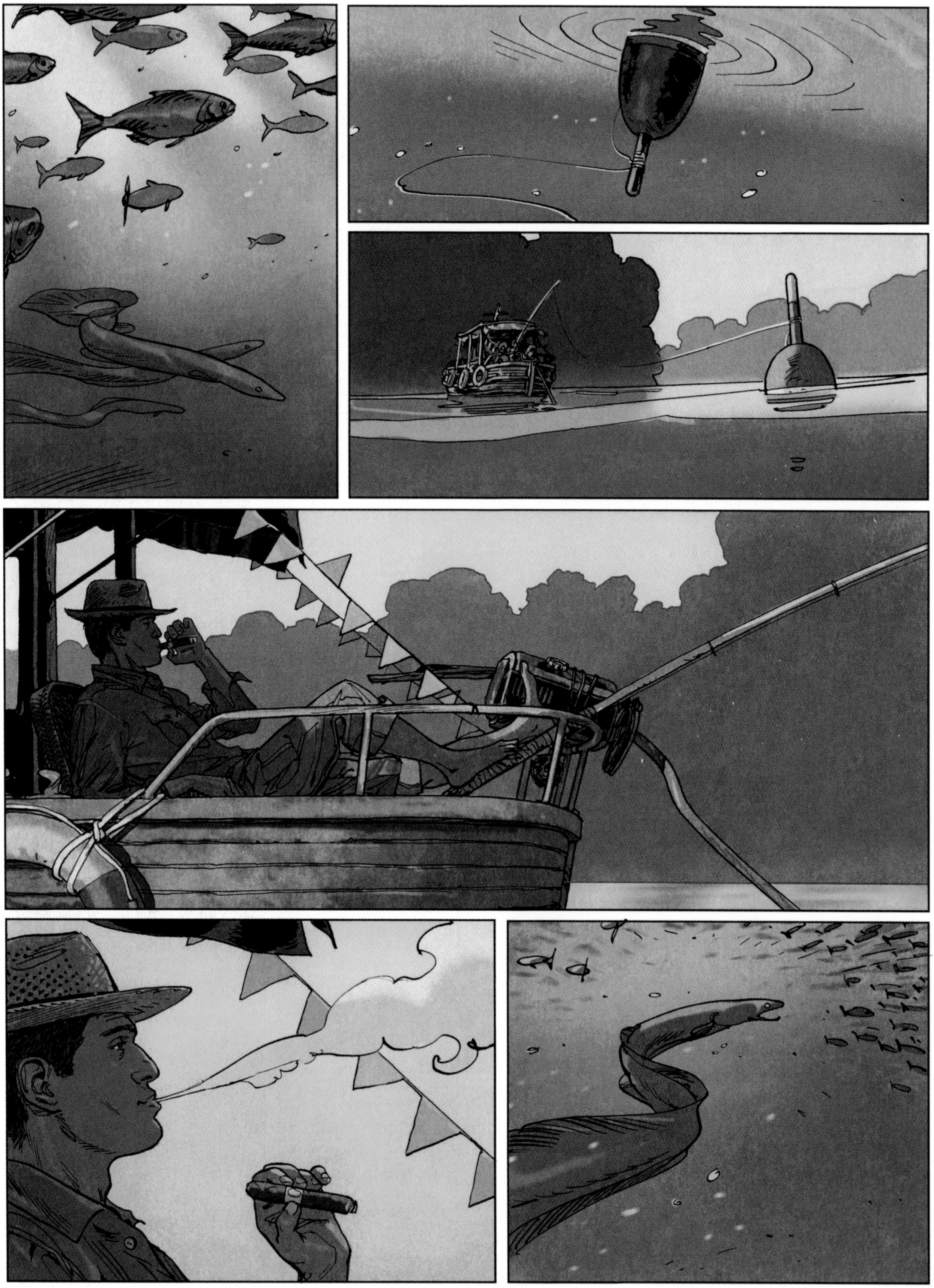

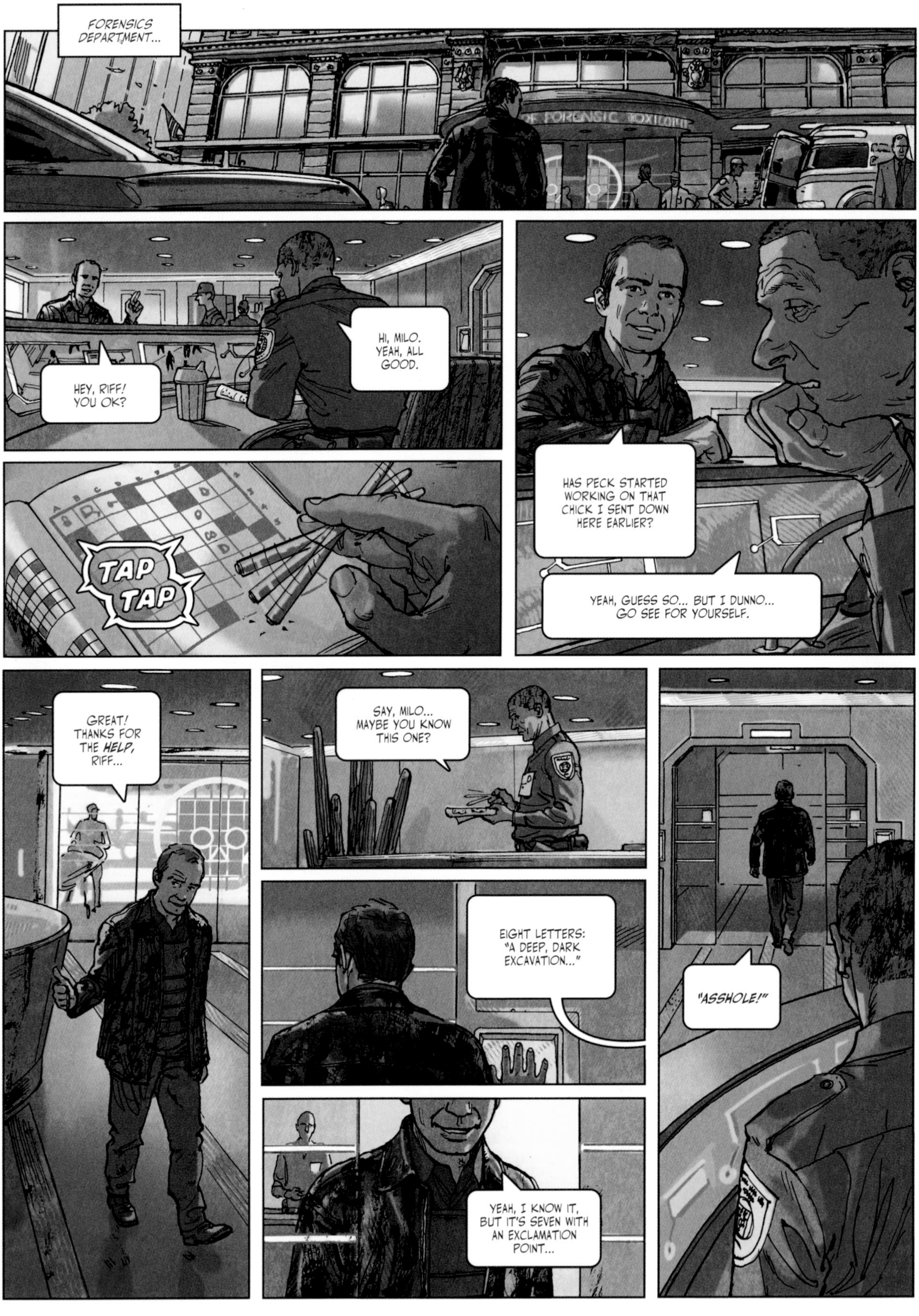
FORENSICS DEPARTMENT...
HEY, RIFF! YOU OK?
HI, MILO. YEAH, ALL GOOD.
HAS PECK STARTED WORKING ON THAT CHICK I SENT DOWN HERE EARLIER?
YEAH, GUESS SO... BUT I DUNNO... GO SEE FOR YOURSELF.
TAP TAP
GREAT! THANKS FOR THE HELP, RIFF...
SAY, MILO... MAYBE YOU KNOW THIS ONE?
EIGHT LETTERS: "A DEEP, DARK EXCAVATION..."
YEAH, I KNOW IT, BUT IT'S SEVEN WITH AN EXCLAMATION POINT...
"ASSHOLE!"

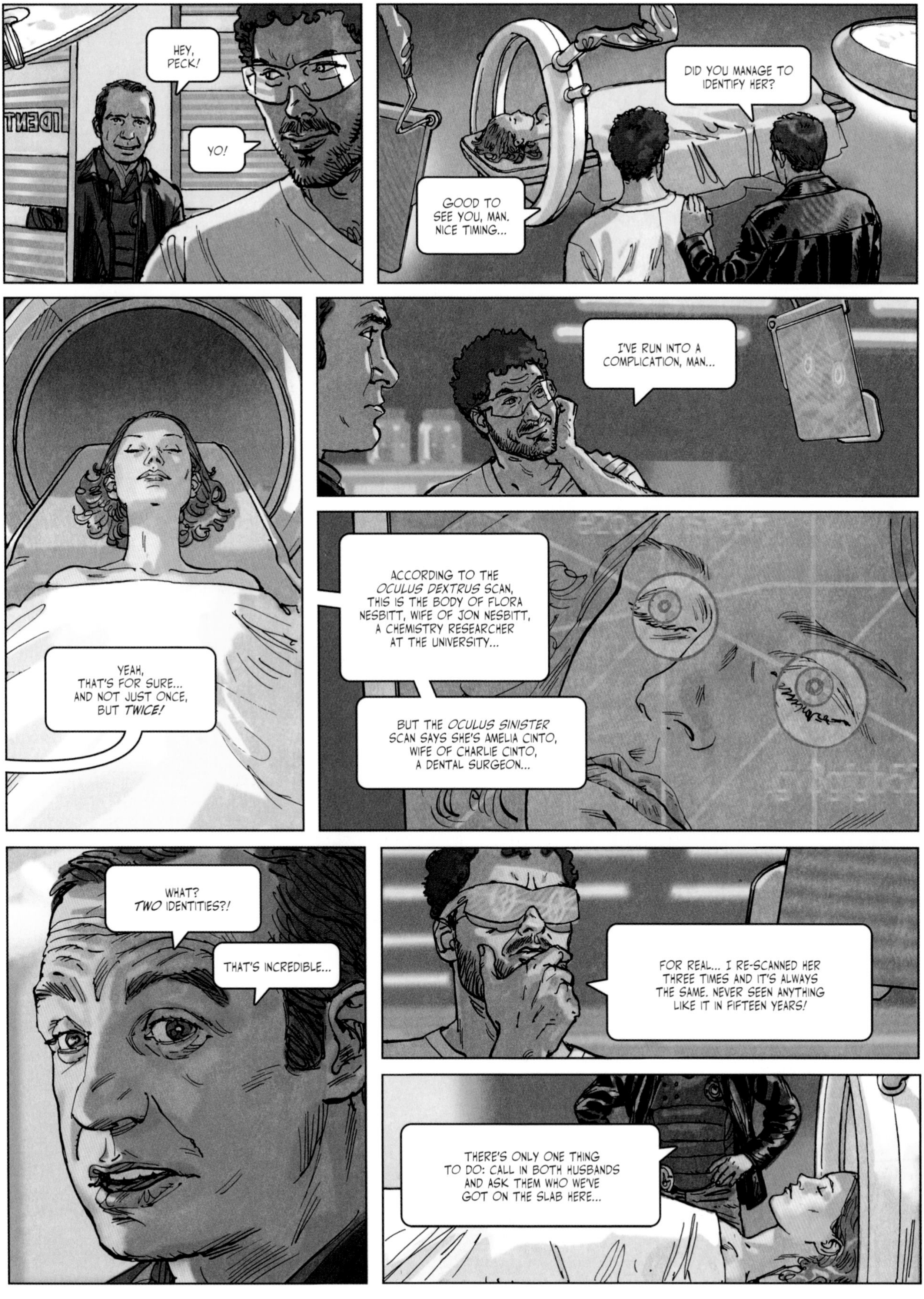
HEY, PECK!
YO!
DID YOU MANAGE TO IDENTIFY HER?
GOOD TO SEE YOU, MAN. NICE TIMING...
I'VE RUN INTO A COMPLICATION, MAN...
YEAH, THAT'S FOR SURE... AND NOT JUST ONCE, BUT *TWICE!*
ACCORDING TO THE *OCULUS DEXTRUS* SCAN, THIS IS THE BODY OF FLORA NESBITT, WIFE OF JON NESBITT, A CHEMISTRY RESEARCHER AT THE UNIVERSITY...
BUT THE *OCULUS SINISTER* SCAN SAYS SHE'S AMELIA CINTO, WIFE OF CHARLIE CINTO, A DENTAL SURGEON...
WHAT? *TWO* IDENTITIES?!
THAT'S INCREDIBLE...
FOR REAL... I RE-SCANNED HER THREE TIMES AND IT'S ALWAYS THE SAME. NEVER SEEN ANYTHING LIKE IT IN FIFTEEN YEARS!
THERE'S ONLY ONE THING TO DO: CALL IN BOTH HUSBANDS AND ASK THEM WHO WE'VE GOT ON THE SLAB HERE...

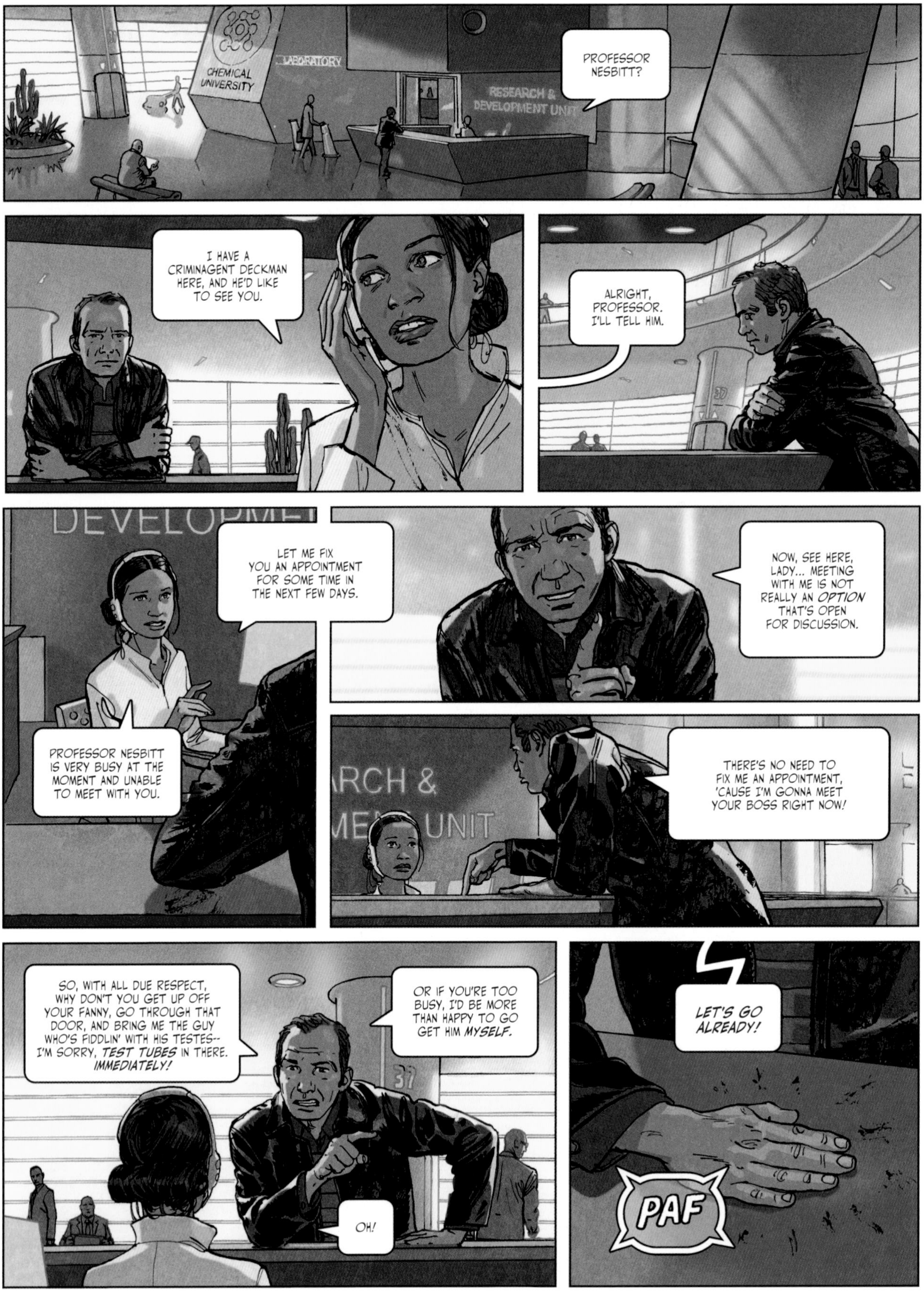
CHEMICAL UNIVERSITY
LABORATORY
RESEARCH & DEVELOPMENT UNIT
PROFESSOR NESBITT?
I HAVE A CRIMINAGENT DECKMAN HERE, AND HE'D LIKE TO SEE YOU.
ALRIGHT, PROFESSOR. I'LL TELL HIM.
LET ME FIX YOU AN APPOINTMENT FOR SOME TIME IN THE NEXT FEW DAYS.
PROFESSOR NESBITT IS VERY BUSY AT THE MOMENT AND UNABLE TO MEET WITH YOU.
NOW, SEE HERE, LADY... MEETING WITH ME IS NOT REALLY AN *OPTION* THAT'S OPEN FOR DISCUSSION.
THERE'S NO NEED TO FIX ME AN APPOINTMENT, 'CAUSE I'M GONNA MEET YOUR BOSS RIGHT NOW!
SO, WITH ALL DUE RESPECT, WHY DON'T YOU GET UP OFF YOUR FANNY, GO THROUGH THAT DOOR, AND BRING ME THE GUY WHO'S FIDDLIN' WITH HIS TESTES-- I'M SORRY, ***TEST TUBES*** IN THERE. ***IMMEDIATELY!***
OR IF YOU'RE TOO BUSY, I'D BE MORE THAN HAPPY TO GO GET HIM ***MYSELF.***
OH!
LET'S GO ALREADY!
PAF

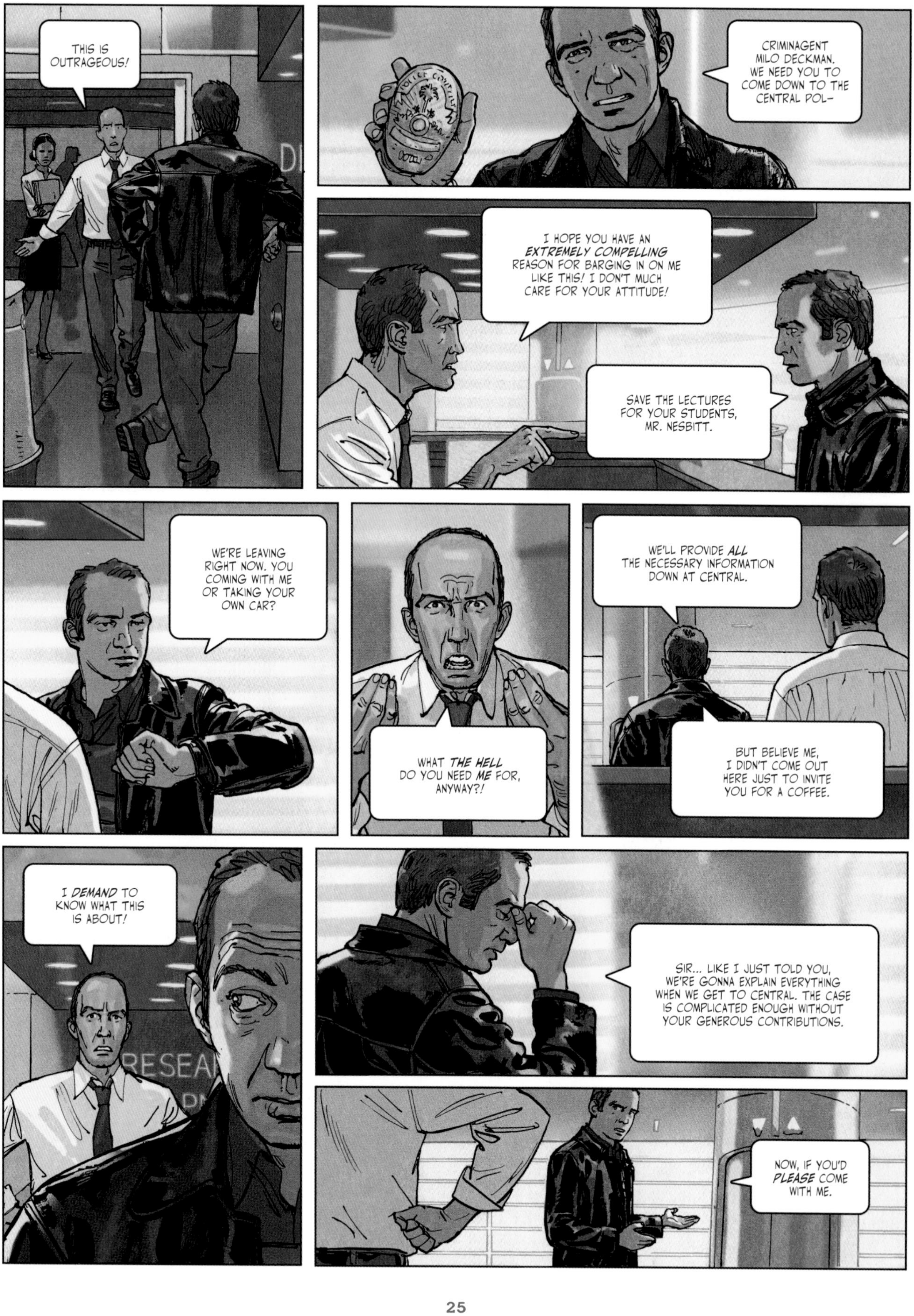
THIS IS OUTRAGEOUS!
CRIMINAGENT MILO DECKMAN. WE NEED YOU TO COME DOWN TO THE CENTRAL POL-
I HOPE YOU HAVE AN **EXTREMELY COMPELLING** REASON FOR BARGING IN ON ME LIKE THIS! I DON'T MUCH CARE FOR YOUR ATTITUDE!
SAVE THE LECTURES FOR YOUR STUDENTS, MR. NESBITT.
WE'RE LEAVING RIGHT NOW. YOU COMING WITH ME OR TAKING YOUR OWN CAR?
WHAT **THE HELL** DO YOU NEED **ME** FOR, ANYWAY?!
WE'LL PROVIDE **ALL** THE NECESSARY INFORMATION DOWN AT CENTRAL.
BUT BELIEVE ME, I DIDN'T COME OUT HERE JUST TO INVITE YOU FOR A COFFEE.
I **DEMAND** TO KNOW WHAT THIS IS ABOUT!
RESEA
SIR... LIKE I JUST TOLD YOU, WE'RE GONNA EXPLAIN EVERYTHING WHEN WE GET TO CENTRAL. THE CASE IS COMPLICATED ENOUGH WITHOUT YOUR GENEROUS CONTRIBUTIONS.
NOW, IF YOU'D **PLEASE** COME WITH ME.

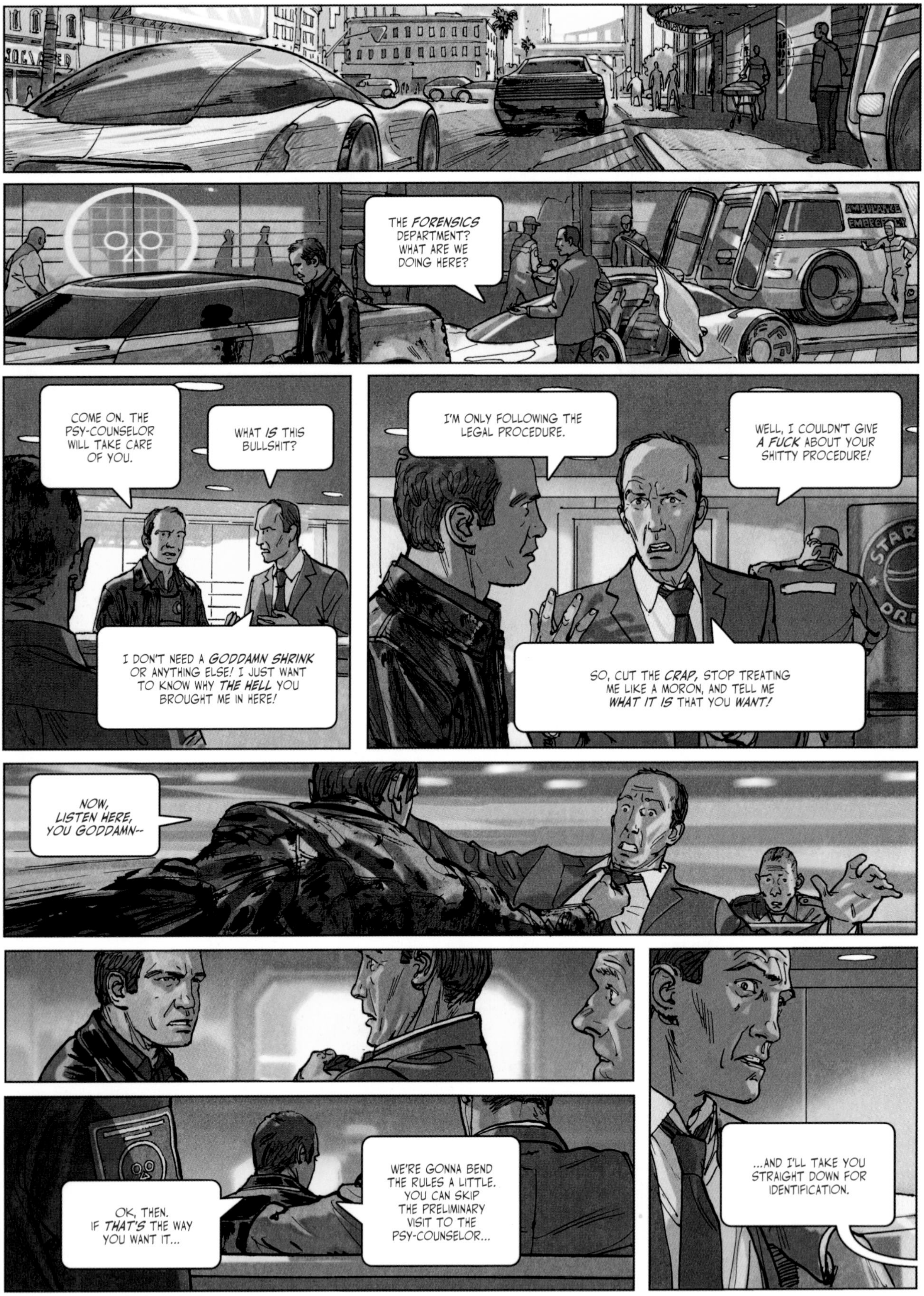
THE *FORENSICS* DEPARTMENT? WHAT ARE WE DOING HERE?
COME ON. THE PSY-COUNSELOR WILL TAKE CARE OF YOU.
WHAT *IS* THIS BULLSHIT?
I DON'T NEED A *GODDAMN SHRINK* OR ANYTHING ELSE! I JUST WANT TO KNOW WHY *THE HELL* YOU BROUGHT ME IN HERE!
I'M ONLY FOLLOWING THE LEGAL PROCEDURE.
WELL, I COULDN'T GIVE *A FUCK* ABOUT YOUR SHITTY PROCEDURE!
SO, CUT THE *CRAP*, STOP TREATING ME LIKE A MORON, AND TELL ME *WHAT IT IS* THAT YOU *WANT!*
NOW, LISTEN HERE, YOU GODDAMN--
OK, THEN. IF *THAT'S* THE WAY YOU WANT IT...
WE'RE GONNA BEND THE RULES A LITTLE. YOU CAN SKIP THE PRELIMINARY VISIT TO THE PSY-COUNSELOR...
...AND I'LL TAKE YOU STRAIGHT DOWN FOR IDENTIFICATION.

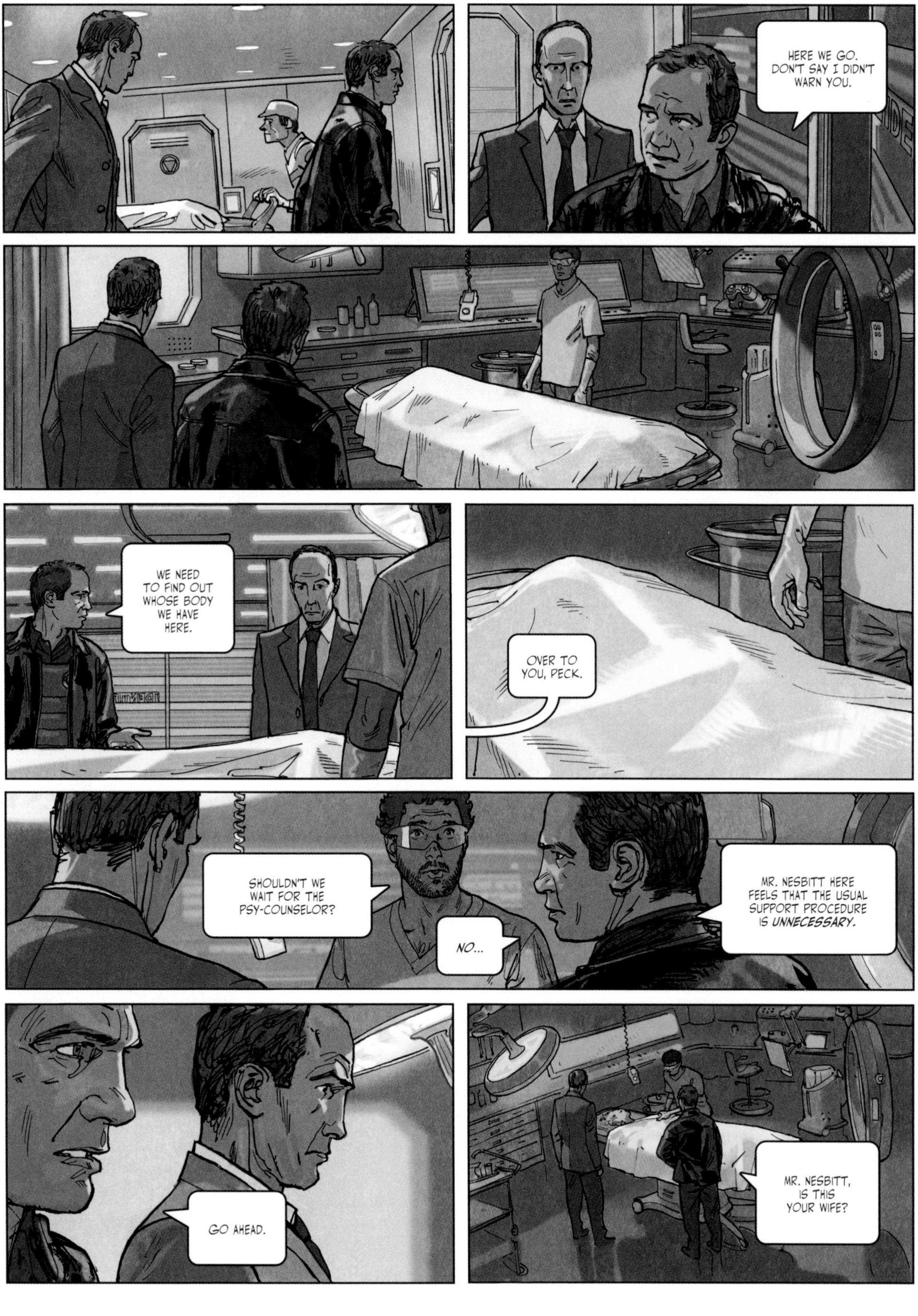
HERE WE GO. DON'T SAY I DIDN'T WARN YOU.
WE NEED TO FIND OUT WHOSE BODY WE HAVE HERE.
OVER TO YOU, PECK.
SHOULDN'T WE WAIT FOR THE PSY-COUNSELOR?
NO...
MR. NESBITT HERE FEELS THAT THE USUAL SUPPORT PROCEDURE IS *UNNECESSARY.*
GO AHEAD.
MR. NESBITT, IS THIS YOUR WIFE?

HELLO? THIS IS NESBITT! I'M JUST LEAVING *THE MORGUE* AT CENTRAL POLICE...

TELL ME WHAT *THE HELL* IS GOING ON! WAS IT *YOU* WHO DID IT?!

COOL DOWN, MR. NESBITT. WHAT EXACTLY DO YOU MEAN?

MY WIFE, GODDAMMIT! SHE'S DEAD!

IT WAS YOU, WASN'T IT?!

IF SHE'S ALREADY DEAD, MR. NESBITT, IT MEANS THAT SOMEBODY *ELSE* GOT TO HER FIRST.

I WON'T DENY THAT WE WERE PLANNING TO DISPOSE OF HER IN THE NEAR FUTURE BECAUSE, ACCORDING TO WHAT YOU TOLD US BEFORE, SHE WAS GETTING FAR TOO *INQUISITIVE*.

BUT... THEN WHO DID IT?!

WE DON'T HAVE A CLUE ABOUT THAT. THE LEAST WE CAN SAY IS THAT YOUR SITUATION IS PRETTY UNSTABLE AT THE MOMENT, TO PUT IT *MILDLY*.

NO MORE PHONE CALLS, MR. NESBITT. WE'LL GET AHOLD OF YOU AGAIN WHEN WE FEEL THE TIME IS RIGHT.

AT LEAST WE KNOW WHO THE WOMAN IS NOW. WE WERE LUCKY TO LAND ON THE RIGHT HUSBAND THE FIRST TIME!

YEAH...

NOW, ALL WE NEED TO DO IS SHOW THE BODY TO THE OTHER GUY, AND WE CAN WRAP THIS JOB UP.

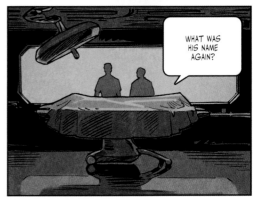

WHAT WAS HIS NAME AGAIN?

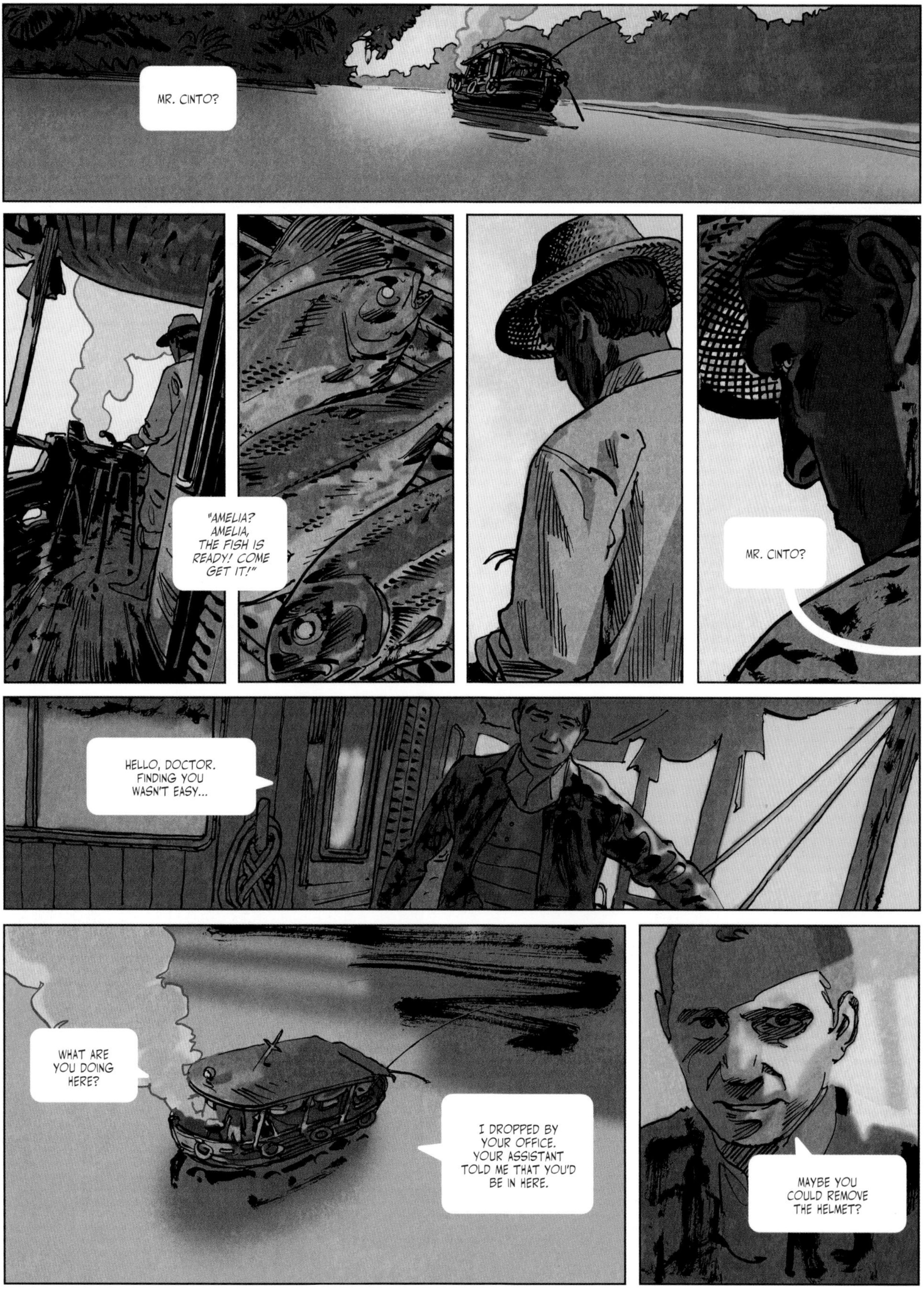
MR. CINTO?
"AMELIA? AMELIA, THE FISH IS READY! COME GET IT!"
MR. CINTO?
HELLO, DOCTOR. FINDING YOU WASN'T EASY...
WHAT ARE YOU DOING HERE?
I DROPPED BY YOUR OFFICE. YOUR ASSISTANT TOLD ME THAT YOU'D BE IN HERE.
MAYBE YOU COULD REMOVE THE HELMET?

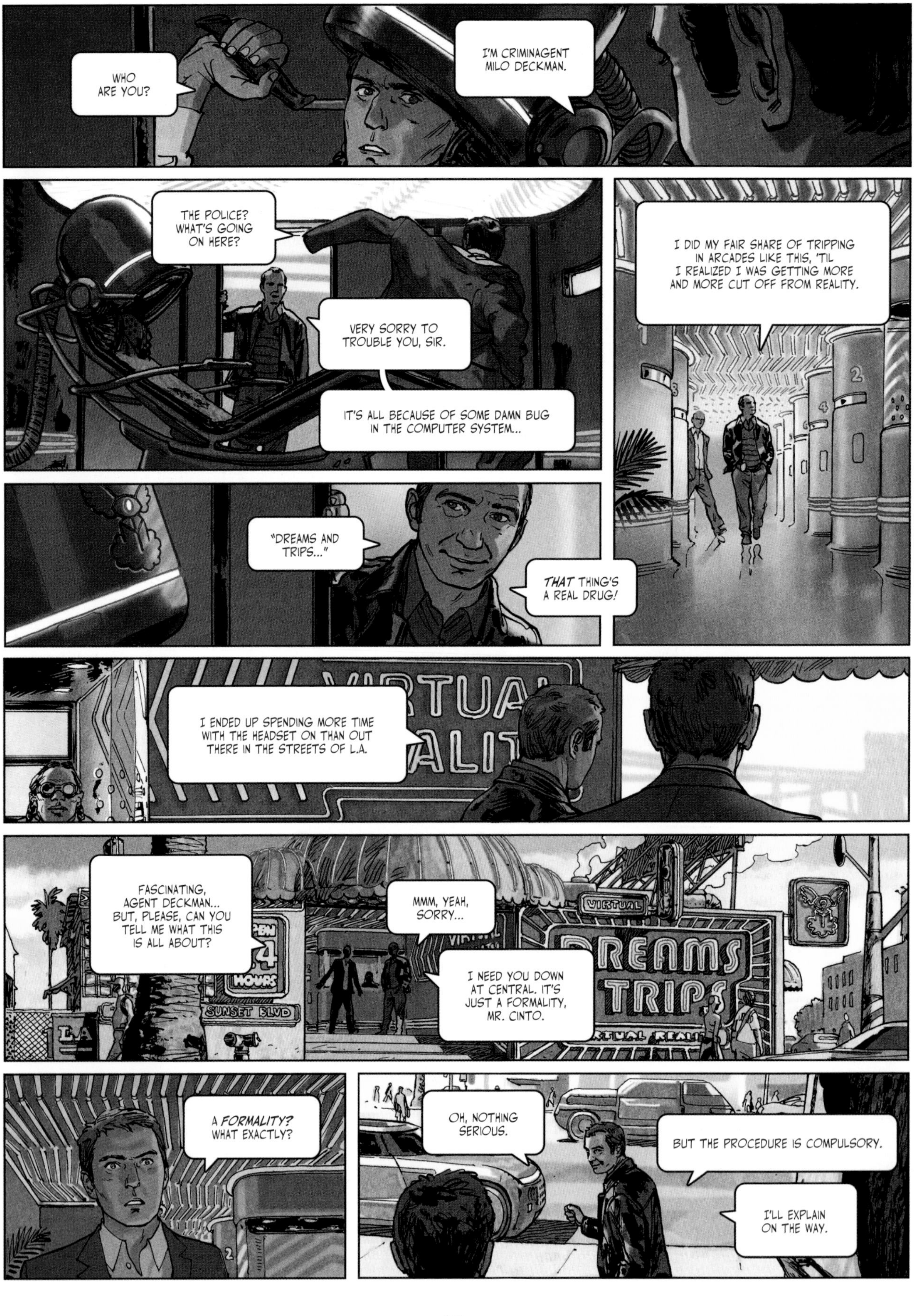
WHO ARE YOU?
I'M CRIMINAGENT MILO DECKMAN.
THE POLICE? WHAT'S GOING ON HERE?
VERY SORRY TO TROUBLE YOU, SIR.
IT'S ALL BECAUSE OF SOME DAMN BUG IN THE COMPUTER SYSTEM...
"DREAMS AND TRIPS..."
THAT THING'S A REAL DRUG!
I DID MY FAIR SHARE OF TRIPPING IN ARCADES LIKE THIS, 'TIL I REALIZED I WAS GETTING MORE AND MORE CUT OFF FROM REALITY.
I ENDED UP SPENDING MORE TIME WITH THE HEADSET ON THAN OUT THERE IN THE STREETS OF L.A.
FASCINATING, AGENT DECKMAN... BUT, PLEASE, CAN YOU TELL ME WHAT THIS IS ALL ABOUT?
MMM, YEAH, SORRY...
I NEED YOU DOWN AT CENTRAL. IT'S JUST A FORMALITY, MR. CINTO.
DREAMS TRIPS
SUNSET BLVD
A *FORMALITY?* WHAT EXACTLY?
OH, NOTHING SERIOUS.
BUT THE PROCEDURE IS COMPULSORY.
I'LL EXPLAIN ON THE WAY.

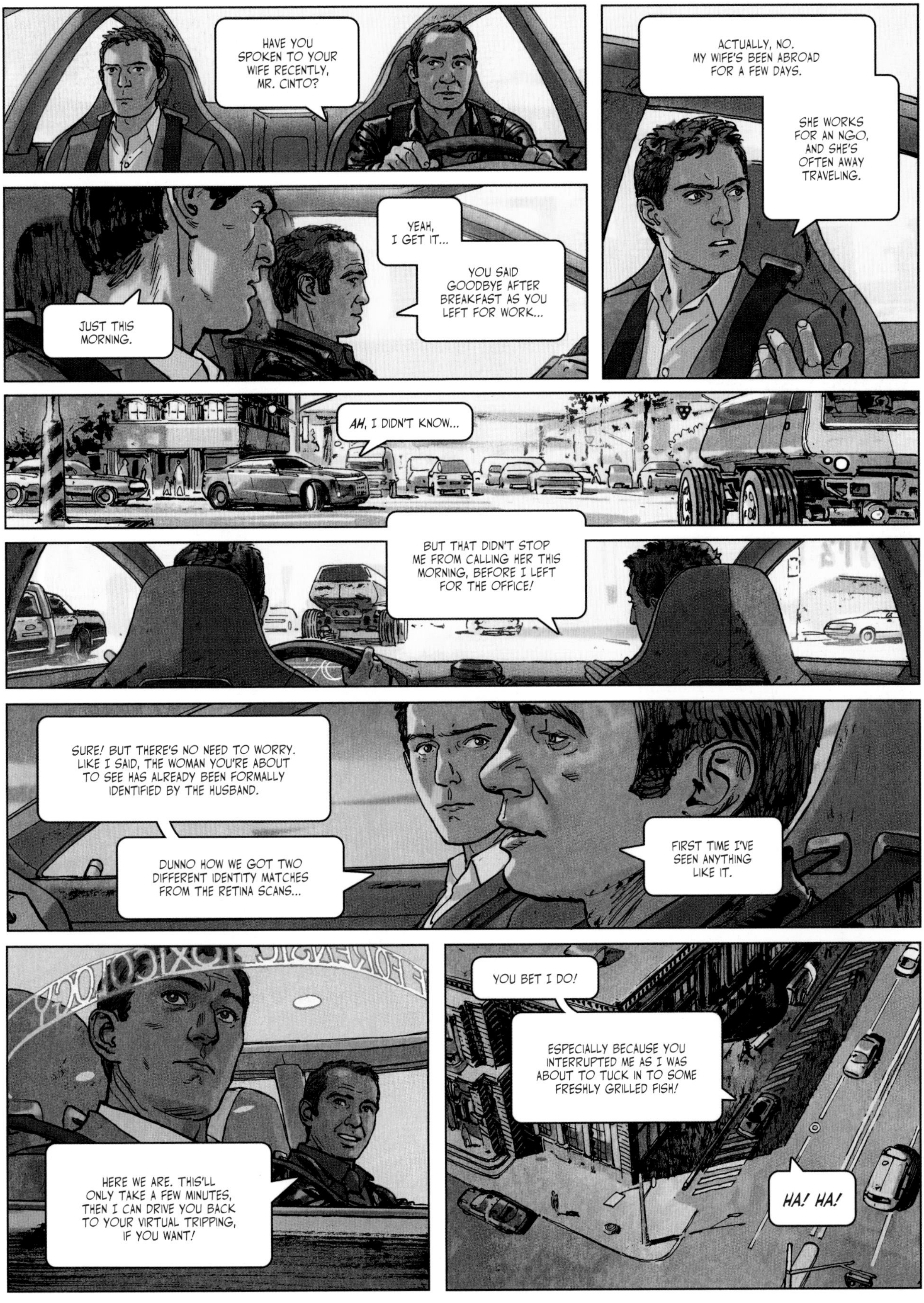
HAVE YOU SPOKEN TO YOUR WIFE RECENTLY, MR. CINTO?
ACTUALLY, NO. MY WIFE'S BEEN ABROAD FOR A FEW DAYS.
SHE WORKS FOR AN NGO, AND SHE'S OFTEN AWAY TRAVELING.
JUST THIS MORNING.
YEAH, I GET IT...
YOU SAID GOODBYE AFTER BREAKFAST AS YOU LEFT FOR WORK...
AH, I DIDN'T KNOW...
BUT THAT DIDN'T STOP ME FROM CALLING HER THIS MORNING, BEFORE I LEFT FOR THE OFFICE!
SURE! BUT THERE'S NO NEED TO WORRY. LIKE I SAID, THE WOMAN YOU'RE ABOUT TO SEE HAS ALREADY BEEN FORMALLY IDENTIFIED BY THE HUSBAND.
DUNNO HOW WE GOT TWO DIFFERENT IDENTITY MATCHES FROM THE RETINA SCANS...
FIRST TIME I'VE SEEN ANYTHING LIKE IT.
HERE WE ARE. THIS'LL ONLY TAKE A FEW MINUTES, THEN I CAN DRIVE YOU BACK TO YOUR VIRTUAL TRIPPING, IF YOU WANT!
YOU BET I DO!
ESPECIALLY BECAUSE YOU INTERRUPTED ME AS I WAS ABOUT TO TUCK IN TO SOME FRESHLY GRILLED FISH!
HA! HA!

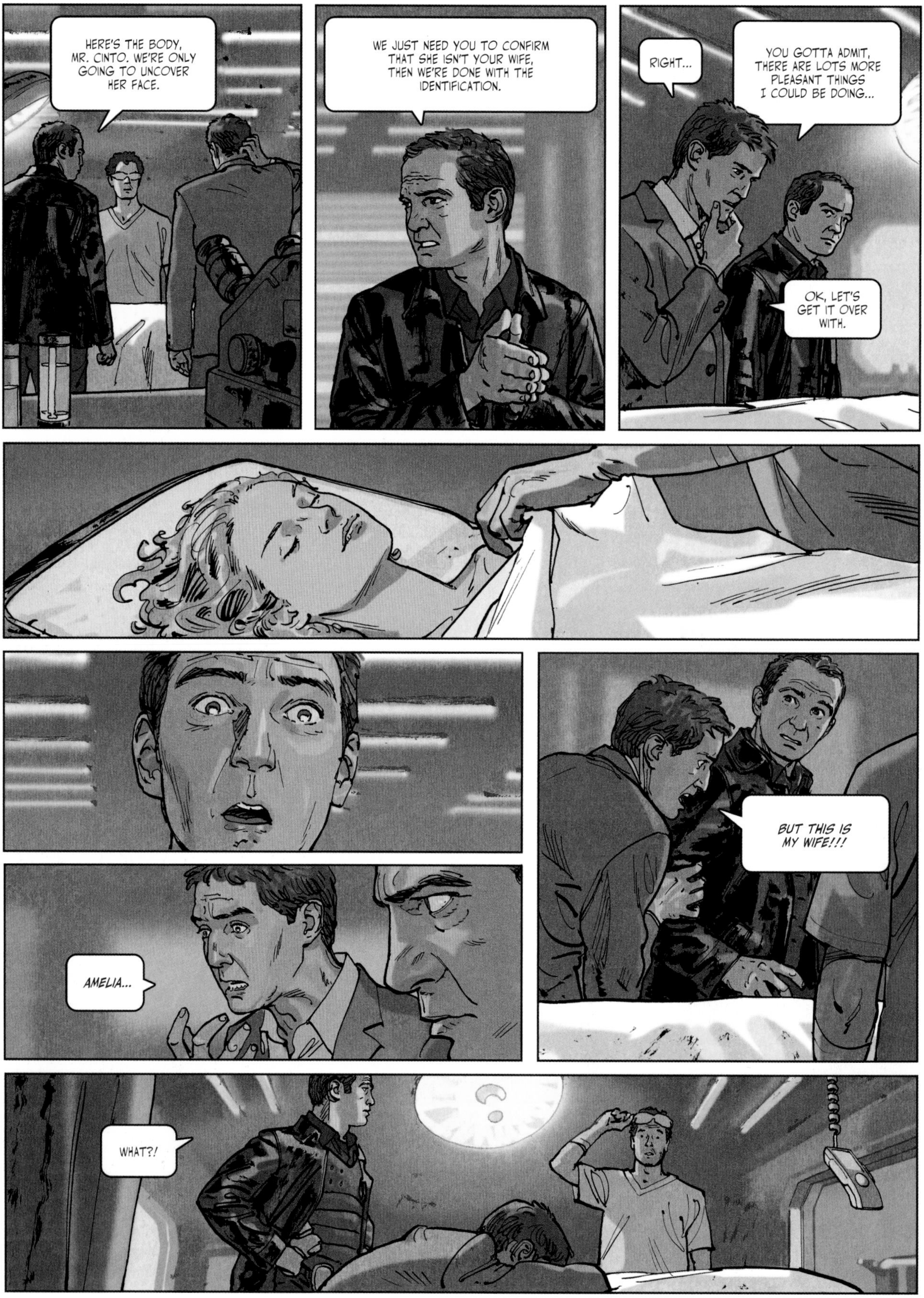
HERE'S THE BODY, MR. CINTO. WE'RE ONLY GOING TO UNCOVER HER FACE.
WE JUST NEED YOU TO CONFIRM THAT SHE ISN'T YOUR WIFE, THEN WE'RE DONE WITH THE IDENTIFICATION.
RIGHT...
YOU GOTTA ADMIT, THERE ARE LOTS MORE PLEASANT THINGS I COULD BE DOING...
OK, LET'S GET IT OVER WITH.
BUT THIS IS MY WIFE!!!
AMELIA...
WHAT?!

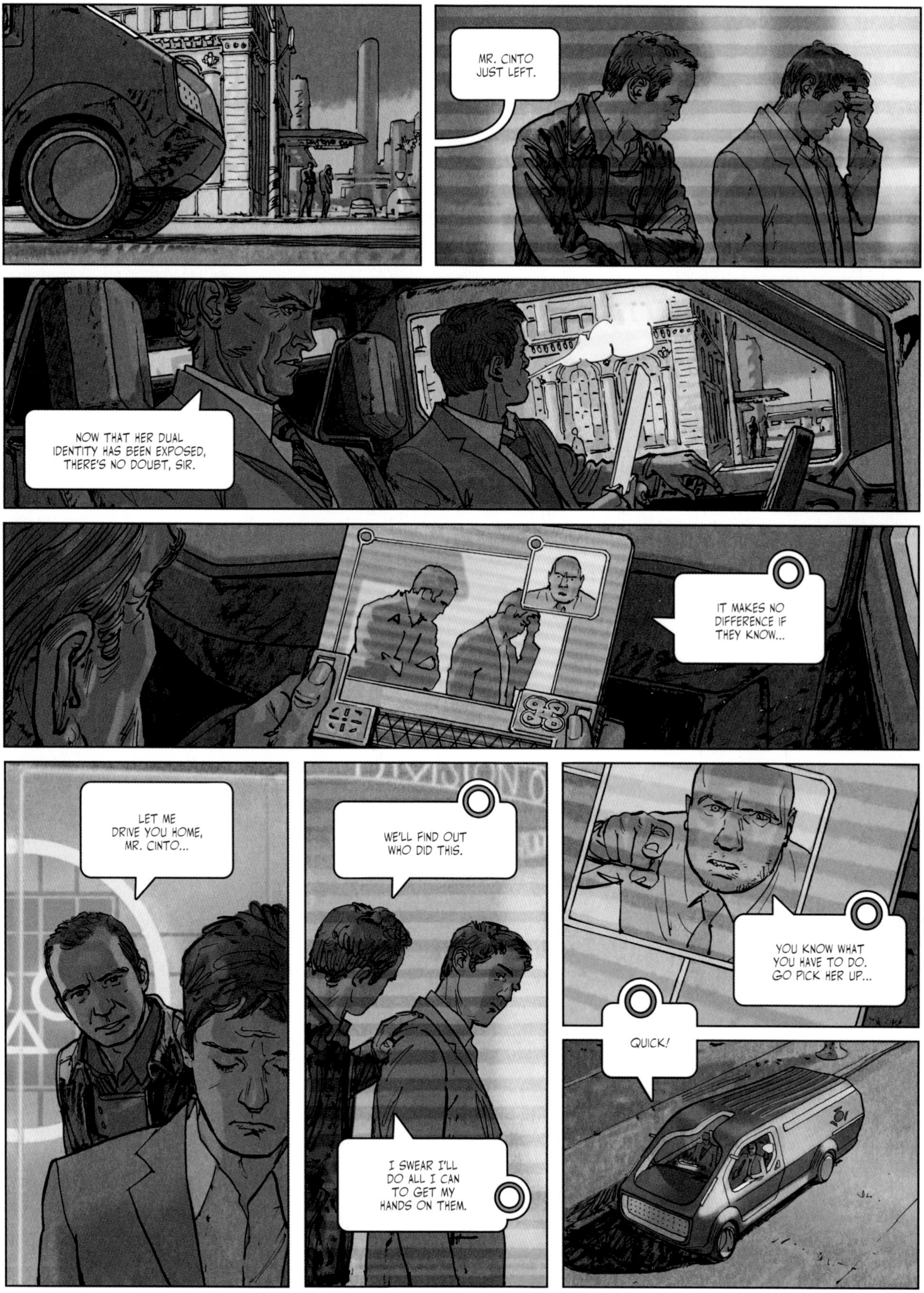
MR. CINTO JUST LEFT.
NOW THAT HER DUAL IDENTITY HAS BEEN EXPOSED, THERE'S NO DOUBT, SIR.
IT MAKES NO DIFFERENCE IF THEY KNOW...
LET ME DRIVE YOU HOME, MR. CINTO...
WE'LL FIND OUT WHO DID THIS.
I SWEAR I'LL DO ALL I CAN TO GET MY HANDS ON THEM.
YOU KNOW WHAT YOU HAVE TO DO. GO PICK HER UP...
QUICK!

HEY, DOC!

MILO! WHAT FAIR WIND BRINGS YOU TO ME?

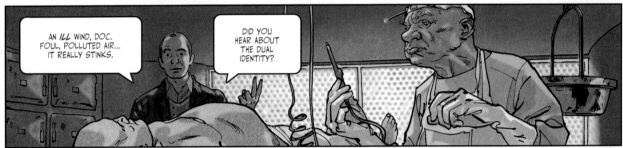

AN *ILL* WIND, DOC. FOUL, POLLUTED AIR... IT REALLY STINKS.

DID YOU HEAR ABOUT THE DUAL IDENTITY?

YEAH, PECK MENTIONED IT BRIEFLY.

I'LL GET ON IT TOMORROW MORNING...

I'VE GOT ANOTHER COUPLE WAITING ON ICE FOR ME TODAY.

PITY... I'M IN A RUSH TO FIND OUT WHAT THE WOMAN'S BODY CAN TELL US. I NEED TO GET A HANDLE ON THIS CASE.

CADAVERS *ALWAYS* HAVE A STORY TO TELL. YOU JUST NEED TO KNOW HOW TO UNLOCK THEIR SECRETS.

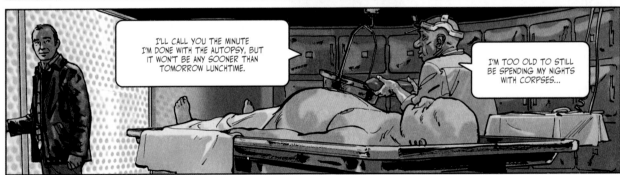

I'LL CALL YOU THE MINUTE I'M DONE WITH THE AUTOPSY, BUT IT WON'T BE ANY SOONER THAN TOMORROW LUNCHTIME.

I'M TOO OLD TO STILL BE SPENDING MY NIGHTS WITH CORPSES...

34

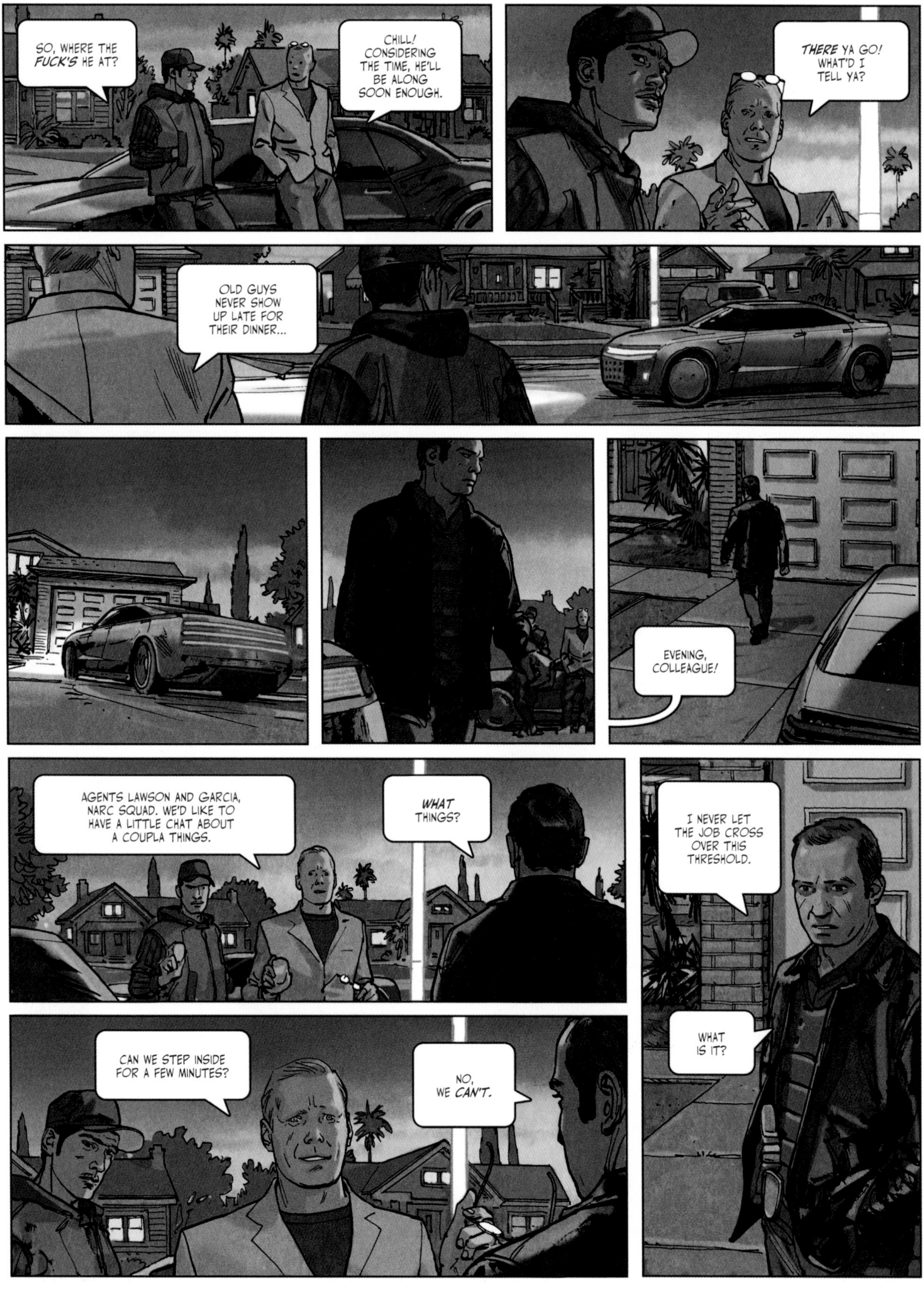
SO, WHERE THE *FUCK'S* HE AT?
CHILL! CONSIDERING THE TIME, HE'LL BE ALONG SOON ENOUGH.
THERE YA GO! WHAT'D I TELL YA?
OLD GUYS NEVER SHOW UP LATE FOR THEIR DINNER...
EVENING, COLLEAGUE!
AGENTS LAWSON AND GARCIA, NARC SQUAD. WE'D LIKE TO HAVE A LITTLE CHAT ABOUT A COUPLA THINGS.
WHAT THINGS?
CAN WE STEP INSIDE FOR A FEW MINUTES?
NO, WE *CAN'T.*
I NEVER LET THE JOB CROSS OVER THIS THRESHOLD.
WHAT IS IT?

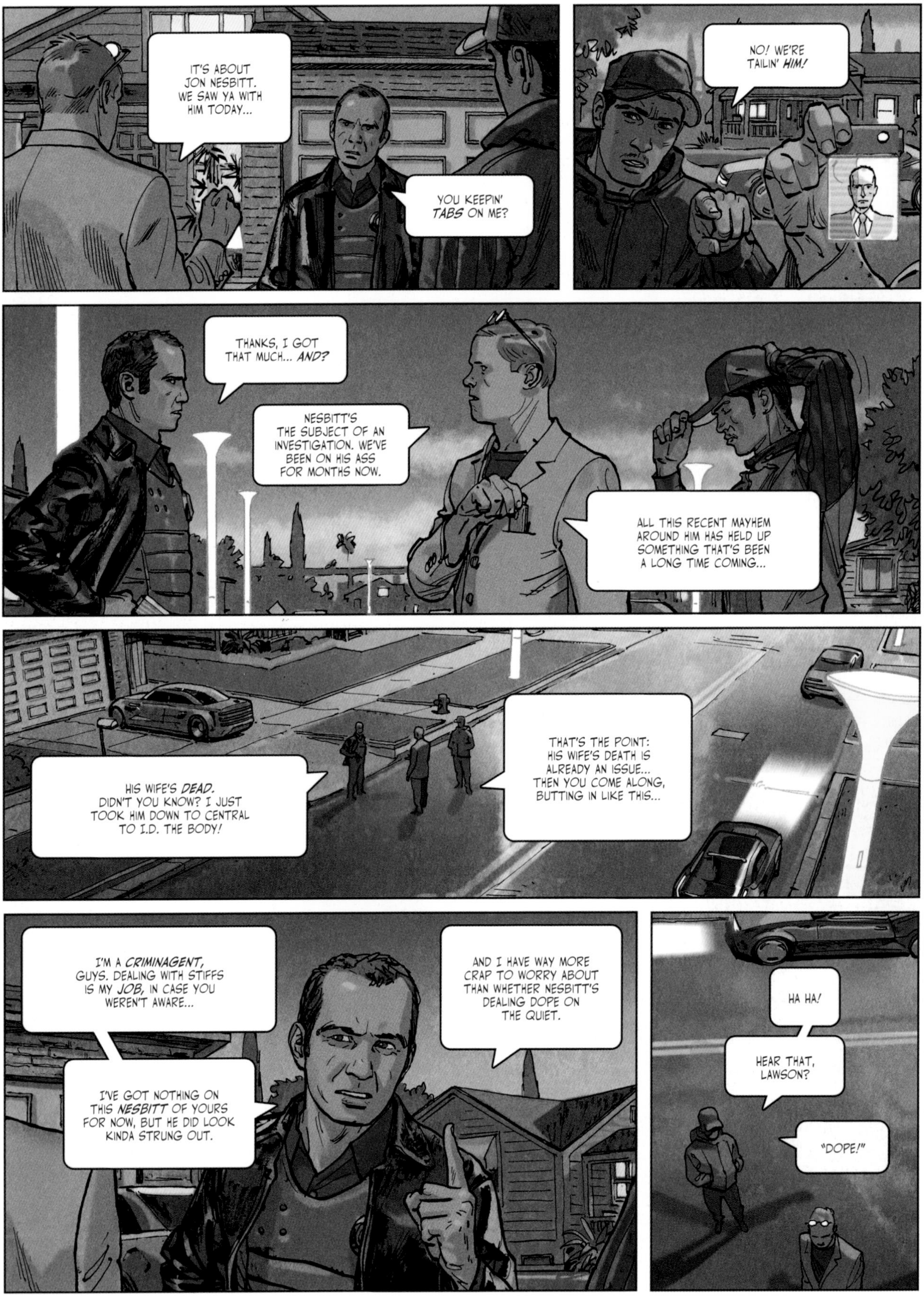

IT'S ABOUT JON NESBITT. WE SAW YA WITH HIM TODAY...
YOU KEEPIN' *TABS* ON ME?
NO! WE'RE TAILIN' *HIM!*
THANKS, I GOT THAT MUCH... *AND?*
NESBITT'S THE SUBJECT OF AN INVESTIGATION. WE'VE BEEN ON HIS ASS FOR MONTHS NOW.
ALL THIS RECENT MAYHEM AROUND HIM HAS HELD UP SOMETHING THAT'S BEEN A LONG TIME COMING...
HIS WIFE'S *DEAD.* DIDN'T YOU KNOW? I JUST TOOK HIM DOWN TO CENTRAL TO I.D. THE BODY!
THAT'S THE POINT: HIS WIFE'S DEATH IS ALREADY AN ISSUE... THEN YOU COME ALONG, BUTTING IN LIKE THIS...
I'M A *CRIMINAGENT,* GUYS. DEALING WITH STIFFS IS MY *JOB,* IN CASE YOU WEREN'T AWARE...
I'VE GOT NOTHING ON THIS *NESBITT* OF YOURS FOR NOW, BUT HE DID LOOK KINDA STRUNG OUT.
AND I HAVE WAY MORE CRAP TO WORRY ABOUT THAN WHETHER NESBITT'S DEALING DOPE ON THE QUIET.
HA HA!
HEAR THAT, LAWSON?
"DOPE!"

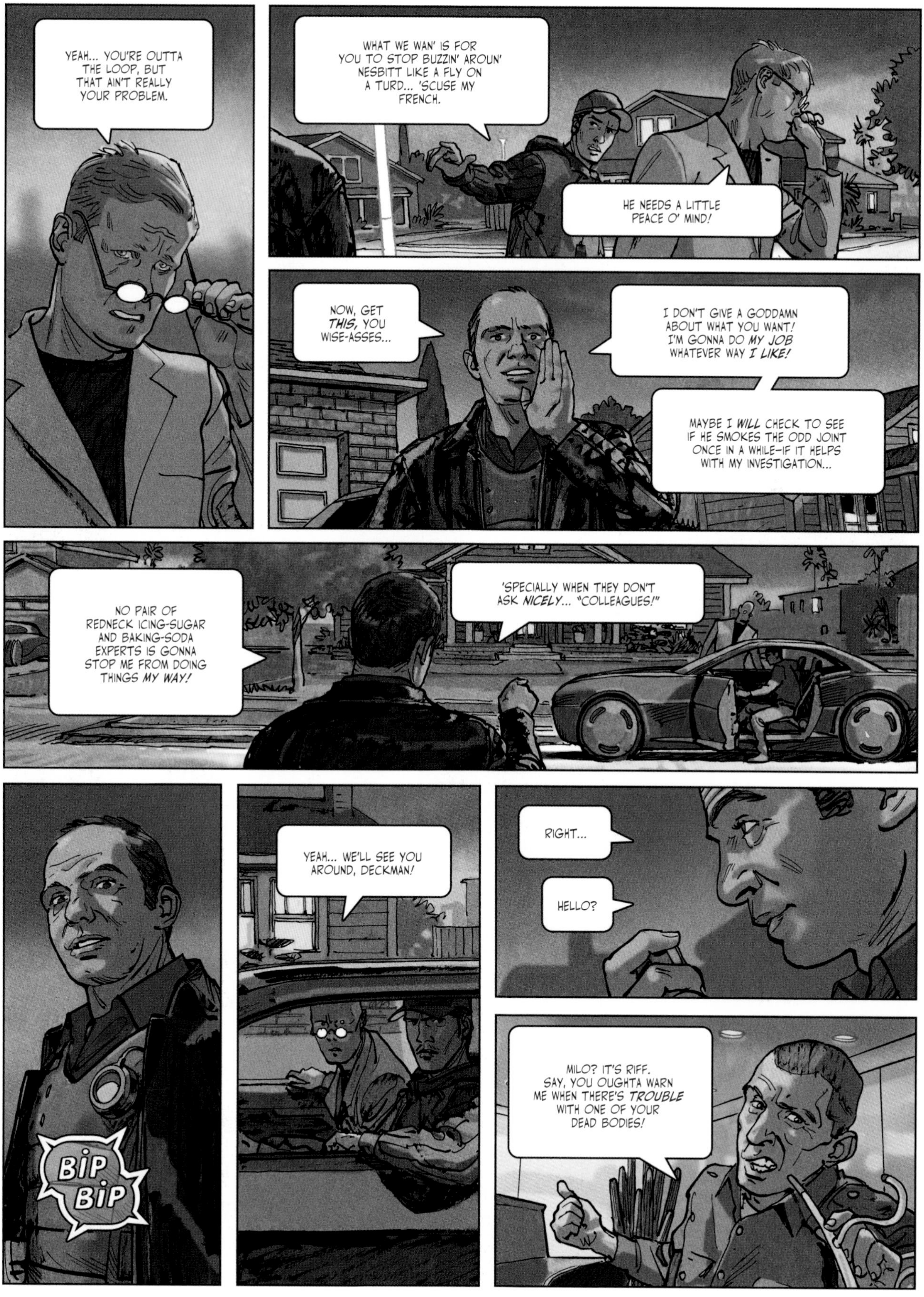
YEAH... YOU'RE OUTTA THE LOOP, BUT THAT AIN'T REALLY YOUR PROBLEM.
WHAT WE WAN' IS FOR YOU TO STOP BUZZIN' AROUN' NESBITT LIKE A FLY ON A TURD... 'SCUSE MY FRENCH.
HE NEEDS A LITTLE PEACE O' MIND!
NOW, GET *THIS,* YOU WISE-ASSES...
I DON'T GIVE A GODDAMN ABOUT WHAT YOU WANT! I'M GONNA DO *MY JOB* WHATEVER WAY *I LIKE!*
MAYBE I *WILL* CHECK TO SEE IF HE SMOKES THE ODD JOINT ONCE IN A WHILE–IF IT HELPS WITH MY INVESTIGATION...
NO PAIR OF REDNECK ICING-SUGAR AND BAKING-SODA EXPERTS IS GONNA STOP ME FROM DOING THINGS *MY WAY!*
'SPECIALLY WHEN THEY DON'T ASK *NICELY*... "COLLEAGUES!"
BIP BIP
YEAH... WE'LL SEE YOU AROUND, DECKMAN!
RIGHT...
HELLO?
MILO? IT'S RIFF. SAY, YOU OUGHTA WARN ME WHEN THERE'S *TROUBLE* WITH ONE OF YOUR DEAD BODIES!

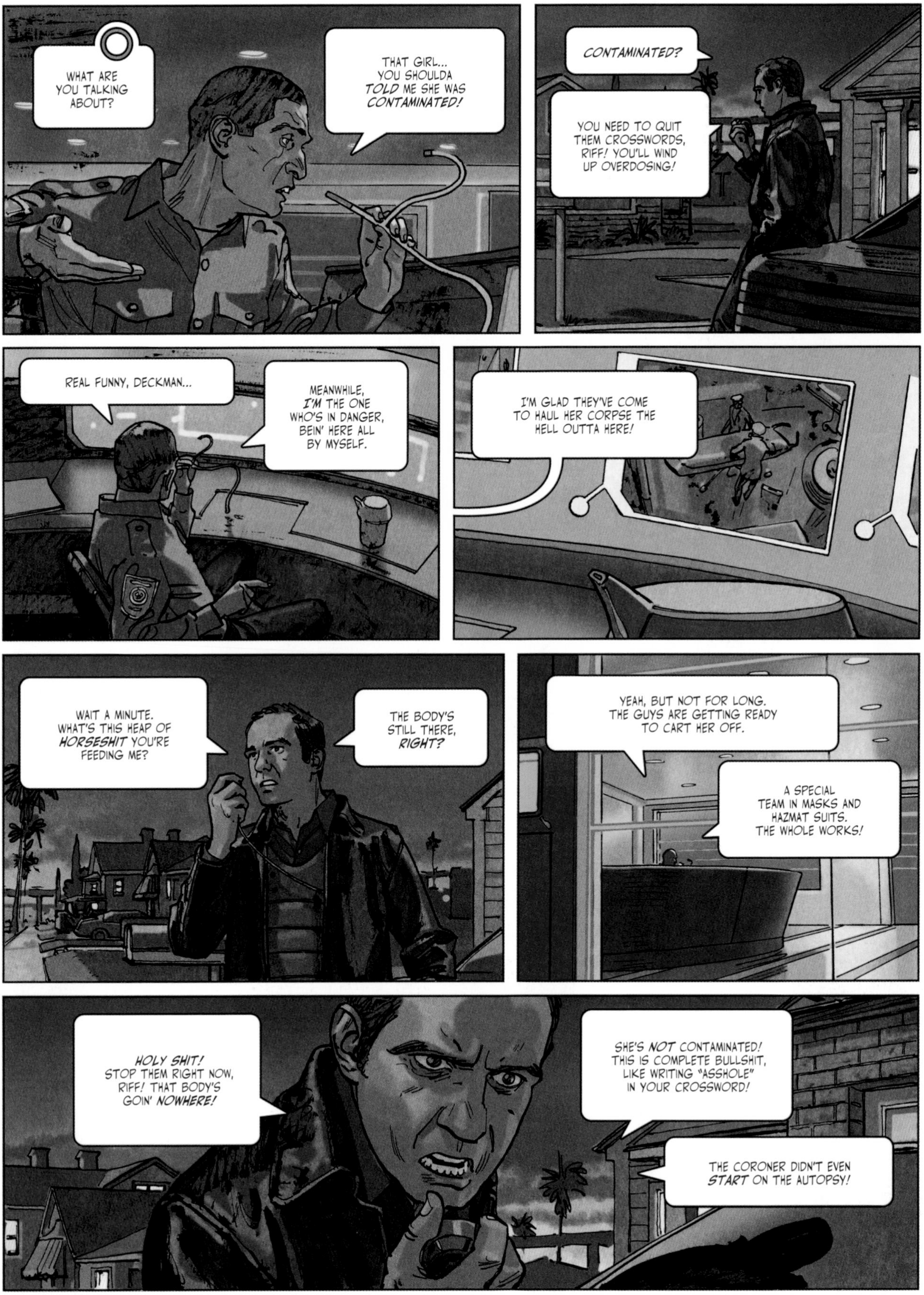

WHAT ARE YOU TALKING ABOUT?
THAT GIRL... YOU SHOULDA *TOLD* ME SHE WAS *CONTAMINATED!*
CONTAMINATED?
YOU NEED TO QUIT THEM CROSSWORDS, RIFF! YOU'LL WIND UP OVERDOSING!
REAL FUNNY, DECKMAN...
MEANWHILE, *I'M* THE ONE WHO'S IN DANGER, BEIN' HERE ALL BY MYSELF.
I'M GLAD THEY'VE COME TO HAUL HER CORPSE THE HELL OUTTA HERE!
WAIT A MINUTE. WHAT'S THIS HEAP OF *HORSESHIT* YOU'RE FEEDING ME?
THE BODY'S STILL THERE, *RIGHT?*
YEAH, BUT NOT FOR LONG. THE GUYS ARE GETTING READY TO CART HER OFF.
A SPECIAL TEAM IN MASKS AND HAZMAT SUITS. THE WHOLE WORKS!
HOLY SHIT! STOP THEM RIGHT NOW, RIFF! THAT BODY'S GOIN' *NOWHERE!*
SHE'S *NOT* CONTAMINATED! THIS IS COMPLETE BULLSHIT, LIKE WRITING "ASSHOLE" IN YOUR CROSSWORD!
THE CORONER DIDN'T EVEN *START* ON THE AUTOPSY!

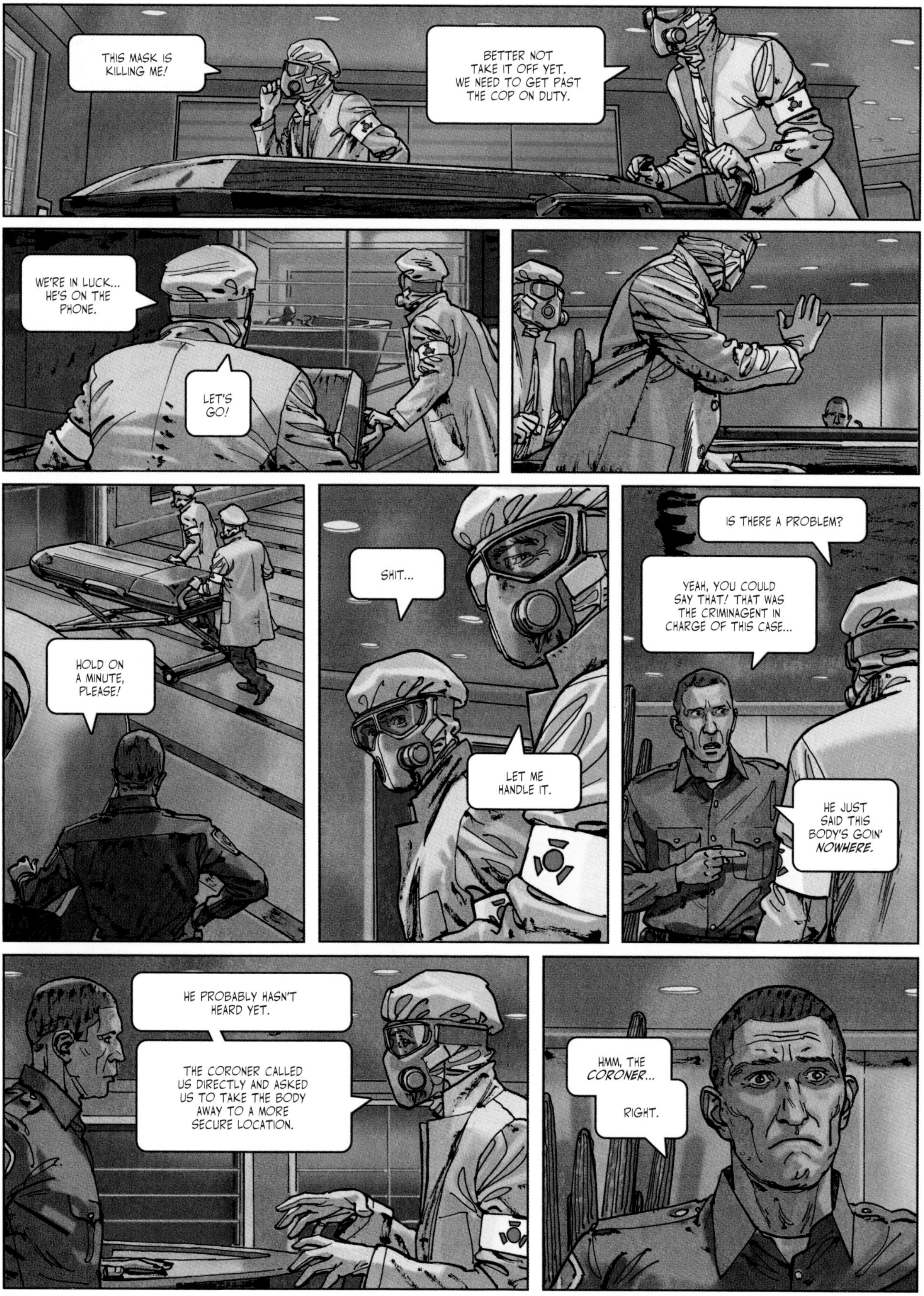
THIS MASK IS KILLING ME!
BETTER NOT TAKE IT OFF YET. WE NEED TO GET PAST THE COP ON DUTY.
WE'RE IN LUCK... HE'S ON THE PHONE.
LET'S GO!
HOLD ON A MINUTE, PLEASE!
SHIT...
LET ME HANDLE IT.
IS THERE A PROBLEM?
YEAH, YOU COULD SAY THAT! THAT WAS THE CRIMINAGENT IN CHARGE OF THIS CASE...
HE JUST SAID THIS BODY'S GOIN' *NOWHERE.*
HE PROBABLY HASN'T HEARD YET.
THE CORONER CALLED US DIRECTLY AND ASKED US TO TAKE THE BODY AWAY TO A MORE SECURE LOCATION.
HMM, THE *CORONER*...
RIGHT.

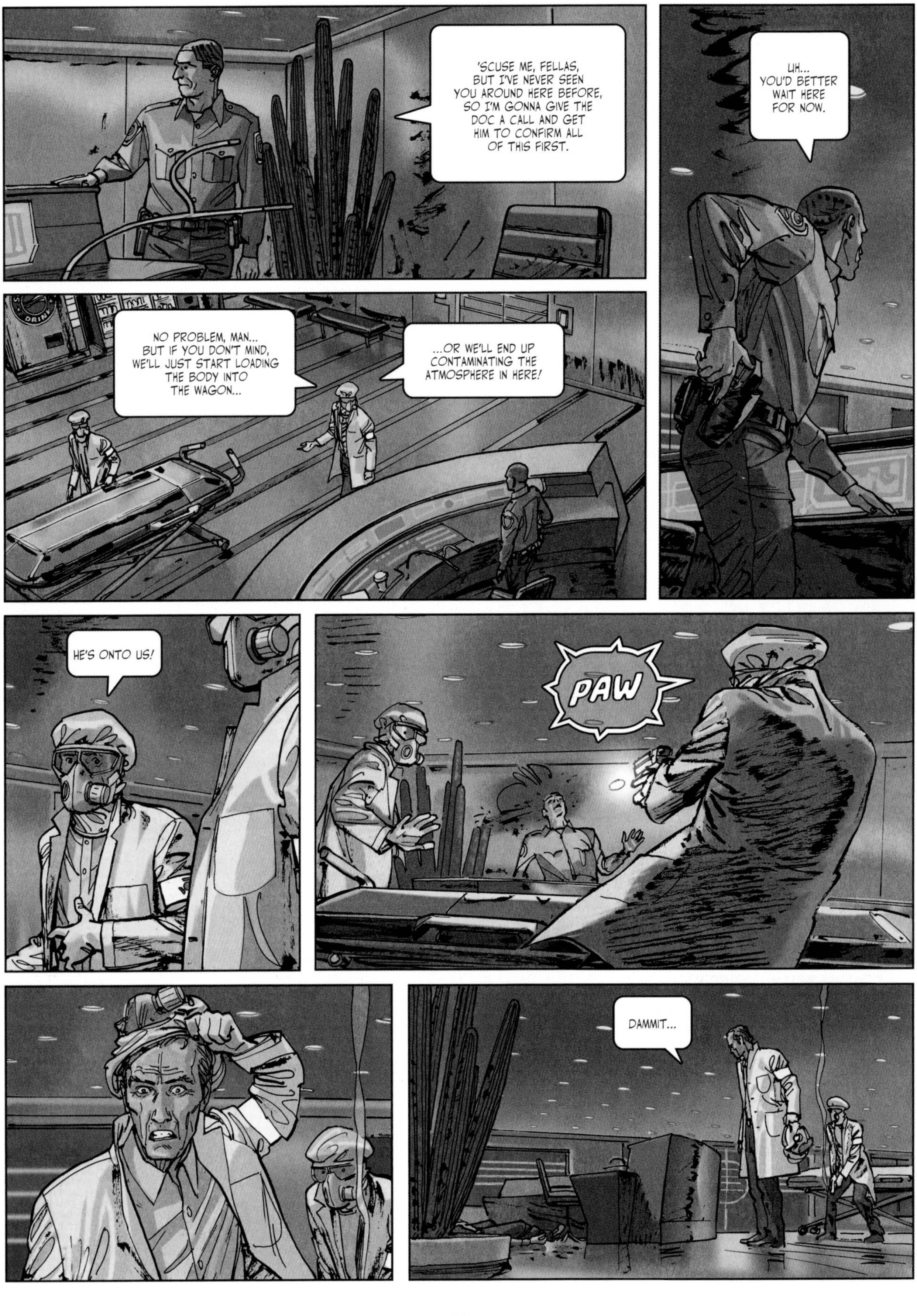
'SCUSE ME, FELLAS, BUT I'VE NEVER SEEN YOU AROUND HERE BEFORE, SO I'M GONNA GIVE THE DOC A CALL AND GET HIM TO CONFIRM ALL OF THIS FIRST.
UH... YOU'D BETTER WAIT HERE FOR NOW.
NO PROBLEM, MAN... BUT IF YOU DON'T MIND, WE'LL JUST START LOADING THE BODY INTO THE WAGON...
...OR WE'LL END UP CONTAMINATING THE ATMOSPHERE IN HERE!
HE'S ONTO US!
PAW
DAMMIT...

WE'RE IN THE SHIT *NOW!* HE SEALED ALL THE DOORS BEFORE I WHACKED HIM.

FUCK... THIS MISSION IS SERIOUSLY STARTING TO STINK!

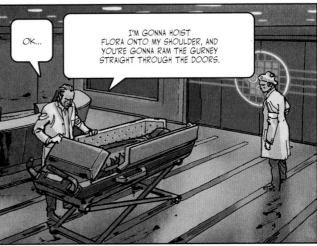

OK...

I'M GONNA HOIST FLORA ONTO MY SHOULDER, AND YOU'RE GONNA RAM THE GURNEY STRAIGHT THROUGH THE DOORS.

ARE YOU *NUTS?* WE'LL HAVE THE WHOLE OF CENTRAL AFTER US— IF THE ONE I WASTED DIDN'T ALREADY WARN 'EM BEFORE HE *CROAKED!*

YOU GOT SOME *OTHER* SOLUTION, EINSTEIN?

NO? THEN DO WHAT I *TELL* YOU!

YOU PISS ME OFF, JOSH!

I KNOW.

DO IT!

41

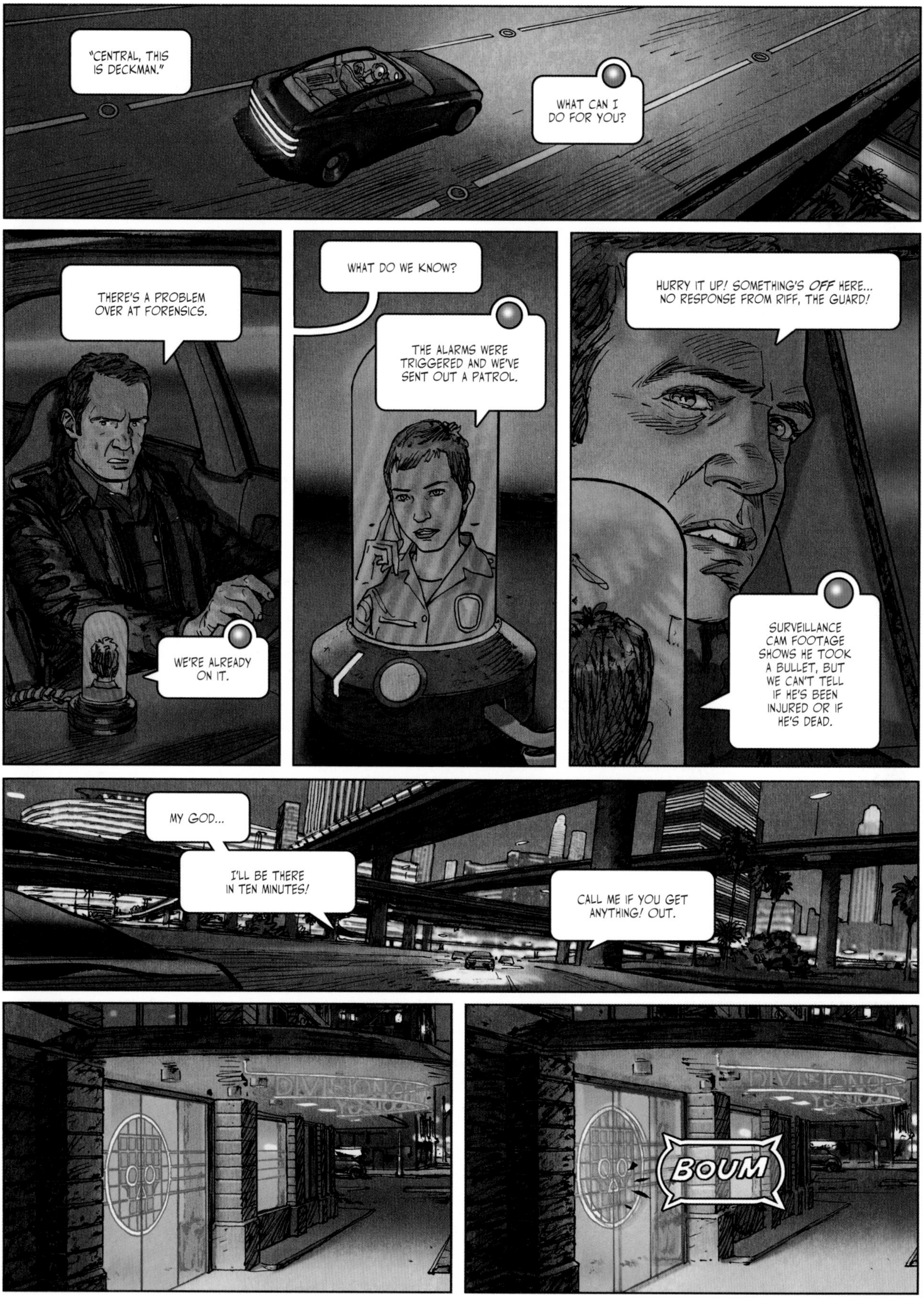

"CENTRAL, THIS IS DECKMAN."
WHAT CAN I DO FOR YOU?
THERE'S A PROBLEM OVER AT FORENSICS.
WE'RE ALREADY ON IT.
WHAT DO WE KNOW?
THE ALARMS WERE TRIGGERED AND WE'VE SENT OUT A PATROL.
HURRY IT UP! SOMETHING'S *OFF* HERE... NO RESPONSE FROM RIFF, THE GUARD!
SURVEILLANCE CAM FOOTAGE SHOWS HE TOOK A BULLET, BUT WE CAN'T TELL IF HE'S BEEN INJURED OR IF HE'S DEAD.
MY GOD...
I'LL BE THERE IN TEN MINUTES!
CALL ME IF YOU GET ANYTHING! OUT.
BOUM

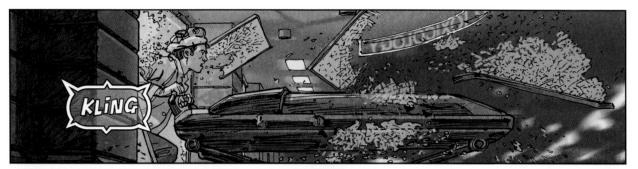

TODAY'S BEEN JUST ONE LONG SCREWUP!

WHAT KINDA JOB *IS* THIS?!

GETTING ALL *PHILOSOPHICAL* NOW? *MOVE* YOUR *ASS!*

SHOULD THANK OUR LUCKY STARS THAT THE WELCOMING COMMITTEE ISN'T HERE YET.

YOU SEE... SPEAK OF THE DEVIL...

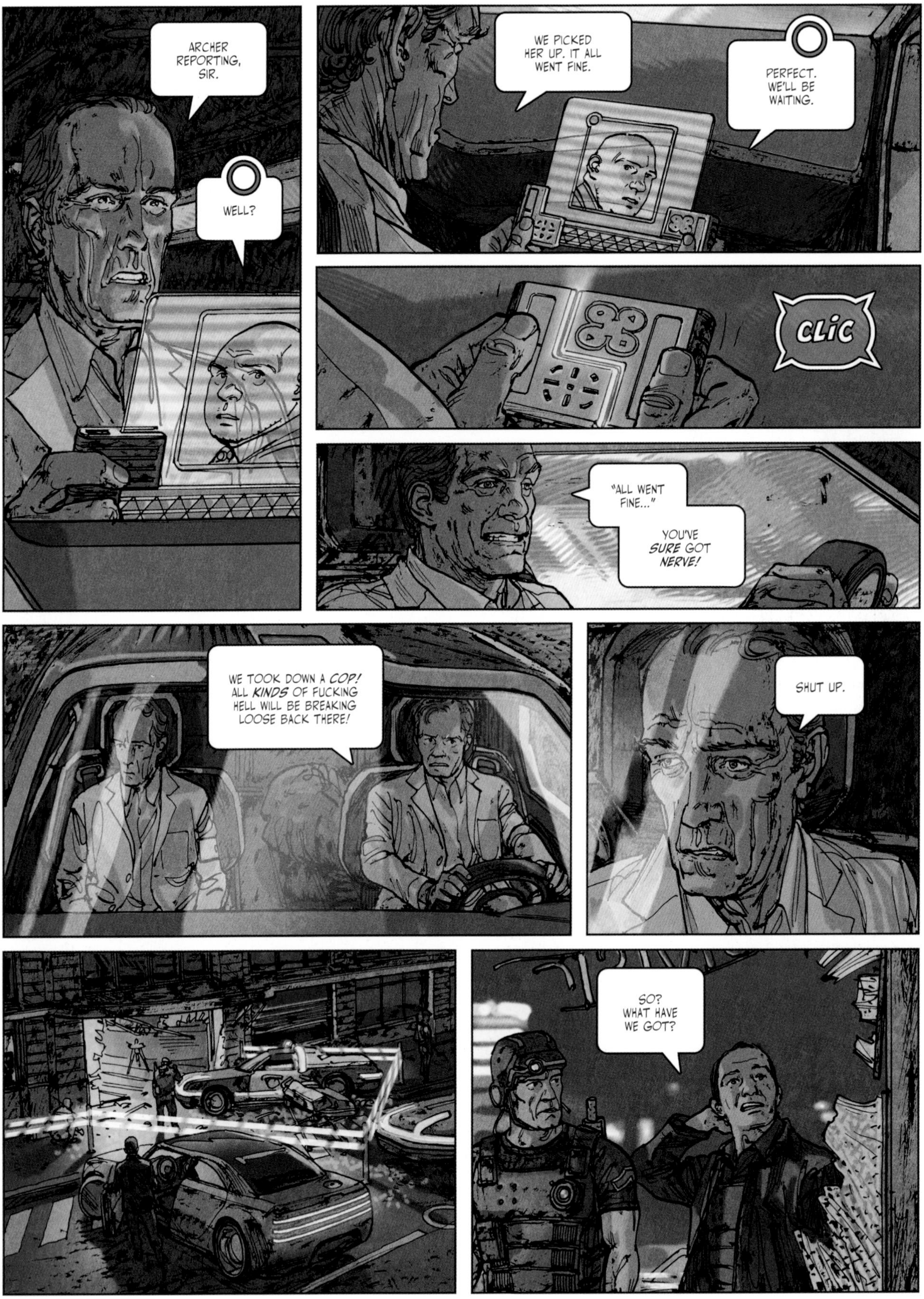
ARCHER REPORTING, SIR.
WELL?
WE PICKED HER UP. IT ALL WENT FINE.
PERFECT. WE'LL BE WAITING.
CLIC
"ALL WENT FINE..."
YOU'VE *SURE* GOT *NERVE!*
WE TOOK DOWN A *COP!* ALL *KINDS* OF FUCKING HELL WILL BE BREAKING LOOSE BACK THERE!
SHUT UP.
SO? WHAT HAVE WE GOT?

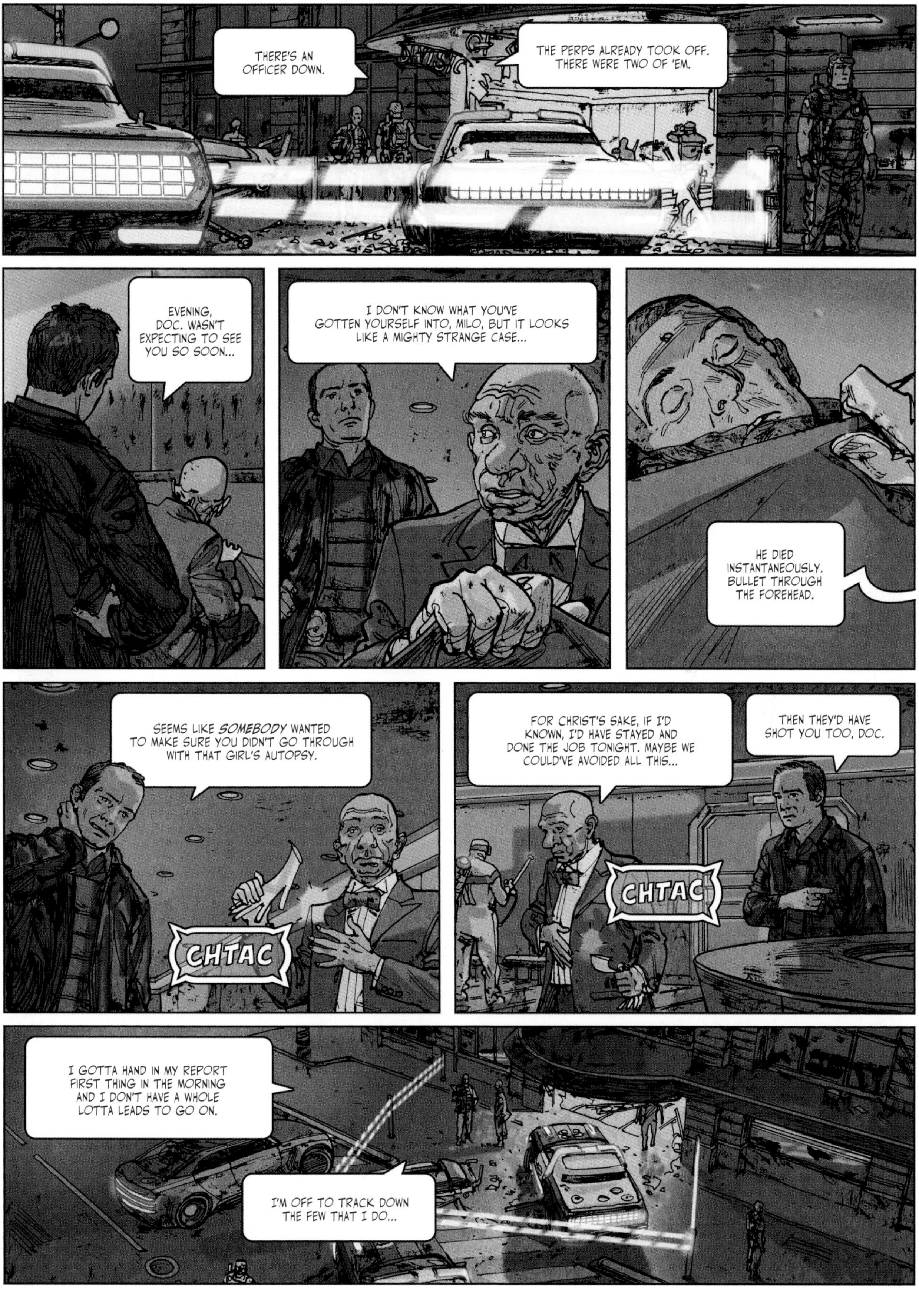
THERE'S AN OFFICER DOWN.
THE PERPS ALREADY TOOK OFF. THERE WERE TWO OF 'EM.
EVENING, DOC. WASN'T EXPECTING TO SEE YOU SO SOON...
I DON'T KNOW WHAT YOU'VE GOTTEN YOURSELF INTO, MILO, BUT IT LOOKS LIKE A MIGHTY STRANGE CASE...
HE DIED INSTANTANEOUSLY. BULLET THROUGH THE FOREHEAD.
SEEMS LIKE *SOMEBODY* WANTED TO MAKE SURE YOU DIDN'T GO THROUGH WITH THAT GIRL'S AUTOPSY.
CHTAC
FOR CHRIST'S SAKE, IF I'D KNOWN, I'D HAVE STAYED AND DONE THE JOB TONIGHT. MAYBE WE COULD'VE AVOIDED ALL THIS...
CHTAC
THEN THEY'D HAVE SHOT YOU TOO, DOC.
I GOTTA HAND IN MY REPORT FIRST THING IN THE MORNING AND I DON'T HAVE A WHOLE LOTTA LEADS TO GO ON.
I'M OFF TO TRACK DOWN THE FEW THAT I DO...

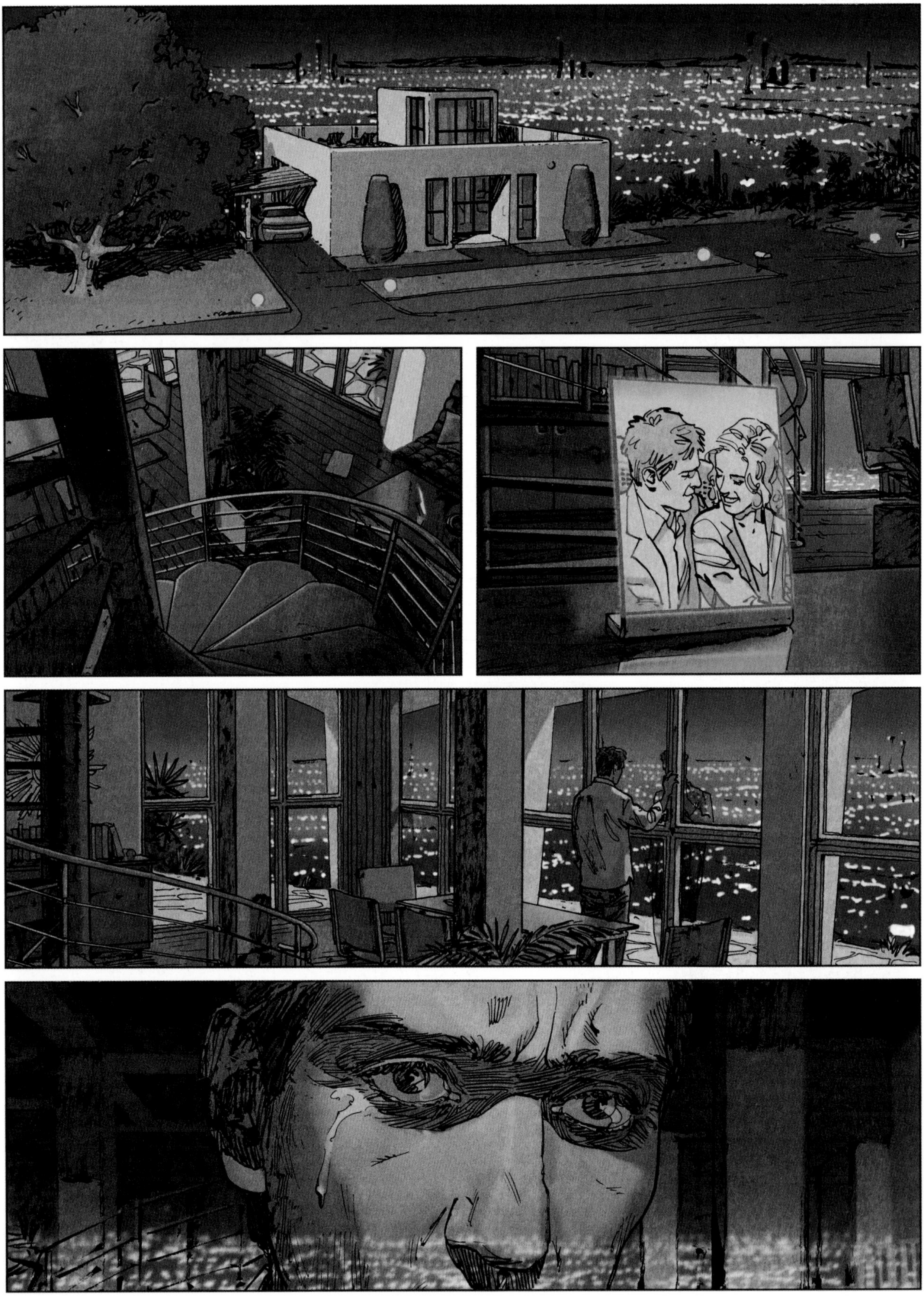

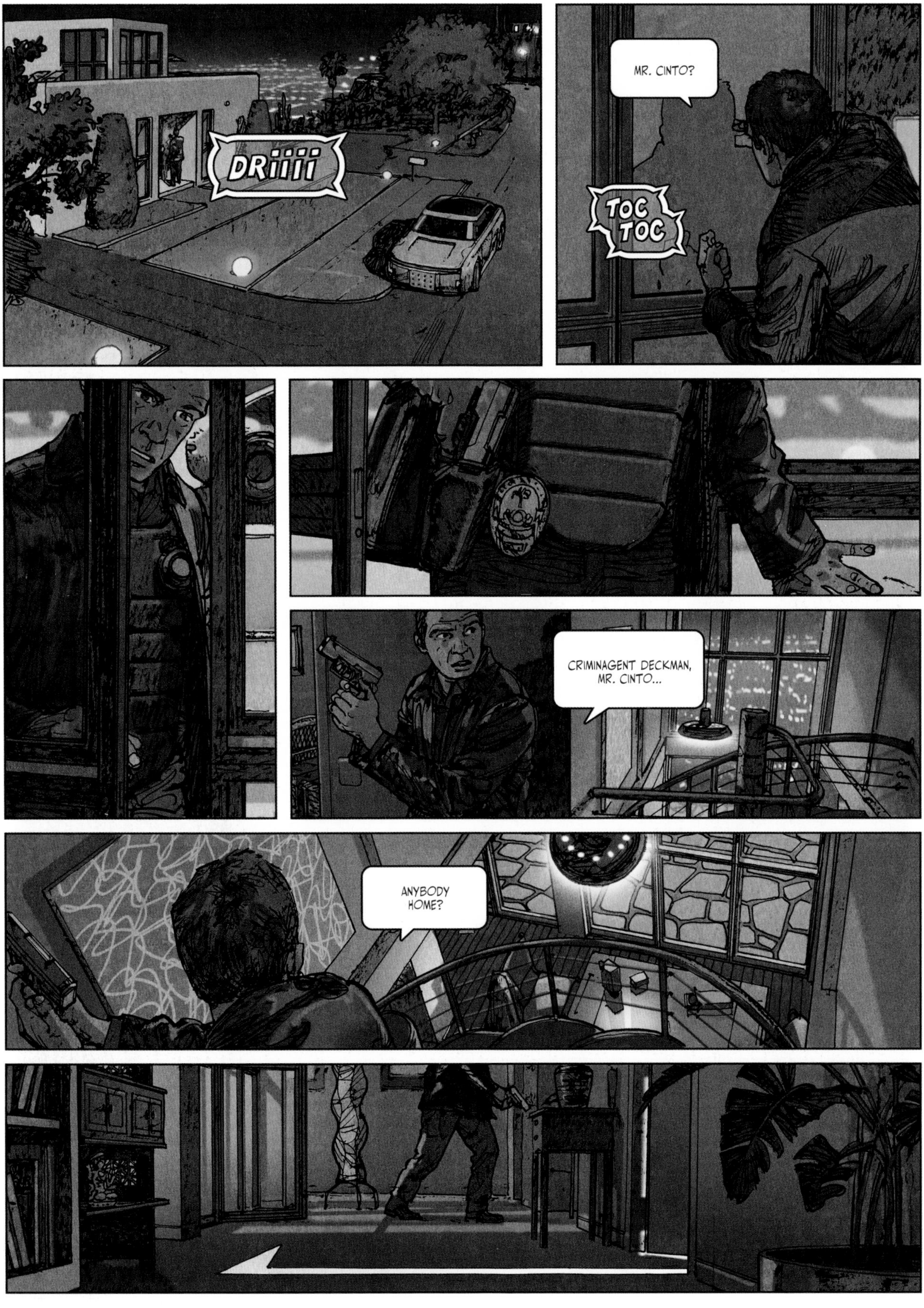
DRiiii
MR. CINTO?
TOC TOC
CRIMINAGENT DECKMAN, MR. CINTO...
ANYBODY HOME?

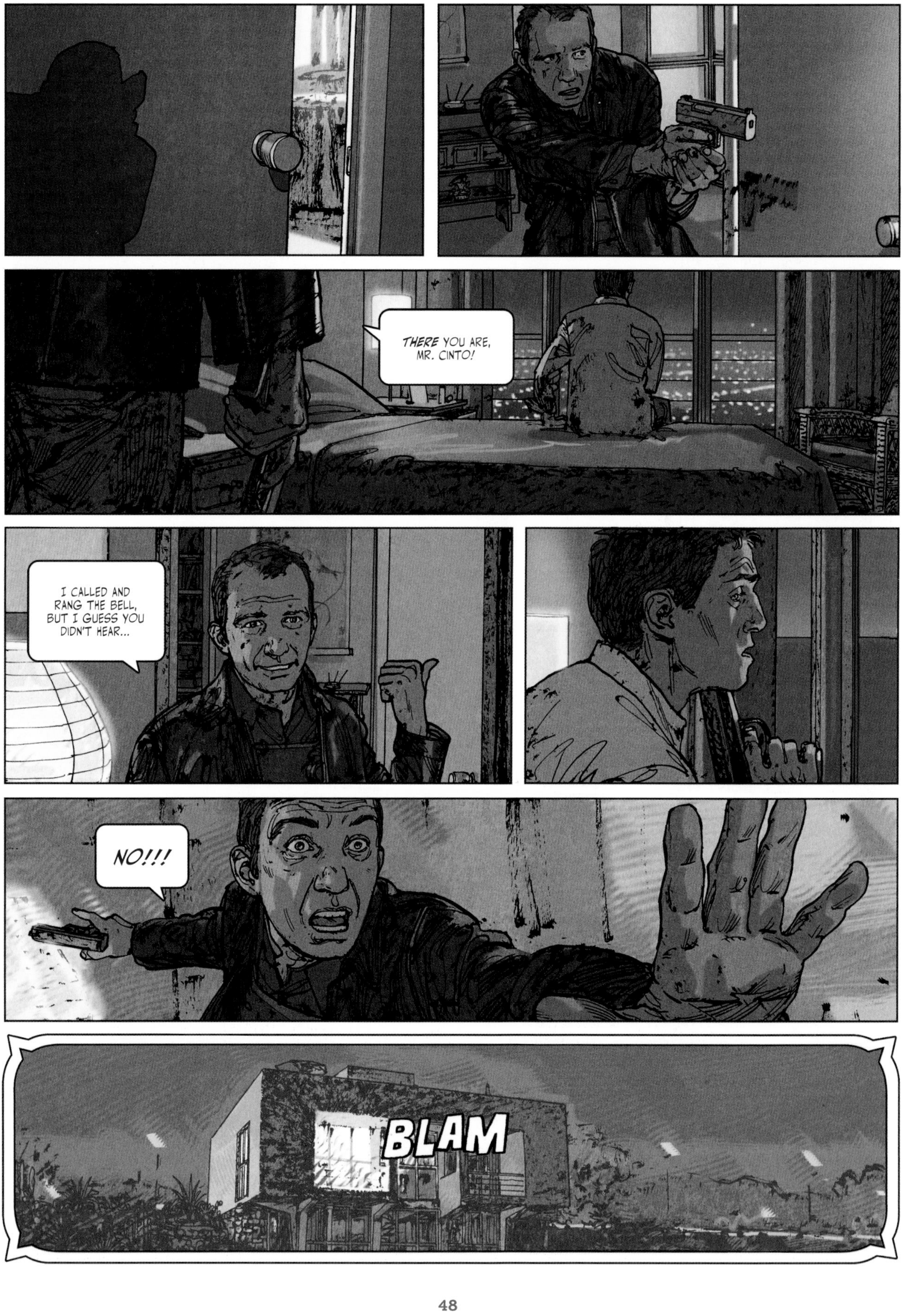

THERE YOU ARE, MR. CINTO!
I CALLED AND RANG THE BELL, BUT I GUESS YOU DIDN'T HEAR...
NO!!!
BLAM

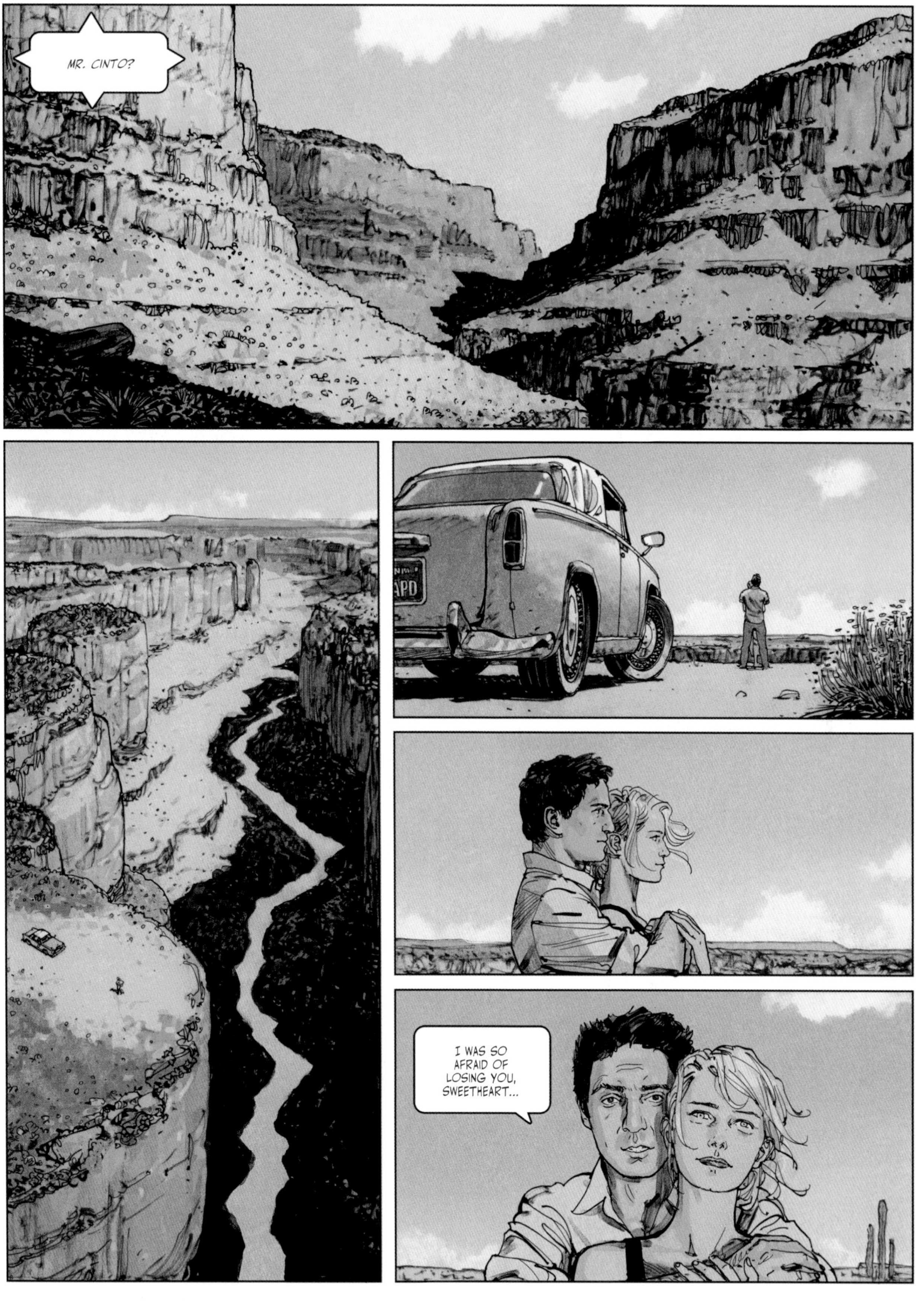
MR. CINTO?
I WAS SO AFRAID OF LOSING YOU, SWEETHEART...

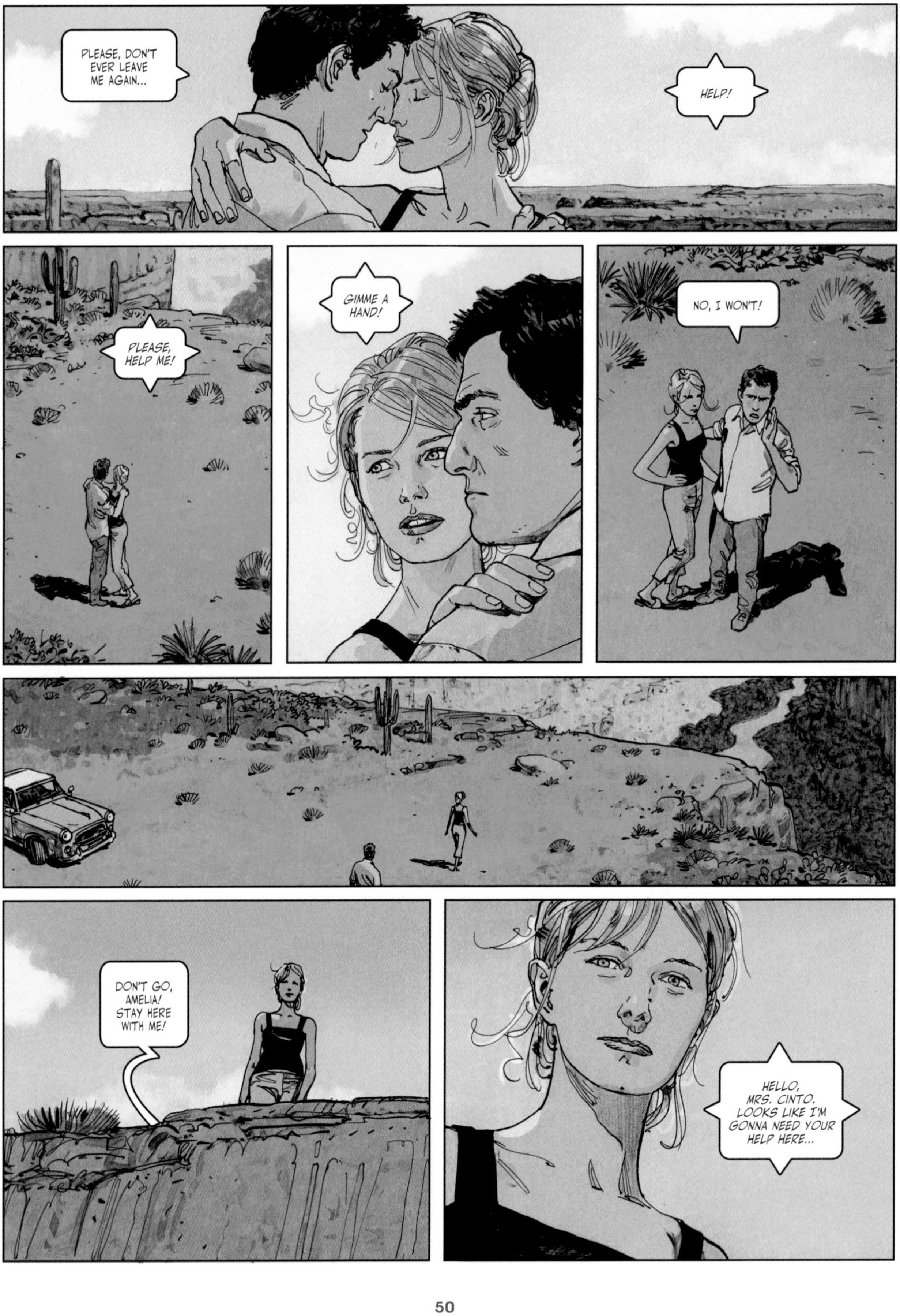
PLEASE, DON'T EVER LEAVE ME AGAIN...
HELP!
PLEASE, HELP ME!
GIMME A HAND!
NO, I WON'T!
DON'T GO, AMELIA! STAY HERE WITH ME!
HELLO, MRS. CINTO. LOOKS LIKE I'M GONNA NEED YOUR HELP HERE...

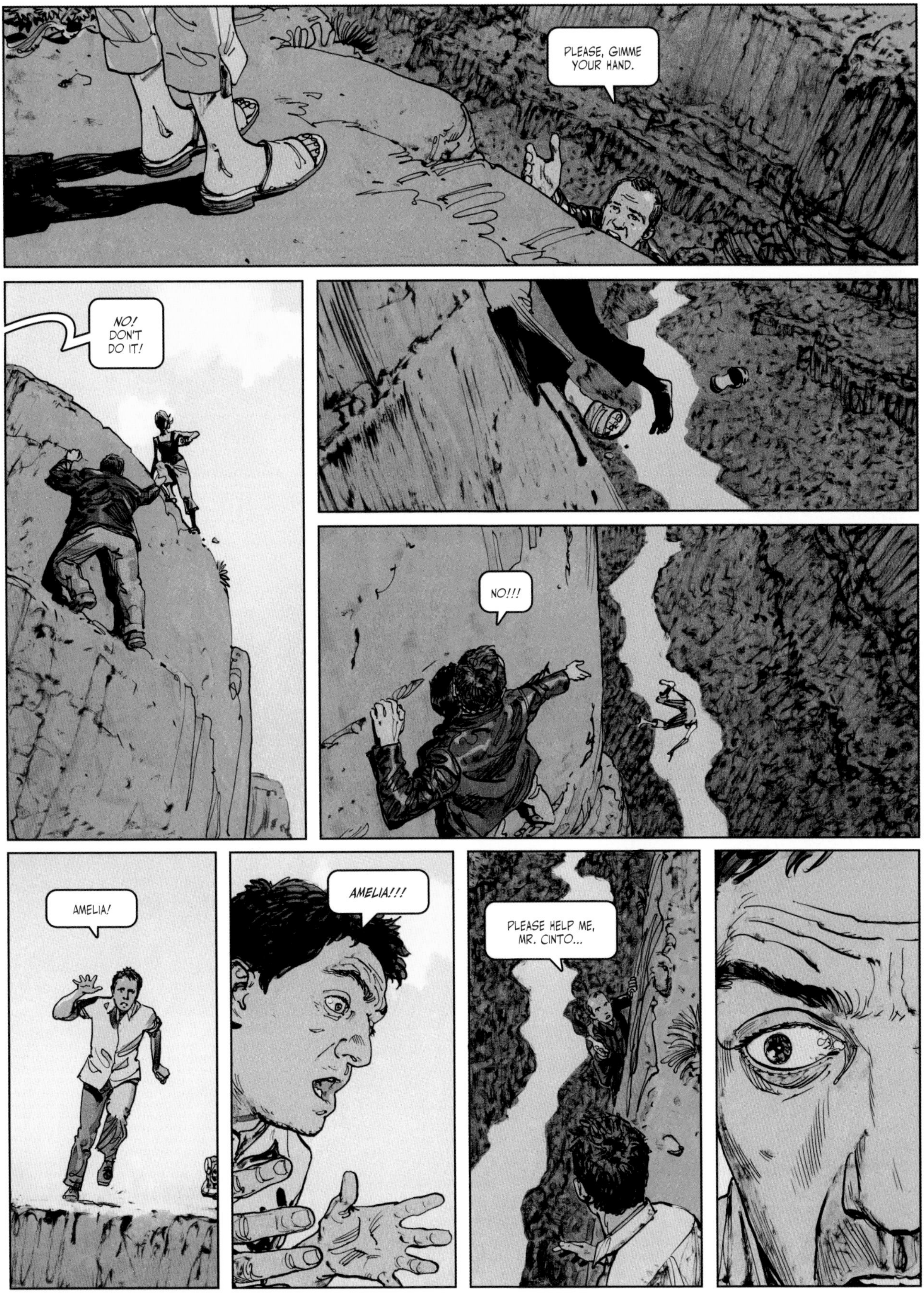
PLEASE, GIMME YOUR HAND.
NO! DON'T DO IT!
NO!!!
AMELIA!
AMELIA!!!
PLEASE HELP ME, MR. CINTO...

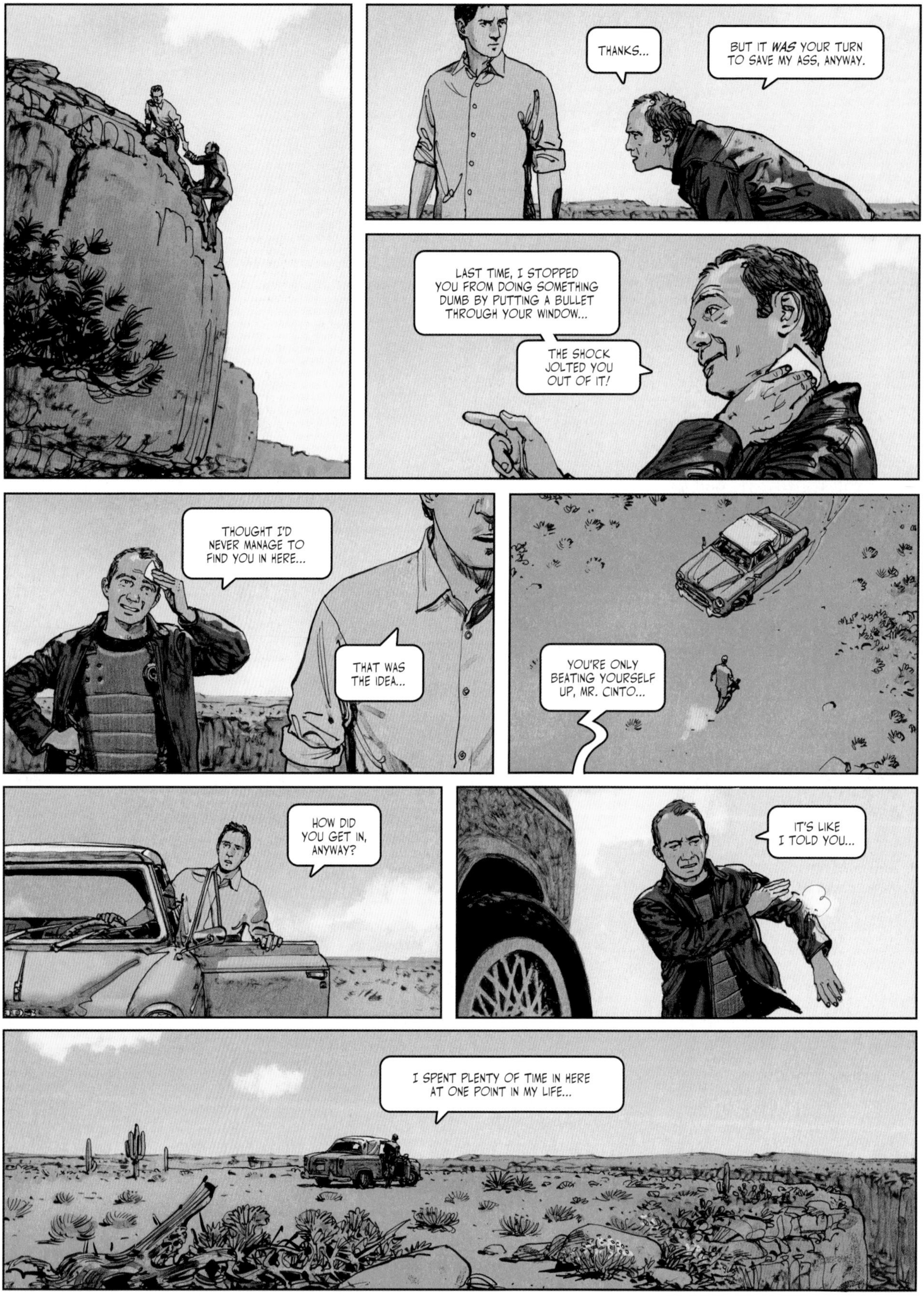
THANKS...
BUT IT WAS YOUR TURN TO SAVE MY ASS, ANYWAY.
LAST TIME, I STOPPED YOU FROM DOING SOMETHING DUMB BY PUTTING A BULLET THROUGH YOUR WINDOW...
THE SHOCK JOLTED YOU OUT OF IT!
THOUGHT I'D NEVER MANAGE TO FIND YOU IN HERE...
THAT WAS THE IDEA...
YOU'RE ONLY BEATING YOURSELF UP, MR. CINTO...
HOW DID YOU GET IN, ANYWAY?
IT'S LIKE I TOLD YOU...
I SPENT PLENTY OF TIME IN HERE AT ONE POINT IN MY LIFE...

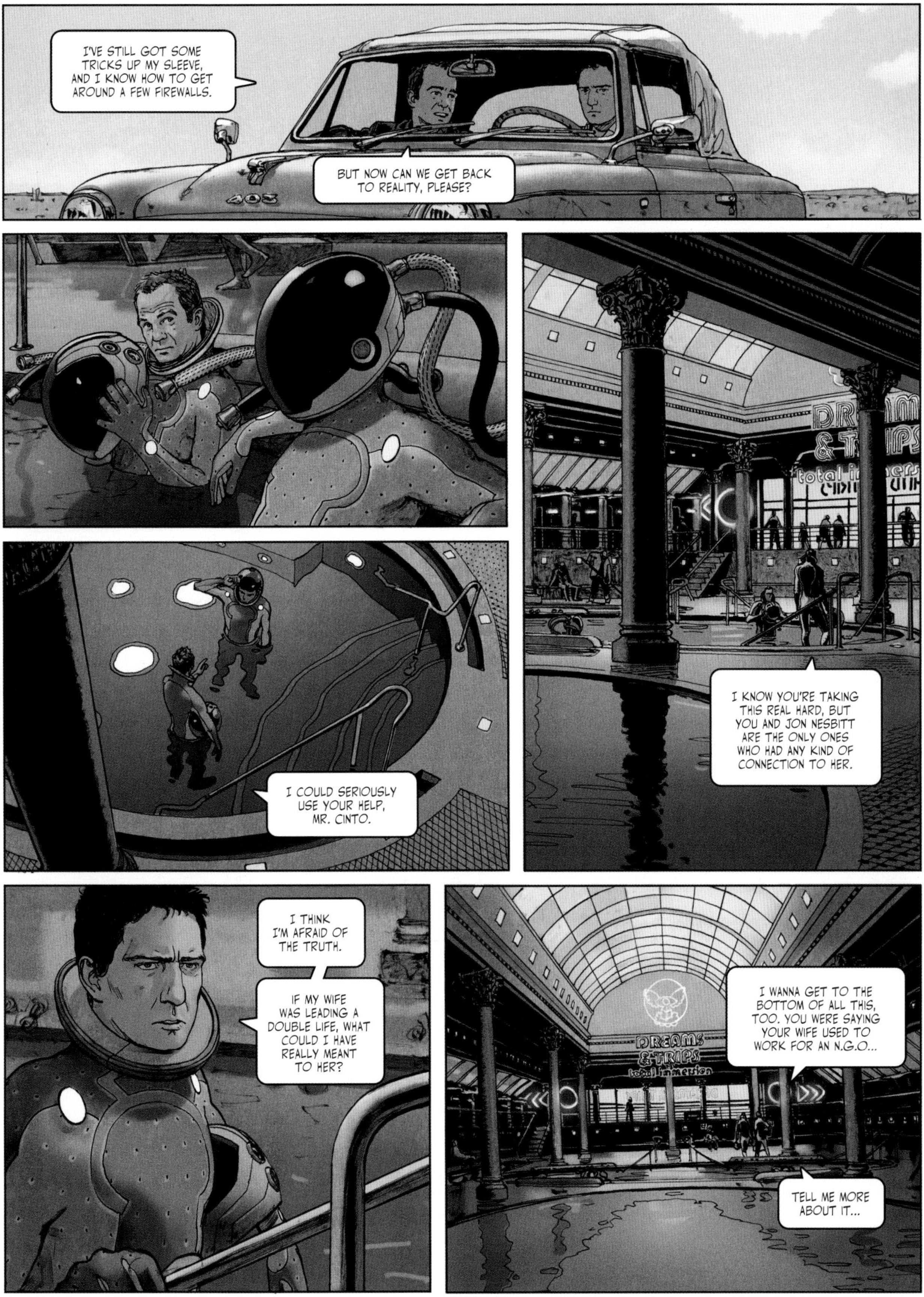
I'VE STILL GOT SOME TRICKS UP MY SLEEVE, AND I KNOW HOW TO GET AROUND A FEW FIREWALLS.
BUT NOW CAN WE GET BACK TO REALITY, PLEASE?
I COULD SERIOUSLY USE YOUR HELP, MR. CINTO.
I KNOW YOU'RE TAKING THIS REAL HARD, BUT YOU AND JON NESBITT ARE THE ONLY ONES WHO HAD ANY KIND OF CONNECTION TO HER.
I THINK I'M AFRAID OF THE TRUTH.
IF MY WIFE WAS LEADING A DOUBLE LIFE, WHAT COULD I HAVE REALLY MEANT TO HER?
I WANNA GET TO THE BOTTOM OF ALL THIS, TOO. YOU WERE SAYING YOUR WIFE USED TO WORK FOR AN N.G.O...
TELL ME MORE ABOUT IT...

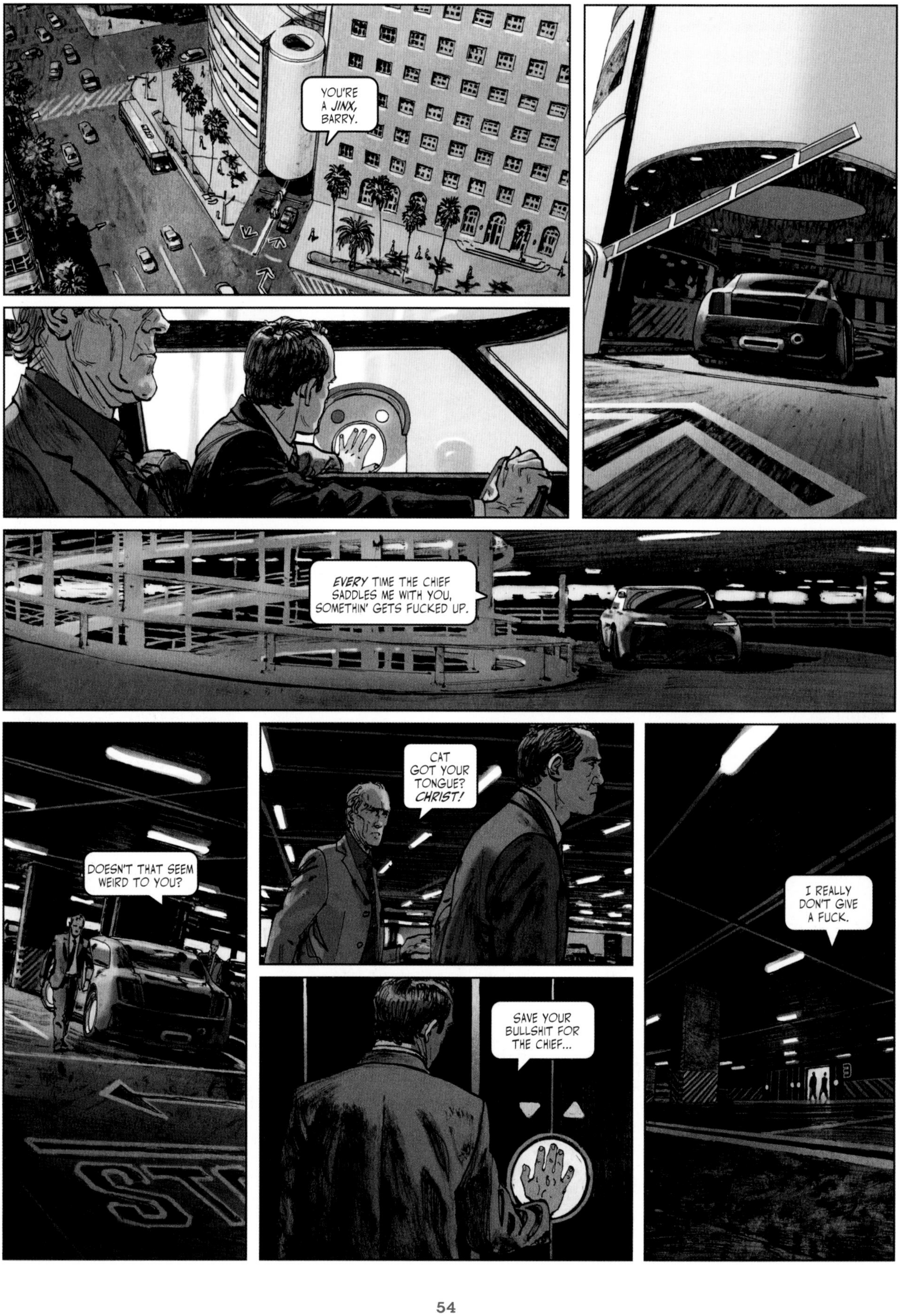
YOU'RE A JINX, BARRY.
EVERY TIME THE CHIEF SADDLES ME WITH YOU, SOMETHIN' GETS FUCKED UP.
DOESN'T THAT SEEM WEIRD TO YOU?
CAT GOT YOUR TONGUE? CHRIST!
SAVE YOUR BULLSHIT FOR THE CHIEF...
I REALLY DON'T GIVE A FUCK.

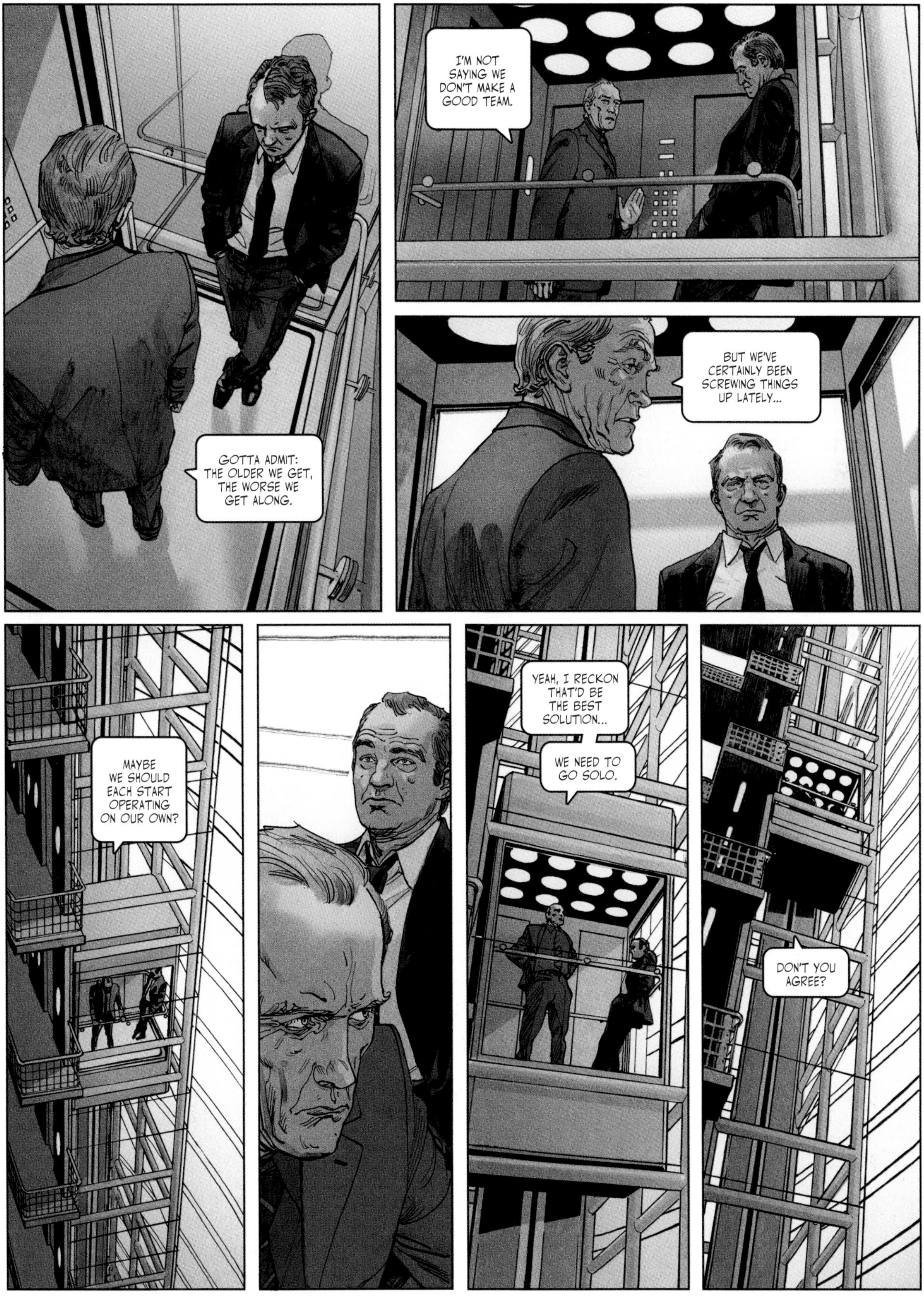
GOTTA ADMIT: THE OLDER WE GET, THE WORSE WE GET ALONG.
I'M NOT SAYING WE DON'T MAKE A GOOD TEAM.
BUT WE'VE CERTAINLY BEEN SCREWING THINGS UP LATELY...
MAYBE WE SHOULD EACH START OPERATING ON OUR OWN?
YEAH, I RECKON THAT'D BE THE BEST SOLUTION...
WE NEED TO GO SOLO.
DON'T YOU AGREE?

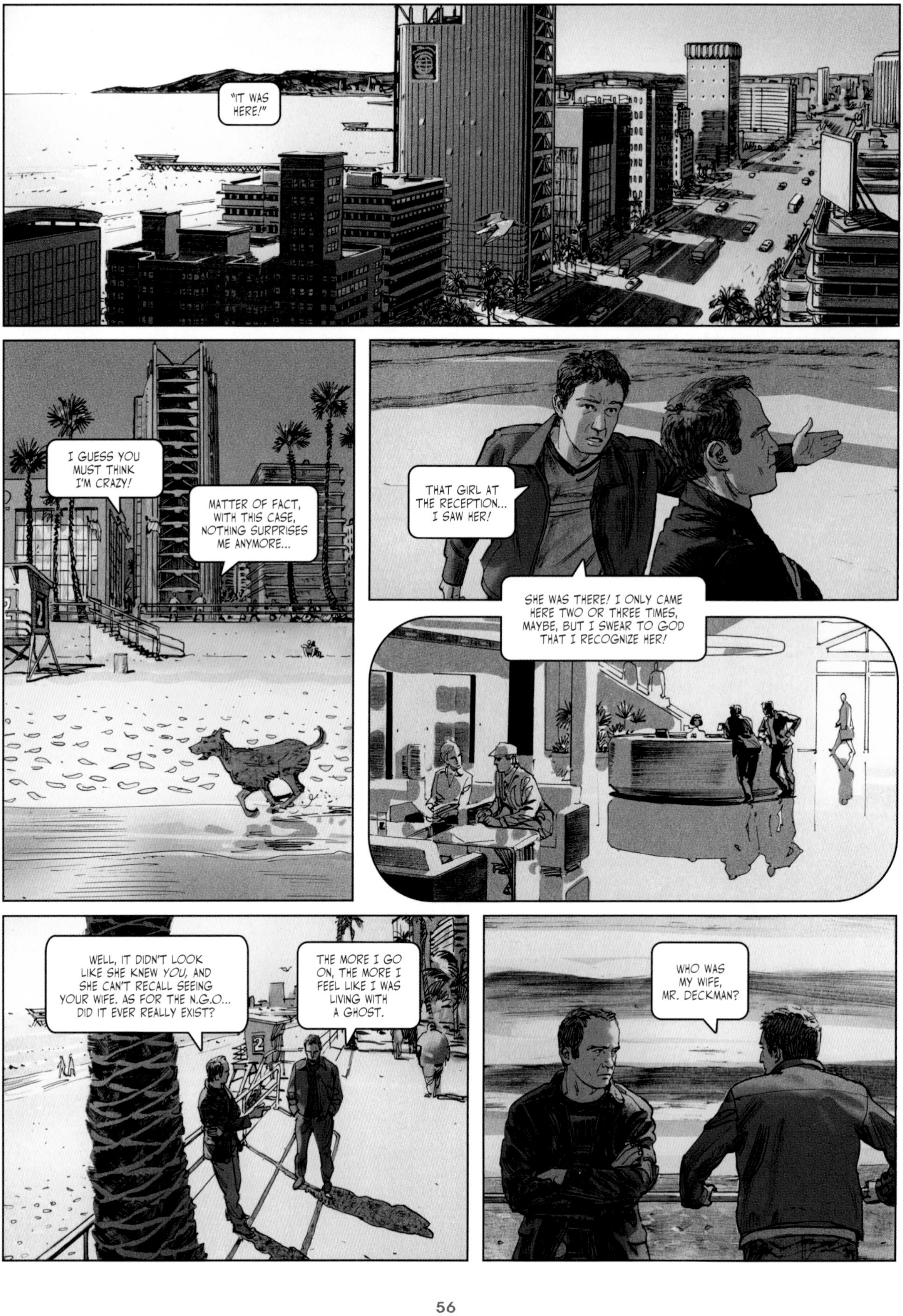
"IT WAS HERE!"
I GUESS YOU MUST THINK I'M CRAZY!
MATTER OF FACT, WITH THIS CASE, NOTHING SURPRISES ME ANYMORE...
THAT GIRL AT THE RECEPTION... I SAW HER!
SHE WAS THERE! I ONLY CAME HERE TWO OR THREE TIMES, MAYBE, BUT I SWEAR TO GOD THAT I RECOGNIZE HER!
WELL, IT DIDN'T LOOK LIKE SHE KNEW *YOU,* AND SHE CAN'T RECALL SEEING YOUR WIFE. AS FOR THE N.G.O... DID IT EVER REALLY EXIST?
THE MORE I GO ON, THE MORE I FEEL LIKE I WAS LIVING WITH A GHOST.
WHO WAS MY WIFE, MR. DECKMAN?

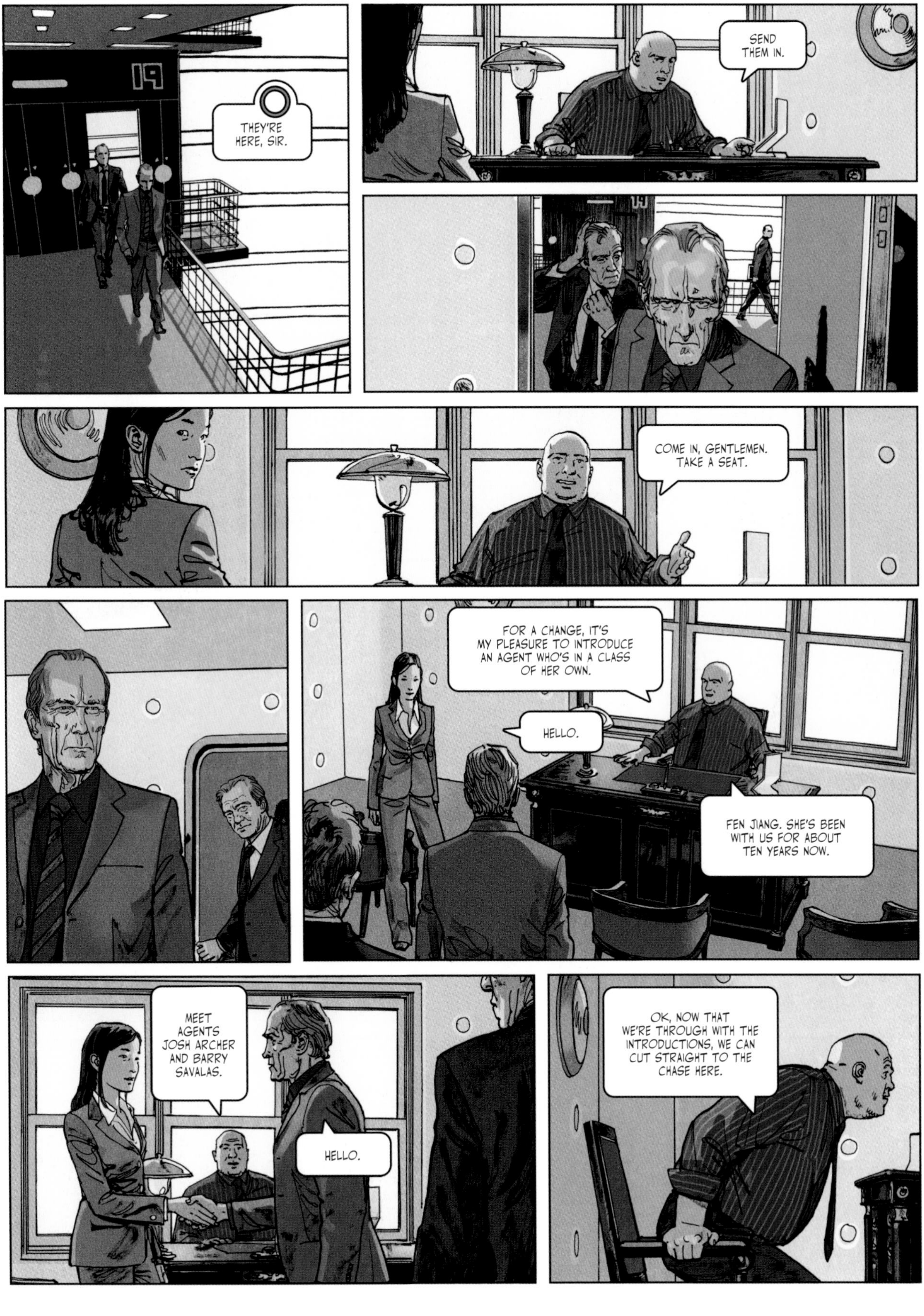
THEY'RE HERE, SIR.
SEND THEM IN.
COME IN, GENTLEMEN. TAKE A SEAT.
FOR A CHANGE, IT'S MY PLEASURE TO INTRODUCE AN AGENT WHO'S IN A CLASS OF HER OWN.
HELLO.
FEN JIANG. SHE'S BEEN WITH US FOR ABOUT TEN YEARS NOW.
MEET AGENTS JOSH ARCHER AND BARRY SAVALAS.
HELLO.
OK, NOW THAT WE'RE THROUGH WITH THE INTRODUCTIONS, WE CAN CUT STRAIGHT TO THE CHASE HERE.

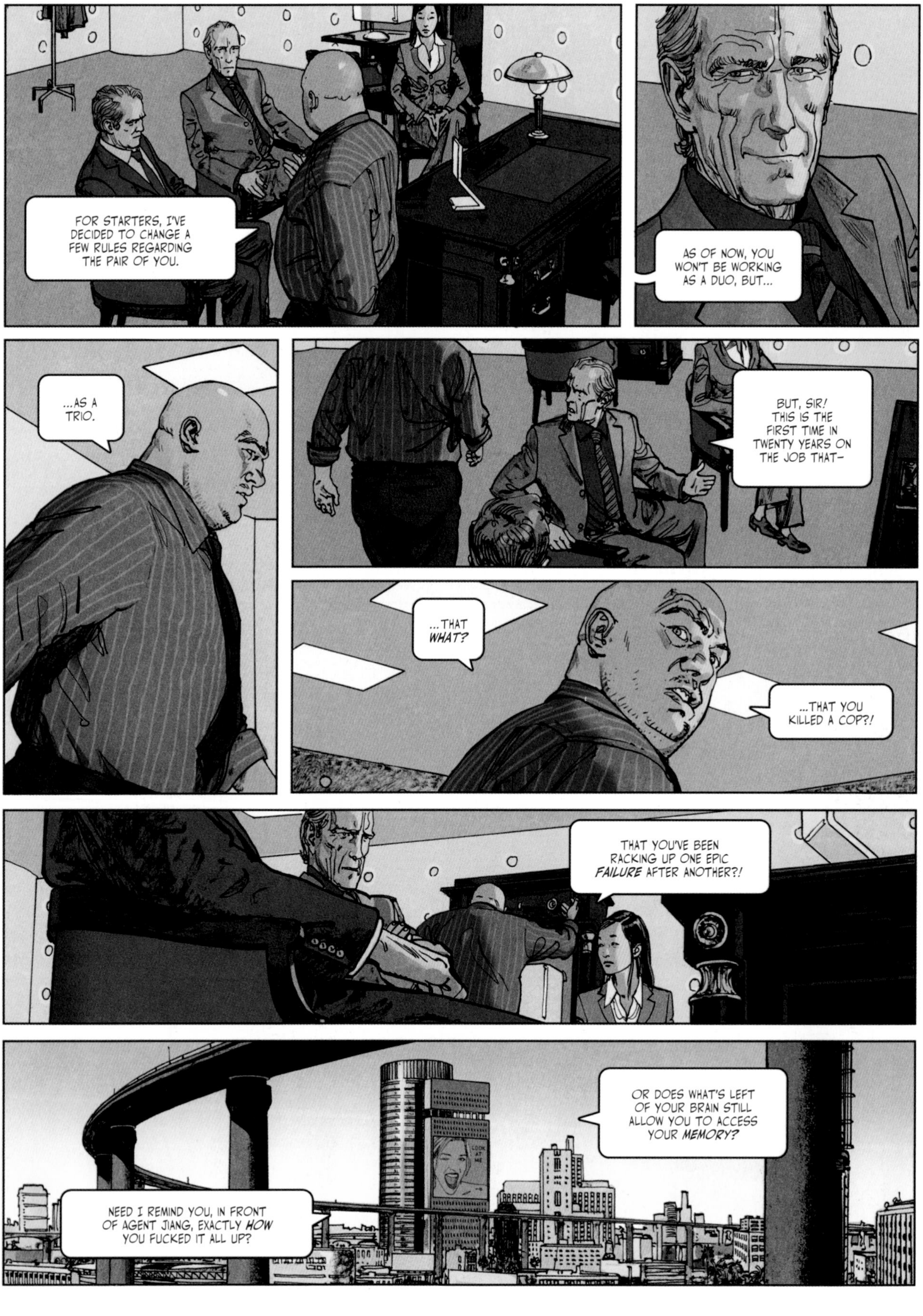

FOR STARTERS, I'VE DECIDED TO CHANGE A FEW RULES REGARDING THE PAIR OF YOU.
AS OF NOW, YOU WON'T BE WORKING AS A DUO, BUT...
...AS A TRIO.
BUT, SIR! THIS IS THE FIRST TIME IN TWENTY YEARS ON THE JOB THAT–
...THAT WHAT?
...THAT YOU KILLED A COP?!
THAT YOU'VE BEEN RACKING UP ONE EPIC FAILURE AFTER ANOTHER?!
OR DOES WHAT'S LEFT OF YOUR BRAIN STILL ALLOW YOU TO ACCESS YOUR MEMORY?
NEED I REMIND YOU, IN FRONT OF AGENT JIANG, EXACTLY HOW YOU FUCKED IT ALL UP?
LOOK AT ME

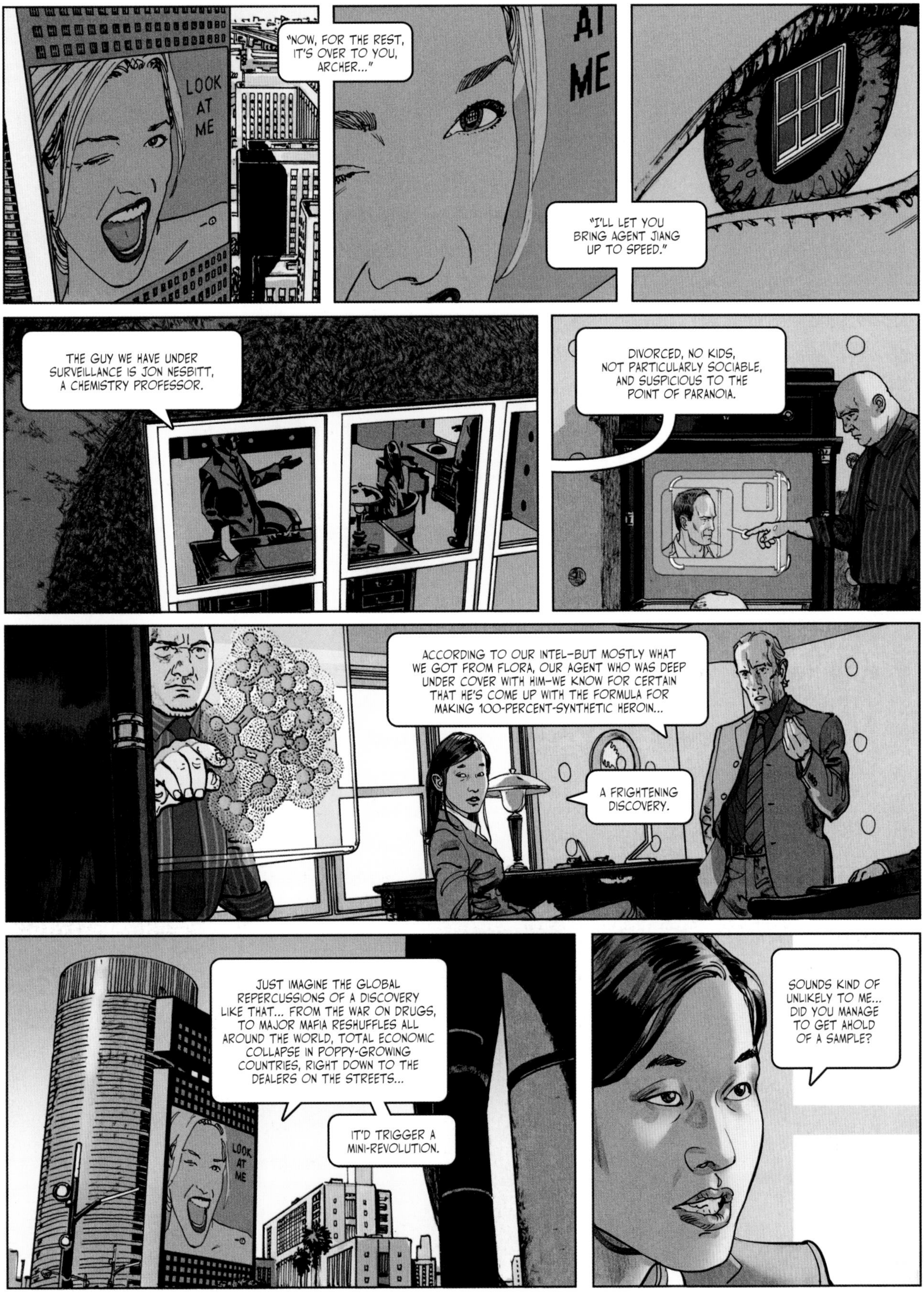
LOOK AT ME
"NOW, FOR THE REST, IT'S OVER TO YOU, ARCHER..."
AT ME
"I'LL LET YOU BRING AGENT JIANG UP TO SPEED."
THE GUY WE HAVE UNDER SURVEILLANCE IS JON NESBITT, A CHEMISTRY PROFESSOR.
DIVORCED, NO KIDS, NOT PARTICULARLY SOCIABLE, AND SUSPICIOUS TO THE POINT OF PARANOIA.
ACCORDING TO OUR INTEL—BUT MOSTLY WHAT WE GOT FROM FLORA, OUR AGENT WHO WAS DEEP UNDER COVER WITH HIM—WE KNOW FOR CERTAIN THAT HE'S COME UP WITH THE FORMULA FOR MAKING 100-PERCENT-SYNTHETIC HEROIN...
A FRIGHTENING DISCOVERY.
JUST IMAGINE THE GLOBAL REPERCUSSIONS OF A DISCOVERY LIKE THAT... FROM THE WAR ON DRUGS, TO MAJOR MAFIA RESHUFFLES ALL AROUND THE WORLD, TOTAL ECONOMIC COLLAPSE IN POPPY-GROWING COUNTRIES, RIGHT DOWN TO THE DEALERS ON THE STREETS...
IT'D TRIGGER A MINI-REVOLUTION.
LOOK AT ME
SOUNDS KIND OF UNLIKELY TO ME... DID YOU MANAGE TO GET AHOLD OF A SAMPLE?

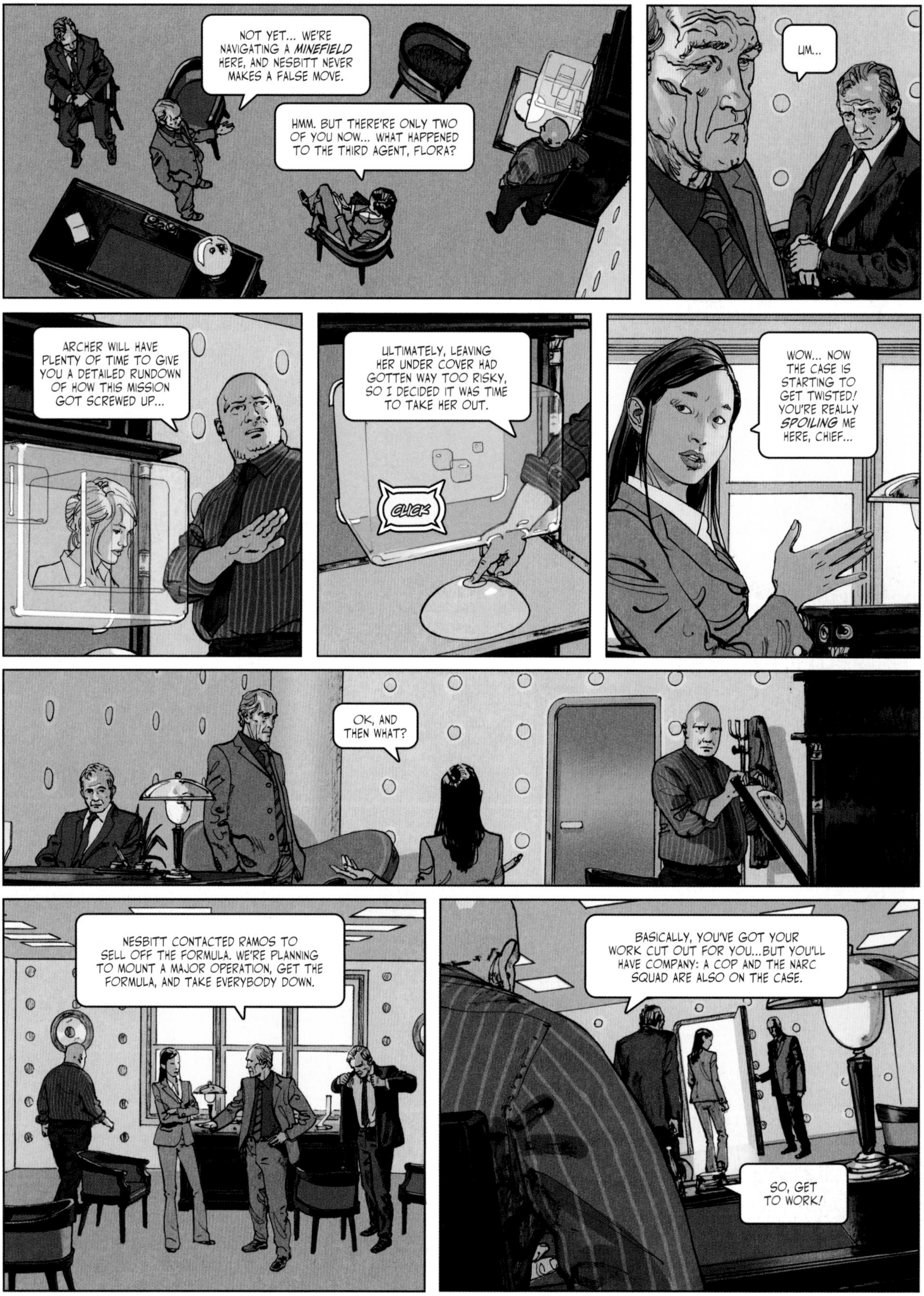
NOT YET... WE'RE NAVIGATING A *MINEFIELD* HERE, AND NESBITT NEVER MAKES A FALSE MOVE.
HMM. BUT THERE'RE ONLY TWO OF YOU NOW... WHAT HAPPENED TO THE THIRD AGENT, FLORA?
UM...
ARCHER WILL HAVE PLENTY OF TIME TO GIVE YOU A DETAILED RUNDOWN OF HOW THIS MISSION GOT SCREWED UP...
ULTIMATELY, LEAVING HER UNDER COVER HAD GOTTEN WAY TOO RISKY, SO I DECIDED IT WAS TIME TO TAKE HER OUT.
CLICK
WOW... NOW THE CASE IS STARTING TO GET TWISTED! YOU'RE REALLY *SPOILING* ME HERE, CHIEF...
OK, AND THEN WHAT?
NESBITT CONTACTED RAMOS TO SELL OFF THE FORMULA. WE'RE PLANNING TO MOUNT A MAJOR OPERATION, GET THE FORMULA, AND TAKE EVERYBODY DOWN.
BASICALLY, YOU'VE GOT YOUR WORK CUT OUT FOR YOU...BUT YOU'LL HAVE COMPANY: A COP AND THE NARC SQUAD ARE ALSO ON THE CASE.
SO, GET TO WORK!

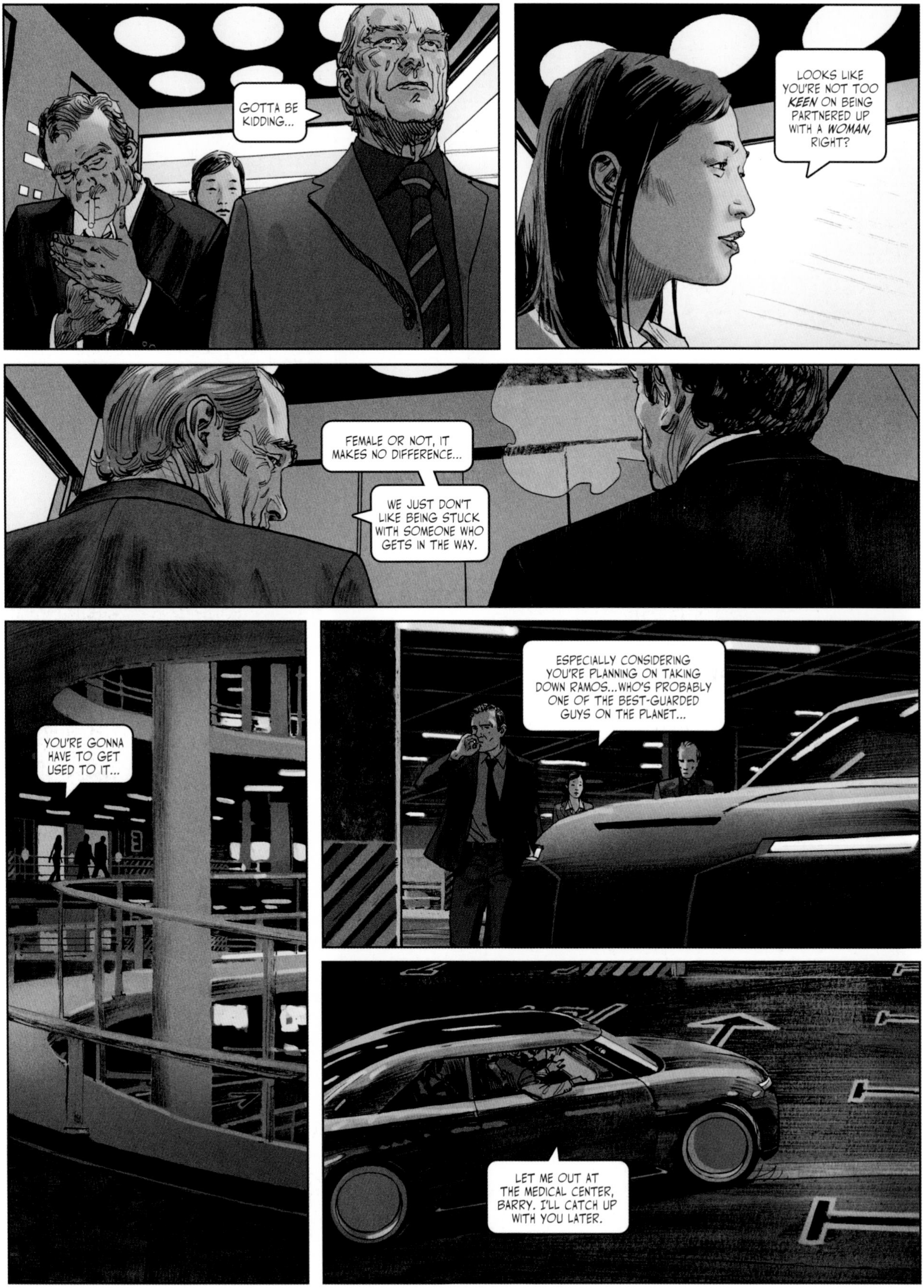
GOTTA BE KIDDING...
LOOKS LIKE YOU'RE NOT TOO *KEEN* ON BEING PARTNERED UP WITH A *WOMAN,* RIGHT?
FEMALE OR NOT, IT MAKES NO DIFFERENCE...
WE JUST DON'T LIKE BEING STUCK WITH SOMEONE WHO GETS IN THE WAY.
YOU'RE GONNA HAVE TO GET USED TO IT...
ESPECIALLY CONSIDERING YOU'RE PLANNING ON TAKING DOWN RAMOS...WHO'S PROBABLY ONE OF THE BEST-GUARDED GUYS ON THE PLANET...
LET ME OUT AT THE MEDICAL CENTER, BARRY. I'LL CATCH UP WITH YOU LATER.

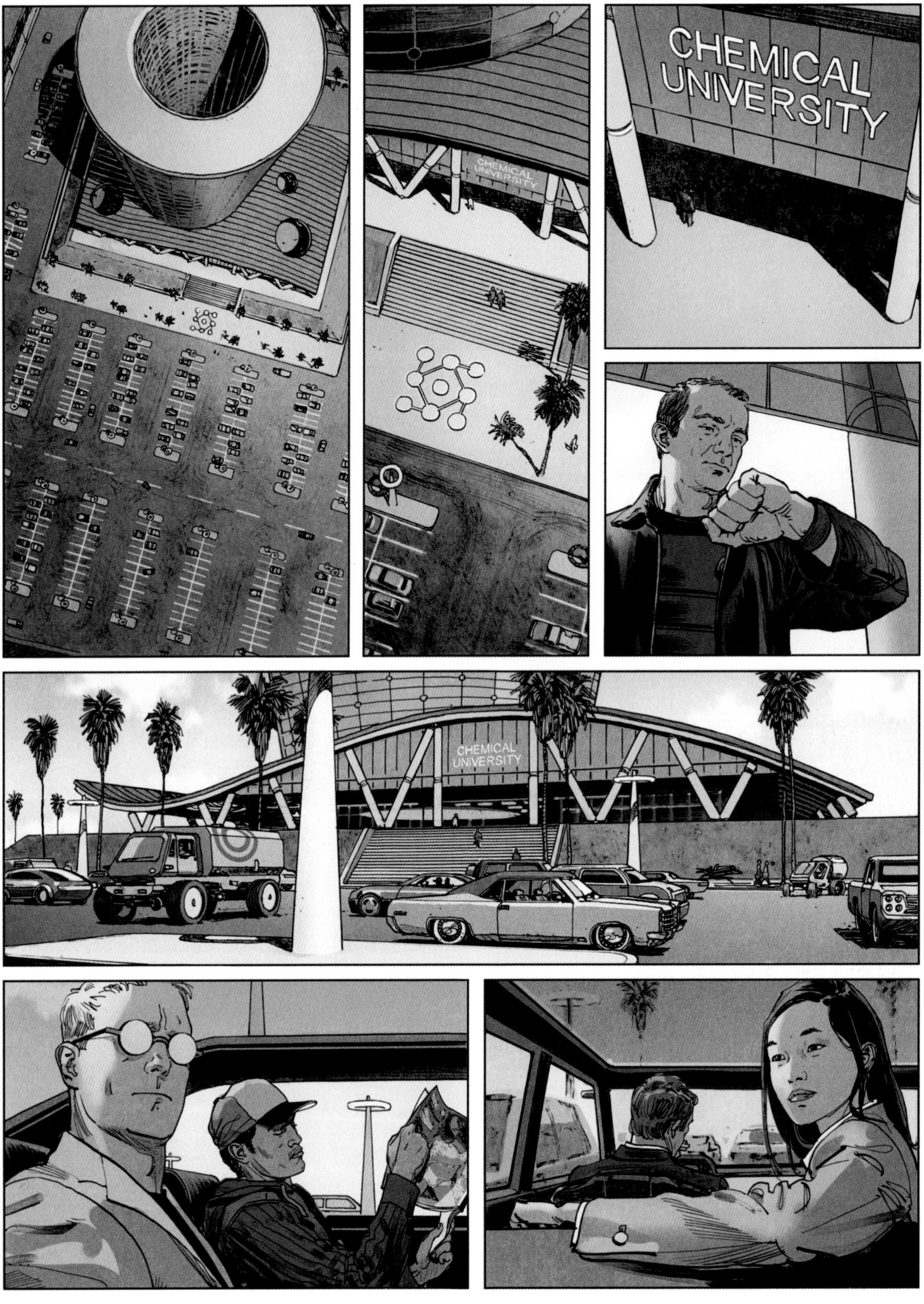
CHEMICAL UNIVERSITY
CHEMICAL UNIVERSITY
CHEMICAL UNIVERSITY

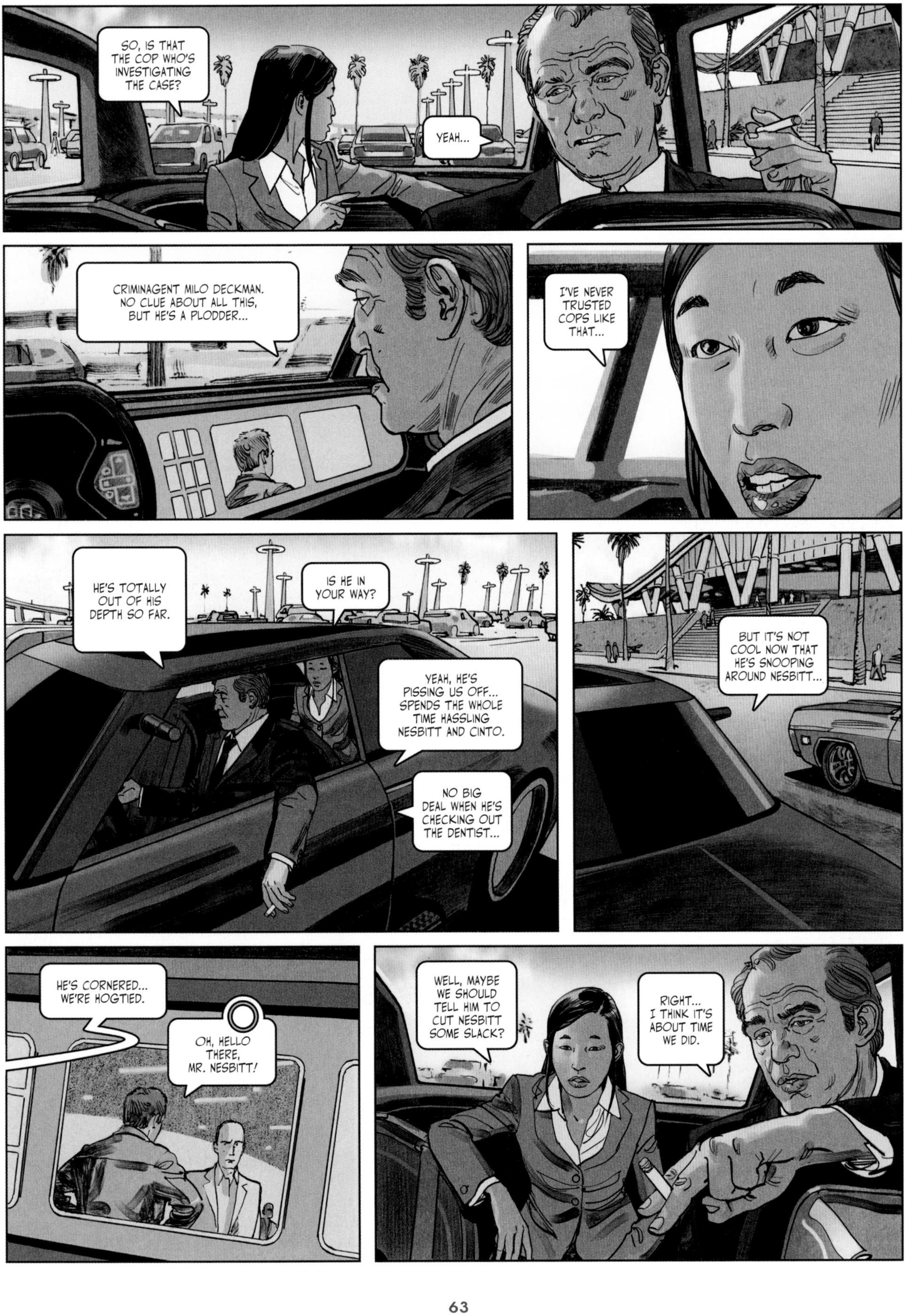
SO, IS THAT THE COP WHO'S INVESTIGATING THE CASE?
YEAH...
CRIMINAGENT MILO DECKMAN. NO CLUE ABOUT ALL THIS, BUT HE'S A PLODDER...
I'VE NEVER TRUSTED COPS LIKE THAT...
HE'S TOTALLY OUT OF HIS DEPTH SO FAR.
IS HE IN YOUR WAY?
YEAH, HE'S PISSING US OFF... SPENDS THE WHOLE TIME HASSLING NESBITT AND CINTO.
NO BIG DEAL WHEN HE'S CHECKING OUT THE DENTIST...
BUT IT'S NOT COOL NOW THAT HE'S SNOOPING AROUND NESBITT...
HE'S CORNERED... WE'RE HOGTIED.
OH, HELLO THERE, MR. NESBITT!
WELL, MAYBE WE SHOULD TELL HIM TO CUT NESBITT SOME SLACK?
RIGHT... I THINK IT'S ABOUT TIME WE DID.

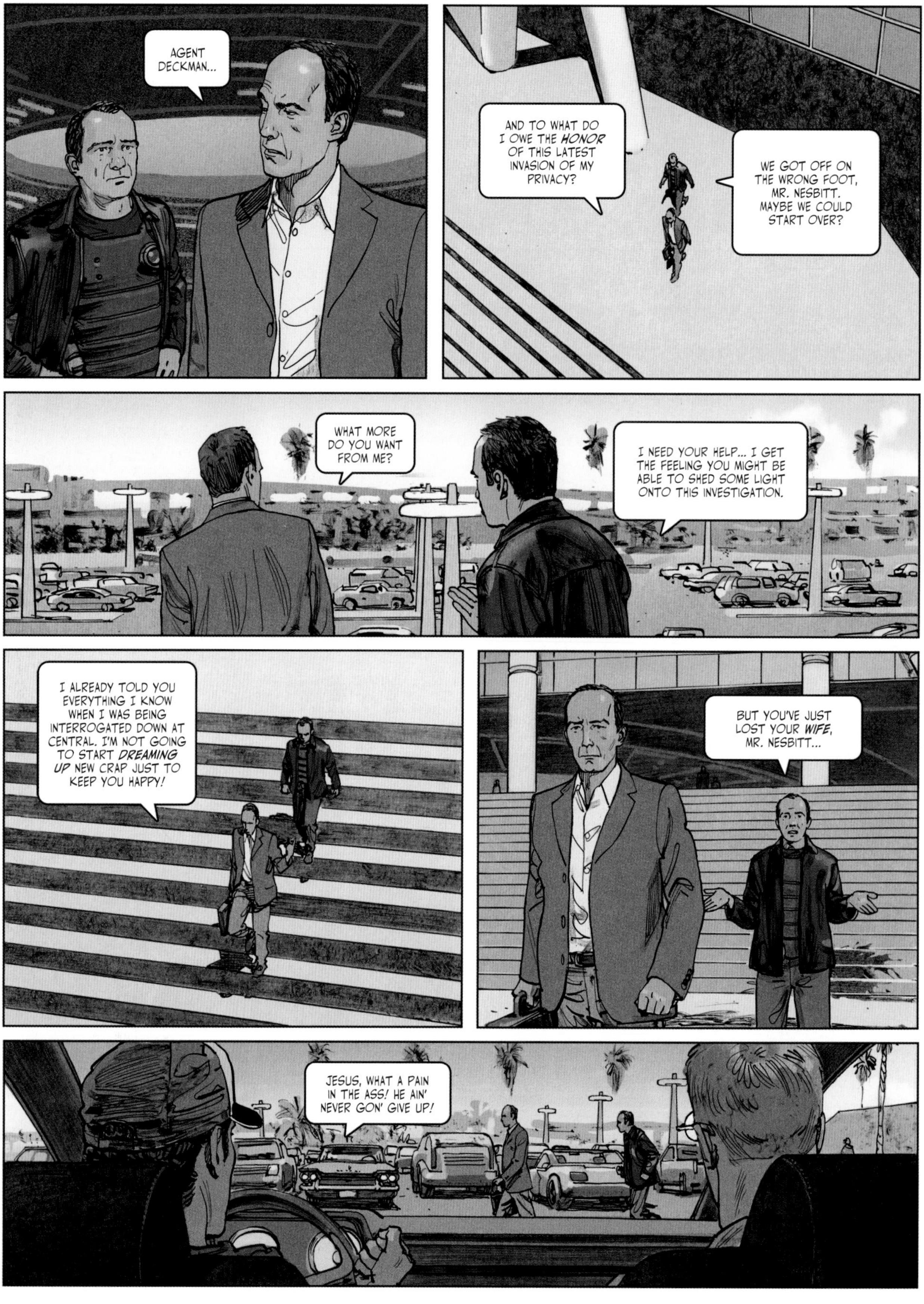
AGENT DECKMAN...
AND TO WHAT DO I OWE THE HONOR OF THIS LATEST INVASION OF MY PRIVACY?
WE GOT OFF ON THE WRONG FOOT, MR. NESBITT. MAYBE WE COULD START OVER?
WHAT MORE DO YOU WANT FROM ME?
I NEED YOUR HELP... I GET THE FEELING YOU MIGHT BE ABLE TO SHED SOME LIGHT ONTO THIS INVESTIGATION.
I ALREADY TOLD YOU EVERYTHING I KNOW WHEN I WAS BEING INTERROGATED DOWN AT CENTRAL. I'M NOT GOING TO START DREAMING UP NEW CRAP JUST TO KEEP YOU HAPPY!
BUT YOU'VE JUST LOST YOUR WIFE, MR. NESBITT...
JESUS, WHAT A PAIN IN THE ASS! HE AIN' NEVER GON' GIVE UP!

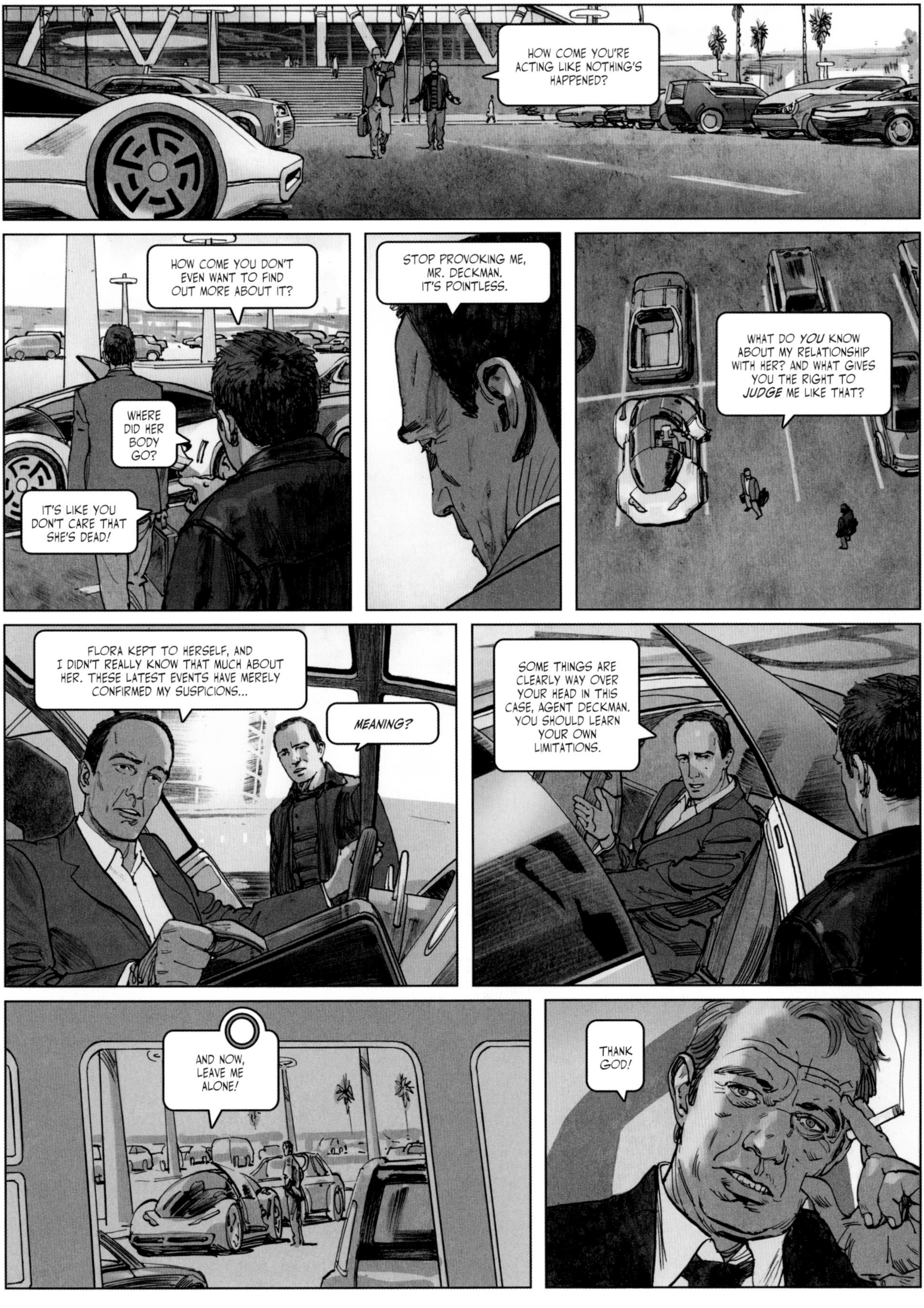
HOW COME YOU'RE ACTING LIKE NOTHING'S HAPPENED?
HOW COME YOU DON'T EVEN WANT TO FIND OUT MORE ABOUT IT?
WHERE DID HER BODY GO?
IT'S LIKE YOU DON'T CARE THAT SHE'S DEAD!
STOP PROVOKING ME, MR. DECKMAN. IT'S POINTLESS.
WHAT DO *YOU* KNOW ABOUT MY RELATIONSHIP WITH HER? AND WHAT GIVES YOU THE RIGHT TO *JUDGE* ME LIKE THAT?
FLORA KEPT TO HERSELF, AND I DIDN'T REALLY KNOW THAT MUCH ABOUT HER. THESE LATEST EVENTS HAVE MERELY CONFIRMED MY SUSPICIONS...
MEANING?
SOME THINGS ARE CLEARLY WAY OVER YOUR HEAD IN THIS CASE, AGENT DECKMAN. YOU SHOULD LEARN YOUR OWN LIMITATIONS.
AND NOW, LEAVE ME ALONE!
THANK GOD!

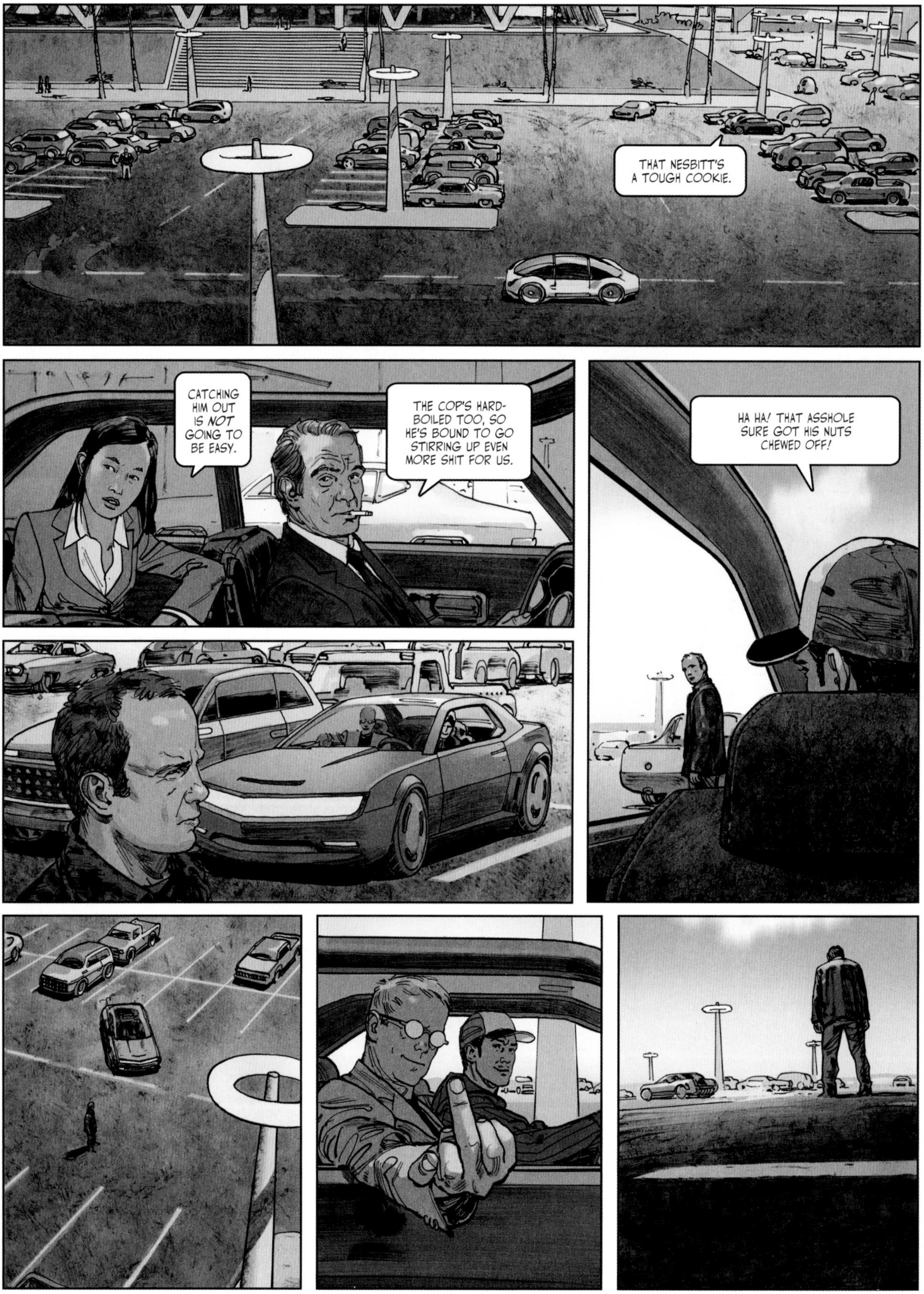
THAT NESBITT'S A TOUGH COOKIE.
CATCHING HIM OUT IS *NOT* GOING TO BE EASY.
THE COP'S HARD-BOILED TOO, SO HE'S BOUND TO GO STIRRING UP EVEN MORE SHIT FOR US.
HA HA! THAT ASSHOLE SURE GOT HIS NUTS CHEWED OFF!

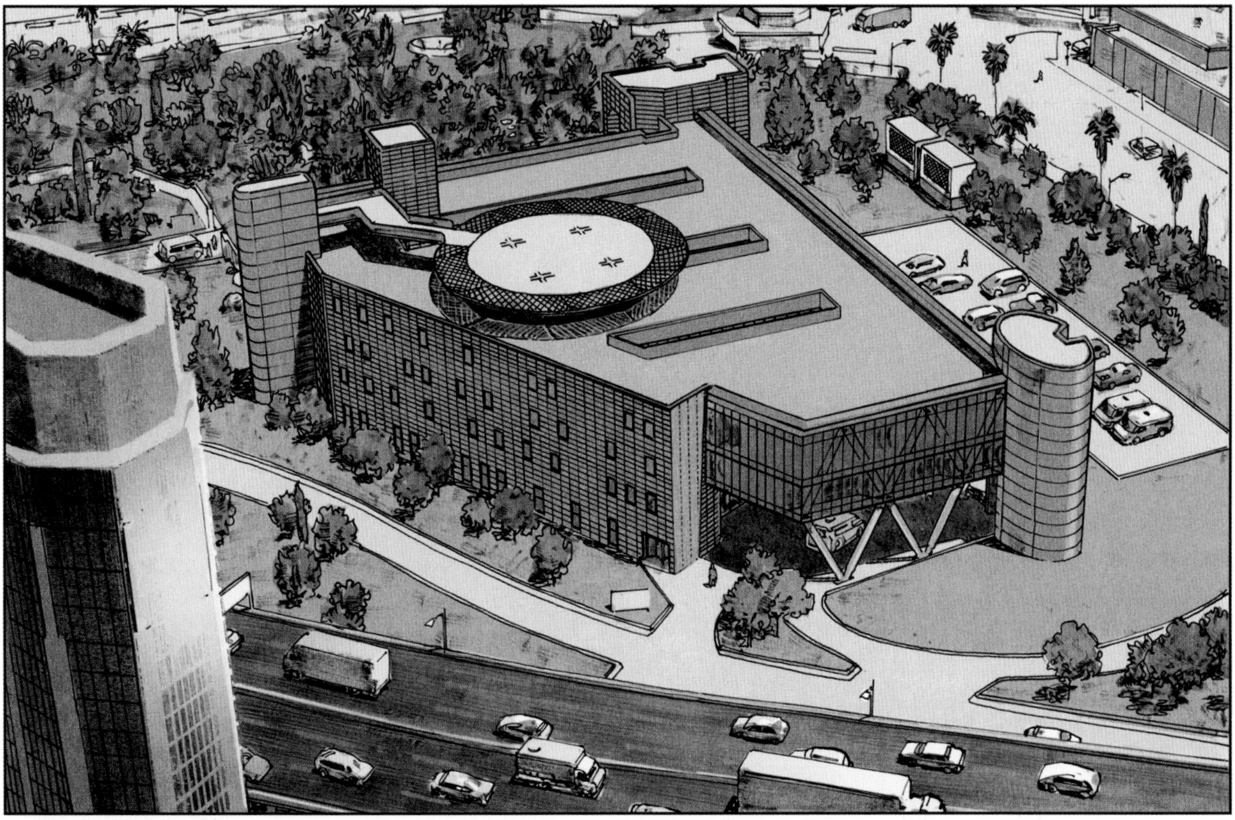

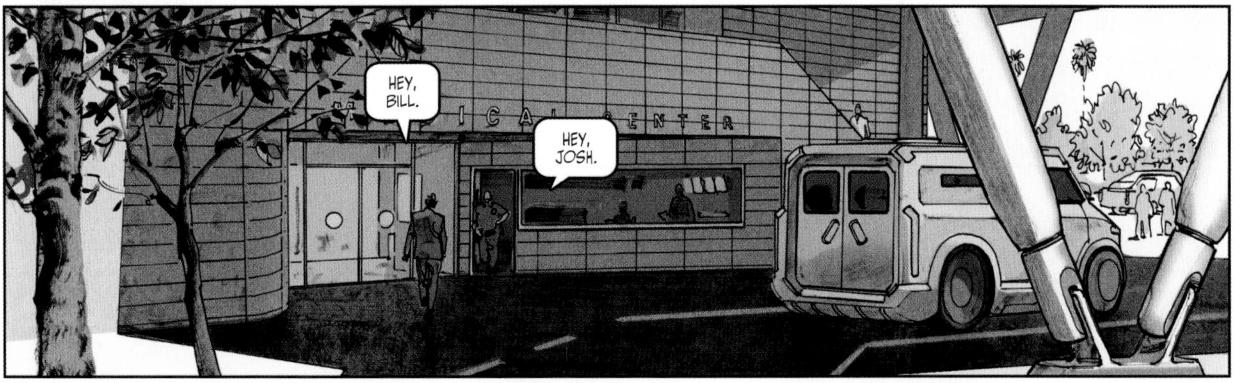
HEY, BILL.
HEY, JOSH.

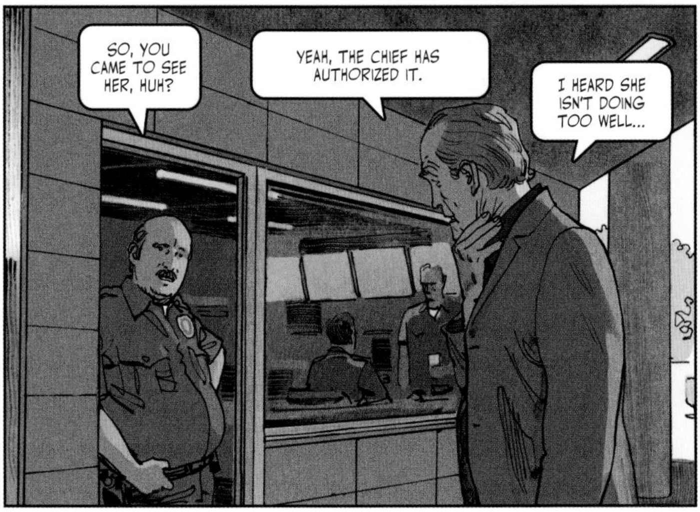
SO, YOU CAME TO SEE HER, HUH?
YEAH, THE CHIEF HAS AUTHORIZED IT.
I HEARD SHE ISN'T DOING TOO WELL...

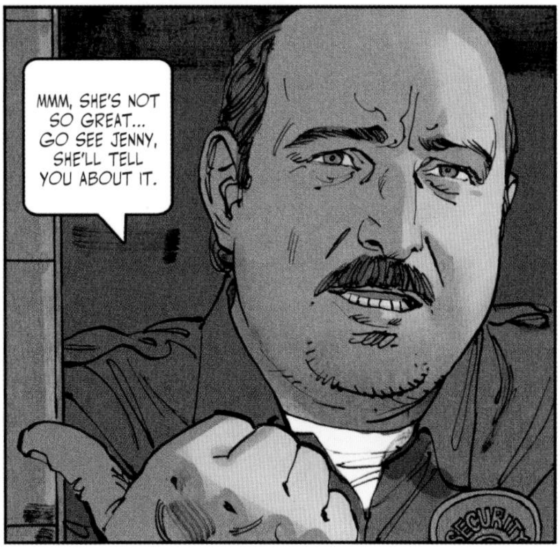
MMM, SHE'S NOT SO GREAT... GO SEE JENNY, SHE'LL TELL YOU ABOUT IT.

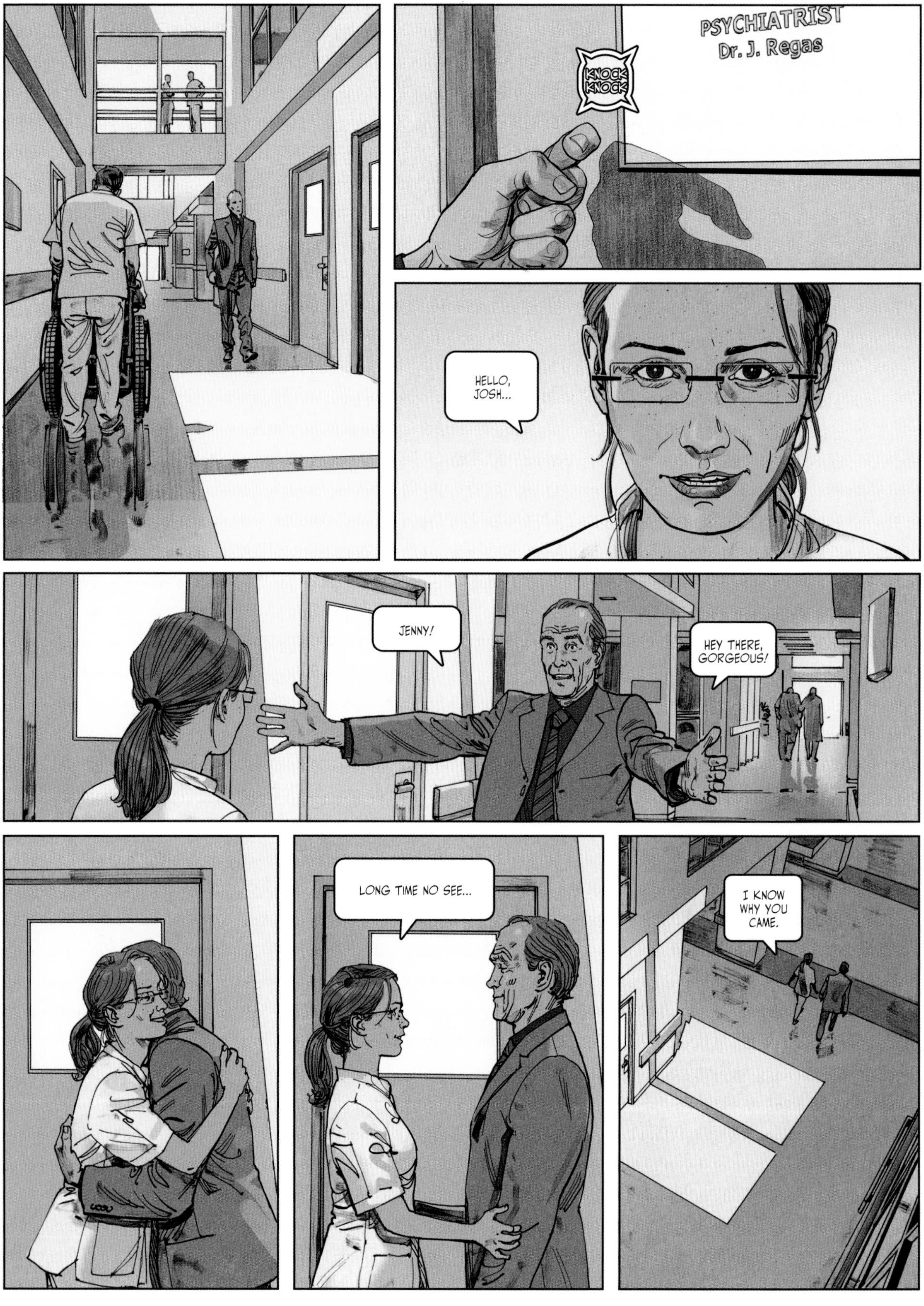
PSYCHIATRIST
Dr. J. Regas
KNOCK KNOCK
HELLO, JOSH...
JENNY!
HEY THERE, GORGEOUS!
LONG TIME NO SEE...
I KNOW WHY YOU CAME.

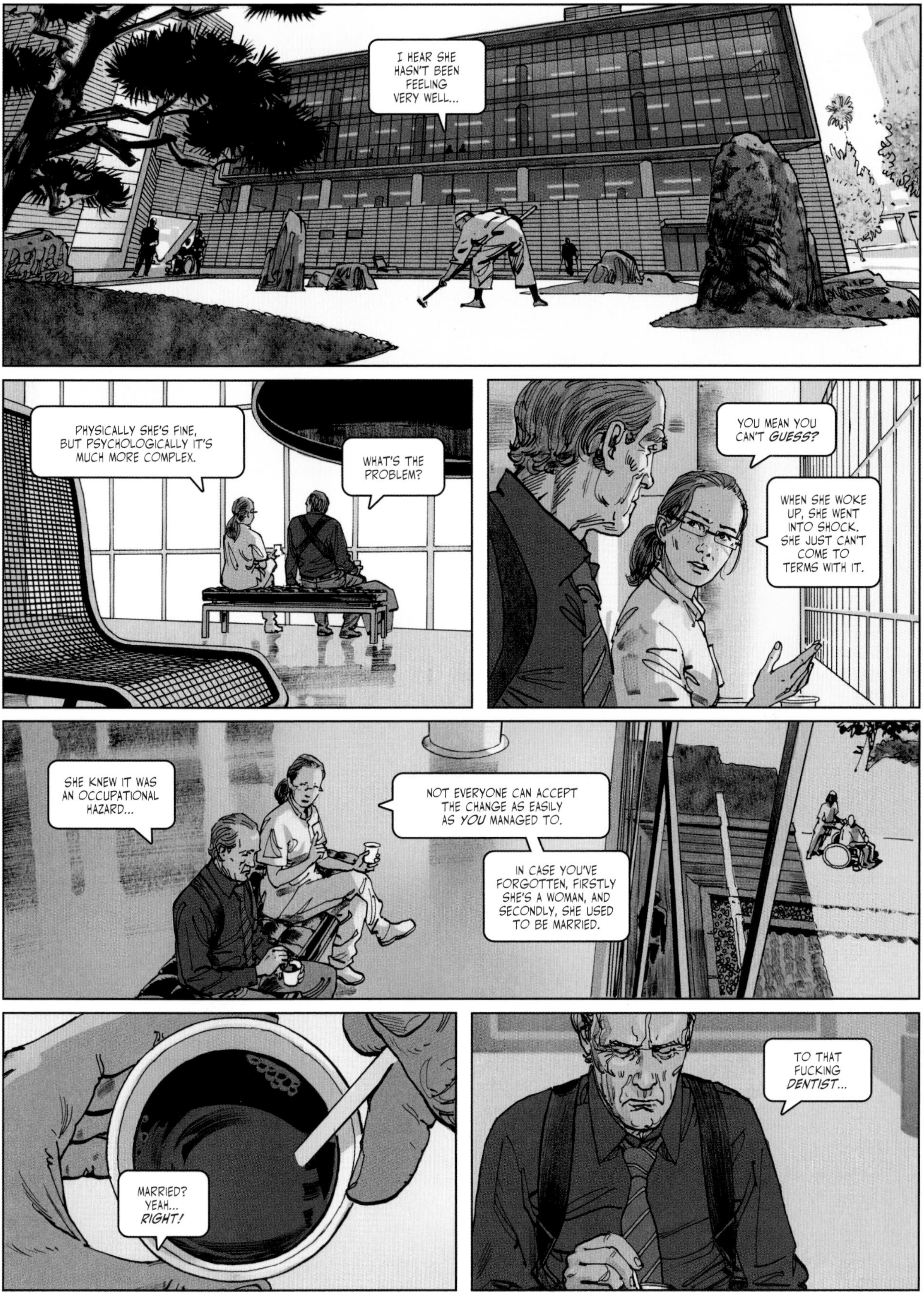
I HEAR SHE HASN'T BEEN FEELING VERY WELL...
PHYSICALLY SHE'S FINE, BUT PSYCHOLOGICALLY IT'S MUCH MORE COMPLEX.
WHAT'S THE PROBLEM?
YOU MEAN YOU CAN'T *GUESS?*
WHEN SHE WOKE UP, SHE WENT INTO SHOCK. SHE JUST CAN'T COME TO TERMS WITH IT.
SHE KNEW IT WAS AN OCCUPATIONAL HAZARD...
NOT EVERYONE CAN ACCEPT THE CHANGE AS EASILY AS *YOU* MANAGED TO.
IN CASE YOU'VE FORGOTTEN, FIRSTLY SHE'S A WOMAN, AND SECONDLY, SHE USED TO BE MARRIED.
MARRIED? YEAH... *RIGHT!*
TO THAT FUCKING *DENTIST*...

I DOUBT SHE'D AGREE WITH YOU THERE...

YOU CAN THINK WHAT YOU LIKE, BUT AT LEAST SHE HAD A LIFE OUTSIDE OF THE AGENCY...

NOT LIKE YOU...

YOU WERE NEVER INTERESTED IN SETTLING DOWN WITH ME...

DON'T GO DIGGING ALL *THAT* UP AGAIN! IT WAS TEN YEARS AGO!

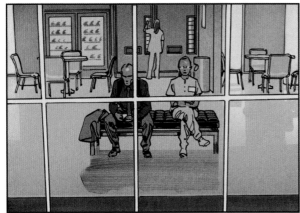

I DIDN'T COME HERE TO TALK ABOUT THAT.

I DON'T THINK IT'D BE WISE FOR YOU TO GO IN AND SEE HER.

HER ROOM NUMBER?

70

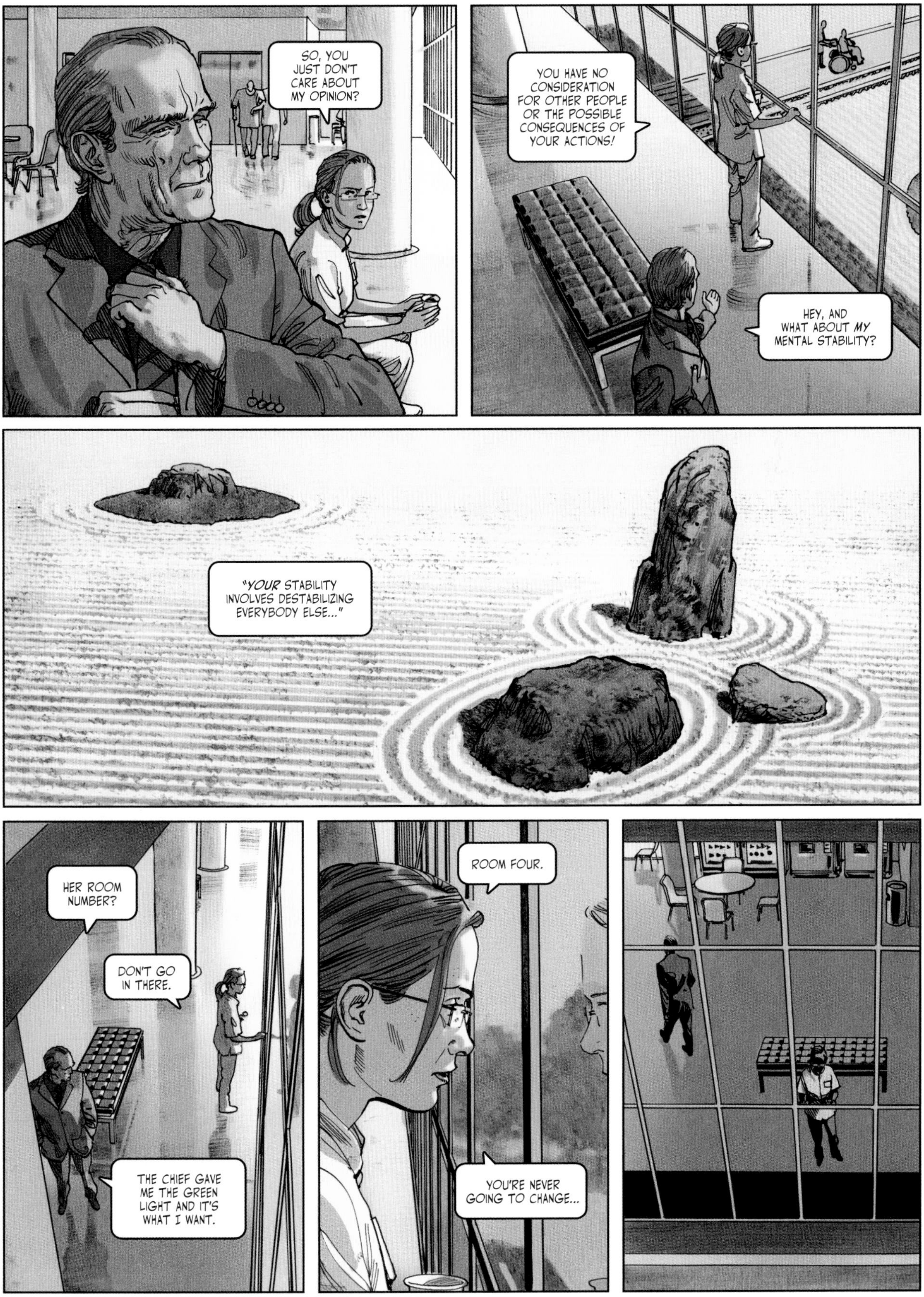
SO, YOU JUST DON'T CARE ABOUT MY OPINION?
YOU HAVE NO CONSIDERATION FOR OTHER PEOPLE OR THE POSSIBLE CONSEQUENCES OF YOUR ACTIONS!
HEY, AND WHAT ABOUT *MY* MENTAL STABILITY?
"*YOUR* STABILITY INVOLVES DESTABILIZING EVERYBODY ELSE..."
HER ROOM NUMBER?
DON'T GO IN THERE.
THE CHIEF GAVE ME THE GREEN LIGHT AND IT'S WHAT I WANT.
ROOM FOUR.
YOU'RE NEVER GOING TO CHANGE...

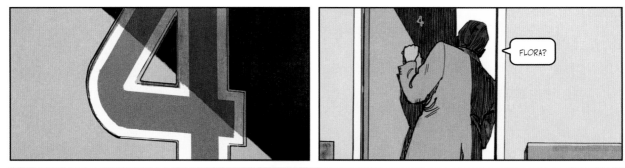

FLORA?

FLORA...

THERE YOU ARE...

WHY?!

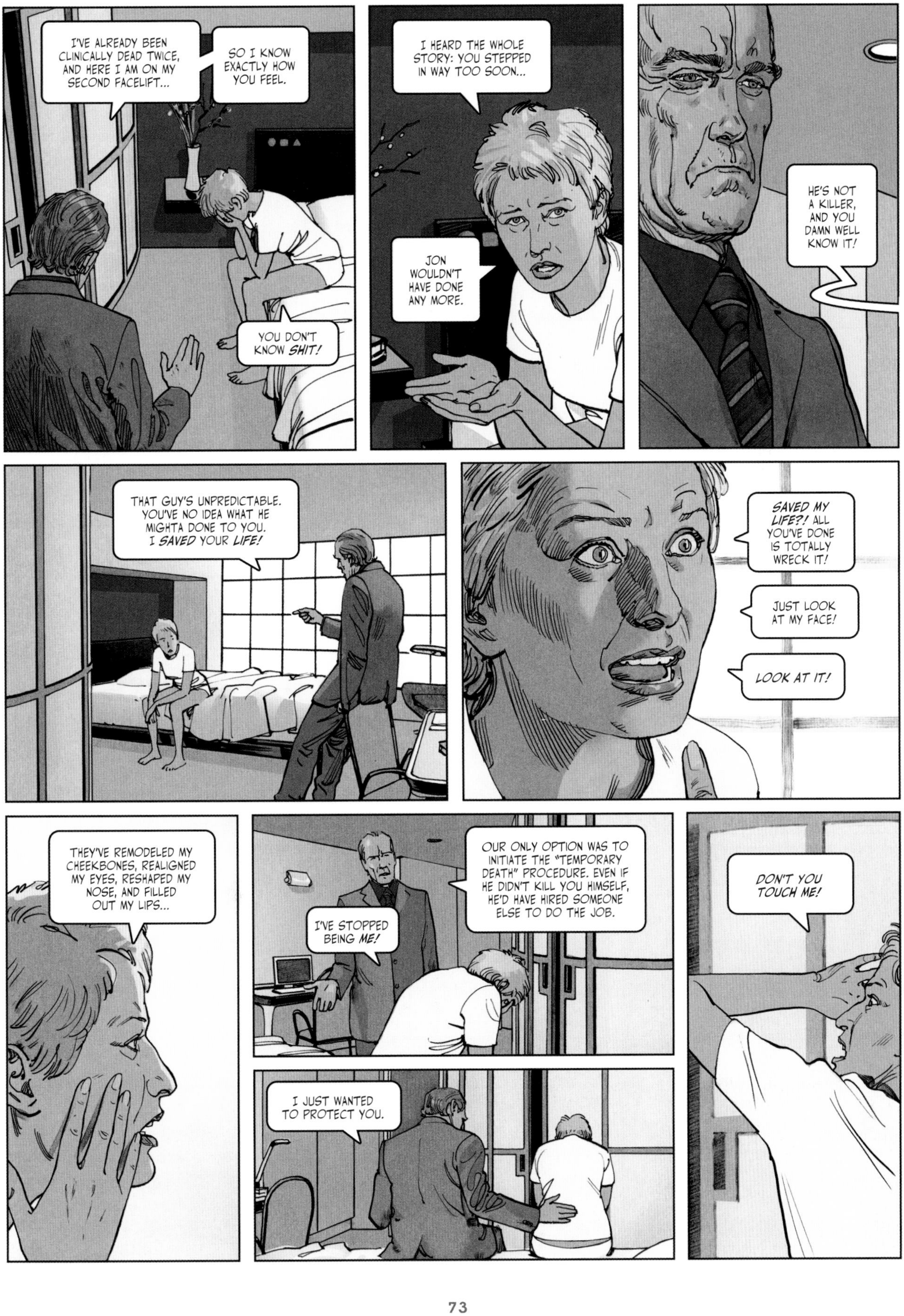
I'VE ALREADY BEEN CLINICALLY DEAD TWICE, AND HERE I AM ON MY SECOND FACELIFT...
SO I KNOW EXACTLY HOW YOU FEEL.
YOU DON'T KNOW SHIT!
I HEARD THE WHOLE STORY: YOU STEPPED IN WAY TOO SOON...
JON WOULDN'T HAVE DONE ANY MORE.
HE'S NOT A KILLER, AND YOU DAMN WELL KNOW IT!
THAT GUY'S UNPREDICTABLE. YOU'VE NO IDEA WHAT HE MIGHTA DONE TO YOU. I SAVED YOUR LIFE!
SAVED MY LIFE?! ALL YOU'VE DONE IS TOTALLY WRECK IT!
JUST LOOK AT MY FACE!
LOOK AT IT!
THEY'VE REMODELED MY CHEEKBONES, REALIGNED MY EYES, RESHAPED MY NOSE, AND FILLED OUT MY LIPS...
I'VE STOPPED BEING ME!
OUR ONLY OPTION WAS TO INITIATE THE "TEMPORARY DEATH" PROCEDURE. EVEN IF HE DIDN'T KILL YOU HIMSELF, HE'D HAVE HIRED SOMEONE ELSE TO DO THE JOB.
I JUST WANTED TO PROTECT YOU.
DON'T YOU TOUCH ME!

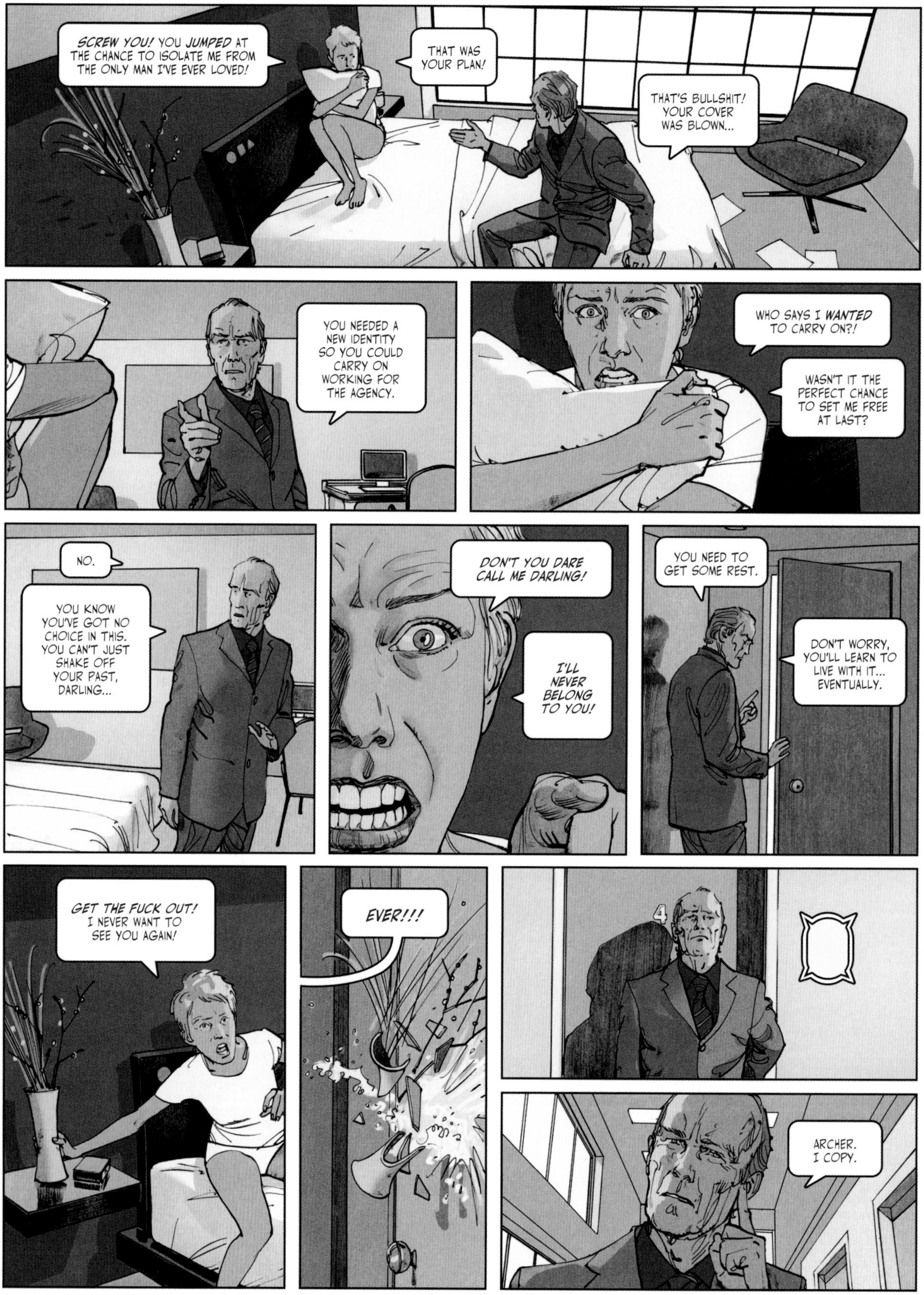

SCREW YOU! YOU JUMPED AT THE CHANCE TO ISOLATE ME FROM THE ONLY MAN I'VE EVER LOVED!
THAT WAS YOUR PLAN!
THAT'S BULLSHIT! YOUR COVER WAS BLOWN...
YOU NEEDED A NEW IDENTITY SO YOU COULD CARRY ON WORKING FOR THE AGENCY.
WHO SAYS I WANTED TO CARRY ON?!
WASN'T IT THE PERFECT CHANCE TO SET ME FREE AT LAST?
NO.
YOU KNOW YOU'VE GOT NO CHOICE IN THIS. YOU CAN'T JUST SHAKE OFF YOUR PAST, DARLING...
DON'T YOU DARE CALL ME DARLING!
I'LL NEVER BELONG TO YOU!
YOU NEED TO GET SOME REST.
DON'T WORRY, YOU'LL LEARN TO LIVE WITH IT... EVENTUALLY.
GET THE FUCK OUT! I NEVER WANT TO SEE YOU AGAIN!
EVER!!!
4
ARCHER. I COPY.

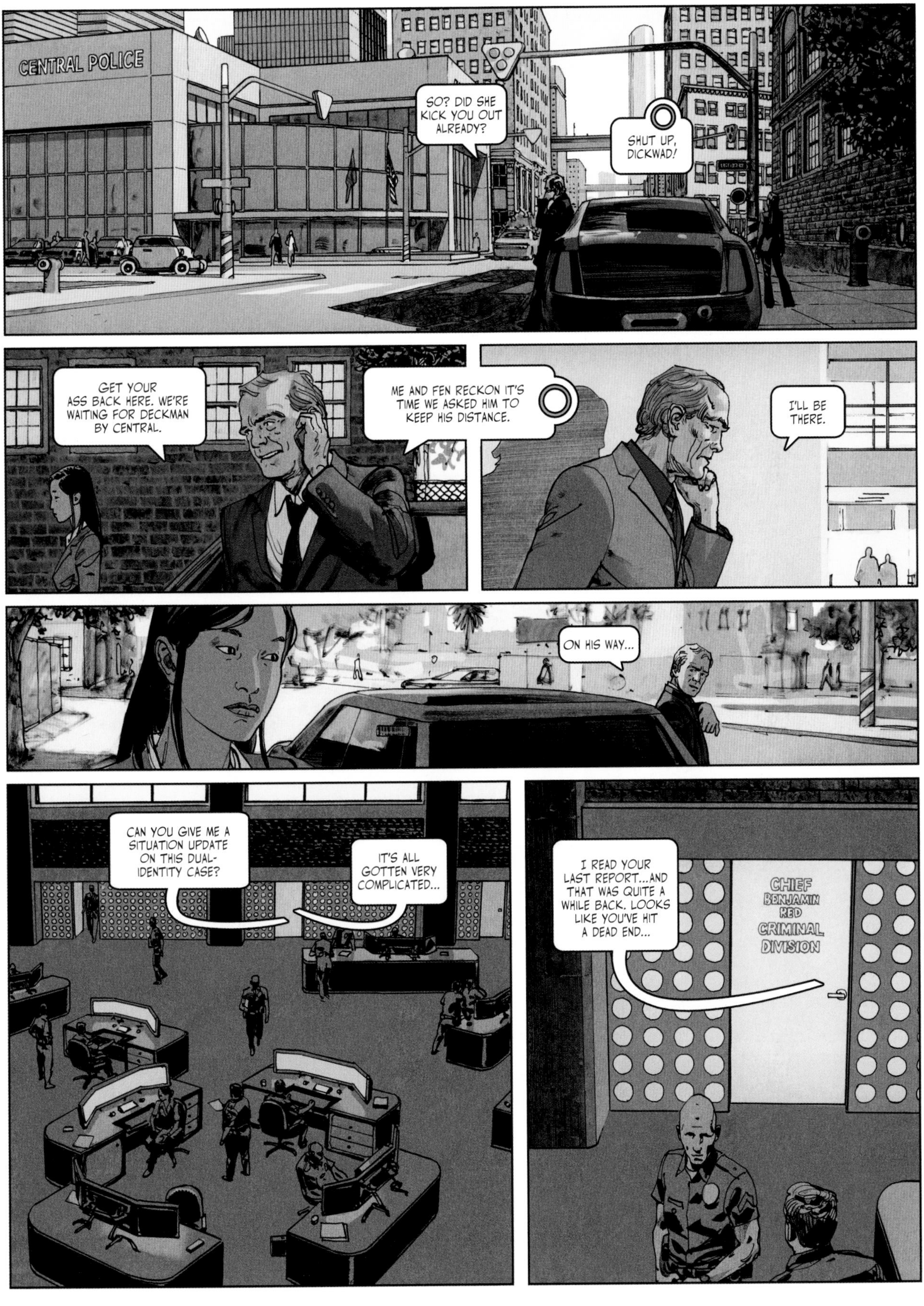
CENTRAL POLICE
SO? DID SHE KICK YOU OUT ALREADY?
SHUT UP, DICKWAD!
GET YOUR ASS BACK HERE. WE'RE WAITING FOR DECKMAN BY CENTRAL.
ME AND FEN RECKON IT'S TIME WE ASKED HIM TO KEEP HIS DISTANCE.
I'LL BE THERE.
ON HIS WAY...
CAN YOU GIVE ME A SITUATION UPDATE ON THIS DUAL-IDENTITY CASE?
IT'S ALL GOTTEN VERY COMPLICATED...
I READ YOUR LAST REPORT...AND THAT WAS QUITE A WHILE BACK. LOOKS LIKE YOU'VE HIT A DEAD END...
CHIEF BENJAMIN RED CRIMINAL DIVISION

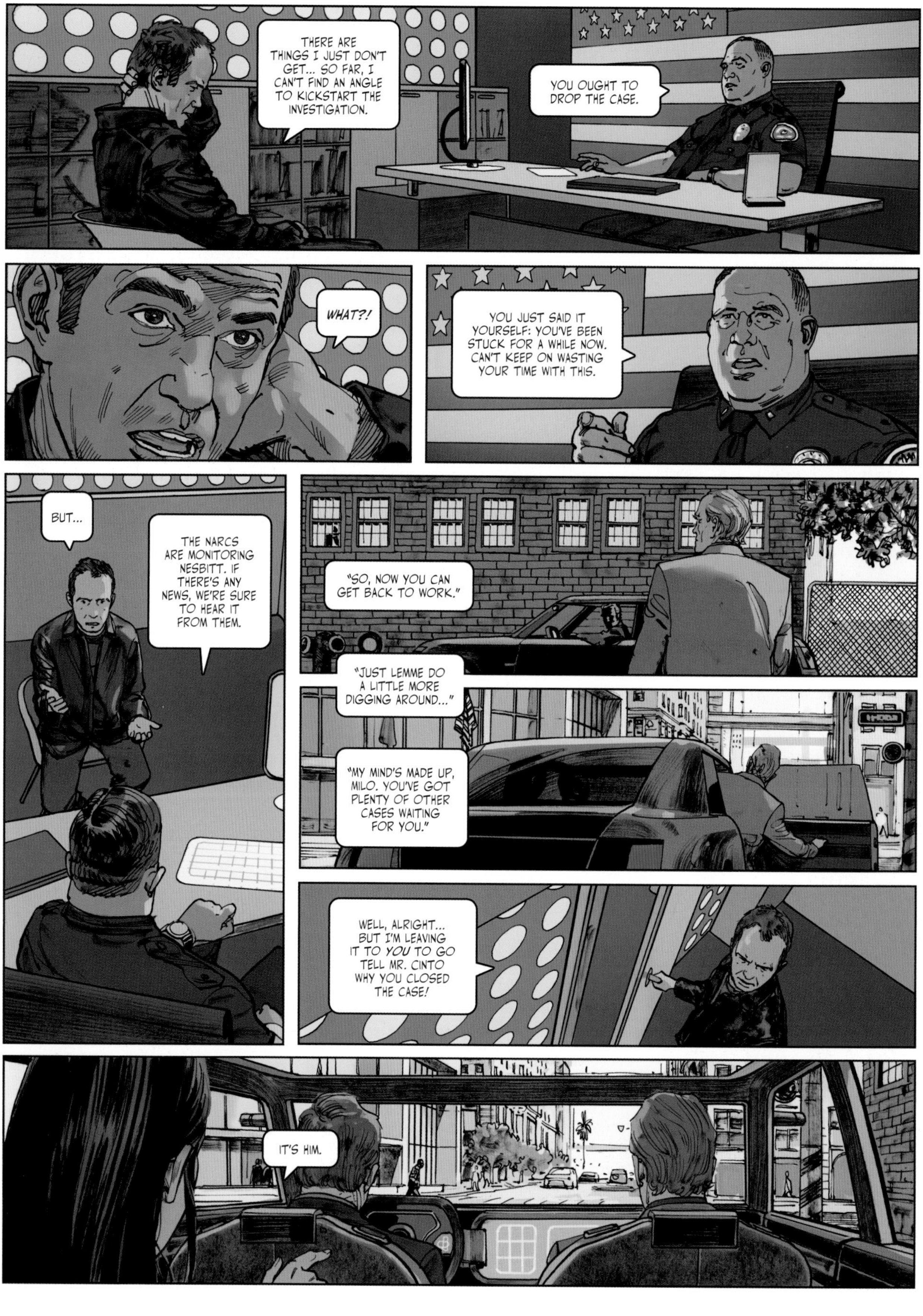
THERE ARE THINGS I JUST DON'T GET... SO FAR, I CAN'T FIND AN ANGLE TO KICKSTART THE INVESTIGATION.
YOU OUGHT TO DROP THE CASE.
WHAT?!
YOU JUST SAID IT YOURSELF: YOU'VE BEEN STUCK FOR A WHILE NOW. CAN'T KEEP ON WASTING YOUR TIME WITH THIS.
BUT...
THE NARCS ARE MONITORING NESBITT. IF THERE'S ANY NEWS, WE'RE SURE TO HEAR IT FROM THEM.
"SO, NOW YOU CAN GET BACK TO WORK."
"JUST LEMME DO A LITTLE MORE DIGGING AROUND..."
"MY MIND'S MADE UP, MILO. YOU'VE GOT PLENTY OF OTHER CASES WAITING FOR YOU."
WELL, ALRIGHT... BUT I'M LEAVING IT TO *YOU* TO GO TELL MR. CINTO WHY YOU CLOSED THE CASE!
IT'S HIM.

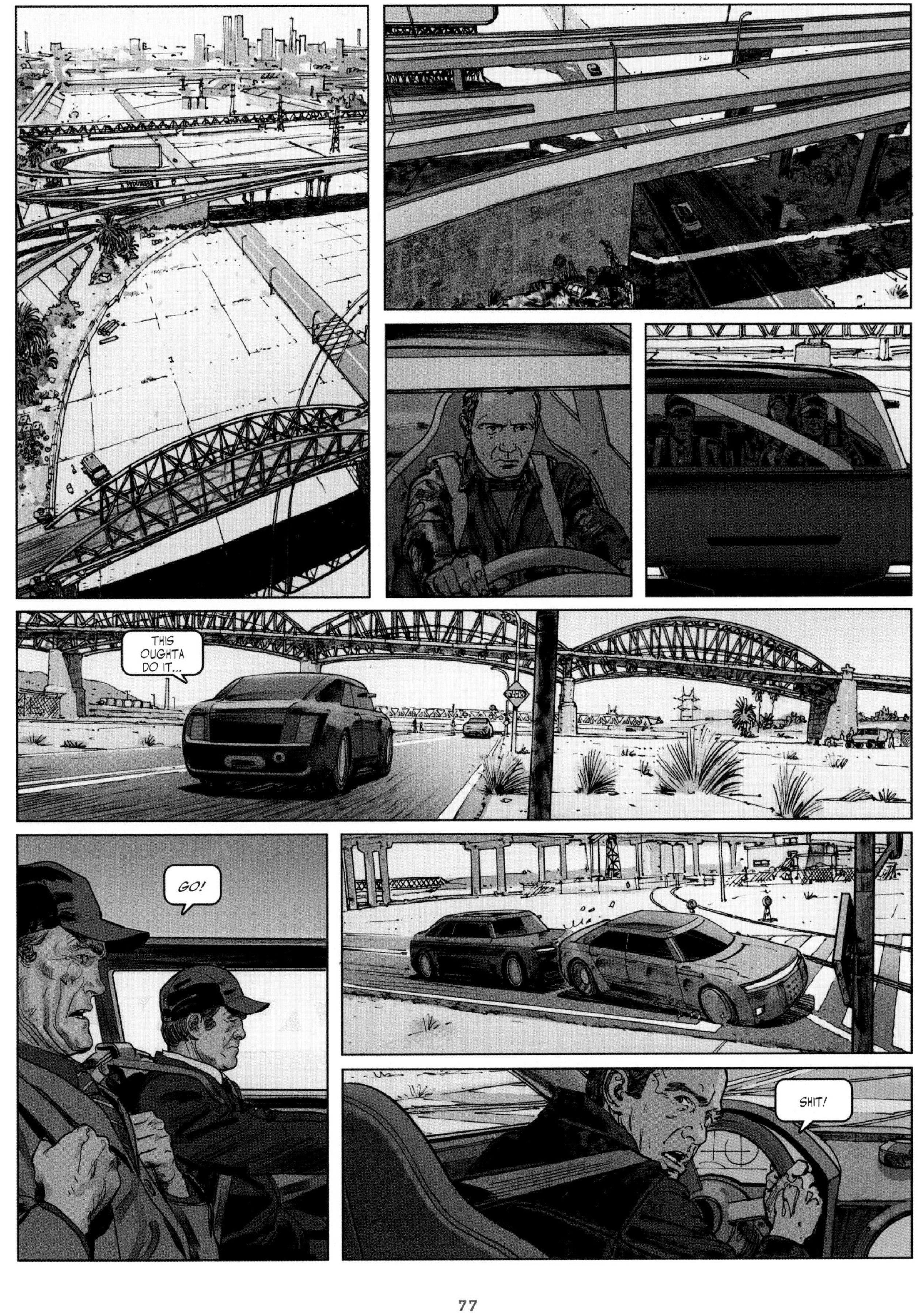
THIS OUGHTA DO IT...
GO!
SHIT!

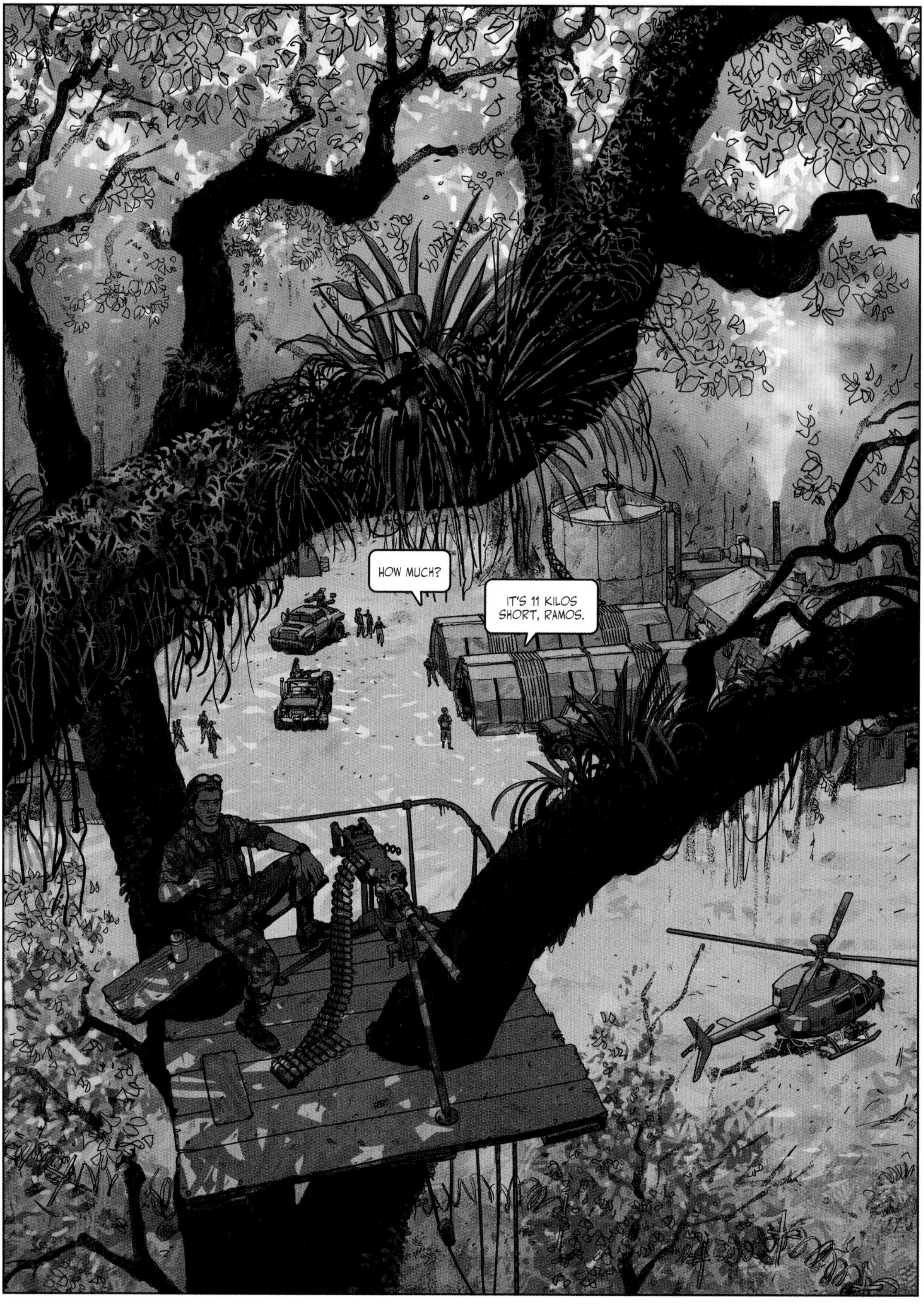
HOW MUCH?
IT'S 11 KILOS SHORT, RAMOS.

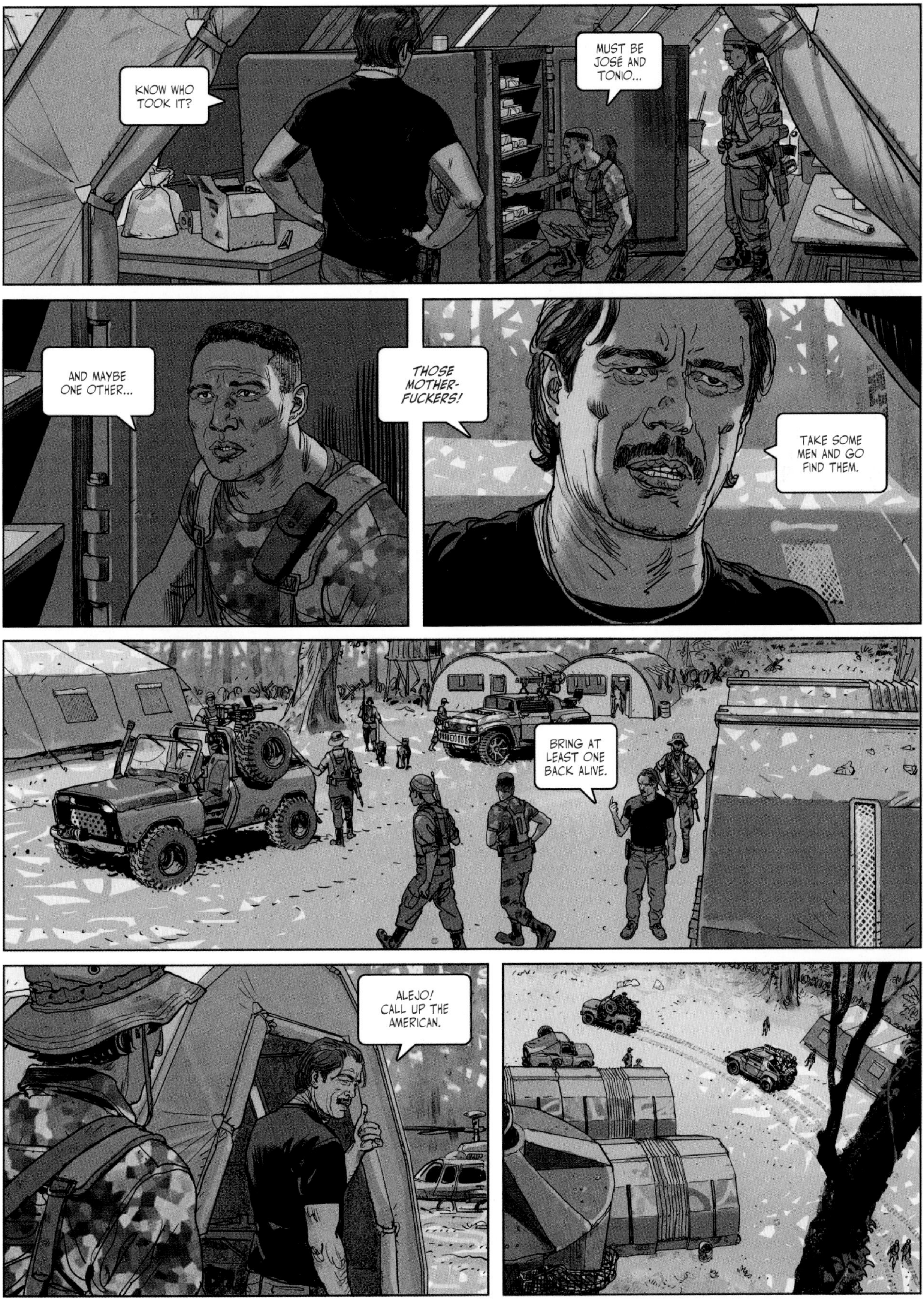
KNOW WHO TOOK IT?
MUST BE JOSÉ AND TONIO...
AND MAYBE ONE OTHER...
THOSE MOTHER-FUCKERS!
TAKE SOME MEN AND GO FIND THEM.
BRING AT LEAST ONE BACK ALIVE.
ALEJO! CALL UP THE AMERICAN.

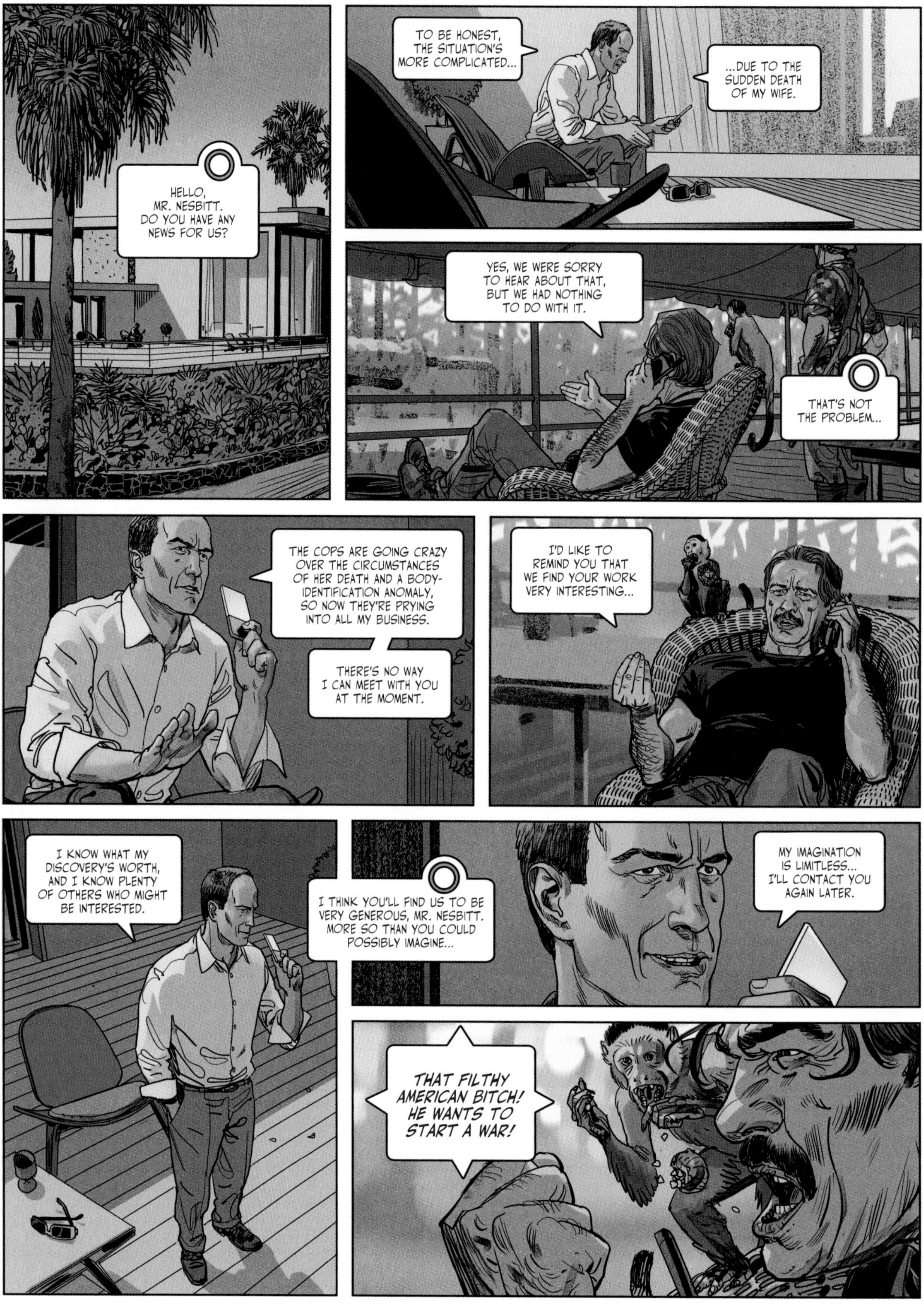
HELLO, MR. NESBITT. DO YOU HAVE ANY NEWS FOR US?
TO BE HONEST, THE SITUATION'S MORE COMPLICATED...
...DUE TO THE SUDDEN DEATH OF MY WIFE.
YES, WE WERE SORRY TO HEAR ABOUT THAT, BUT WE HAD NOTHING TO DO WITH IT.
THAT'S NOT THE PROBLEM...
THE COPS ARE GOING CRAZY OVER THE CIRCUMSTANCES OF HER DEATH AND A BODY-IDENTIFICATION ANOMALY, SO NOW THEY'RE PRYING INTO ALL MY BUSINESS.
THERE'S NO WAY I CAN MEET WITH YOU AT THE MOMENT.
I'D LIKE TO REMIND YOU THAT WE FIND YOUR WORK VERY INTERESTING...
I KNOW WHAT MY DISCOVERY'S WORTH, AND I KNOW PLENTY OF OTHERS WHO MIGHT BE INTERESTED.
I THINK YOU'LL FIND US TO BE VERY GENEROUS, MR. NESBITT. MORE SO THAN YOU COULD POSSIBLY IMAGINE...
MY IMAGINATION IS LIMITLESS... I'LL CONTACT YOU AGAIN LATER.
THAT FILTHY AMERICAN BITCH! HE WANTS TO START A WAR!

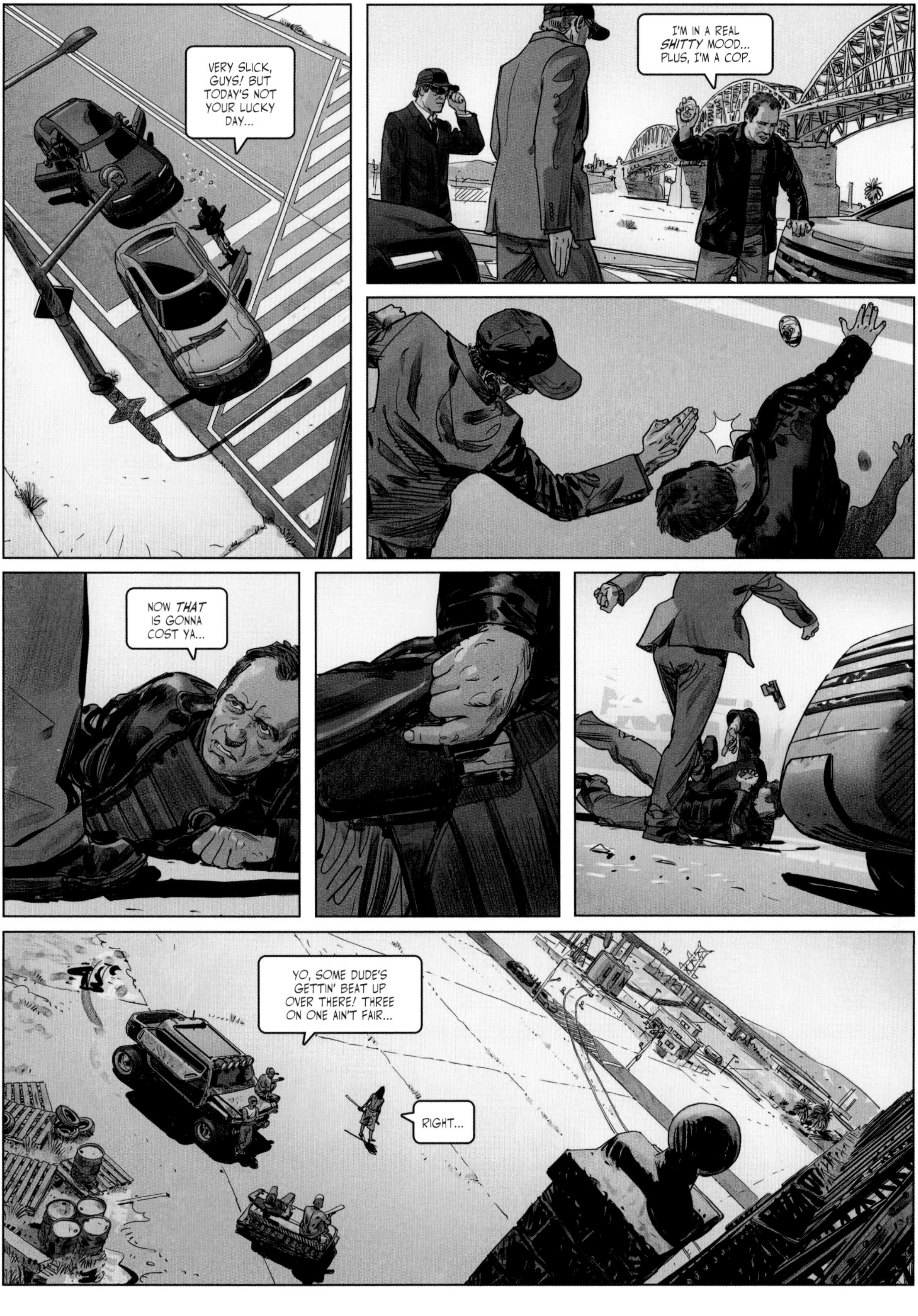
VERY SLICK, GUYS! BUT TODAY'S NOT YOUR LUCKY DAY...
I'M IN A REAL SHITTY MOOD... PLUS, I'M A COP.
NOW THAT IS GONNA COST YA...
YO, SOME DUDE'S GETTIN' BEAT UP OVER THERE! THREE ON ONE AIN'T FAIR...
RIGHT...

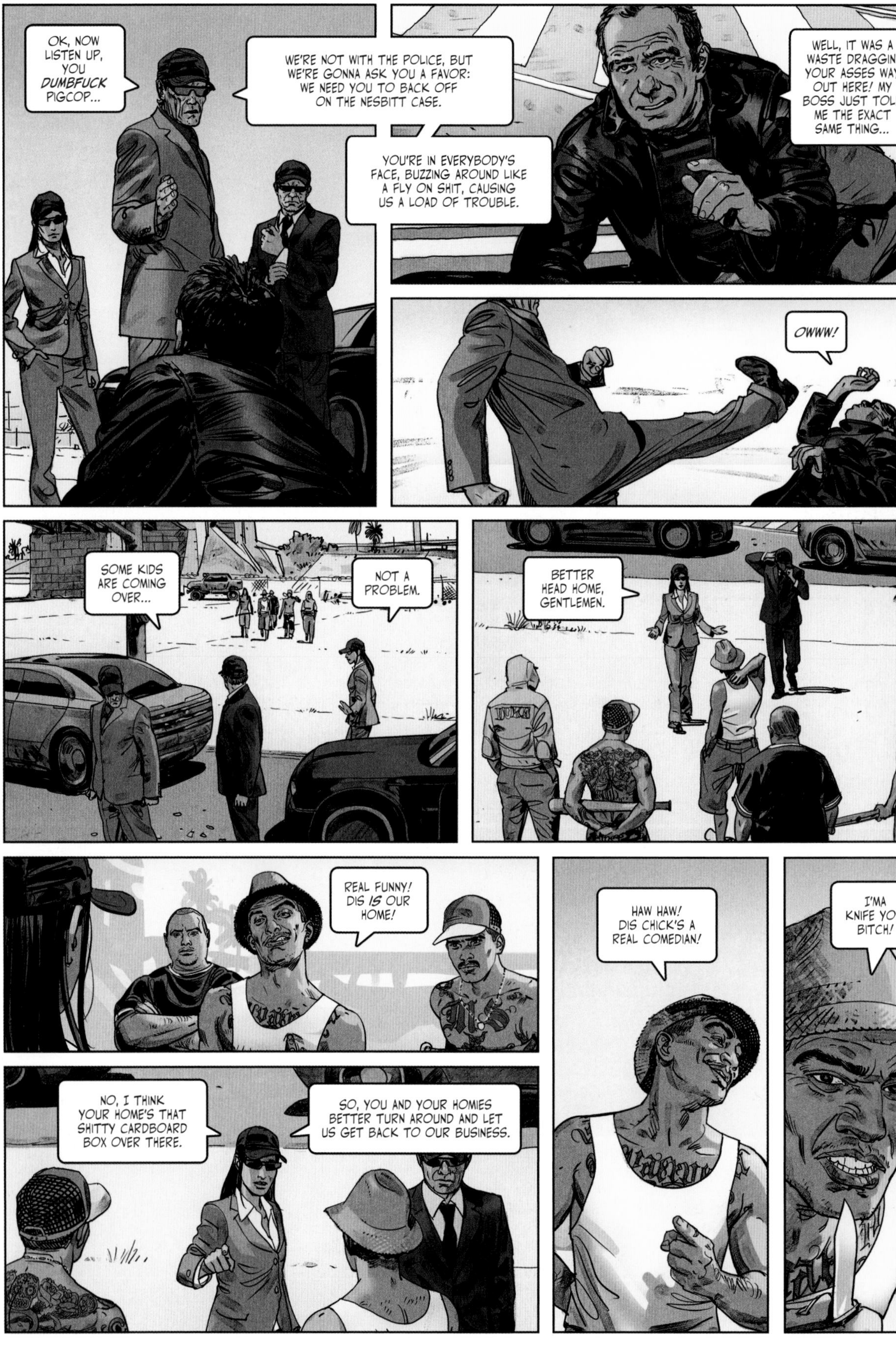
OK, NOW LISTEN UP, YOU *DUMBFUCK* PIGCOP...
WE'RE NOT WITH THE POLICE, BUT WE'RE GONNA ASK YOU A FAVOR: WE NEED YOU TO BACK OFF ON THE NESBITT CASE.
YOU'RE IN EVERYBODY'S FACE, BUZZING AROUND LIKE A FLY ON SHIT, CAUSING US A LOAD OF TROUBLE.
WELL, IT WAS A WASTE DRAGGIN' YOUR ASSES WAY OUT HERE! MY BOSS JUST TOLD ME THE EXACT SAME THING...
OWWW!
SOME KIDS ARE COMING OVER...
NOT A PROBLEM.
BETTER HEAD HOME, GENTLEMEN.
REAL FUNNY! DIS *IS* OUR HOME!
NO, I THINK YOUR HOME'S THAT SHITTY CARDBOARD BOX OVER THERE.
SO, YOU AND YOUR HOMIES BETTER TURN AROUND AND LET US GET BACK TO OUR BUSINESS.
HAW HAW! DIS CHICK'S A REAL COMEDIAN!
I'MA KNIFE YOU, BITCH!

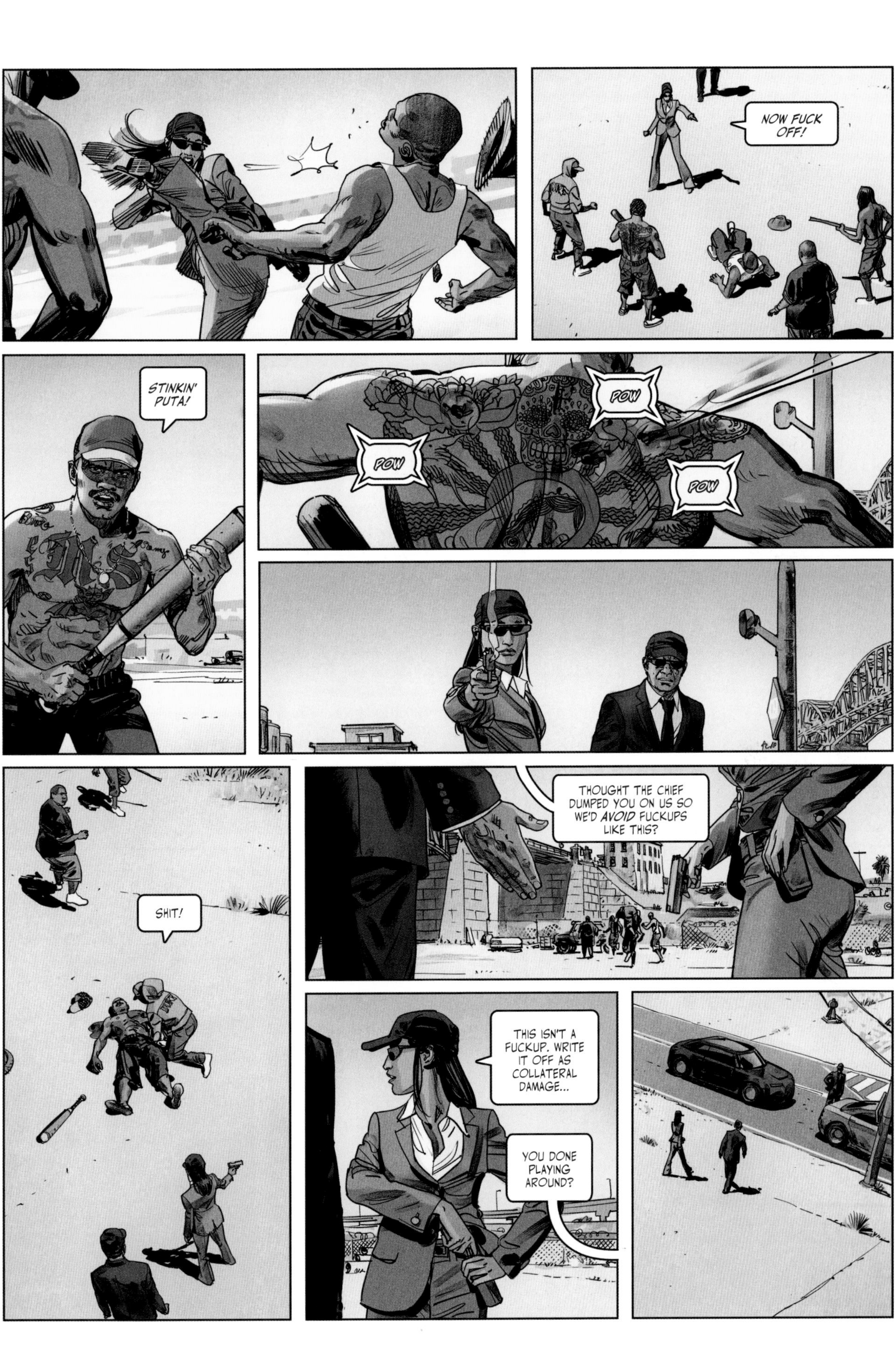
NOW FUCK OFF!
STINKIN' PUTA!
POW
POW
POW
SHIT!
THOUGHT THE CHIEF DUMPED YOU ON US SO WE'D AVOID FUCKUPS LIKE THIS?
THIS ISN'T A FUCKUP. WRITE IT OFF AS COLLATERAL DAMAGE...
YOU DONE PLAYING AROUND?

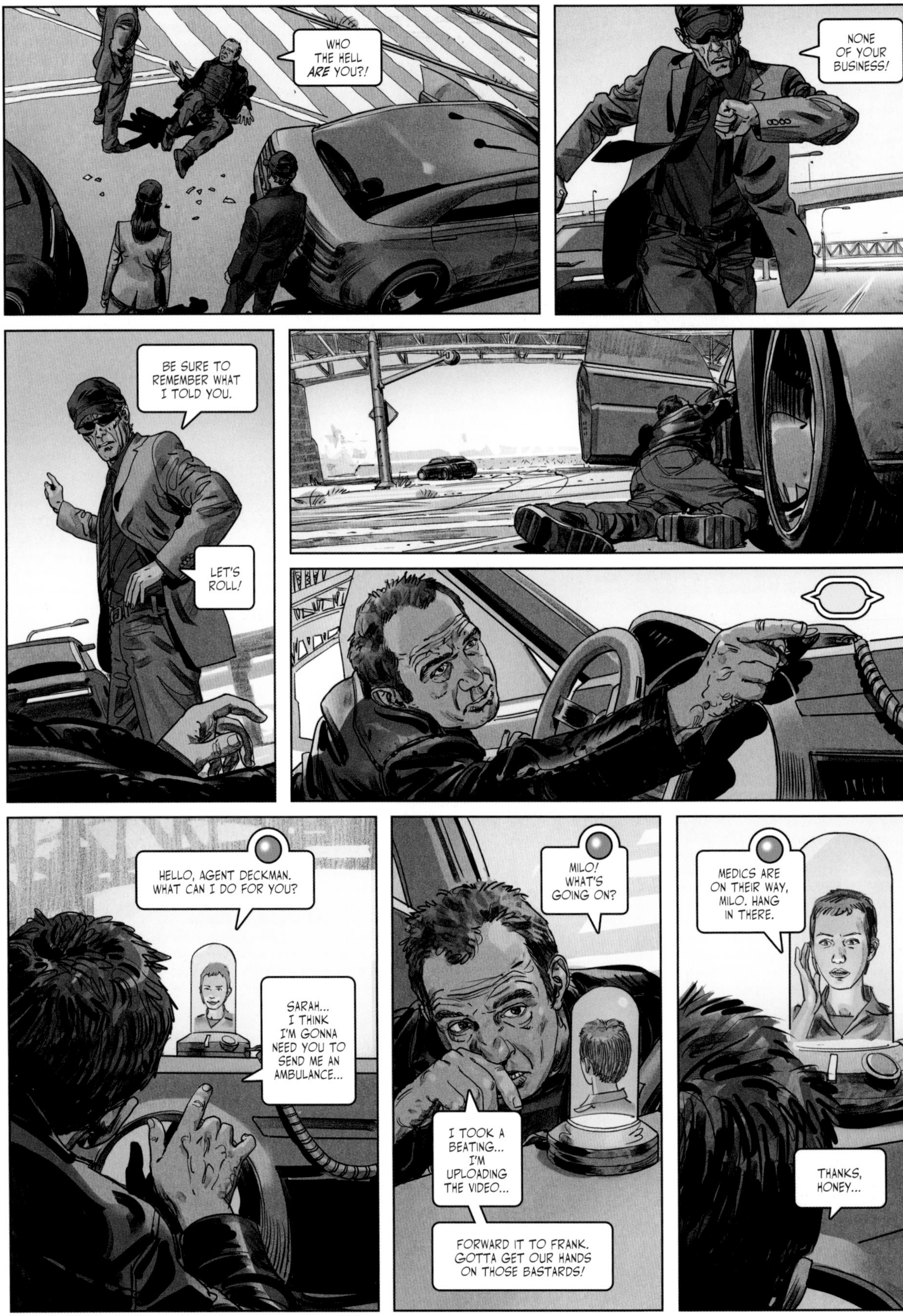
WHO THE HELL *ARE* YOU?!
NONE OF YOUR BUSINESS!
BE SURE TO REMEMBER WHAT I TOLD YOU.
LET'S ROLL!
HELLO, AGENT DECKMAN. WHAT CAN I DO FOR YOU?
SARAH... I THINK I'M GONNA NEED YOU TO SEND ME AN AMBULANCE...
MILO! WHAT'S GOING ON?
I TOOK A BEATING... I'M UPLOADING THE VIDEO...
FORWARD IT TO FRANK. GOTTA GET OUR HANDS ON THOSE BASTARDS!
MEDICS ARE ON THEIR WAY, MILO. HANG IN THERE.
THANKS, HONEY...

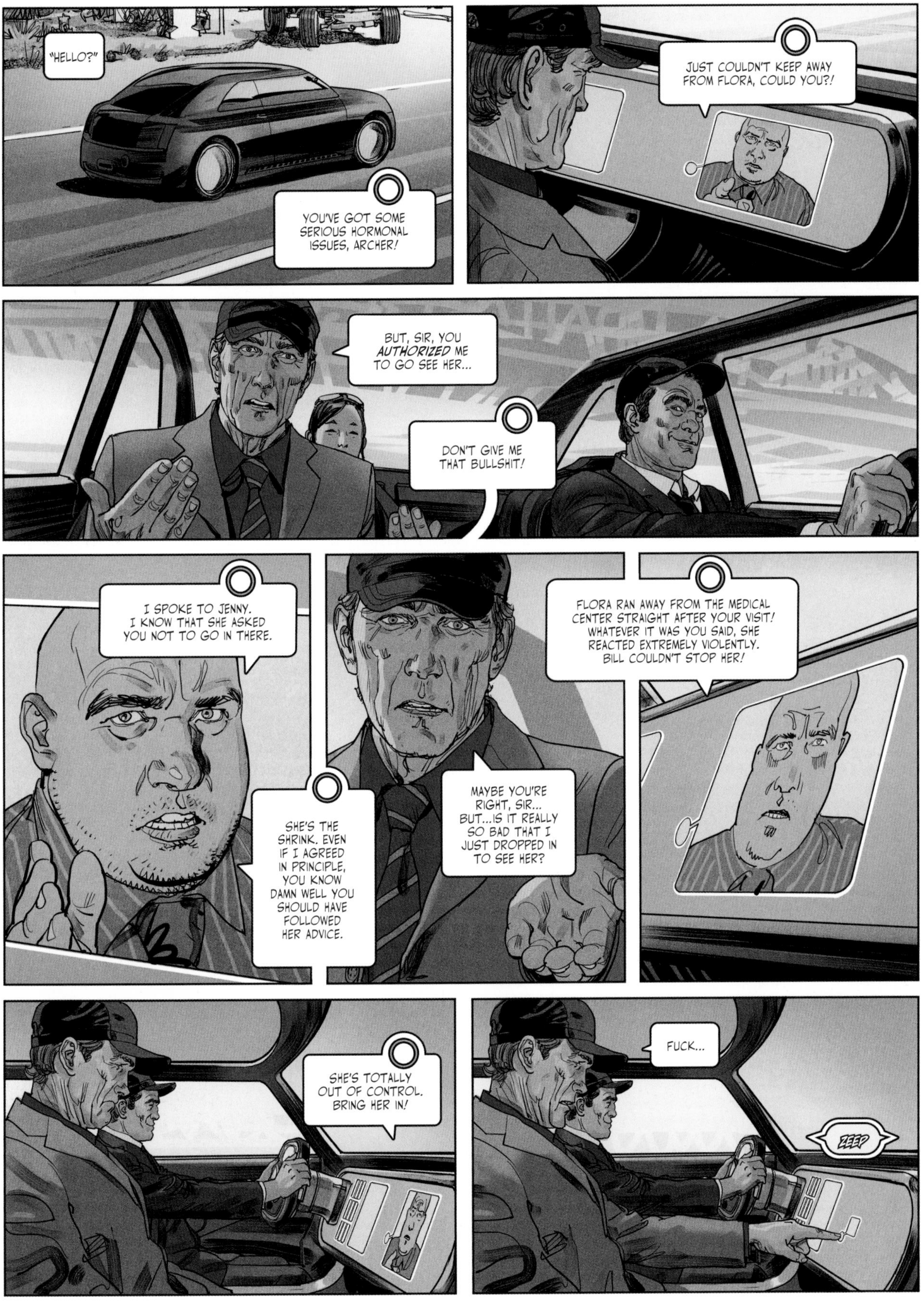
"HELLO?"
YOU'VE GOT SOME SERIOUS HORMONAL ISSUES, ARCHER!
JUST COULDN'T KEEP AWAY FROM FLORA, COULD YOU?!
BUT, SIR, YOU *AUTHORIZED* ME TO GO SEE HER...
DON'T GIVE ME THAT BULLSHIT!
I SPOKE TO JENNY. I KNOW THAT SHE ASKED YOU NOT TO GO IN THERE.
SHE'S THE SHRINK. EVEN IF I AGREED IN PRINCIPLE, YOU KNOW DAMN WELL YOU SHOULD HAVE FOLLOWED HER ADVICE.
MAYBE YOU'RE RIGHT, SIR... BUT...IS IT REALLY SO BAD THAT I JUST DROPPED IN TO SEE HER?
FLORA RAN AWAY FROM THE MEDICAL CENTER STRAIGHT AFTER YOUR VISIT! WHATEVER IT WAS YOU SAID, SHE REACTED EXTREMELY VIOLENTLY. BILL COULDN'T STOP HER!
SHE'S TOTALLY OUT OF CONTROL. BRING HER IN!
FUCK...
ZEEP

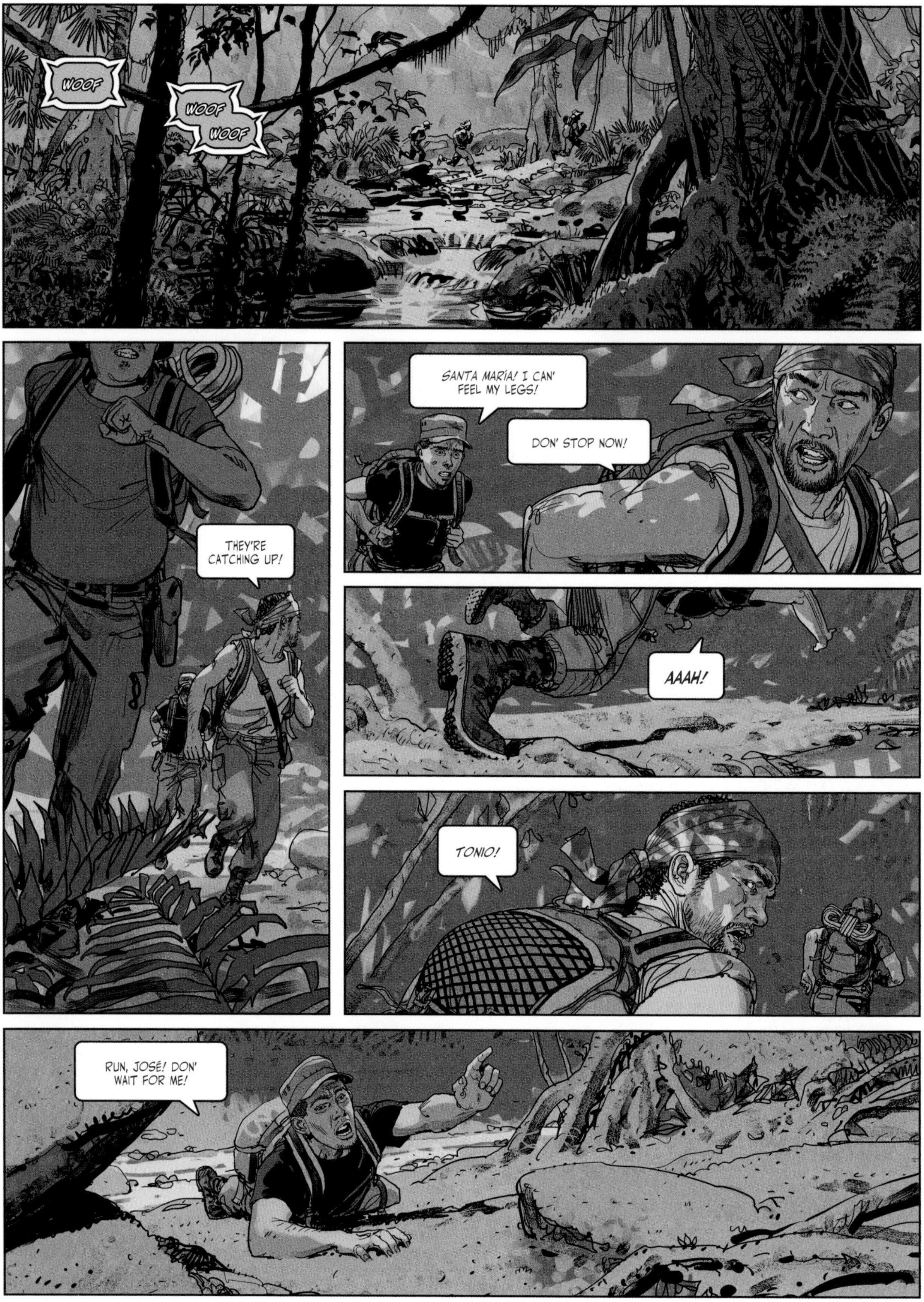
WOOF
WOOF
WOOF
THEY'RE CATCHING UP!
SANTA MARÍA! I CAN' FEEL MY LEGS!
DON' STOP NOW!
AAAH!
TONIO!
RUN, JOSÉ! DON' WAIT FOR ME!

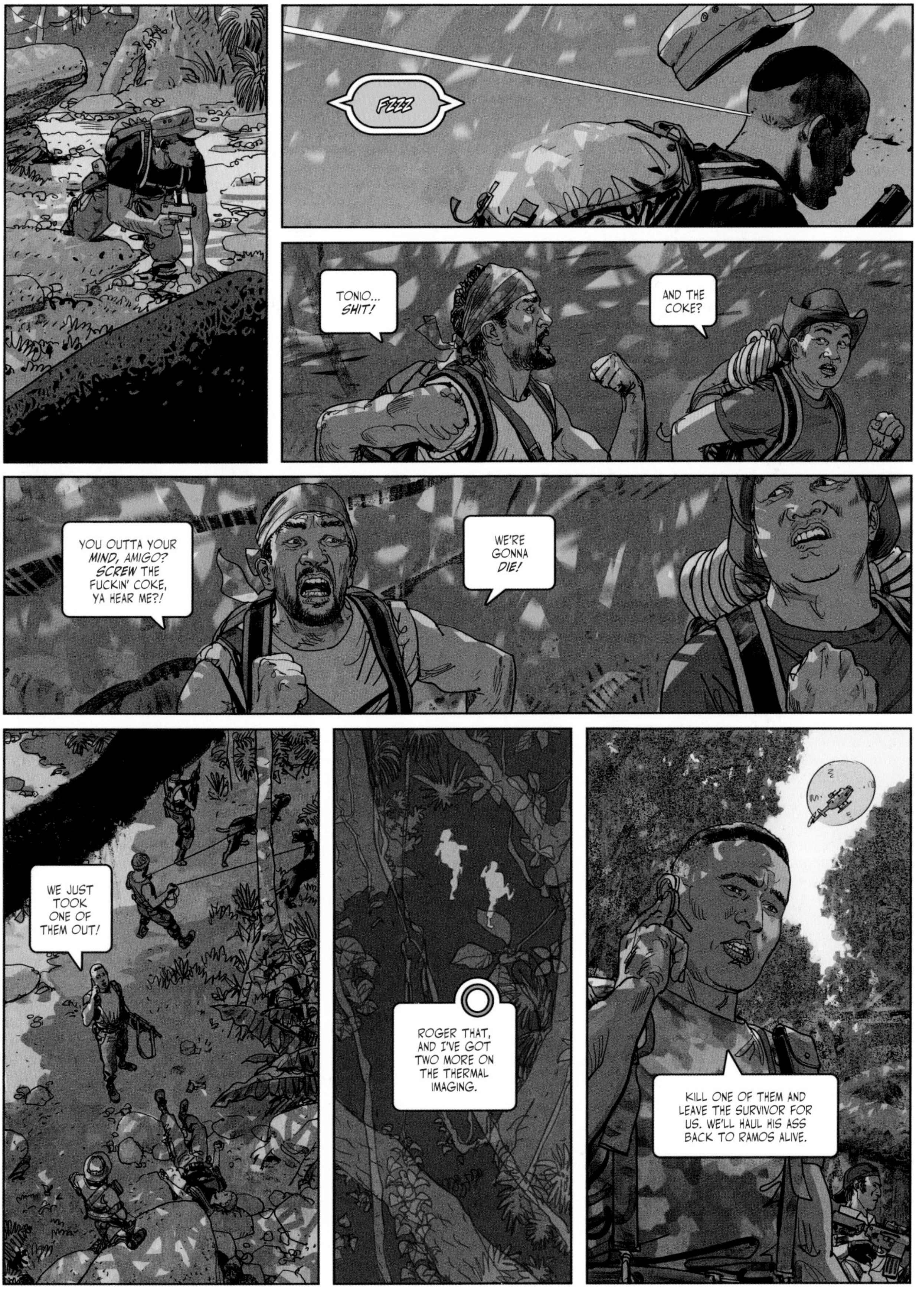
FZZZ
TONIO... SHIT!
AND THE COKE?
YOU OUTTA YOUR MIND, AMIGO? SCREW THE FUCKIN' COKE, YA HEAR ME?!
WE'RE GONNA DIE!
WE JUST TOOK ONE OF THEM OUT!
ROGER THAT, AND I'VE GOT TWO MORE ON THE THERMAL IMAGING.
KILL ONE OF THEM AND LEAVE THE SURVIVOR FOR US. WE'LL HAUL HIS ASS BACK TO RAMOS ALIVE.

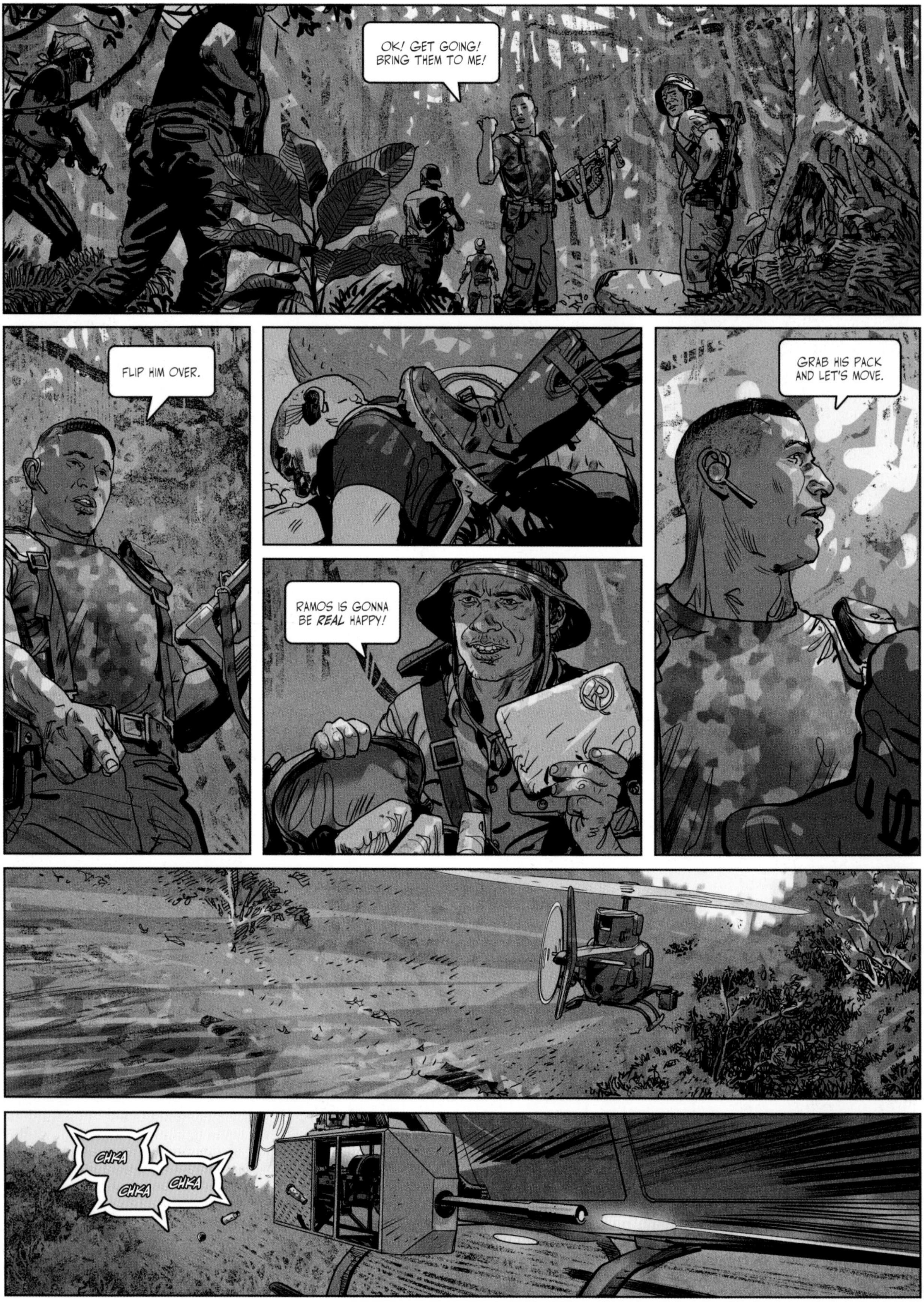
OK! GET GOING! BRING THEM TO ME!
FLIP HIM OVER.
RAMOS IS GONNA BE ***REAL*** HAPPY!
GRAB HIS PACK AND LET'S MOVE.
CHKA
CHKA
CHKA

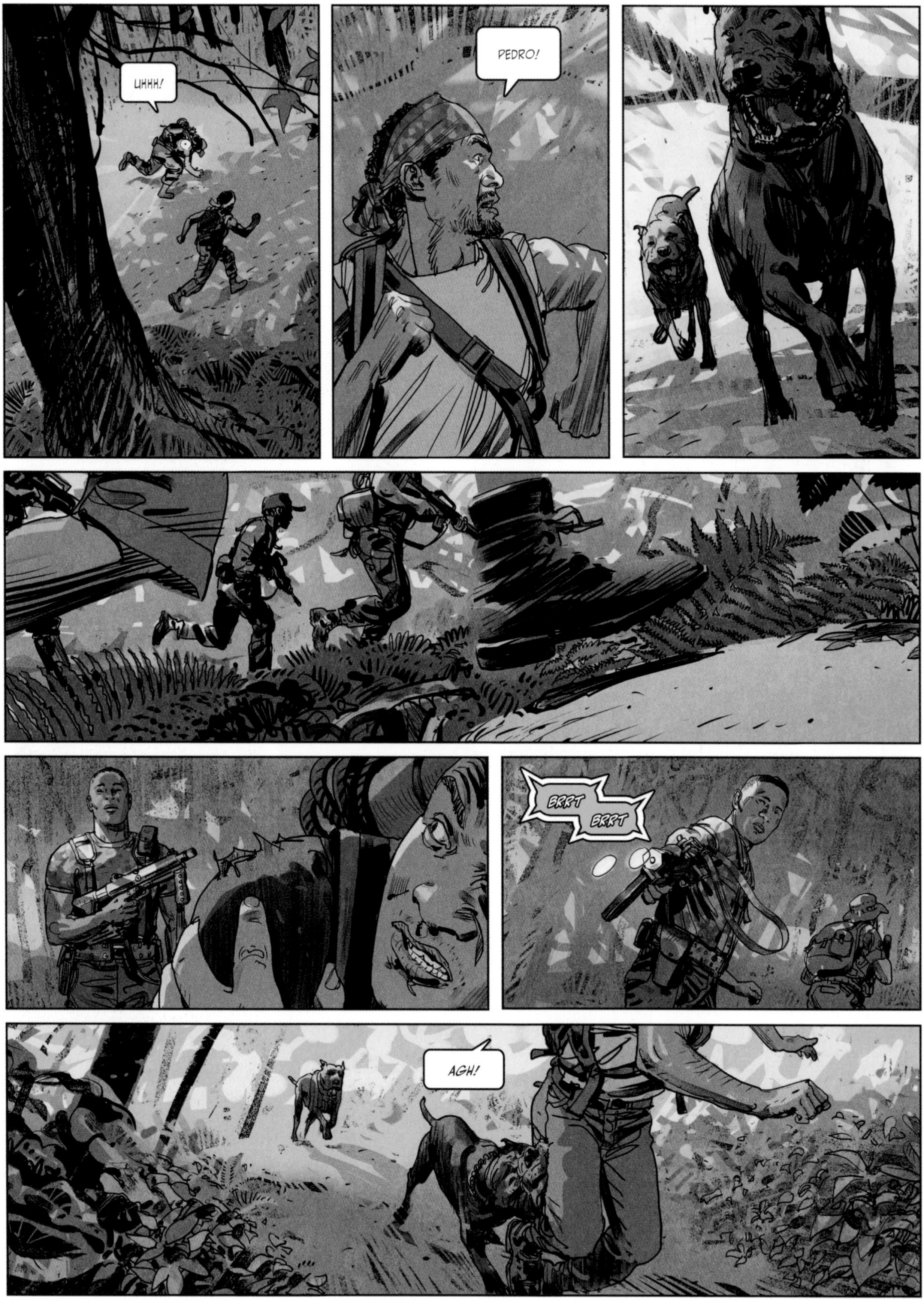
UHHH!
PEDRO!
BRRT
BRRT
AGH!

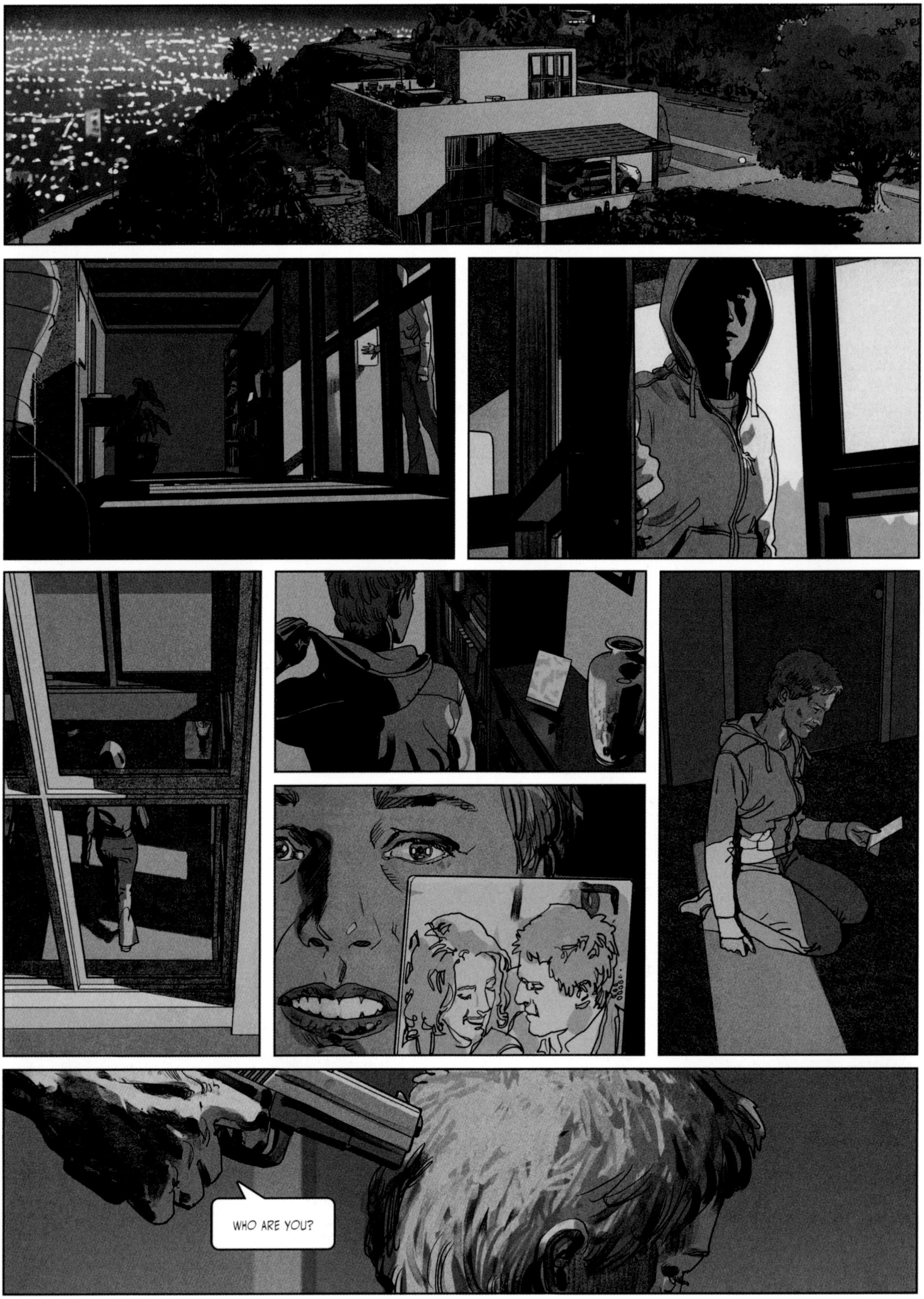
WHO ARE YOU?

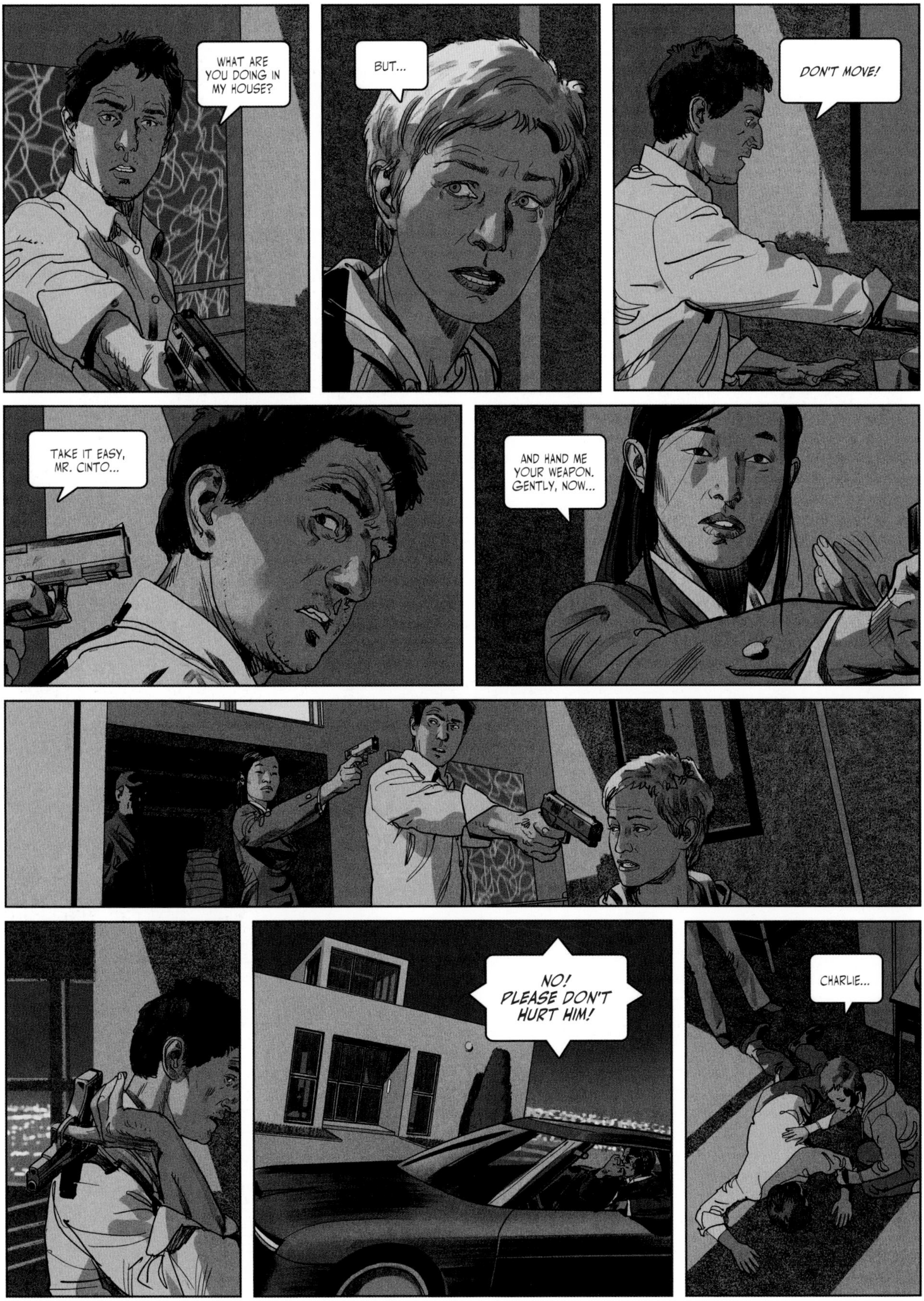
WHAT ARE YOU DOING IN MY HOUSE?
BUT...
DON'T MOVE!
TAKE IT EASY, MR. CINTO...
AND HAND ME YOUR WEAPON. GENTLY, NOW...
NO! PLEASE DON'T HURT HIM!
CHARLIE...

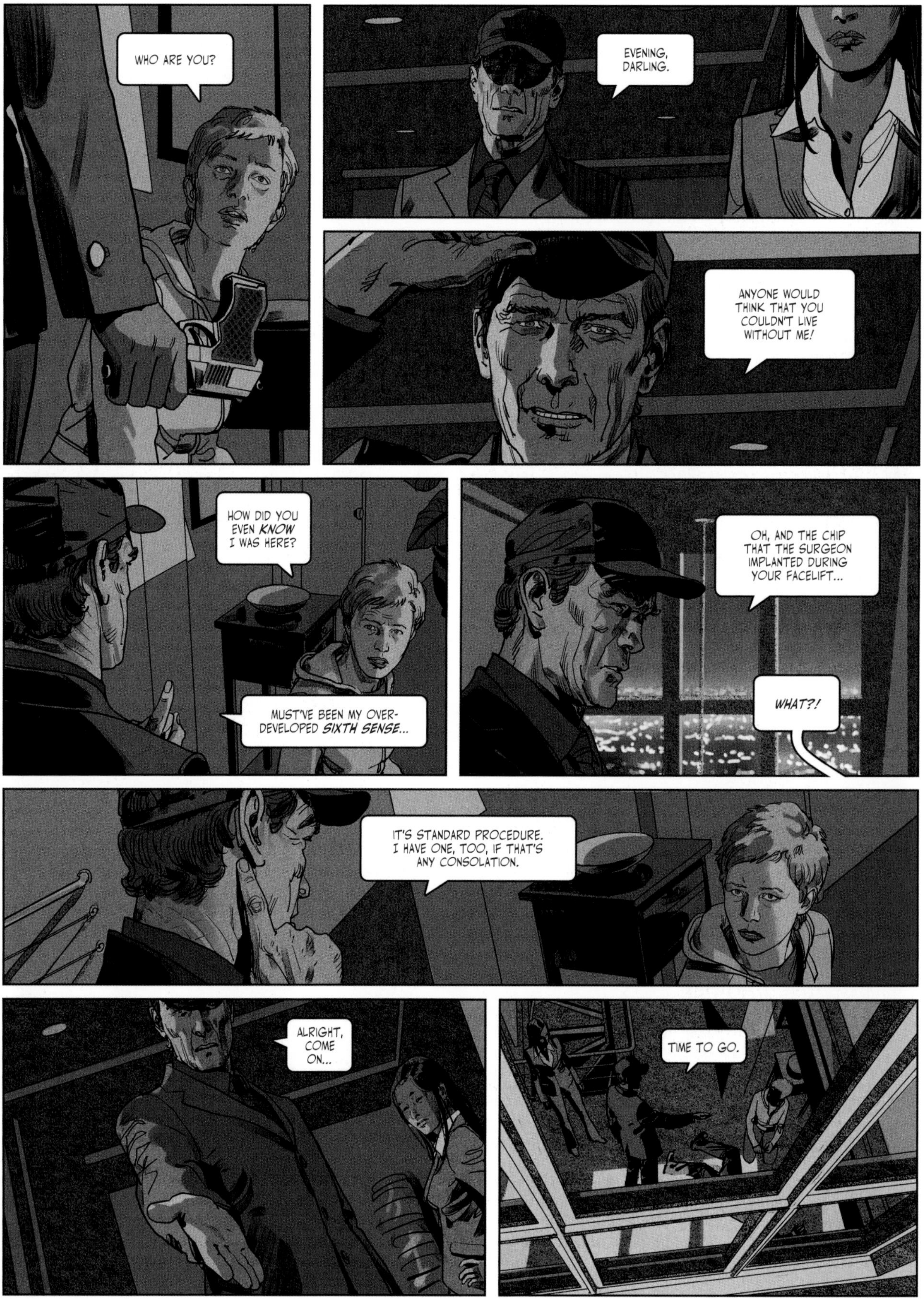
WHO ARE YOU?
EVENING, DARLING.
ANYONE WOULD THINK THAT YOU COULDN'T LIVE WITHOUT ME!
HOW DID YOU EVEN KNOW I WAS HERE?
MUST'VE BEEN MY OVER-DEVELOPED SIXTH SENSE...
OH, AND THE CHIP THAT THE SURGEON IMPLANTED DURING YOUR FACELIFT...
WHAT?!
IT'S STANDARD PROCEDURE. I HAVE ONE, TOO, IF THAT'S ANY CONSOLATION.
ALRIGHT, COME ON...
TIME TO GO.

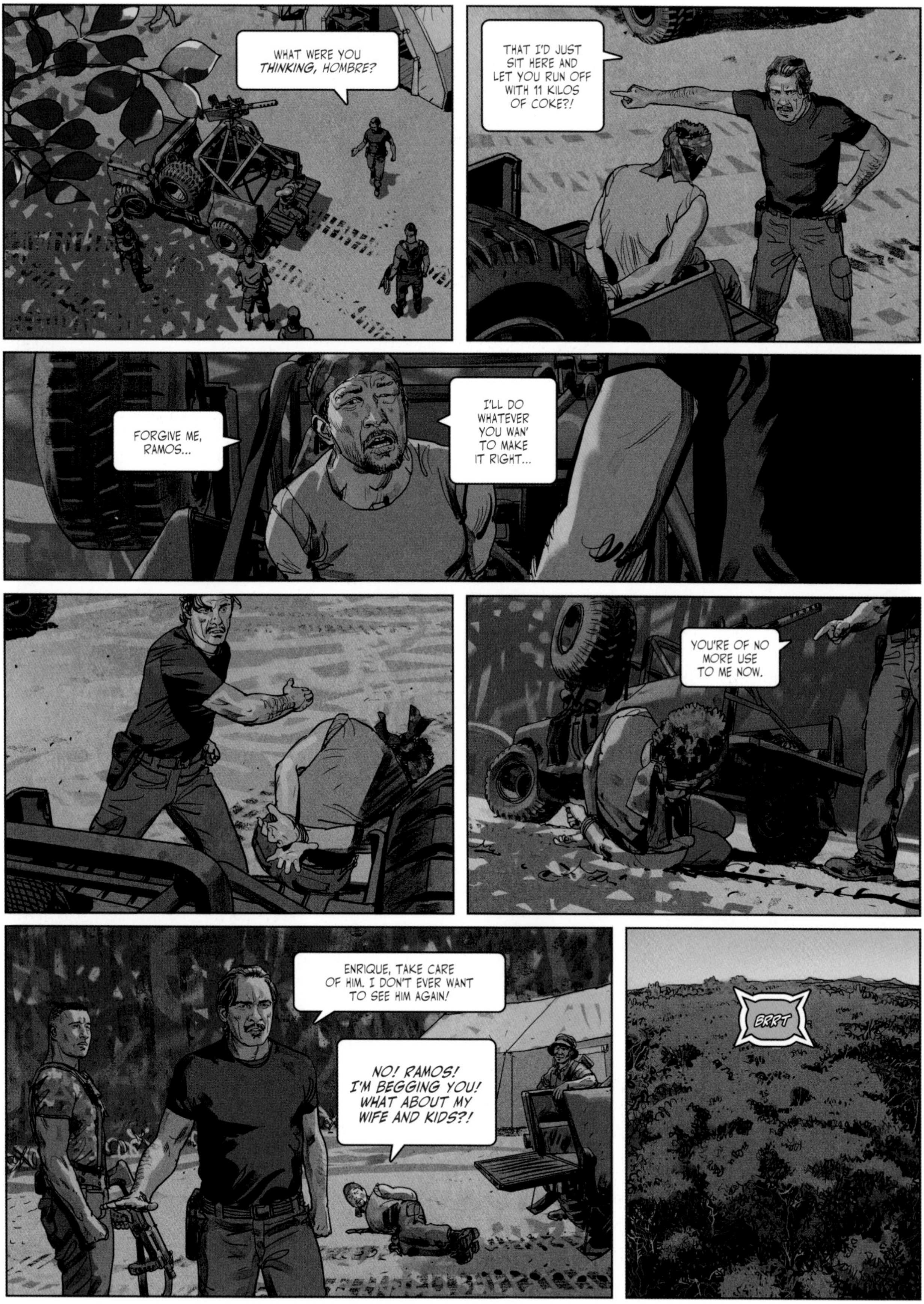
WHAT WERE YOU *THINKING*, HOMBRE?
THAT I'D JUST SIT HERE AND LET YOU RUN OFF WITH 11 KILOS OF COKE?!
FORGIVE ME, RAMOS...
I'LL DO WHATEVER YOU WAN' TO MAKE IT RIGHT...
YOU'RE OF NO MORE USE TO ME NOW.
ENRIQUE, TAKE CARE OF HIM. I DON'T EVER WANT TO SEE HIM AGAIN!
NO! RAMOS! I'M BEGGING YOU! WHAT ABOUT MY WIFE AND KIDS?!
BRRT

IT'S TIME WE SHIFTED THIS OPERATION UP A GEAR.

"I DON'T TRUST THIS NESBITT GUY AT ALL..."

"GOTTA MAKE OUR MOVE OR HE'S GONNA SLIP THROUGH OUR FINGERS."

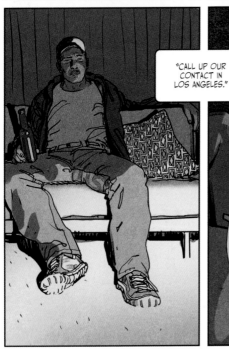

"CALL UP OUR CONTACT IN LOS ANGELES."

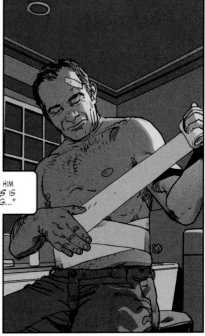

"TELL HIM *RAMOS* IS COMING..."

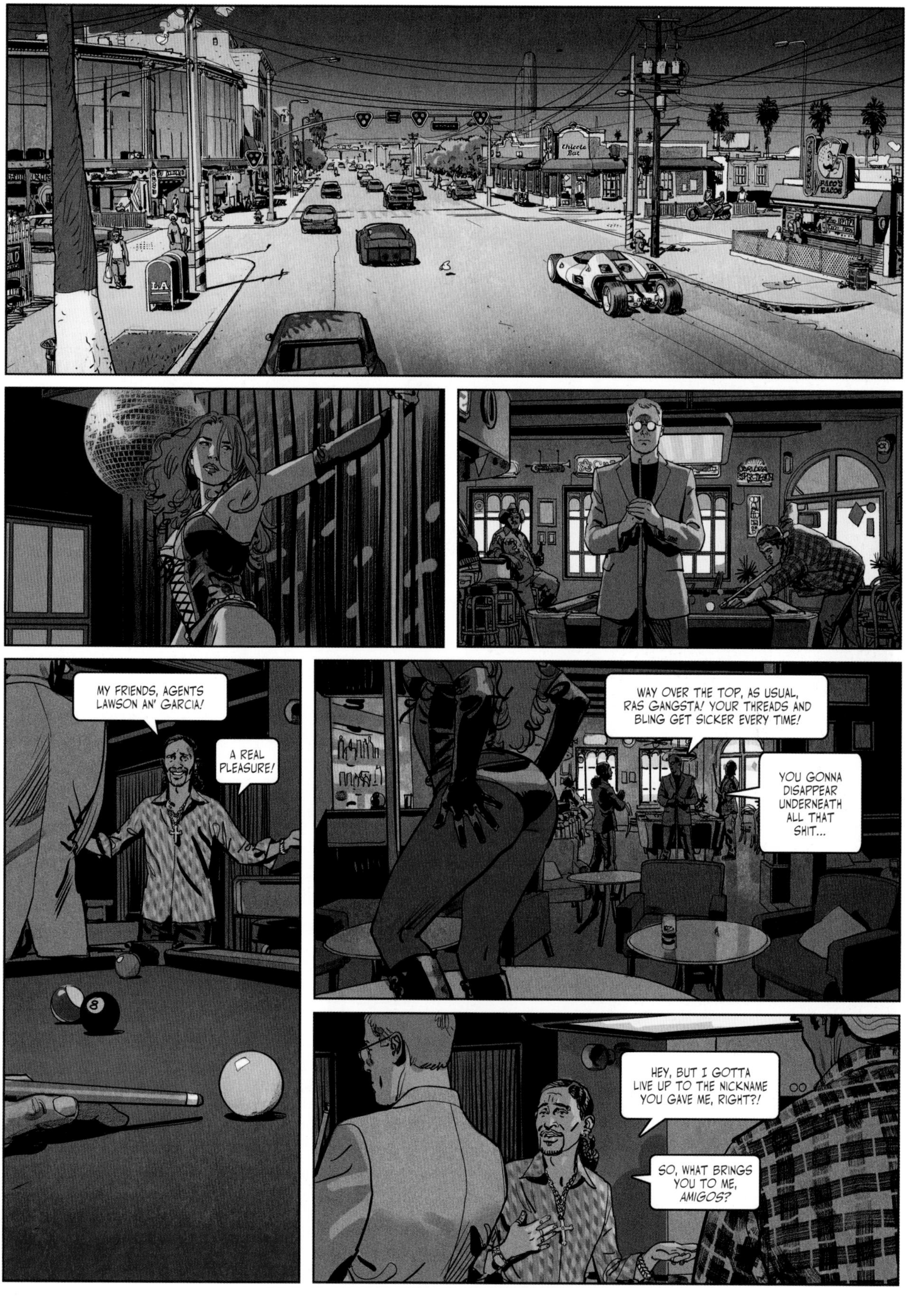
MY FRIENDS, AGENTS LAWSON AN' GARCIA!
A REAL PLEASURE!
WAY OVER THE TOP, AS USUAL, RAS GANGSTA! YOUR THREADS AND BLING GET SICKER EVERY TIME!
YOU GONNA DISAPPEAR UNDERNEATH ALL THAT SHIT...
HEY, BUT I GOTTA LIVE UP TO THE NICKNAME YOU GAVE ME, RIGHT?!
SO, WHAT BRINGS YOU TO ME, *AMIGOS?*

AH... SHE'S A HOTTIE, RIGHT?

"SHE JUST CAME UP FROM MEXICO..."

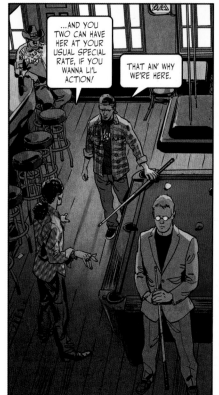

...AND YOU TWO CAN HAVE HER AT YOUR USUAL SPECIAL RATE, IF YOU WANNA LI'L ACTION!

THAT AIN' WHY WE'RE HERE.

GIMME THE LOWDOWN ON RAMOS.

DAMN, AMIGO! HEAVY SHIT!

YOU *KNOW* EVERYTHIN' ABOUT RAMOS IS TOP SECRET, MAN...

DON' SCREW WITH ME, RAS!

I GOT ENOUGH ON YOU TO SHUT THIS JOINT DOWN AN' TURN YOU BACK INTO THE GREASY LI'L RASTA YOU WAS JUST A FEW YEARS AGO!

WHATCHA WAN' ME TO SAY? THAT HE'S RIGHT HERE IN L.A.? I'M GUESSIN' YOU DON' NEED ME TO FILL YOU IN ON THAT...

ANY OL' PUTA CAN TELL YOU THAT!

THAT'S IT! JUST COS I'M LATINO, IT DON' MEAN THAT I KNOW WHO THE GUY'S FUCKIN' OR WHEN!

YEAH, AND WHAT *ELSE* DO YOU KNOW, *ASSHOLE?*

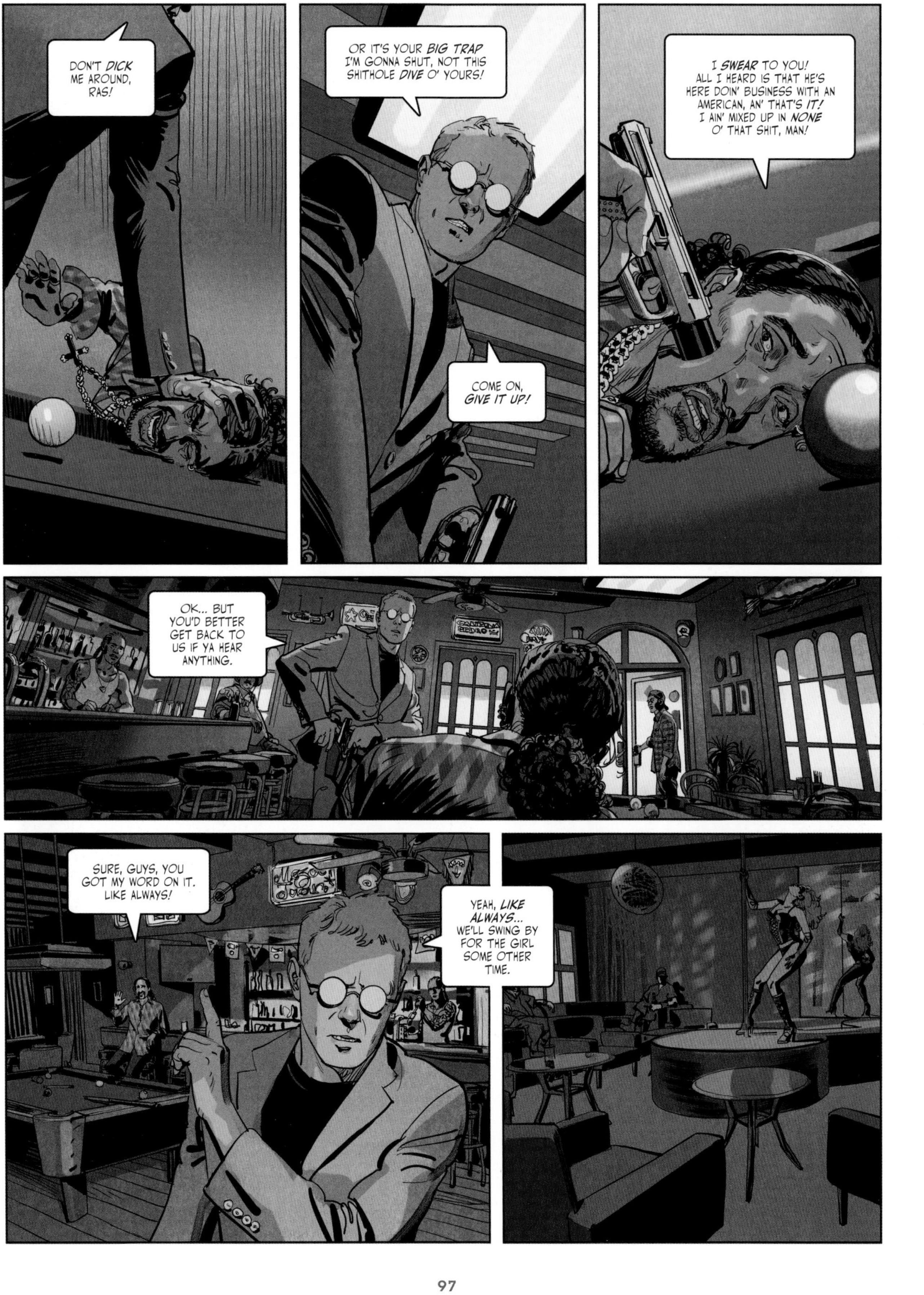
DON'T DICK ME AROUND, RAS!
OR IT'S YOUR BIG TRAP I'M GONNA SHUT, NOT THIS SHITHOLE DIVE O' YOURS!
COME ON, GIVE IT UP!
I SWEAR TO YOU! ALL I HEARD IS THAT HE'S HERE DOIN' BUSINESS WITH AN AMERICAN, AN' THAT'S IT! I AIN' MIXED UP IN NONE O' THAT SHIT, MAN!
OK... BUT YOU'D BETTER GET BACK TO US IF YA HEAR ANYTHING.
SURE, GUYS, YOU GOT MY WORD ON IT. LIKE ALWAYS!
YEAH, LIKE ALWAYS... WE'LL SWING BY FOR THE GIRL SOME OTHER TIME.

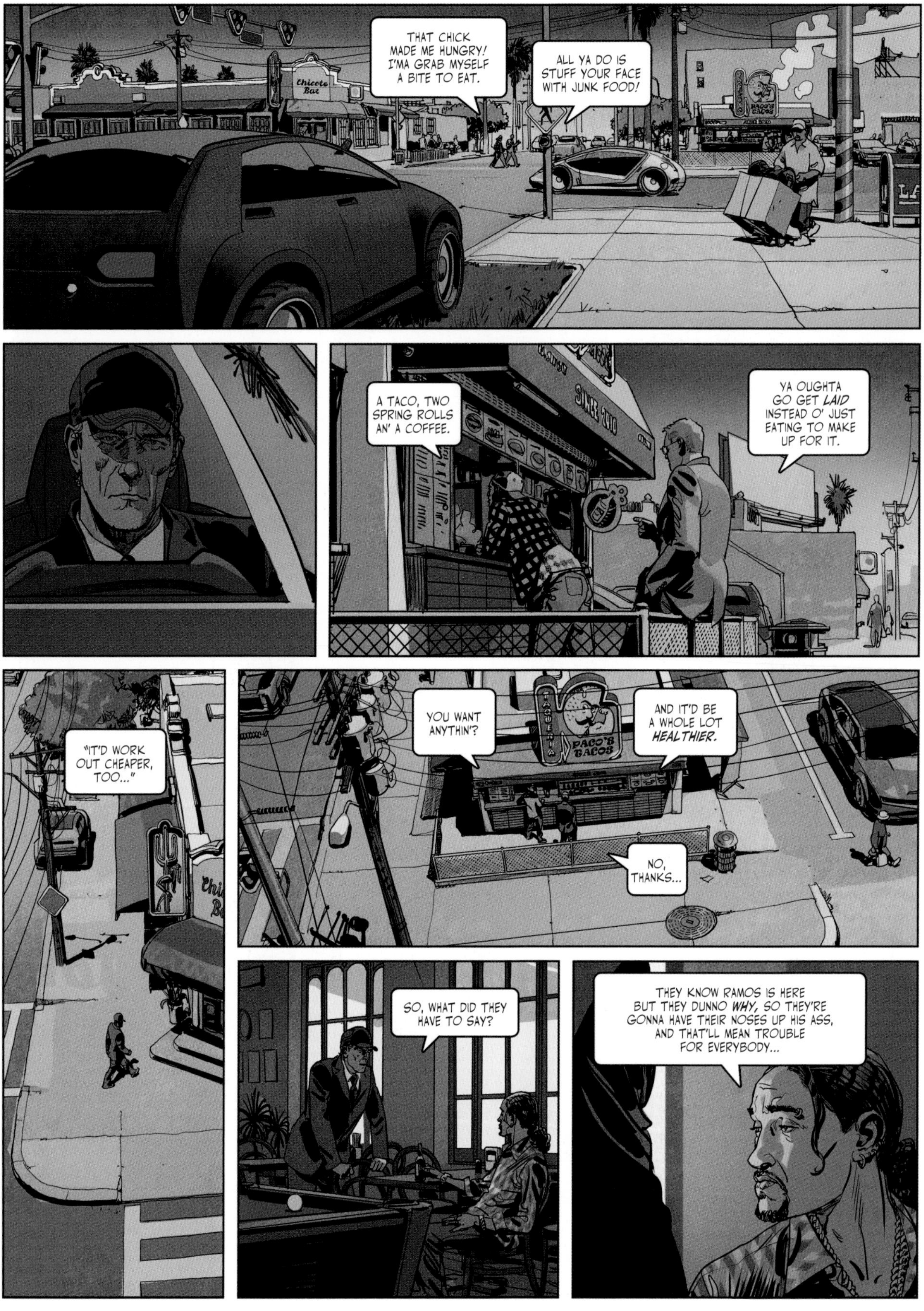
THAT CHICK MADE ME HUNGRY! I'MA GRAB MYSELF A BITE TO EAT.
ALL YA DO IS STUFF YOUR FACE WITH JUNK FOOD!
A TACO, TWO SPRING ROLLS AN' A COFFEE.
YA OUGHTA GO GET *LAID* INSTEAD O' JUST EATING TO MAKE UP FOR IT.
"IT'D WORK OUT CHEAPER, TOO..."
YOU WANT ANYTHIN'?
AND IT'D BE A WHOLE LOT *HEALTHIER.*
NO, THANKS...
SO, WHAT DID THEY HAVE TO SAY?
THEY KNOW RAMOS IS HERE BUT THEY DUNNO *WHY,* SO THEY'RE GONNA HAVE THEIR NOSES UP HIS ASS, AND THAT'LL MEAN TROUBLE FOR EVERYBODY...

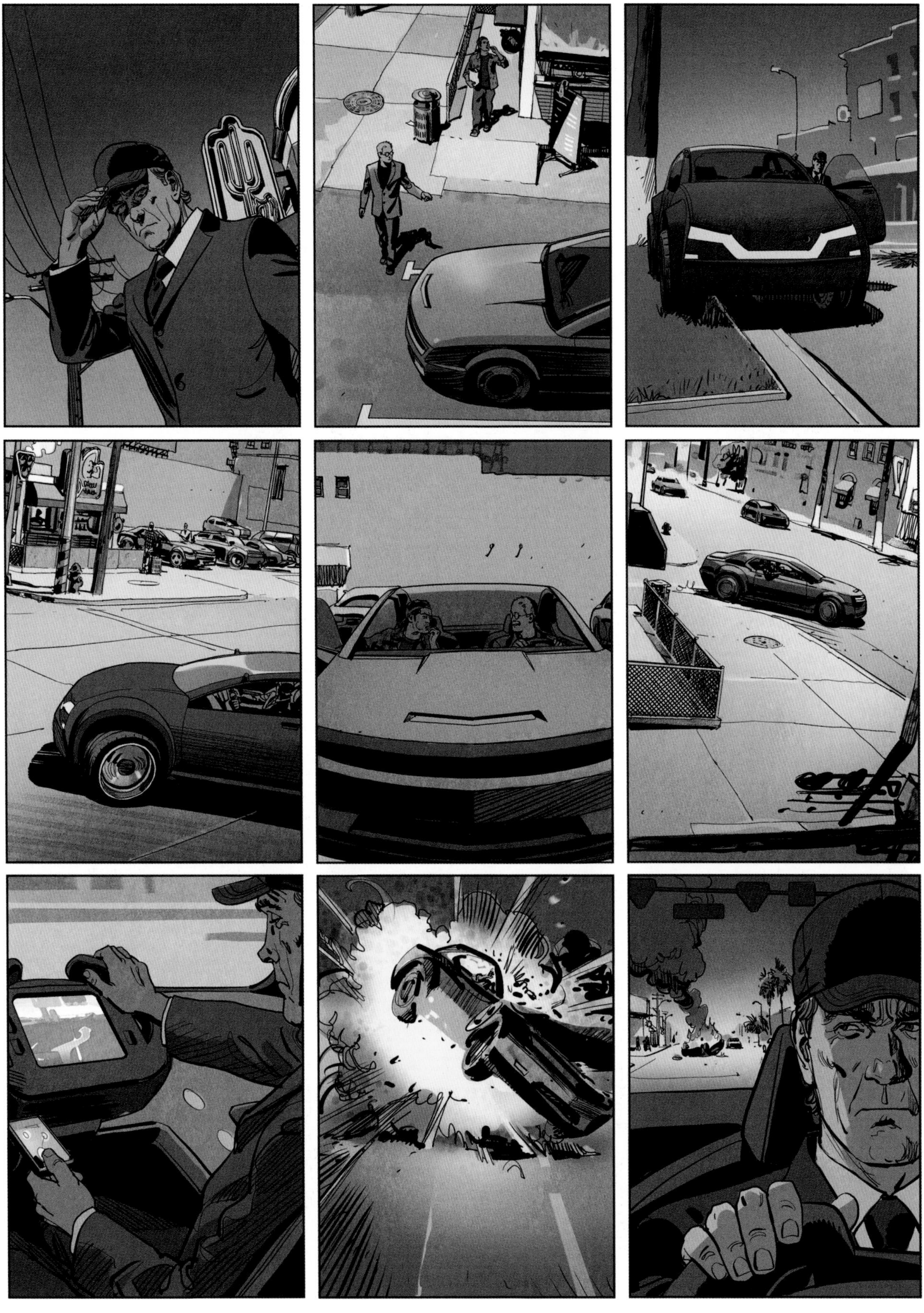

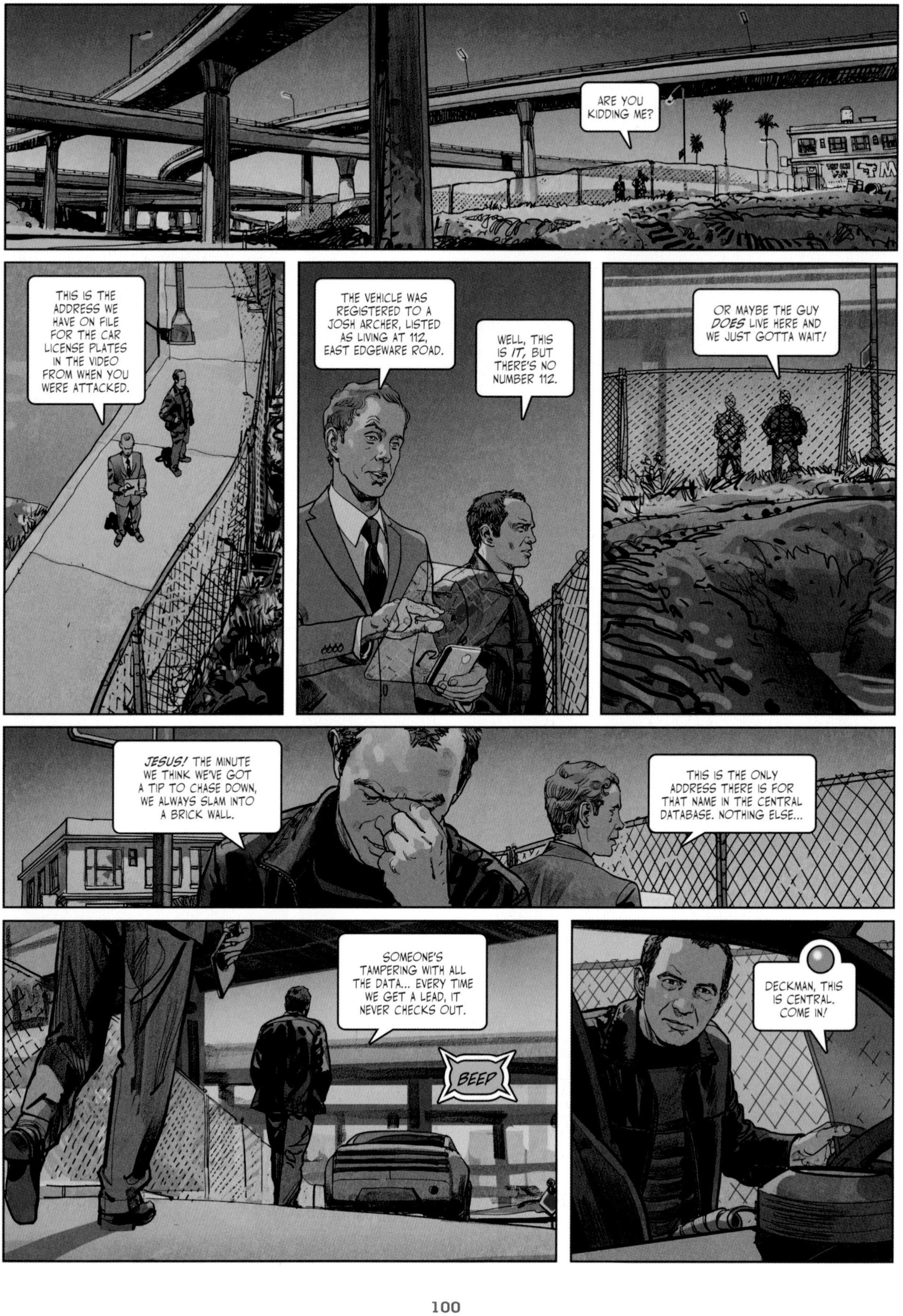
ARE YOU KIDDING ME?
THIS IS THE ADDRESS WE HAVE ON FILE FOR THE CAR LICENSE PLATES IN THE VIDEO FROM WHEN YOU WERE ATTACKED.
THE VEHICLE WAS REGISTERED TO A JOSH ARCHER, LISTED AS LIVING AT 112, EAST EDGEWARE ROAD.
WELL, THIS IS *IT*, BUT THERE'S NO NUMBER 112.
OR MAYBE THE GUY *DOES* LIVE HERE AND WE JUST GOTTA WAIT!
JESUS! THE MINUTE WE THINK WE'VE GOT A TIP TO CHASE DOWN, WE ALWAYS SLAM INTO A BRICK WALL.
THIS IS THE ONLY ADDRESS THERE IS FOR THAT NAME IN THE CENTRAL DATABASE. NOTHING ELSE...
SOMEONE'S TAMPERING WITH ALL THE DATA... EVERY TIME WE GET A LEAD, IT NEVER CHECKS OUT.
BEEP
DECKMAN, THIS IS CENTRAL. COME IN!

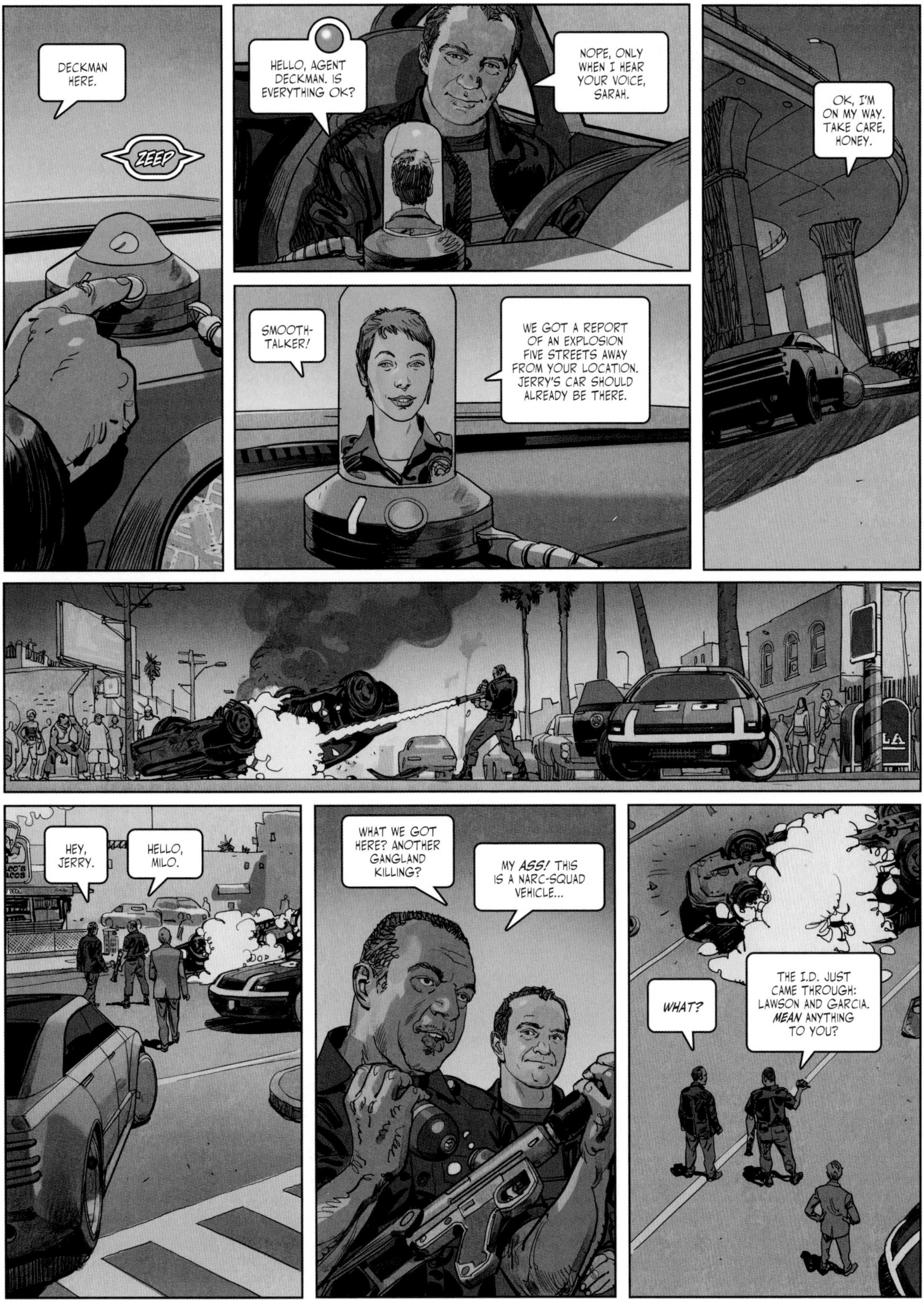
DECKMAN HERE.
ZEEP
HELLO, AGENT DECKMAN. IS EVERYTHING OK?
NOPE, ONLY WHEN I HEAR YOUR VOICE, SARAH.
SMOOTH-TALKER!
WE GOT A REPORT OF AN EXPLOSION FIVE STREETS AWAY FROM YOUR LOCATION. JERRY'S CAR SHOULD ALREADY BE THERE.
OK, I'M ON MY WAY. TAKE CARE, HONEY.
HEY, JERRY.
HELLO, MILO.
WHAT WE GOT HERE? ANOTHER GANGLAND KILLING?
MY ASS! THIS IS A NARC-SQUAD VEHICLE...
WHAT?
THE I.D. JUST CAME THROUGH: LAWSON AND GARCIA. MEAN ANYTHING TO YOU?

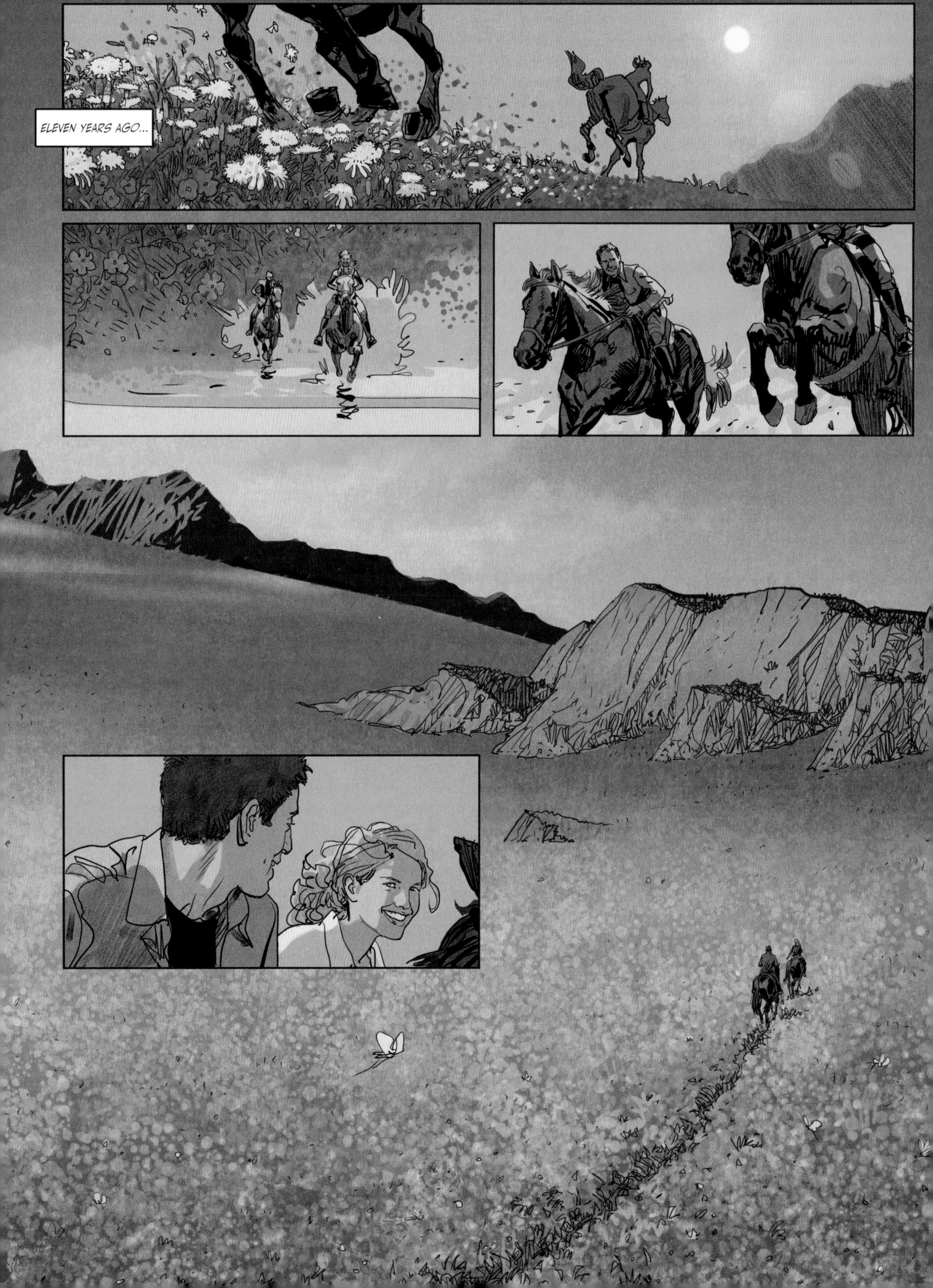
ELEVEN YEARS AGO...

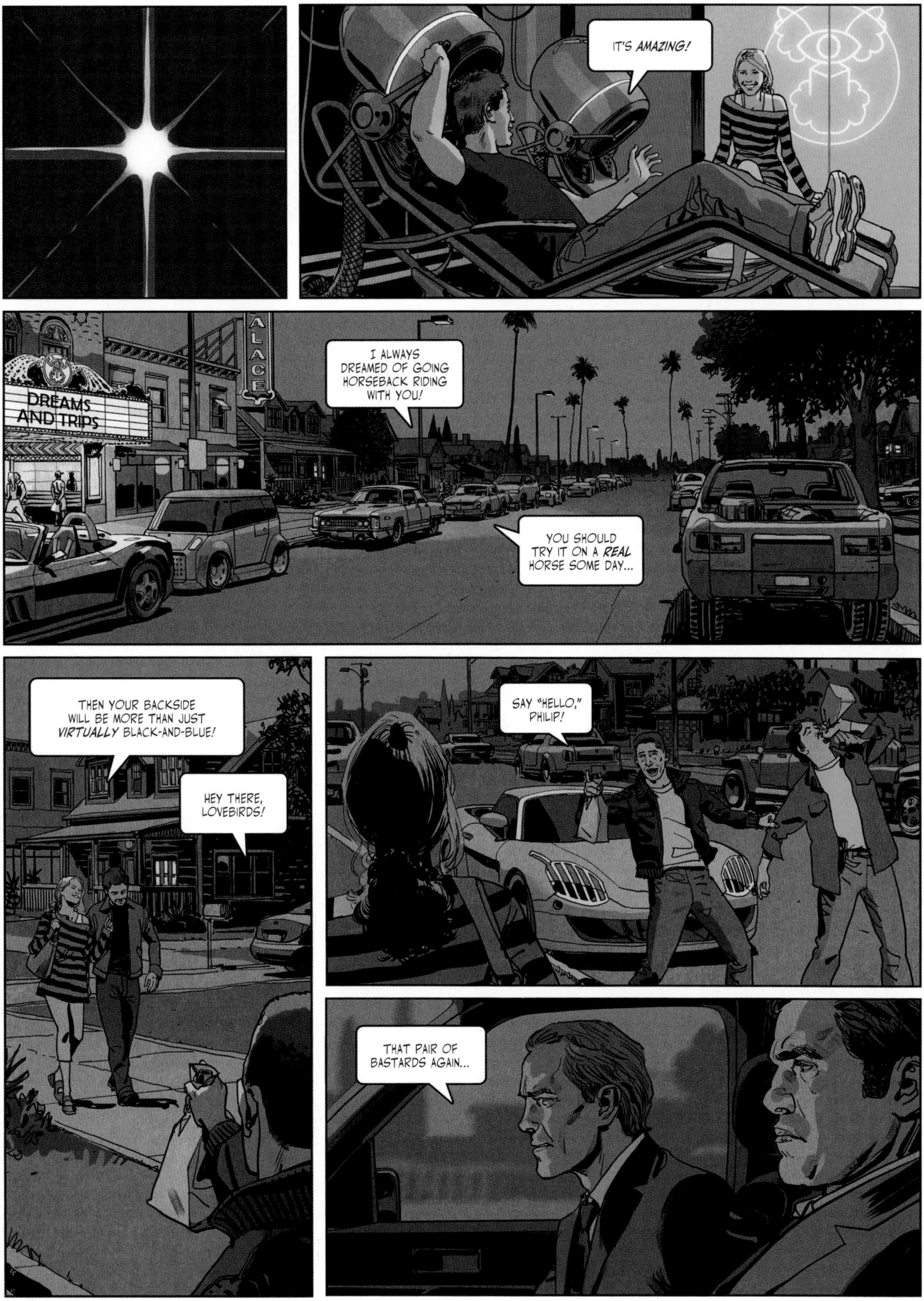
IT'S AMAZING!
DREAMS AND TRIPS
PALACE
I ALWAYS DREAMED OF GOING HORSEBACK RIDING WITH YOU!
YOU SHOULD TRY IT ON A REAL HORSE SOME DAY...
THEN YOUR BACKSIDE WILL BE MORE THAN JUST VIRTUALLY BLACK-AND-BLUE!
HEY THERE, LOVEBIRDS!
SAY "HELLO," PHILIP!
THAT PAIR OF BASTARDS AGAIN...

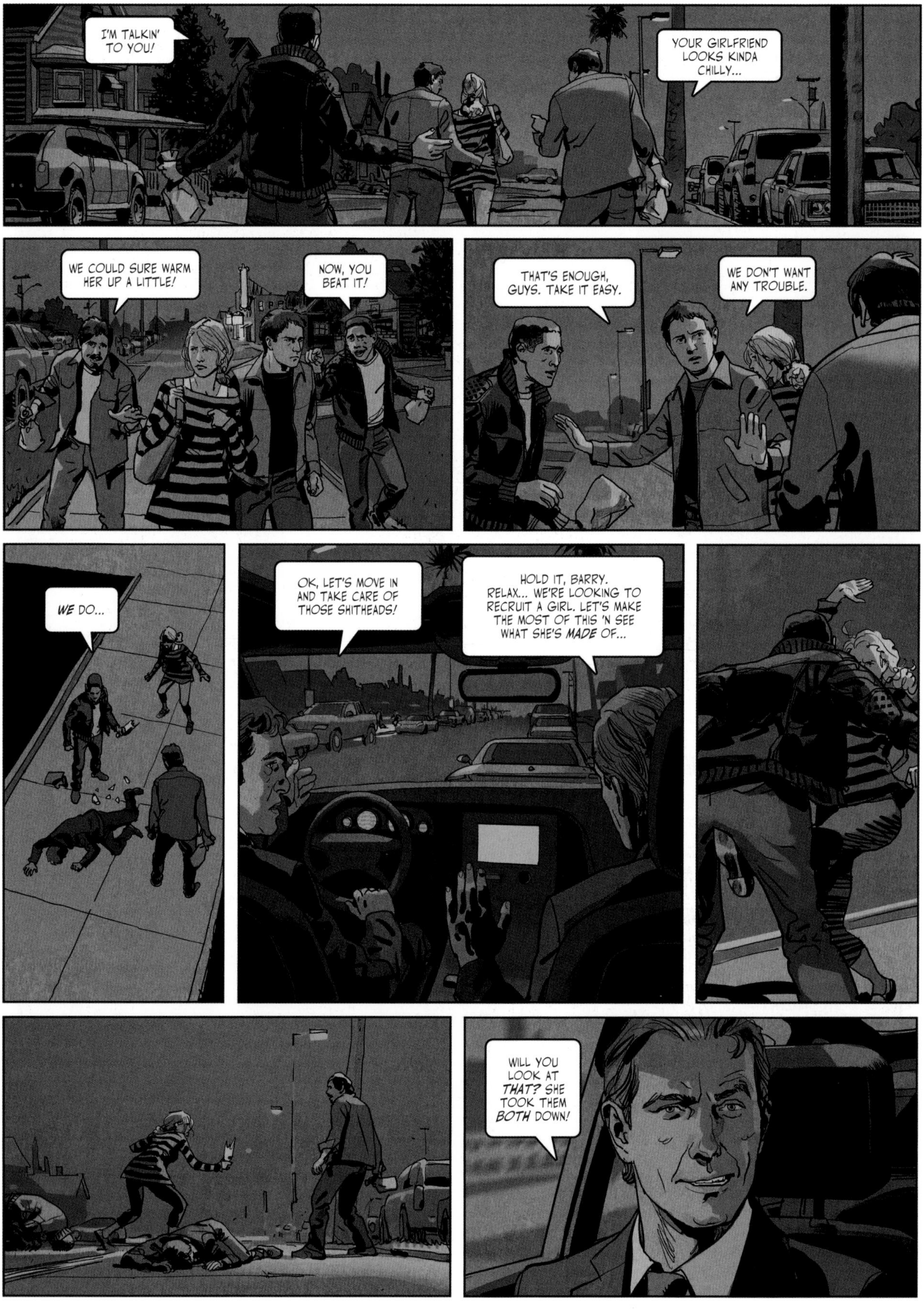
I'M TALKIN' TO YOU!
YOUR GIRLFRIEND LOOKS KINDA CHILLY...
WE COULD SURE WARM HER UP A LITTLE!
NOW, YOU BEAT IT!
THAT'S ENOUGH, GUYS. TAKE IT EASY.
WE DON'T WANT ANY TROUBLE.
WE DO...
OK, LET'S MOVE IN AND TAKE CARE OF THOSE SHITHEADS!
HOLD IT, BARRY. RELAX... WE'RE LOOKING TO RECRUIT A GIRL. LET'S MAKE THE MOST OF THIS 'N SEE WHAT SHE'S *MADE* OF...
WILL YOU LOOK AT *THAT?* SHE TOOK THEM *BOTH* DOWN!

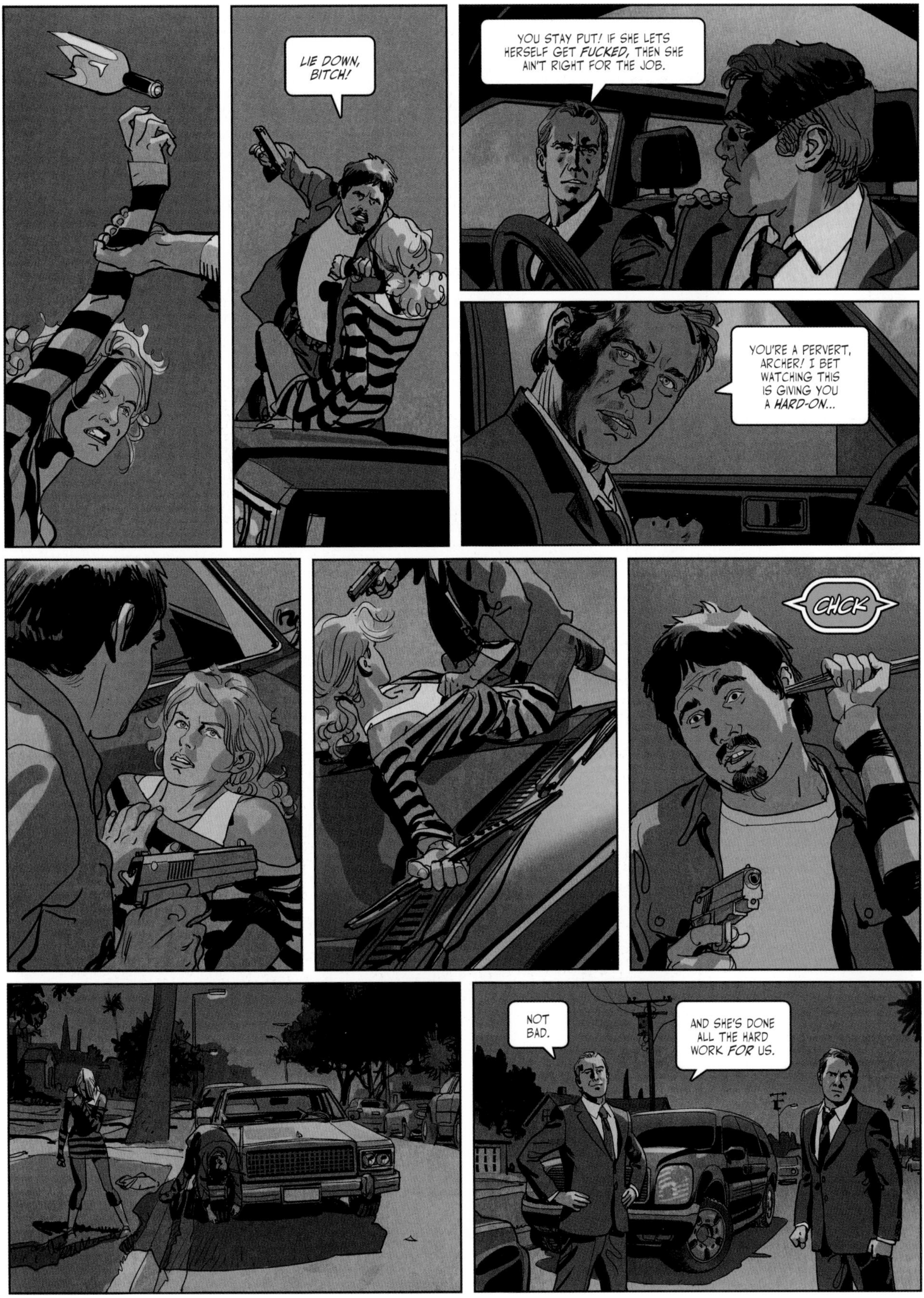
LIE DOWN, BITCH!
YOU STAY PUT! IF SHE LETS HERSELF GET FUCKED, THEN SHE AIN'T RIGHT FOR THE JOB.
YOU'RE A PERVERT, ARCHER! I BET WATCHING THIS IS GIVING YOU A HARD-ON...
CHCK
NOT BAD.
AND SHE'S DONE ALL THE HARD WORK FOR US.

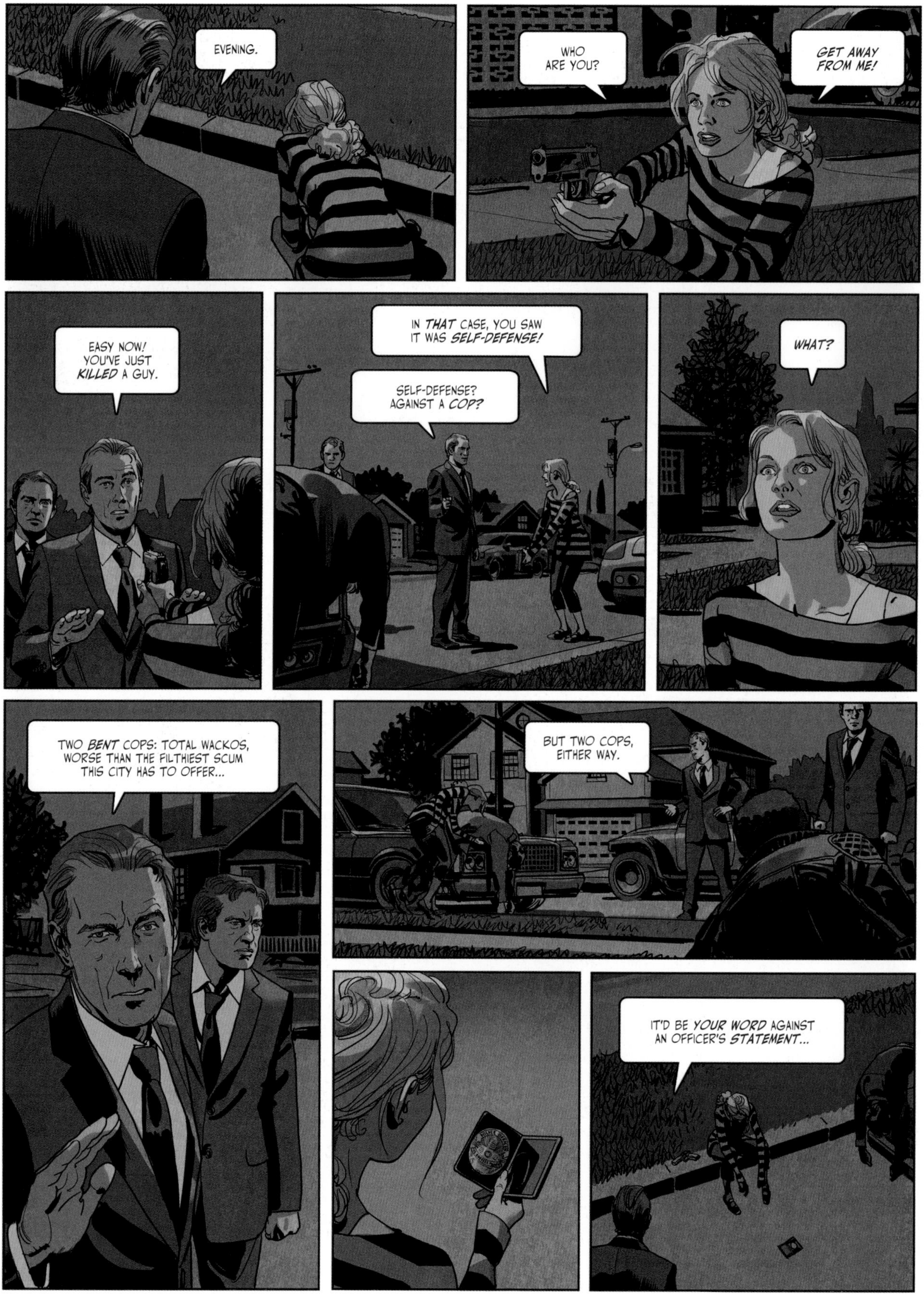

EVENING.
WHO ARE YOU?
GET AWAY FROM ME!
EASY NOW! YOU'VE JUST KILLED A GUY.
IN THAT CASE, YOU SAW IT WAS SELF-DEFENSE!
SELF-DEFENSE? AGAINST A COP?
WHAT?
TWO BENT COPS: TOTAL WACKOS, WORSE THAN THE FILTHIEST SCUM THIS CITY HAS TO OFFER...
BUT TWO COPS, EITHER WAY.
IT'D BE YOUR WORD AGAINST AN OFFICER'S STATEMENT...

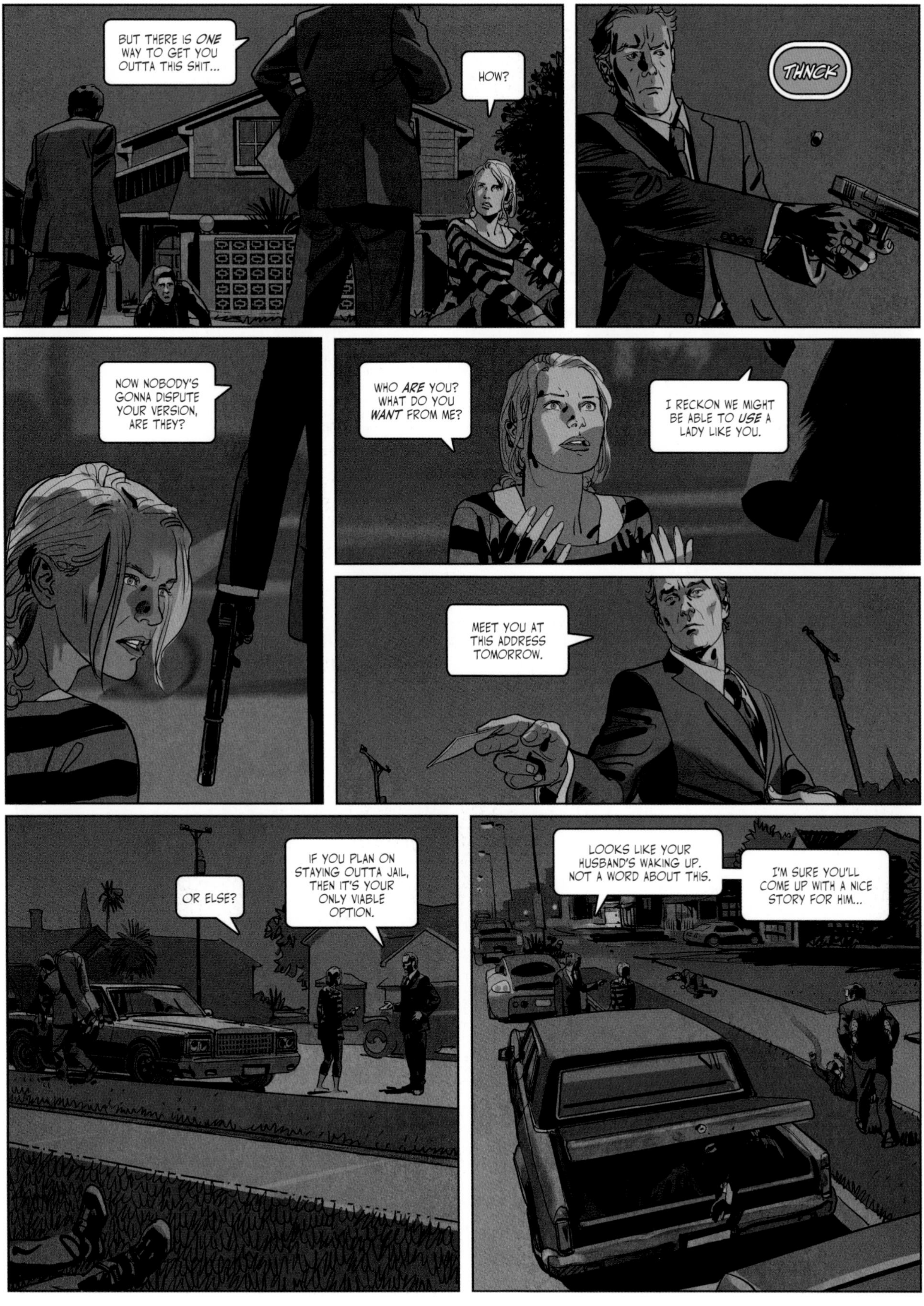
BUT THERE IS ONE WAY TO GET YOU OUTTA THIS SHIT...
HOW?
THNCK
NOW NOBODY'S GONNA DISPUTE YOUR VERSION, ARE THEY?
WHO ARE YOU? WHAT DO YOU WANT FROM ME?
I RECKON WE MIGHT BE ABLE TO USE A LADY LIKE YOU.
MEET YOU AT THIS ADDRESS TOMORROW.
OR ELSE?
IF YOU PLAN ON STAYING OUTTA JAIL, THEN IT'S YOUR ONLY VIABLE OPTION.
LOOKS LIKE YOUR HUSBAND'S WAKING UP. NOT A WORD ABOUT THIS.
I'M SURE YOU'LL COME UP WITH A NICE STORY FOR HIM...

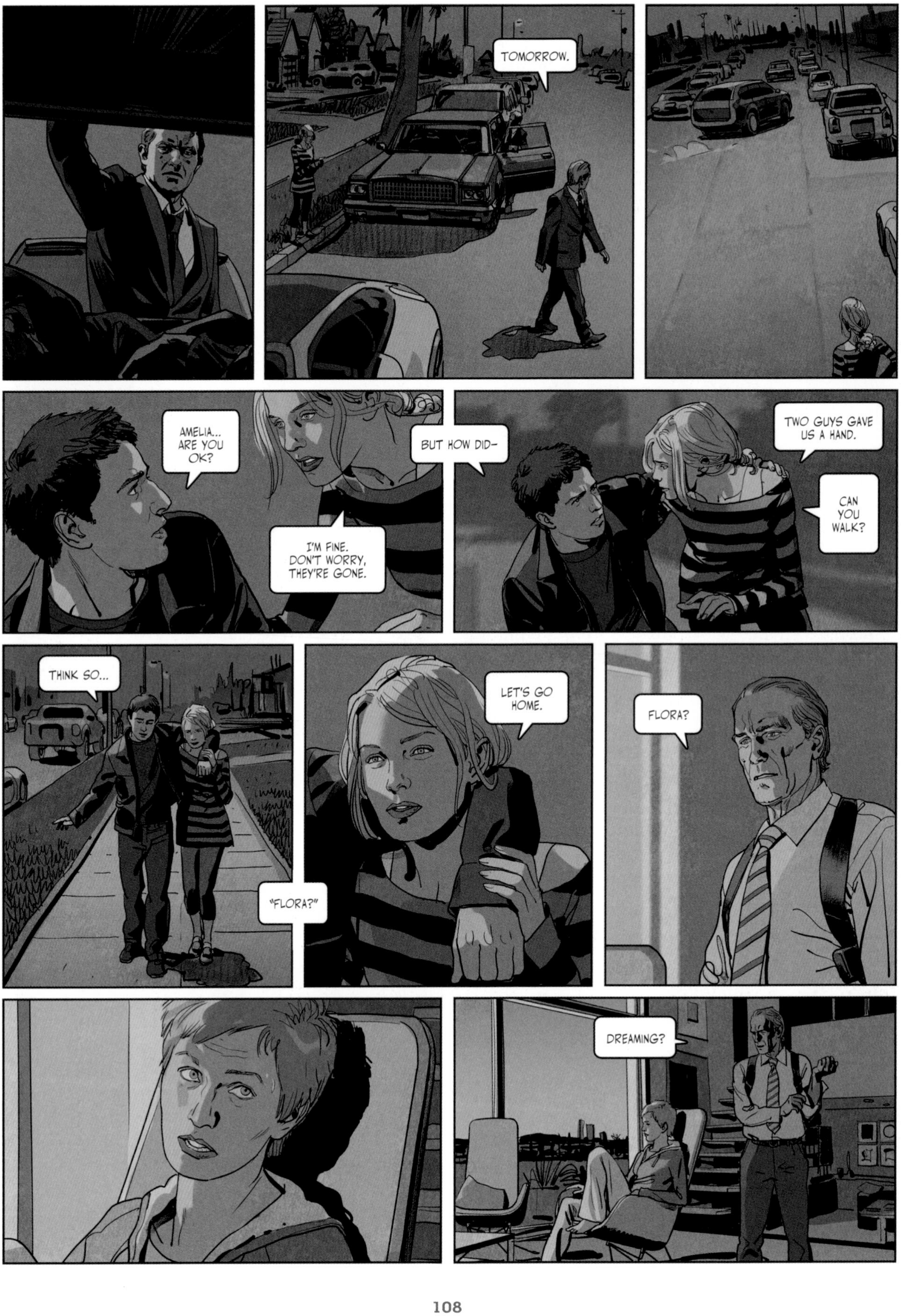
TOMORROW.
AMELIA... ARE YOU OK?
I'M FINE. DON'T WORRY, THEY'RE GONE.
BUT HOW DID-
TWO GUYS GAVE US A HAND.
CAN YOU WALK?
THINK SO...
LET'S GO HOME.
"FLORA?"
FLORA?
DREAMING?

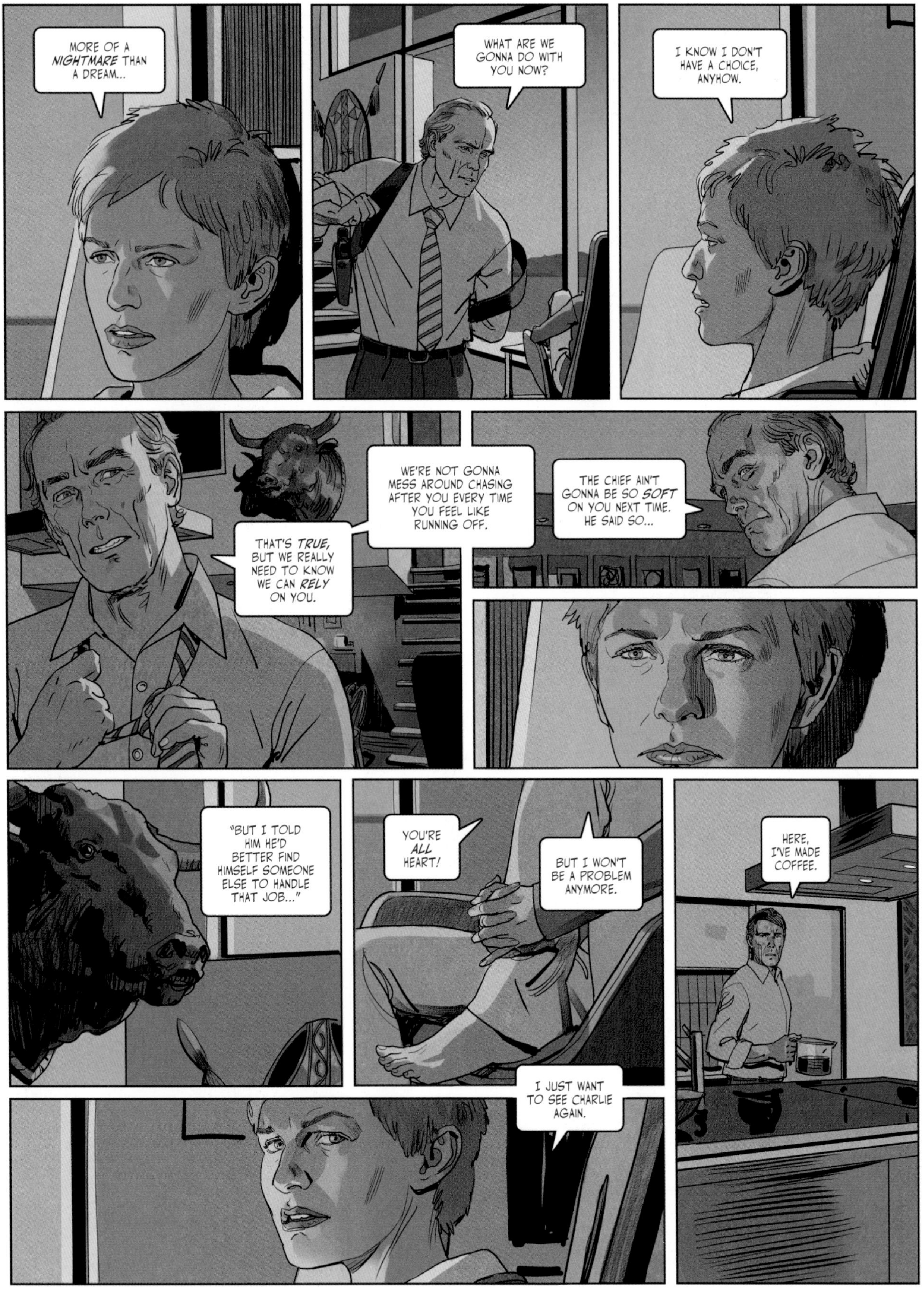
MORE OF A NIGHTMARE THAN A DREAM...
WHAT ARE WE GONNA DO WITH YOU NOW?
I KNOW I DON'T HAVE A CHOICE, ANYHOW.
THAT'S TRUE, BUT WE REALLY NEED TO KNOW WE CAN RELY ON YOU.
WE'RE NOT GONNA MESS AROUND CHASING AFTER YOU EVERY TIME YOU FEEL LIKE RUNNING OFF.
THE CHIEF AIN'T GONNA BE SO SOFT ON YOU NEXT TIME. HE SAID SO...
"BUT I TOLD HIM HE'D BETTER FIND HIMSELF SOMEONE ELSE TO HANDLE THAT JOB..."
YOU'RE ALL HEART!
BUT I WON'T BE A PROBLEM ANYMORE.
I JUST WANT TO SEE CHARLIE AGAIN.
HERE, I'VE MADE COFFEE.

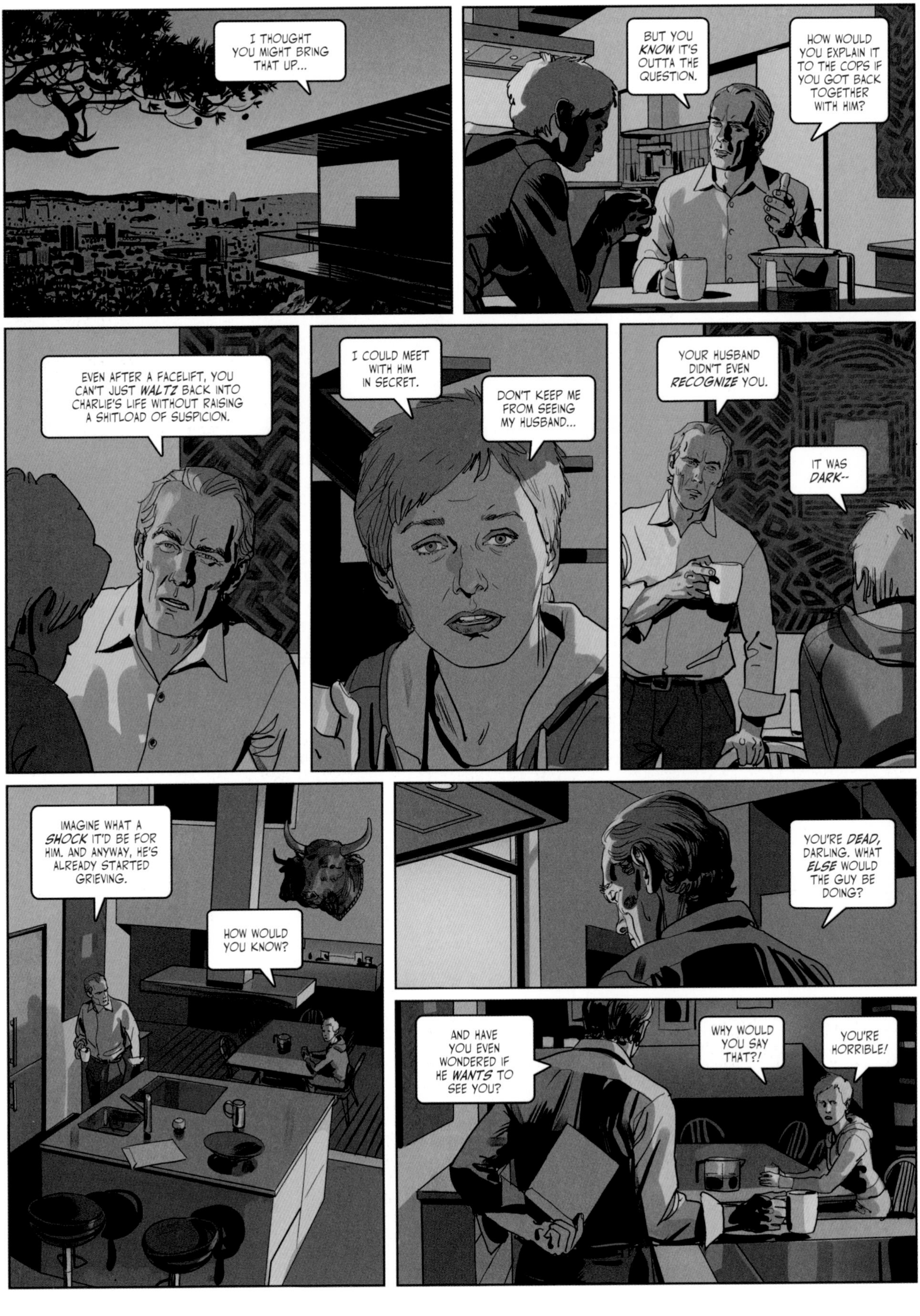

I THOUGHT YOU MIGHT BRING THAT UP...
BUT YOU *KNOW* IT'S OUTTA THE QUESTION.
HOW WOULD YOU EXPLAIN IT TO THE COPS IF YOU GOT BACK TOGETHER WITH HIM?
EVEN AFTER A FACELIFT, YOU CAN'T JUST *WALTZ* BACK INTO CHARLIE'S LIFE WITHOUT RAISING A SHITLOAD OF SUSPICION.
I COULD MEET WITH HIM IN SECRET.
DON'T KEEP ME FROM SEEING MY HUSBAND...
YOUR HUSBAND DIDN'T EVEN *RECOGNIZE* YOU.
IT WAS *DARK*--
IMAGINE WHAT A *SHOCK* IT'D BE FOR HIM. AND ANYWAY, HE'S ALREADY STARTED GRIEVING.
HOW WOULD YOU KNOW?
YOU'RE *DEAD*, DARLING. WHAT *ELSE* WOULD THE GUY BE DOING?
AND HAVE YOU EVEN WONDERED IF HE *WANTS* TO SEE YOU?
WHY WOULD YOU SAY THAT?!
YOU'RE HORRIBLE!

HORRIBLE? *ME?* I WOULDN'T KNOW...

BUT I'M PRETTY SURE *HE'S* THE HORRIBLE ONE...

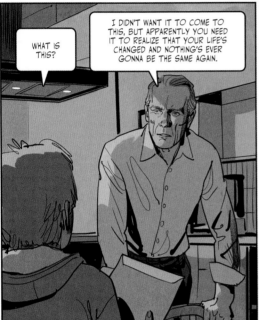

WHAT IS THIS?

I DIDN'T WANT IT TO COME TO THIS, BUT APPARENTLY YOU NEED IT TO REALIZE THAT YOUR LIFE'S CHANGED AND NOTHING'S EVER GONNA BE THE SAME AGAIN.

YOU'RE DEAD, AND YOUR HUSBAND IS CLEAR ON THAT...

SEEMS HE GOT OVER YOU PRETTY QUICK...

OK, I'M READY.

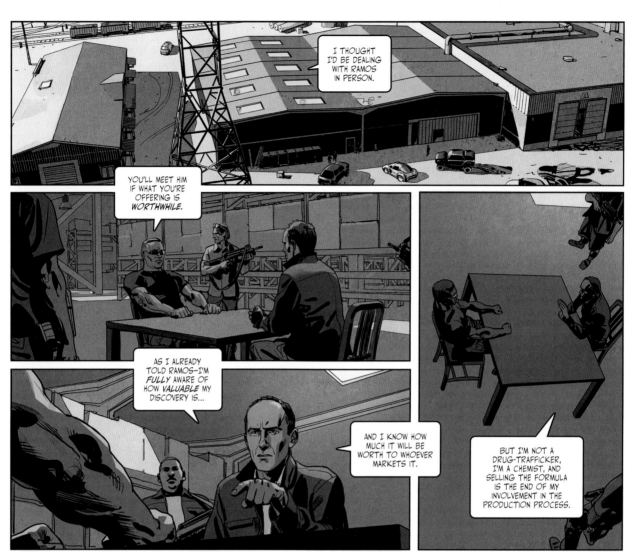

I THOUGHT I'D BE DEALING WITH RAMOS IN PERSON.

YOU'LL MEET HIM IF WHAT YOU'RE OFFERING IS *WORTHWHILE*.

AS I ALREADY TOLD RAMOS—I'M *FULLY* AWARE OF HOW *VALUABLE* MY DISCOVERY IS...

AND I KNOW HOW MUCH IT WILL BE WORTH TO WHOEVER MARKETS IT.

BUT I'M NOT A DRUG-TRAFFICKER, I'M A CHEMIST, AND SELLING THE FORMULA IS THE END OF MY INVOLVEMENT IN THE PRODUCTION PROCESS.

WELL, SINCE YOU'RE ALREADY TALKING PRICES, HOW MUCH DO YOU WANT FOR IT?

100 MILLION US DOLLARS.

RAMOS TOLD ME YOU'D BE *GREEDY*, MR. NESBITT, BUT I HAD NO IDEA *HOW* GREEDY...

YOU KNOW PERFECTLY WELL THAT IT'S GOING TO BRING YOU MUCH MORE THAN THAT.

DON'T GET AHEAD OF YOURSELF... YOU HAVEN'T EVEN SHOWN US ANYTHING YET.

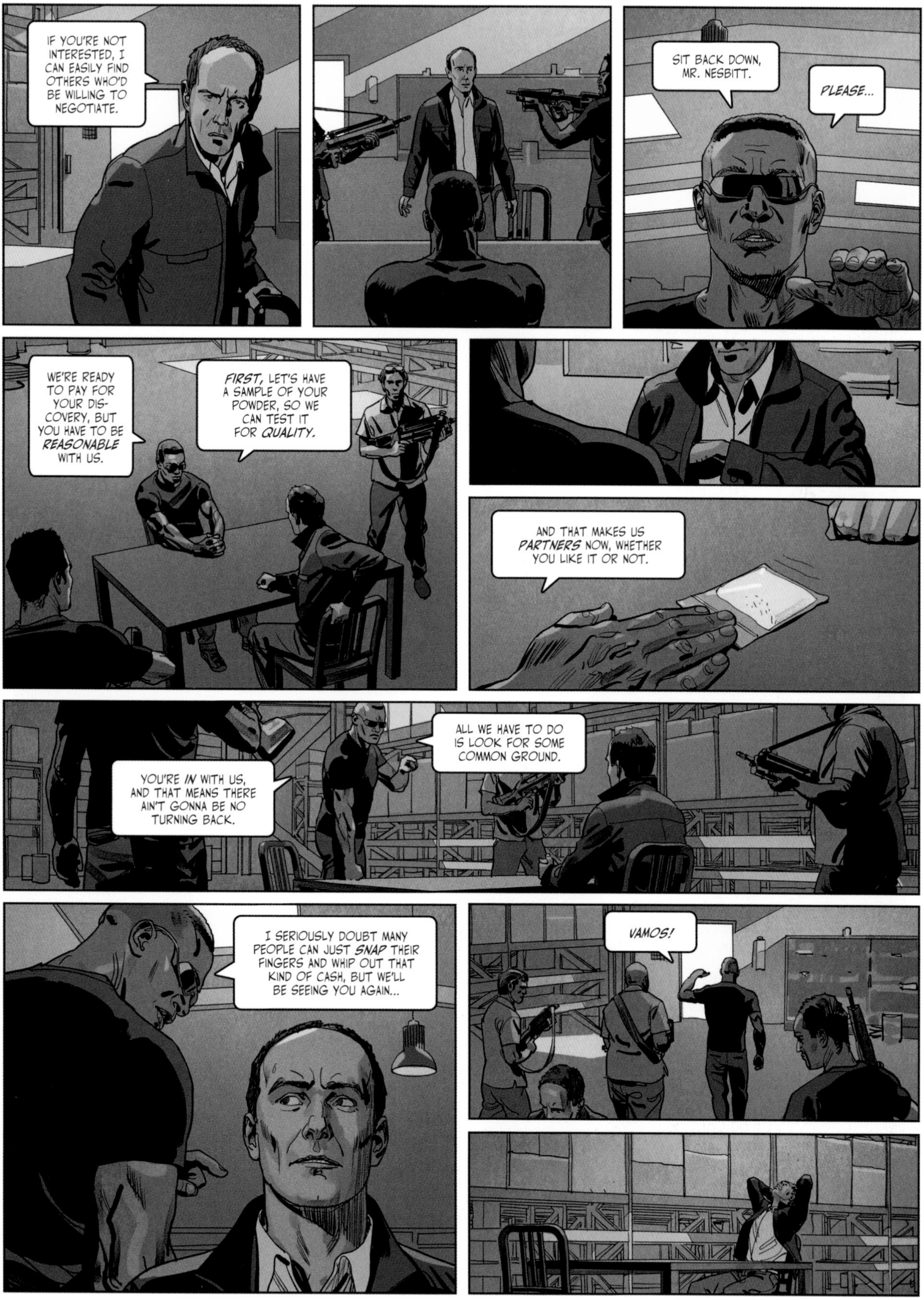
IF YOU'RE NOT INTERESTED, I CAN EASILY FIND OTHERS WHO'D BE WILLING TO NEGOTIATE.
SIT BACK DOWN, MR. NESBITT.
PLEASE...
WE'RE READY TO PAY FOR YOUR DIS-COVERY, BUT YOU HAVE TO BE REASONABLE WITH US.
FIRST, LET'S HAVE A SAMPLE OF YOUR POWDER, SO WE CAN TEST IT FOR QUALITY.
AND THAT MAKES US PARTNERS NOW, WHETHER YOU LIKE IT OR NOT.
YOU'RE IN WITH US, AND THAT MEANS THERE AIN'T GONNA BE NO TURNING BACK.
ALL WE HAVE TO DO IS LOOK FOR SOME COMMON GROUND.
I SERIOUSLY DOUBT MANY PEOPLE CAN JUST SNAP THEIR FINGERS AND WHIP OUT THAT KIND OF CASH, BUT WE'LL BE SEEING YOU AGAIN...
VAMOS!

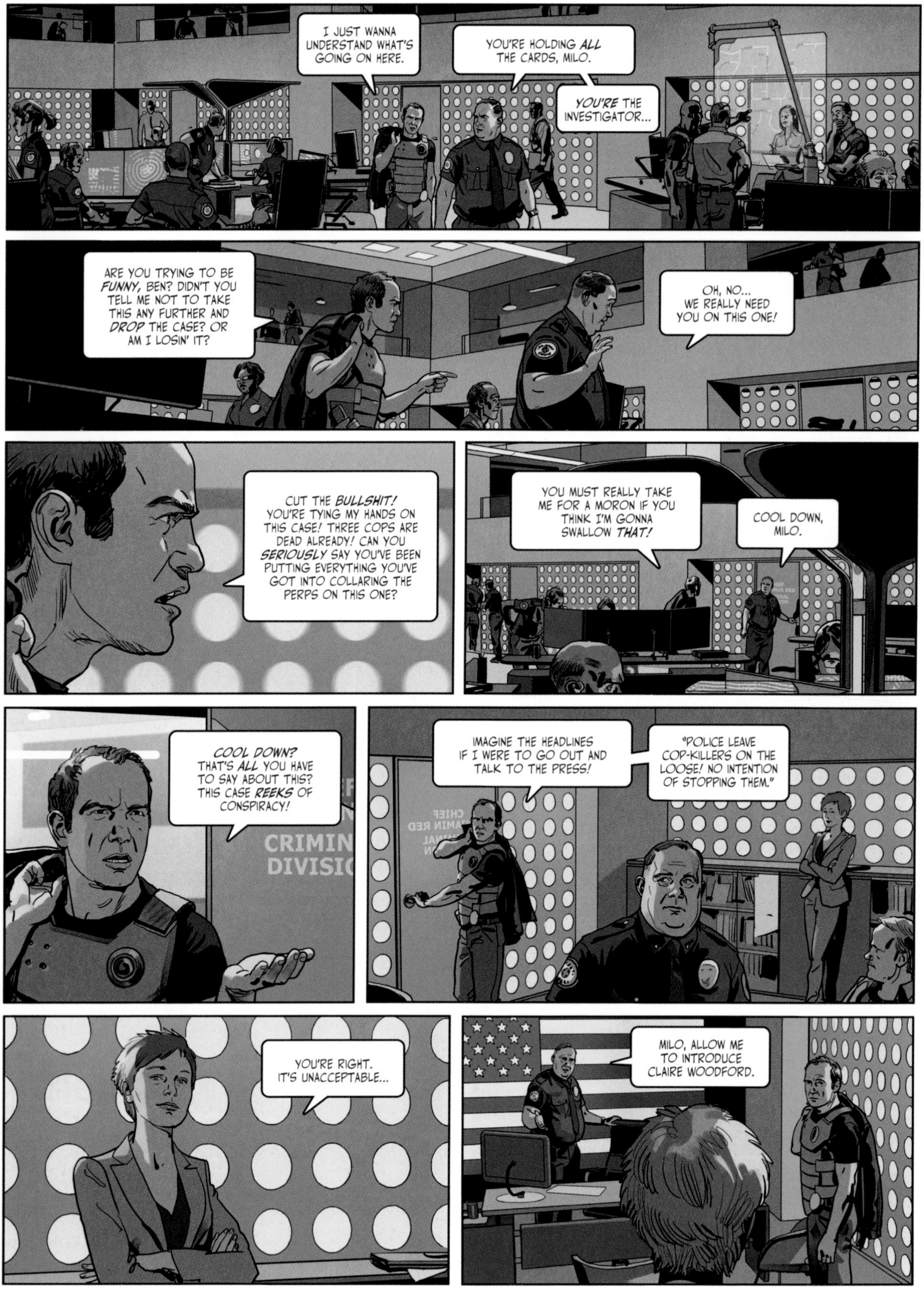
I JUST WANNA UNDERSTAND WHAT'S GOING ON HERE.
YOU'RE HOLDING *ALL* THE CARDS, MILO.
YOU'RE THE INVESTIGATOR...
ARE YOU TRYING TO BE *FUNNY*, BEN? DIDN'T YOU TELL ME NOT TO TAKE THIS ANY FURTHER AND *DROP* THE CASE? OR AM I LOSIN' IT?
OH, NO... WE REALLY NEED YOU ON THIS ONE!
CUT THE *BULLSHIT!* YOU'RE TYING MY HANDS ON THIS CASE! THREE COPS ARE DEAD ALREADY! CAN YOU *SERIOUSLY* SAY YOU'VE BEEN PUTTING EVERYTHING YOU'VE GOT INTO COLLARING THE PERPS ON THIS ONE?
YOU MUST REALLY TAKE ME FOR A MORON IF YOU THINK I'M GONNA SWALLOW *THAT!*
COOL DOWN, MILO.
COOL DOWN? THAT'S *ALL* YOU HAVE TO SAY ABOUT THIS? THIS CASE *REEKS* OF CONSPIRACY!
IMAGINE THE HEADLINES IF I WERE TO GO OUT AND TALK TO THE PRESS!
"POLICE LEAVE COP-KILLERS ON THE LOOSE! NO INTENTION OF STOPPING THEM."
YOU'RE RIGHT. IT'S UNACCEPTABLE...
MILO, ALLOW ME TO INTRODUCE CLAIRE WOODFORD.

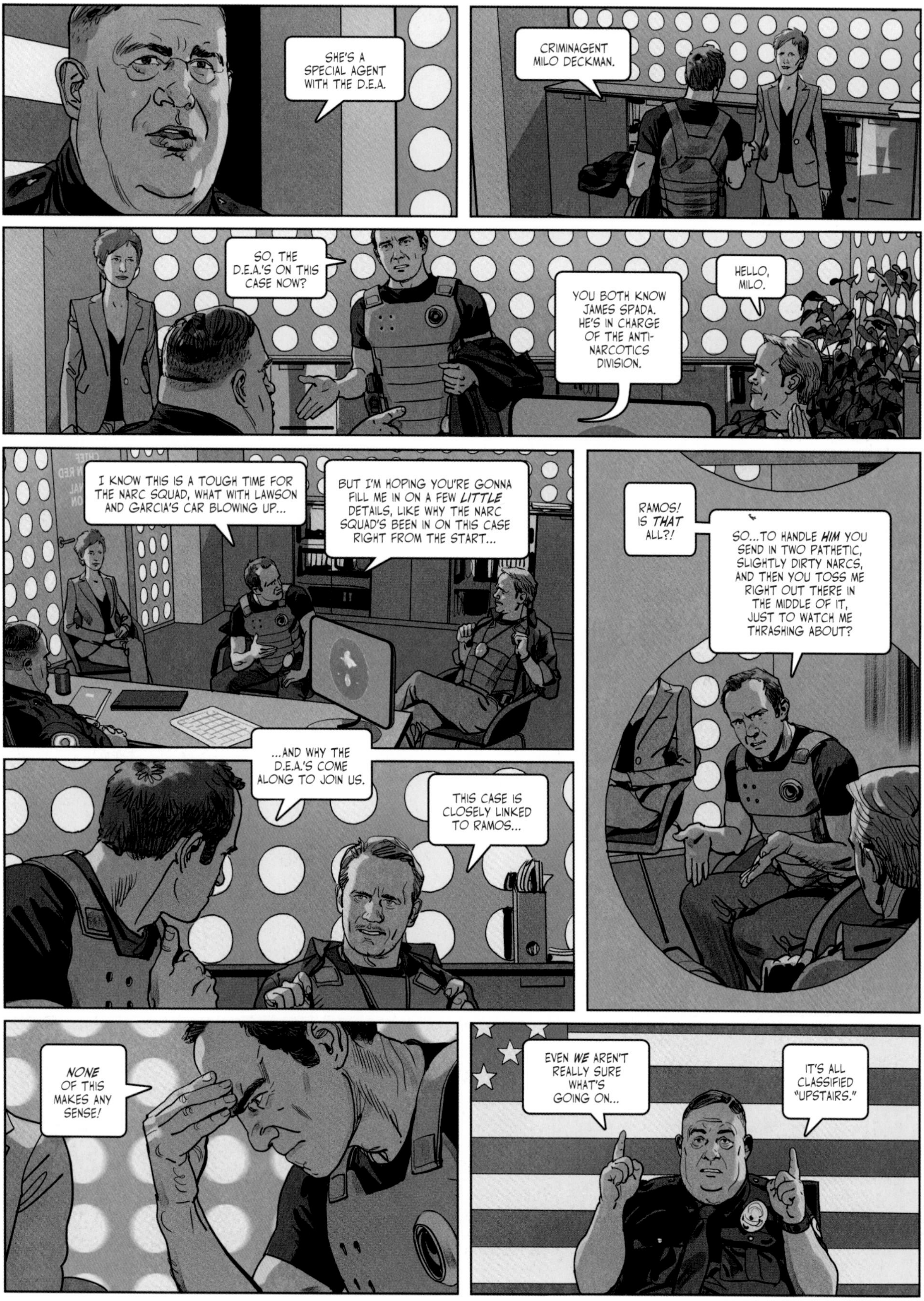
SHE'S A SPECIAL AGENT WITH THE D.E.A.
CRIMINAGENT MILO DECKMAN.
SO, THE D.E.A.'S ON THIS CASE NOW?
YOU BOTH KNOW JAMES SPADA. HE'S IN CHARGE OF THE ANTI-NARCOTICS DIVISION.
HELLO, MILO.
I KNOW THIS IS A TOUGH TIME FOR THE NARC SQUAD, WHAT WITH LAWSON AND GARCIA'S CAR BLOWING UP...
BUT I'M HOPING YOU'RE GONNA FILL ME IN ON A FEW *LITTLE* DETAILS, LIKE WHY THE NARC SQUAD'S BEEN IN ON THIS CASE RIGHT FROM THE START...
...AND WHY THE D.E.A.'S COME ALONG TO JOIN US.
THIS CASE IS CLOSELY LINKED TO RAMOS...
RAMOS! IS *THAT* ALL?!
SO...TO HANDLE *HIM* YOU SEND IN TWO PATHETIC, SLIGHTLY DIRTY NARCS, AND THEN YOU TOSS ME RIGHT OUT THERE IN THE MIDDLE OF IT, JUST TO WATCH ME THRASHING ABOUT?
NONE OF THIS MAKES ANY SENSE!
EVEN *WE* AREN'T REALLY SURE WHAT'S GOING ON...
IT'S ALL CLASSIFIED "UPSTAIRS."

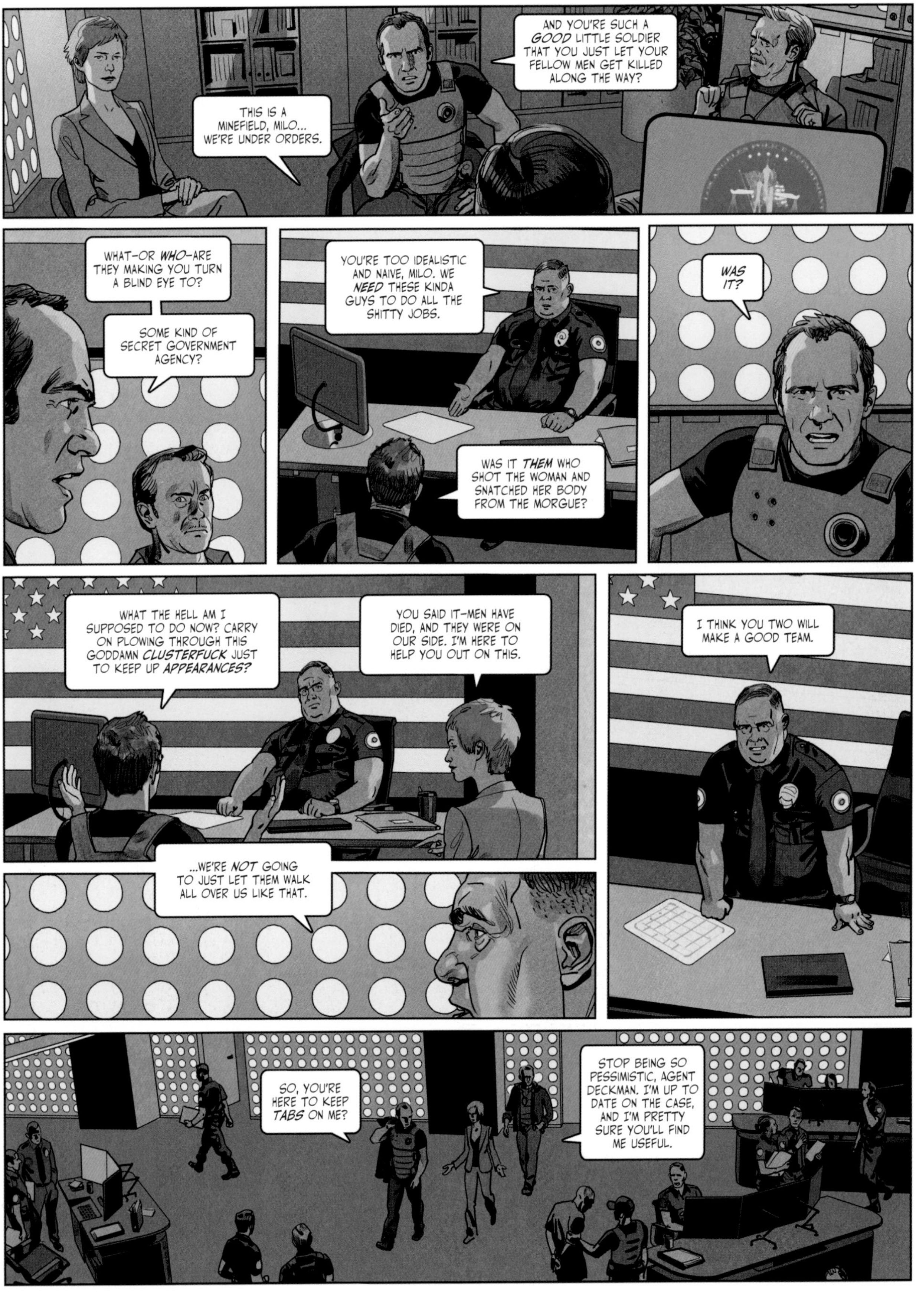

THIS IS A MINEFIELD, MILO... WE'RE UNDER ORDERS.
AND YOU'RE SUCH A GOOD LITTLE SOLDIER THAT YOU JUST LET YOUR FELLOW MEN GET KILLED ALONG THE WAY?
WHAT–OR WHO–ARE THEY MAKING YOU TURN A BLIND EYE TO?
SOME KIND OF SECRET GOVERNMENT AGENCY?
YOU'RE TOO IDEALISTIC AND NAIVE, MILO. WE NEED THESE KINDA GUYS TO DO ALL THE SHITTY JOBS.
WAS IT THEM WHO SHOT THE WOMAN AND SNATCHED HER BODY FROM THE MORGUE?
WAS IT?
WHAT THE HELL AM I SUPPOSED TO DO NOW? CARRY ON PLOWING THROUGH THIS GODDAMN CLUSTERFUCK JUST TO KEEP UP APPEARANCES?
YOU SAID IT–MEN HAVE DIED, AND THEY WERE ON OUR SIDE. I'M HERE TO HELP YOU OUT ON THIS.
...WE'RE NOT GOING TO JUST LET THEM WALK ALL OVER US LIKE THAT.
I THINK YOU TWO WILL MAKE A GOOD TEAM.
SO, YOU'RE HERE TO KEEP TABS ON ME?
STOP BEING SO PESSIMISTIC, AGENT DECKMAN. I'M UP TO DATE ON THE CASE, AND I'M PRETTY SURE YOU'LL FIND ME USEFUL.

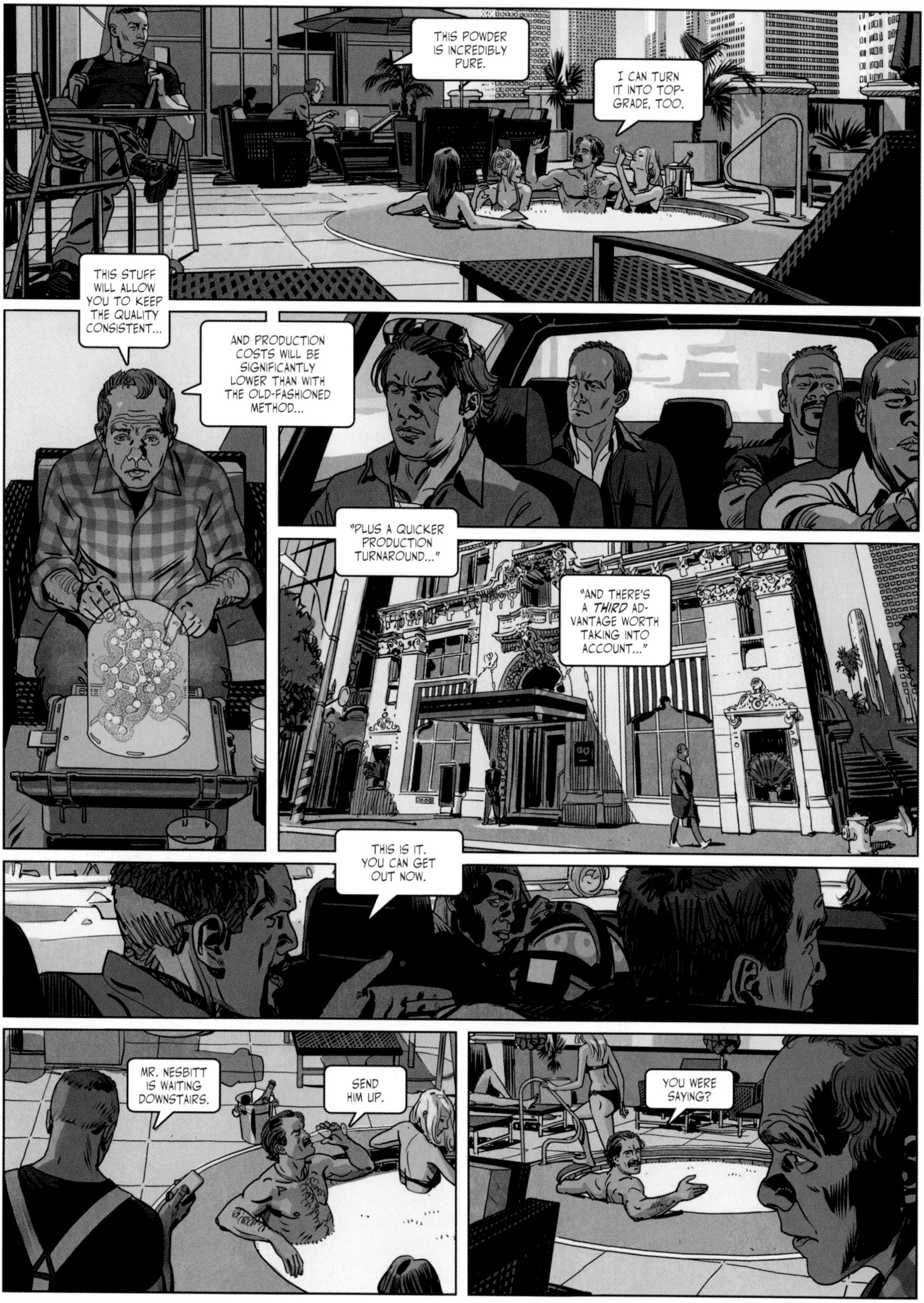
THIS POWDER IS INCREDIBLY PURE.
I CAN TURN IT INTO TOP-GRADE, TOO.
THIS STUFF WILL ALLOW YOU TO KEEP THE QUALITY CONSISTENT...
AND PRODUCTION COSTS WILL BE SIGNIFICANTLY LOWER THAN WITH THE OLD-FASHIONED METHOD...
"PLUS A QUICKER PRODUCTION TURNAROUND..."
"AND THERE'S A *THIRD* ADVANTAGE WORTH TAKING INTO ACCOUNT..."
THIS IS IT. YOU CAN GET OUT NOW.
MR. NESBITT IS WAITING DOWNSTAIRS.
SEND HIM UP.
YOU WERE SAYING?

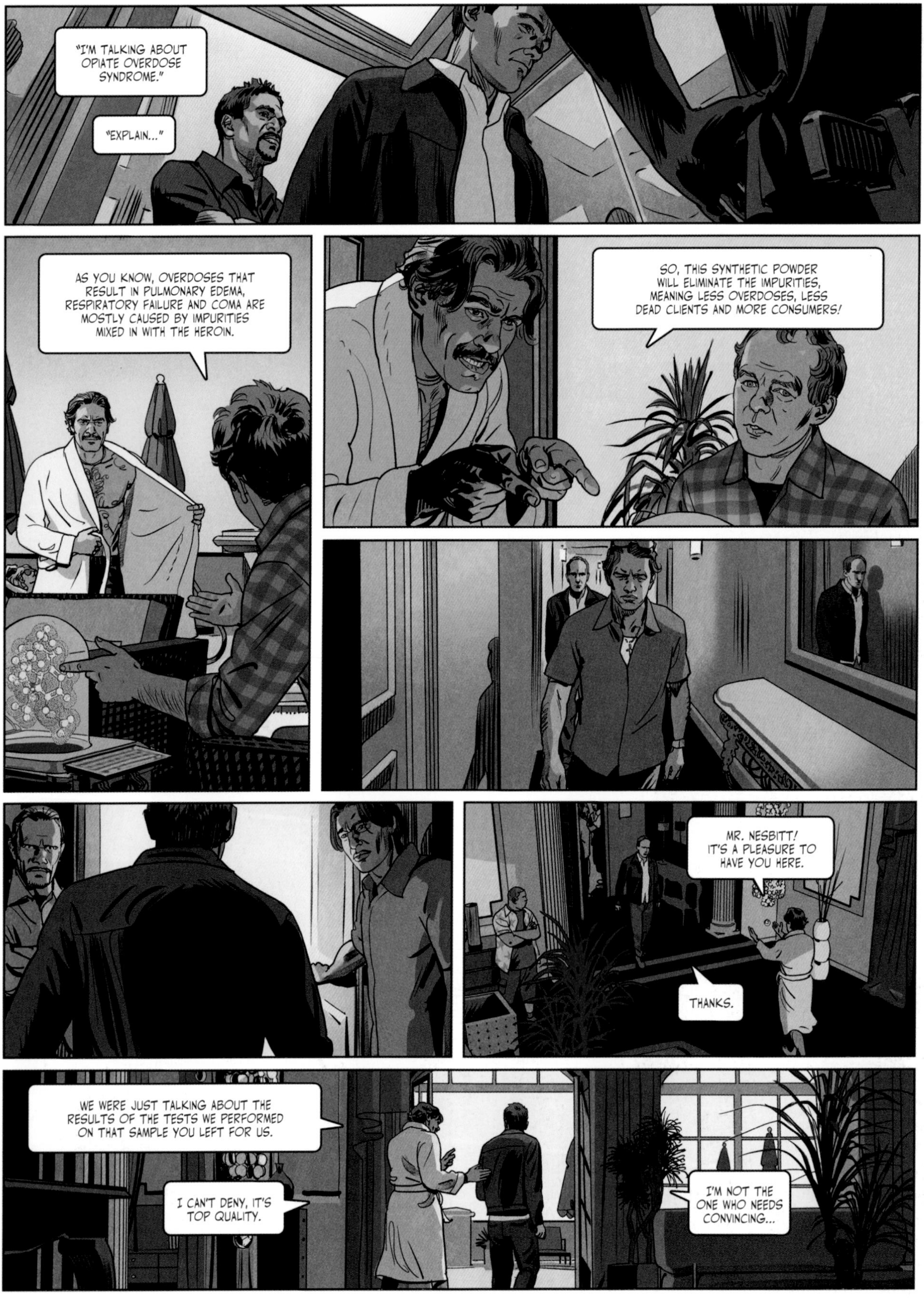
"I'M TALKING ABOUT OPIATE OVERDOSE SYNDROME."
"EXPLAIN..."
AS YOU KNOW, OVERDOSES THAT RESULT IN PULMONARY EDEMA, RESPIRATORY FAILURE AND COMA ARE MOSTLY CAUSED BY IMPURITIES MIXED IN WITH THE HEROIN.
SO, THIS SYNTHETIC POWDER WILL ELIMINATE THE IMPURITIES, MEANING LESS OVERDOSES, LESS DEAD CLIENTS AND MORE CONSUMERS!
MR. NESBITT! IT'S A PLEASURE TO HAVE YOU HERE.
THANKS.
WE WERE JUST TALKING ABOUT THE RESULTS OF THE TESTS WE PERFORMED ON THAT SAMPLE YOU LEFT FOR US.
I CAN'T DENY, IT'S TOP QUALITY.
I'M NOT THE ONE WHO NEEDS CONVINCING...

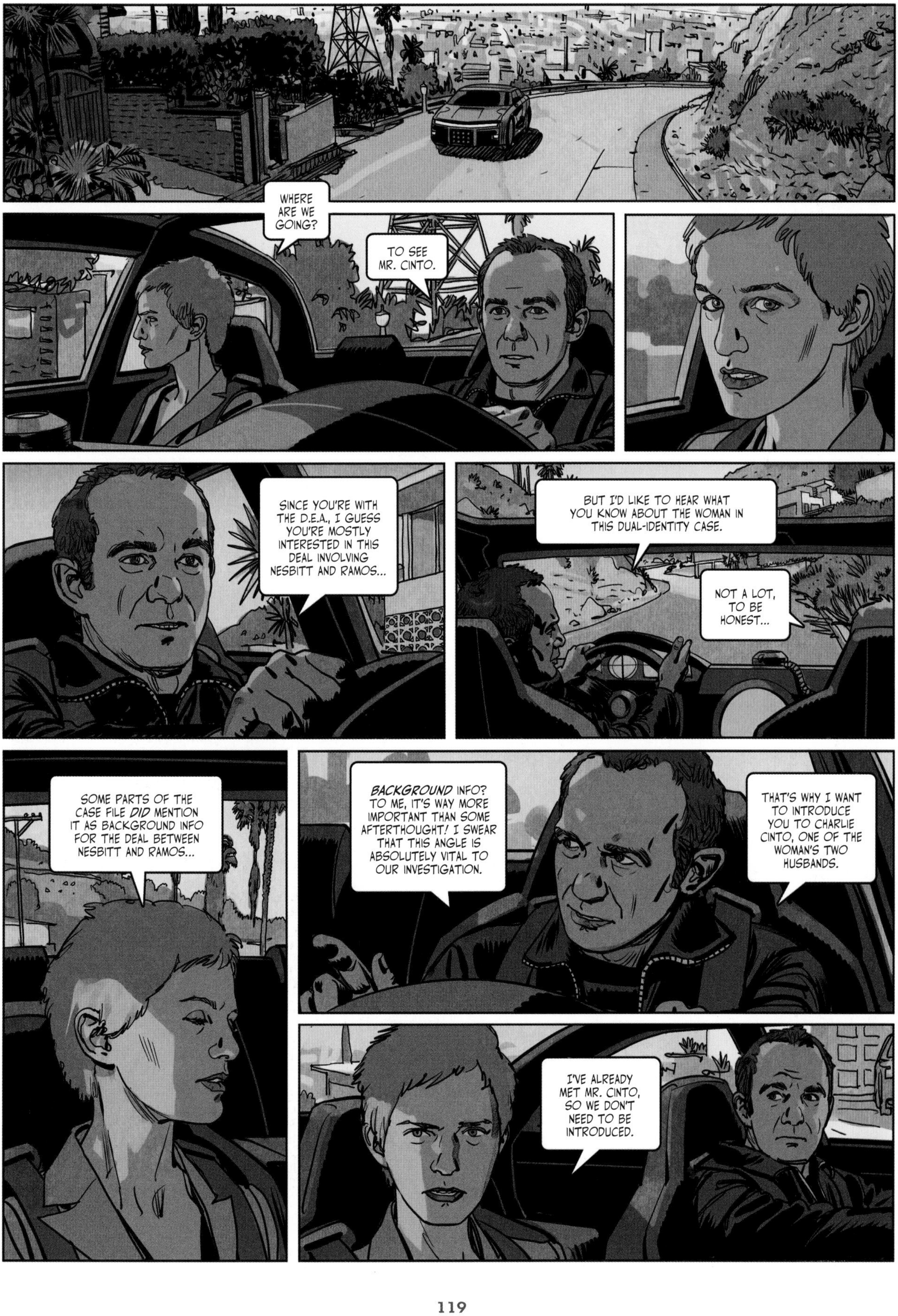
WHERE ARE WE GOING?
TO SEE MR. CINTO.
SINCE YOU'RE WITH THE D.E.A., I GUESS YOU'RE MOSTLY INTERESTED IN THIS DEAL INVOLVING NESBITT AND RAMOS...
BUT I'D LIKE TO HEAR WHAT YOU KNOW ABOUT THE WOMAN IN THIS DUAL-IDENTITY CASE.
NOT A LOT, TO BE HONEST...
SOME PARTS OF THE CASE FILE *DID* MENTION IT AS BACKGROUND INFO FOR THE DEAL BETWEEN NESBITT AND RAMOS...
BACKGROUND INFO? TO ME, IT'S WAY MORE IMPORTANT THAN SOME AFTERTHOUGHT! I SWEAR THAT THIS ANGLE IS ABSOLUTELY VITAL TO OUR INVESTIGATION.
THAT'S WHY I WANT TO INTRODUCE YOU TO CHARLIE CINTO, ONE OF THE WOMAN'S TWO HUSBANDS.
I'VE ALREADY MET MR. CINTO, SO WE DON'T NEED TO BE INTRODUCED.

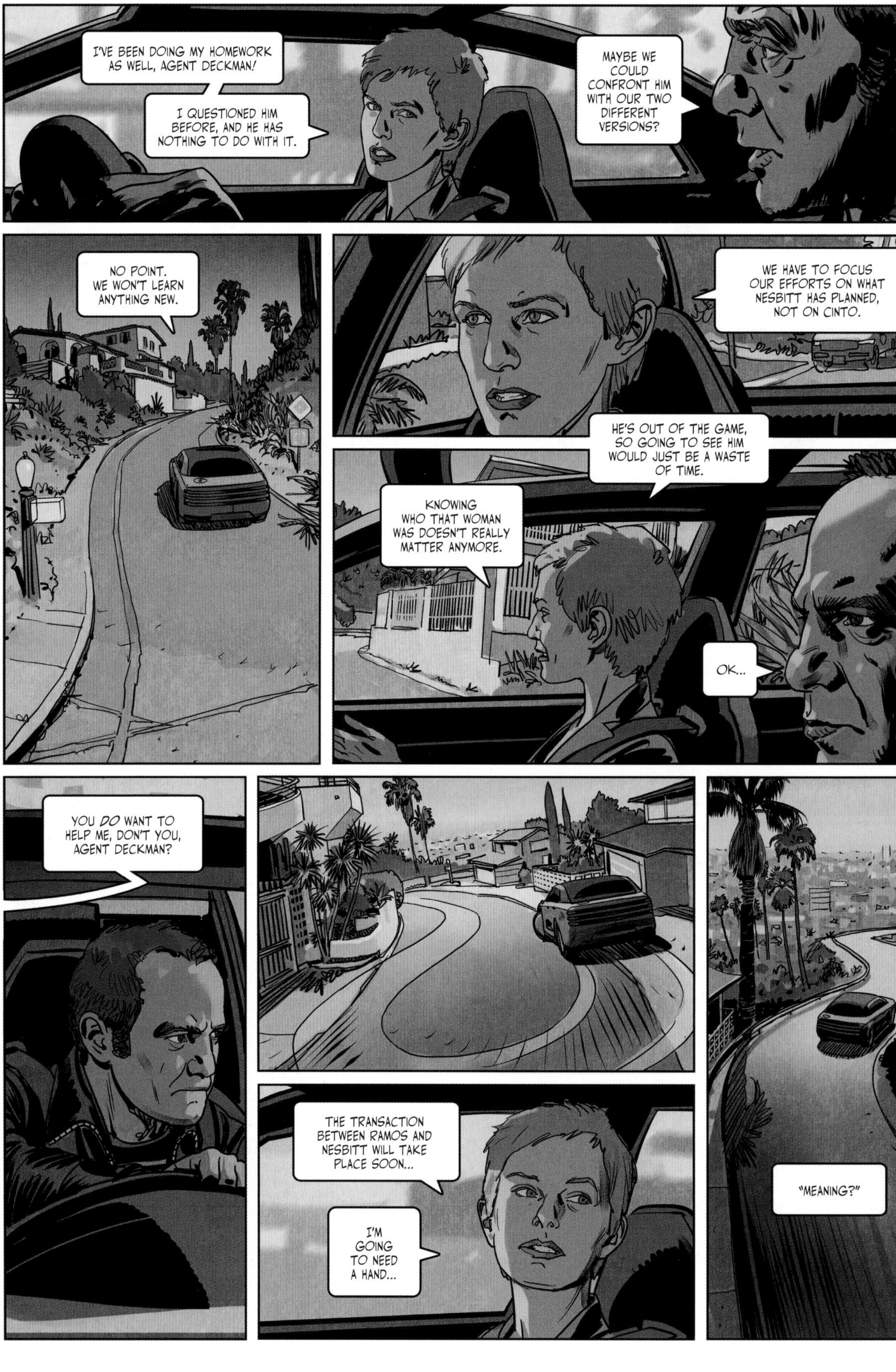
I'VE BEEN DOING MY HOMEWORK AS WELL, AGENT DECKMAN!
I QUESTIONED HIM BEFORE, AND HE HAS NOTHING TO DO WITH IT.
MAYBE WE COULD CONFRONT HIM WITH OUR TWO DIFFERENT VERSIONS?
NO POINT. WE WON'T LEARN ANYTHING NEW.
WE HAVE TO FOCUS OUR EFFORTS ON WHAT NESBITT HAS PLANNED, NOT ON CINTO.
HE'S OUT OF THE GAME, SO GOING TO SEE HIM WOULD JUST BE A WASTE OF TIME.
KNOWING WHO THAT WOMAN WAS DOESN'T REALLY MATTER ANYMORE.
OK...
YOU *DO* WANT TO HELP ME, DON'T YOU, AGENT DECKMAN?
THE TRANSACTION BETWEEN RAMOS AND NESBITT WILL TAKE PLACE SOON...
I'M GOING TO NEED A HAND...
"MEANING?"

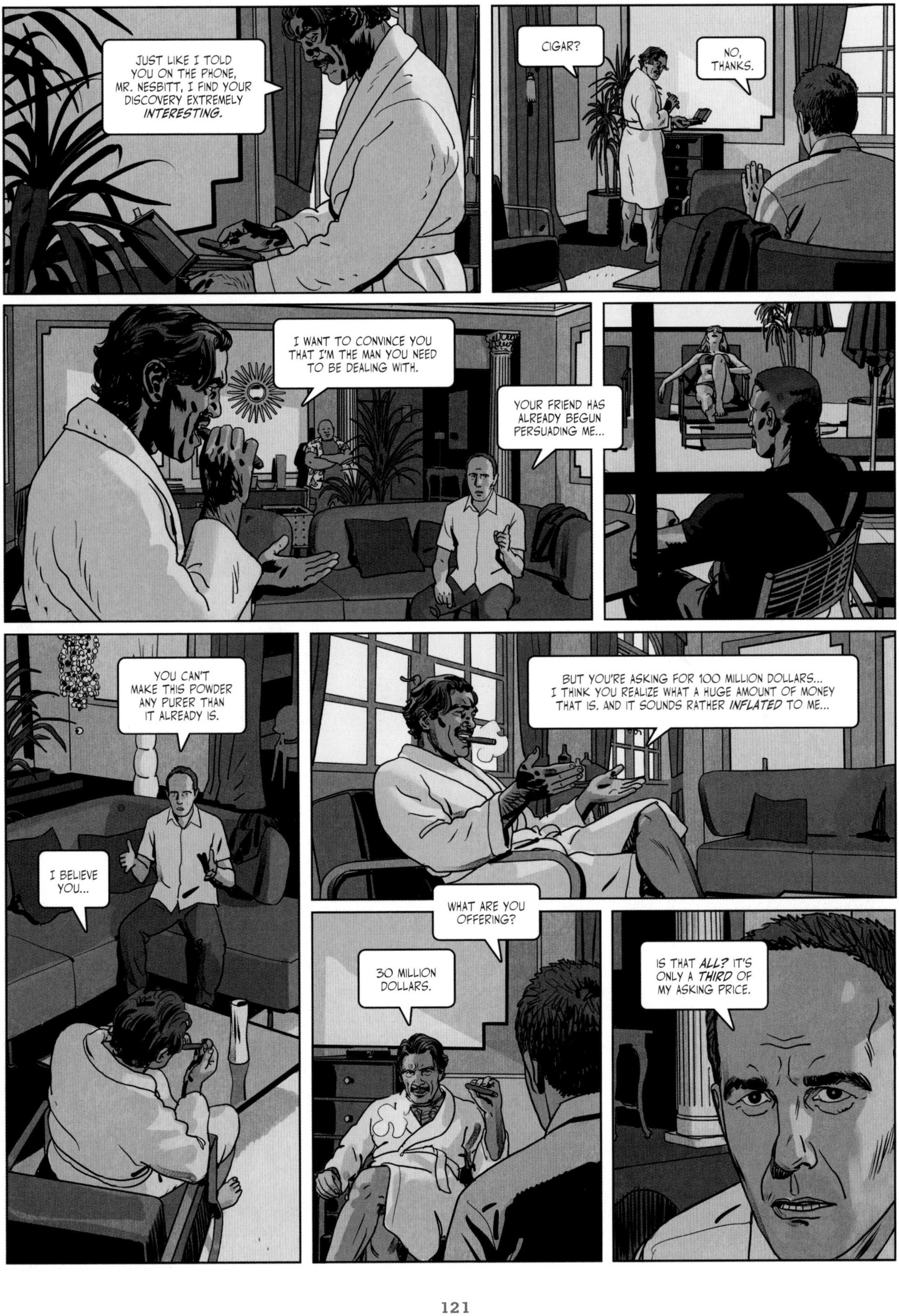
JUST LIKE I TOLD YOU ON THE PHONE, MR. NESBITT, I FIND YOUR DISCOVERY EXTREMELY *INTERESTING.*
CIGAR?
NO, THANKS.
I WANT TO CONVINCE YOU THAT I'M THE MAN YOU NEED TO BE DEALING WITH.
YOUR FRIEND HAS ALREADY BEGUN PERSUADING ME...
YOU CAN'T MAKE THIS POWDER ANY PURER THAN IT ALREADY IS.
I BELIEVE YOU...
BUT YOU'RE ASKING FOR 100 MILLION DOLLARS... I THINK YOU REALIZE WHAT A HUGE AMOUNT OF MONEY THAT IS. AND IT SOUNDS RATHER *INFLATED* TO ME...
WHAT ARE YOU OFFERING?
30 MILLION DOLLARS.
IS THAT *ALL?* IT'S ONLY A *THIRD* OF MY ASKING PRICE.

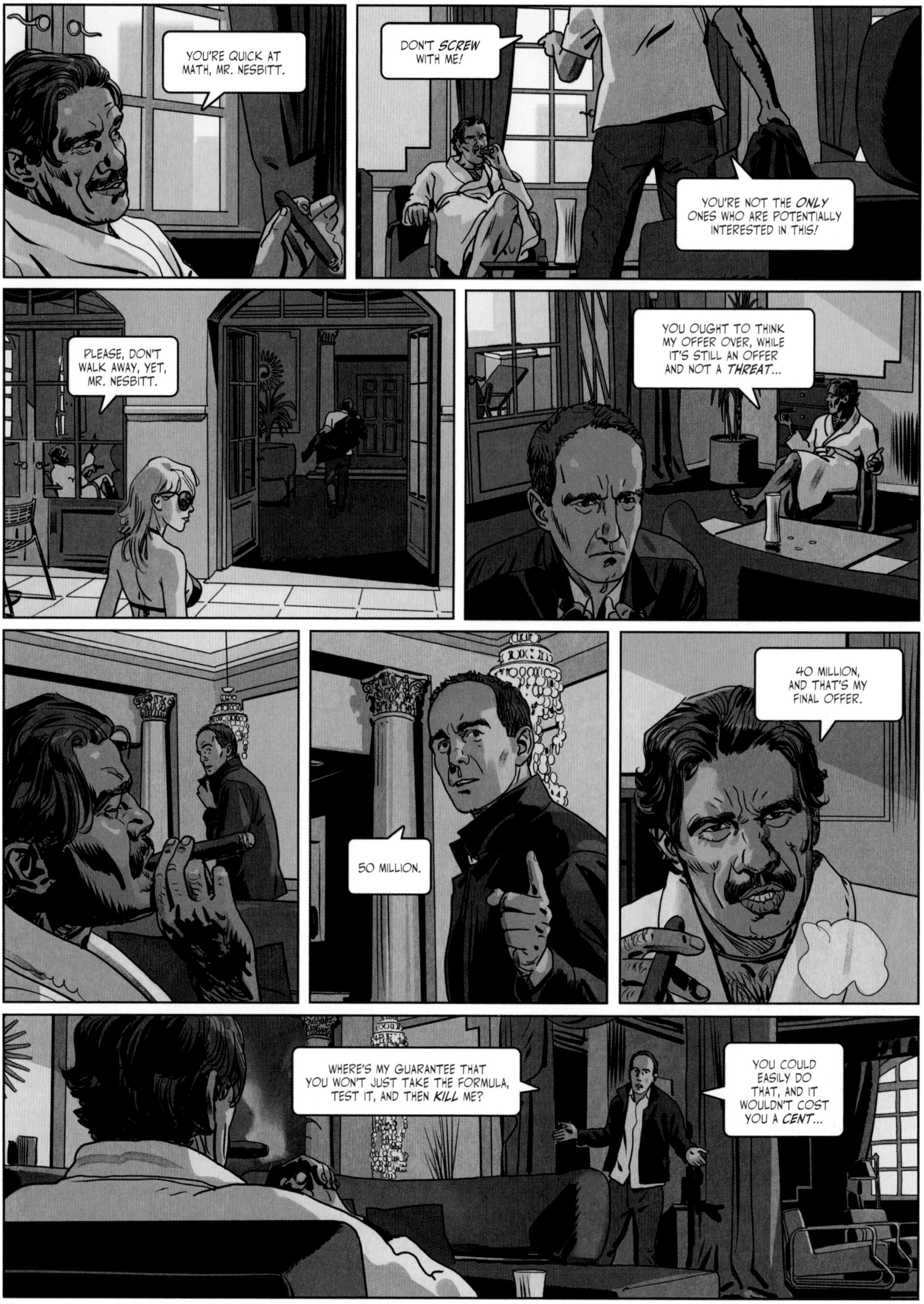

YOU'RE QUICK AT MATH, MR. NESBITT.
DON'T SCREW WITH ME!
YOU'RE NOT THE ONLY ONES WHO ARE POTENTIALLY INTERESTED IN THIS!
PLEASE, DON'T WALK AWAY, YET, MR. NESBITT.
YOU OUGHT TO THINK MY OFFER OVER, WHILE IT'S STILL AN OFFER AND NOT A THREAT...
50 MILLION.
40 MILLION, AND THAT'S MY FINAL OFFER.
WHERE'S MY GUARANTEE THAT YOU WON'T JUST TAKE THE FORMULA, TEST IT, AND THEN KILL ME?
YOU COULD EASILY DO THAT, AND IT WOULDN'T COST YOU A CENT...

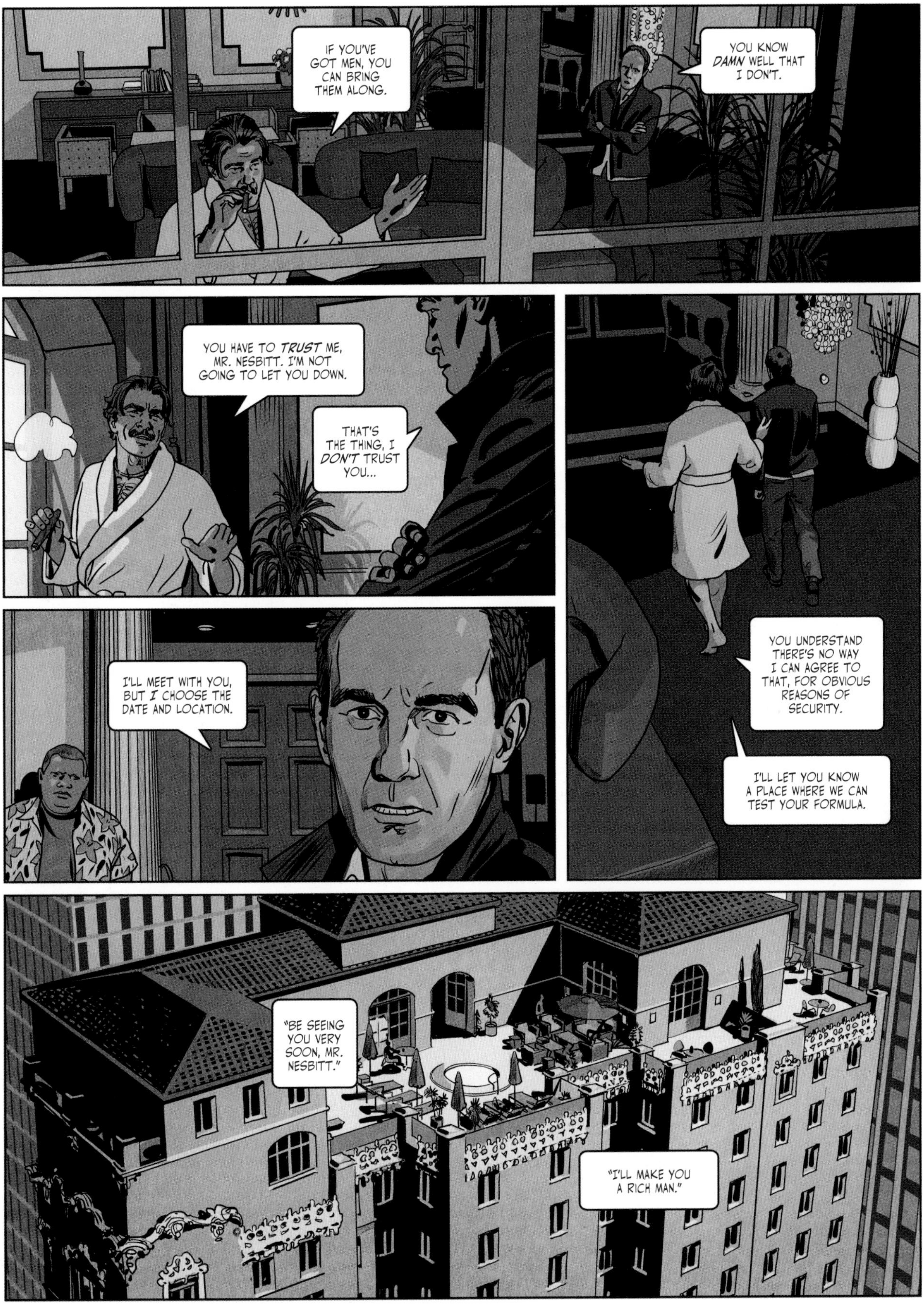
IF YOU'VE GOT MEN, YOU CAN BRING THEM ALONG.
YOU KNOW DAMN WELL THAT I DON'T.
YOU HAVE TO TRUST ME, MR. NESBITT. I'M NOT GOING TO LET YOU DOWN.
THAT'S THE THING, I DON'T TRUST YOU...
I'LL MEET WITH YOU, BUT I CHOOSE THE DATE AND LOCATION.
YOU UNDERSTAND THERE'S NO WAY I CAN AGREE TO THAT, FOR OBVIOUS REASONS OF SECURITY.
I'LL LET YOU KNOW A PLACE WHERE WE CAN TEST YOUR FORMULA.
"BE SEEING YOU VERY SOON, MR. NESBITT."
"I'LL MAKE YOU A RICH MAN."

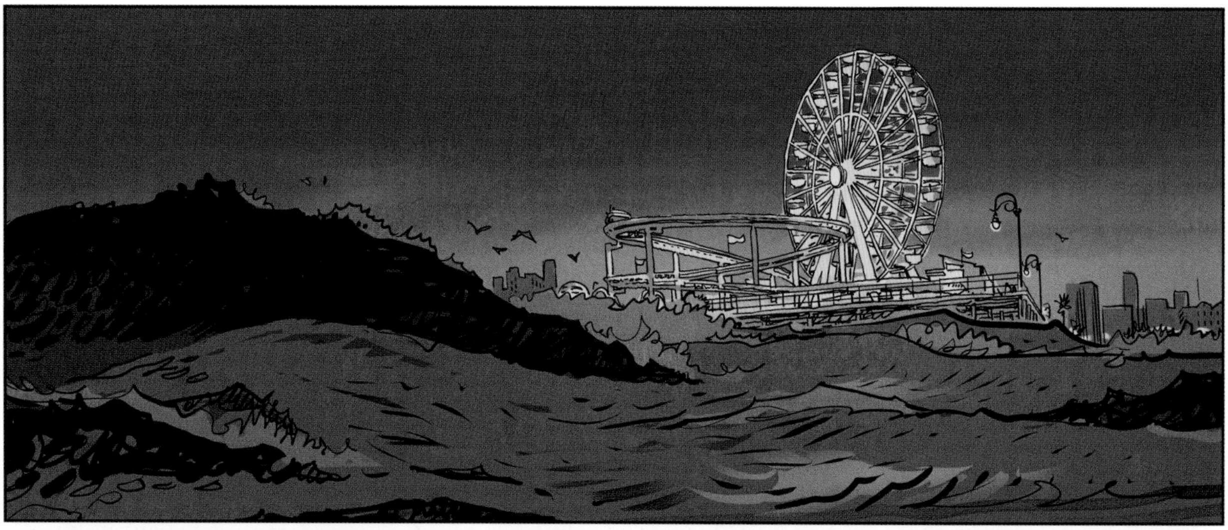

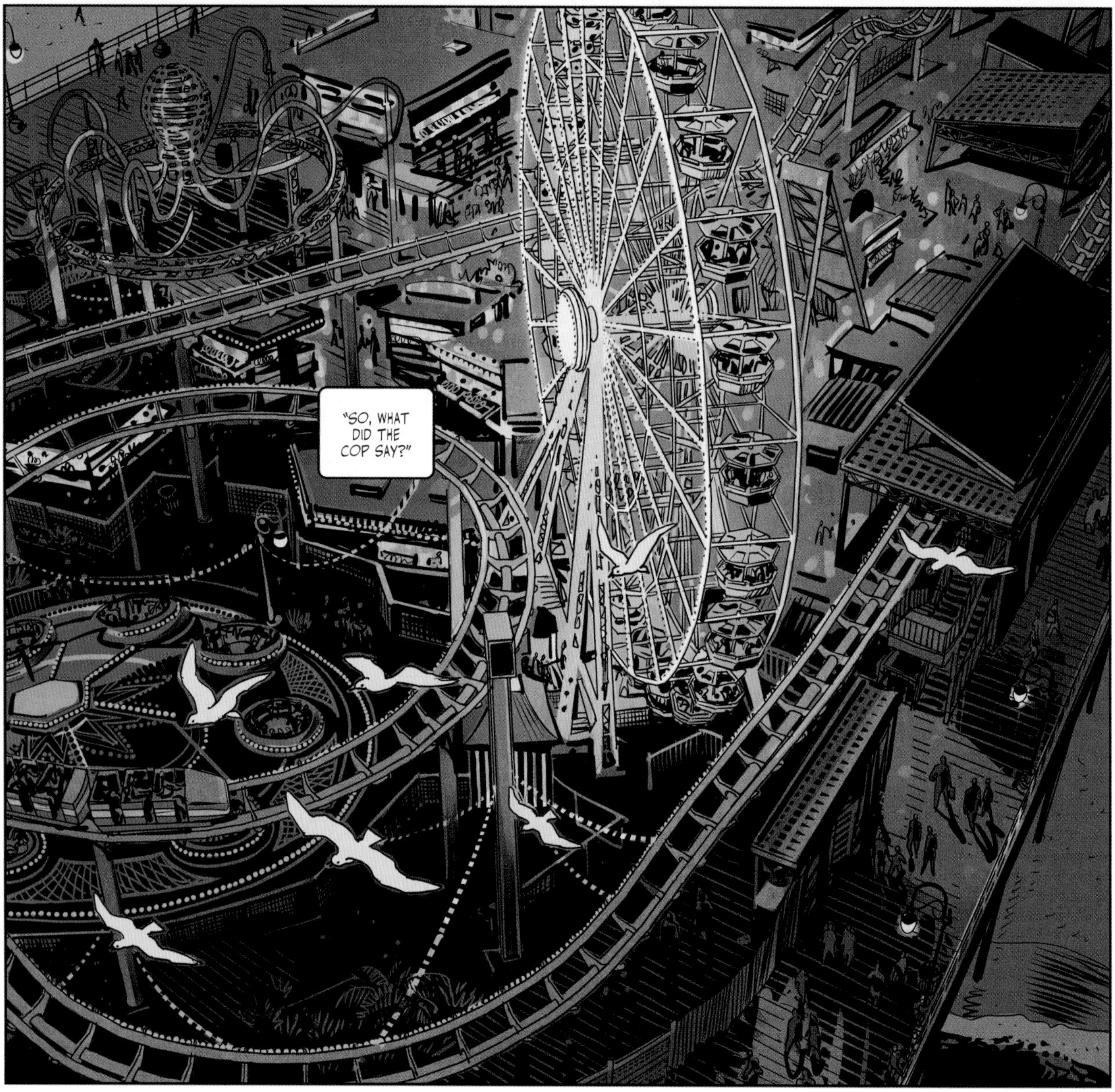
"SO, WHAT DID THE COP SAY?"

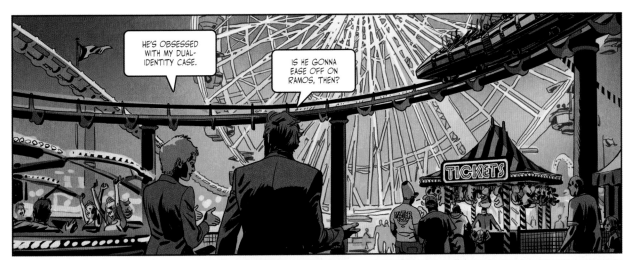

HE'S OBSESSED WITH MY DUAL-IDENTITY CASE.

IS HE GONNA EASE OFF ON RAMOS, THEN?

PROBABLY, BUT IT WON'T BE DIFFICULT FOR HIM TO PIECE IT ALL TOGETHER FROM THERE.

IT WON'T BE MUCH LONGER NOW.

NESBITT MET WITH RAMOS. THE DEAL'S GOING DOWN TOMORROW.

THE CHIEF AGREED TO LET US TAKE A BREAK AFTER THIS.

IT'S ABOUT TIME...

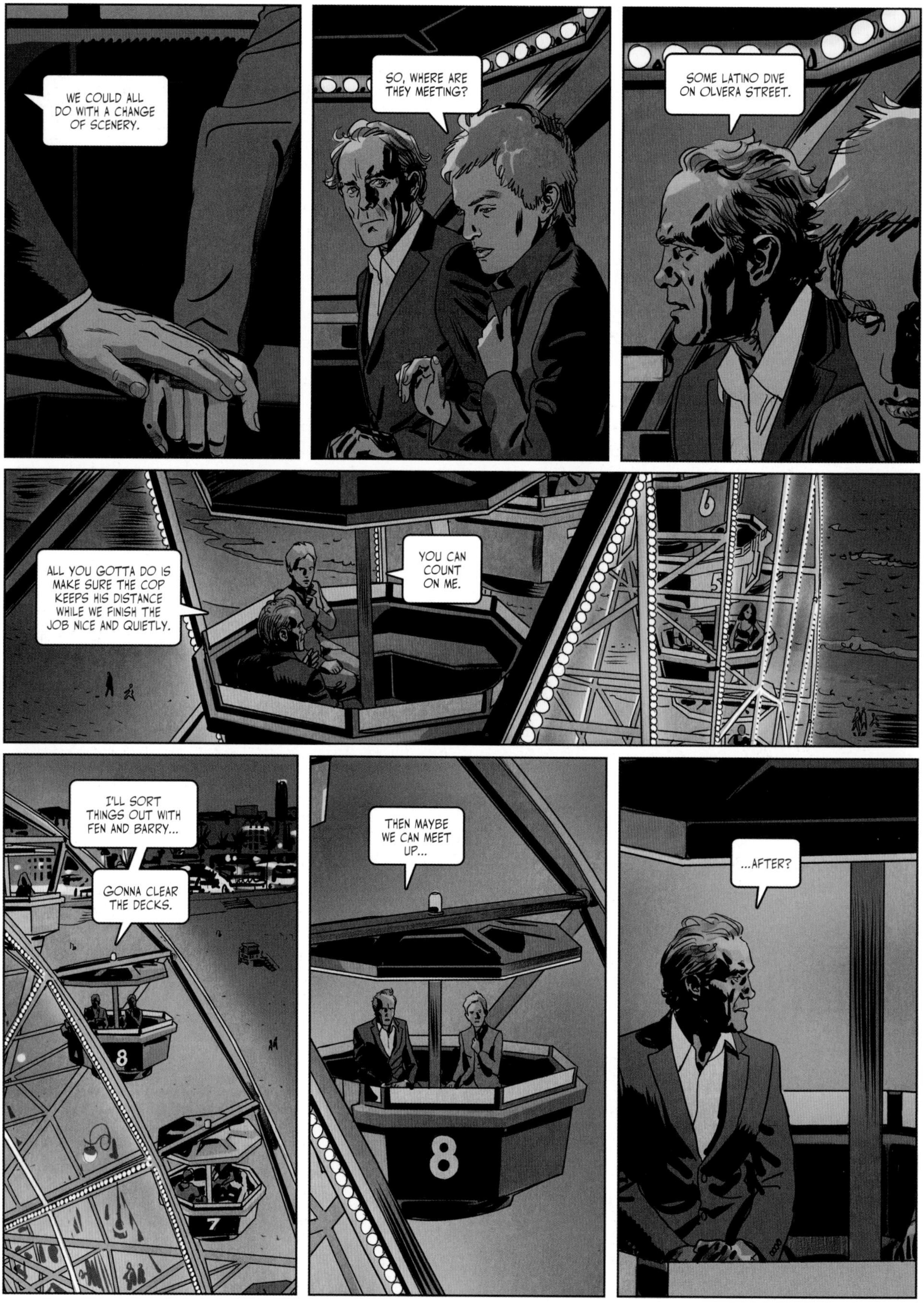
WE COULD ALL DO WITH A CHANGE OF SCENERY.
SO, WHERE ARE THEY MEETING?
SOME LATINO DIVE ON OLVERA STREET.
ALL YOU GOTTA DO IS MAKE SURE THE COP KEEPS HIS DISTANCE WHILE WE FINISH THE JOB NICE AND QUIETLY.
YOU CAN COUNT ON ME.
6
5
I'LL SORT THINGS OUT WITH FEN AND BARRY...
GONNA CLEAR THE DECKS.
8
7
THEN MAYBE WE CAN MEET UP...
8
...AFTER?

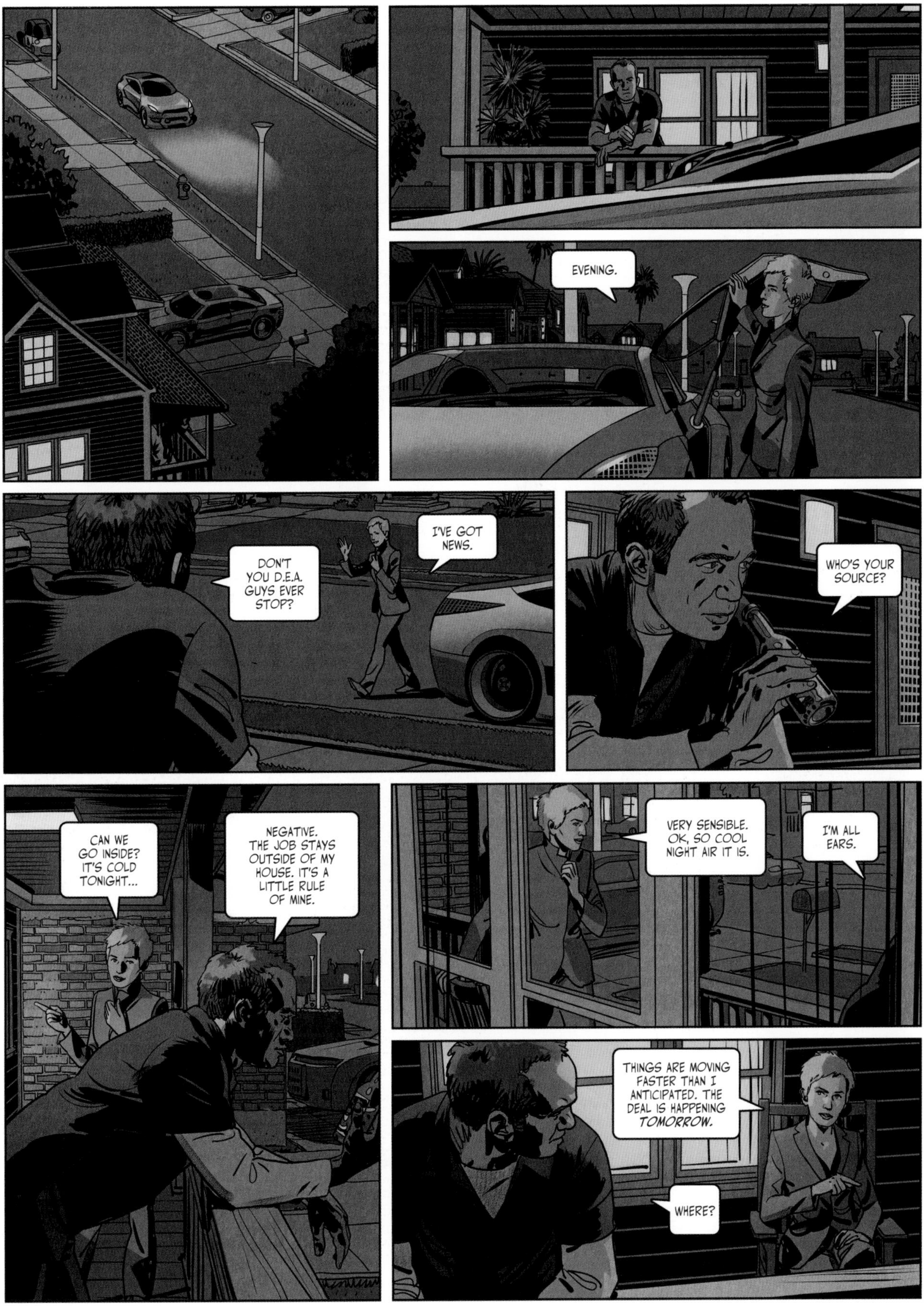
EVENING.
DON'T YOU D.E.A. GUYS EVER STOP?
I'VE GOT NEWS.
WHO'S YOUR SOURCE?
CAN WE GO INSIDE? IT'S COLD TONIGHT...
NEGATIVE. THE JOB STAYS OUTSIDE OF MY HOUSE. IT'S A LITTLE RULE OF MINE.
VERY SENSIBLE. OK, SO COOL NIGHT AIR IT IS.
I'M ALL EARS.
THINGS ARE MOVING FASTER THAN I ANTICIPATED. THE DEAL IS HAPPENING *TOMORROW.*
WHERE?

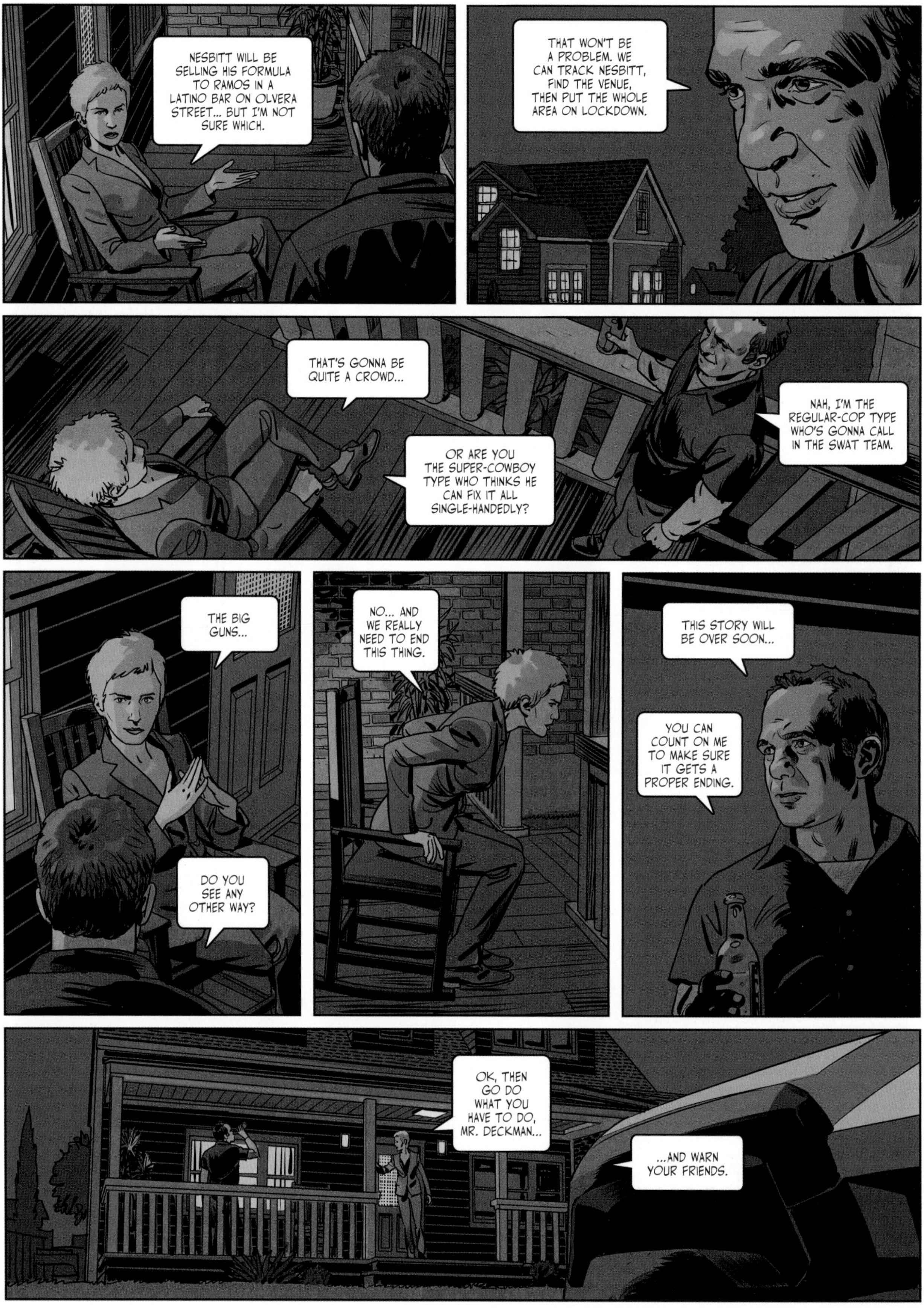
NESBITT WILL BE SELLING HIS FORMULA TO RAMOS IN A LATINO BAR ON OLVERA STREET... BUT I'M NOT SURE WHICH.
THAT WON'T BE A PROBLEM. WE CAN TRACK NESBITT, FIND THE VENUE, THEN PUT THE WHOLE AREA ON LOCKDOWN.
THAT'S GONNA BE QUITE A CROWD...
OR ARE YOU THE SUPER-COWBOY TYPE WHO THINKS HE CAN FIX IT ALL SINGLE-HANDEDLY?
NAH, I'M THE REGULAR-COP TYPE WHO'S GONNA CALL IN THE SWAT TEAM.
THE BIG GUNS...
DO YOU SEE ANY OTHER WAY?
NO... AND WE REALLY NEED TO END THIS THING.
THIS STORY WILL BE OVER SOON...
YOU CAN COUNT ON ME TO MAKE SURE IT GETS A PROPER ENDING.
OK, THEN GO DO WHAT YOU HAVE TO DO, MR. DECKMAN...
...AND WARN YOUR FRIENDS.

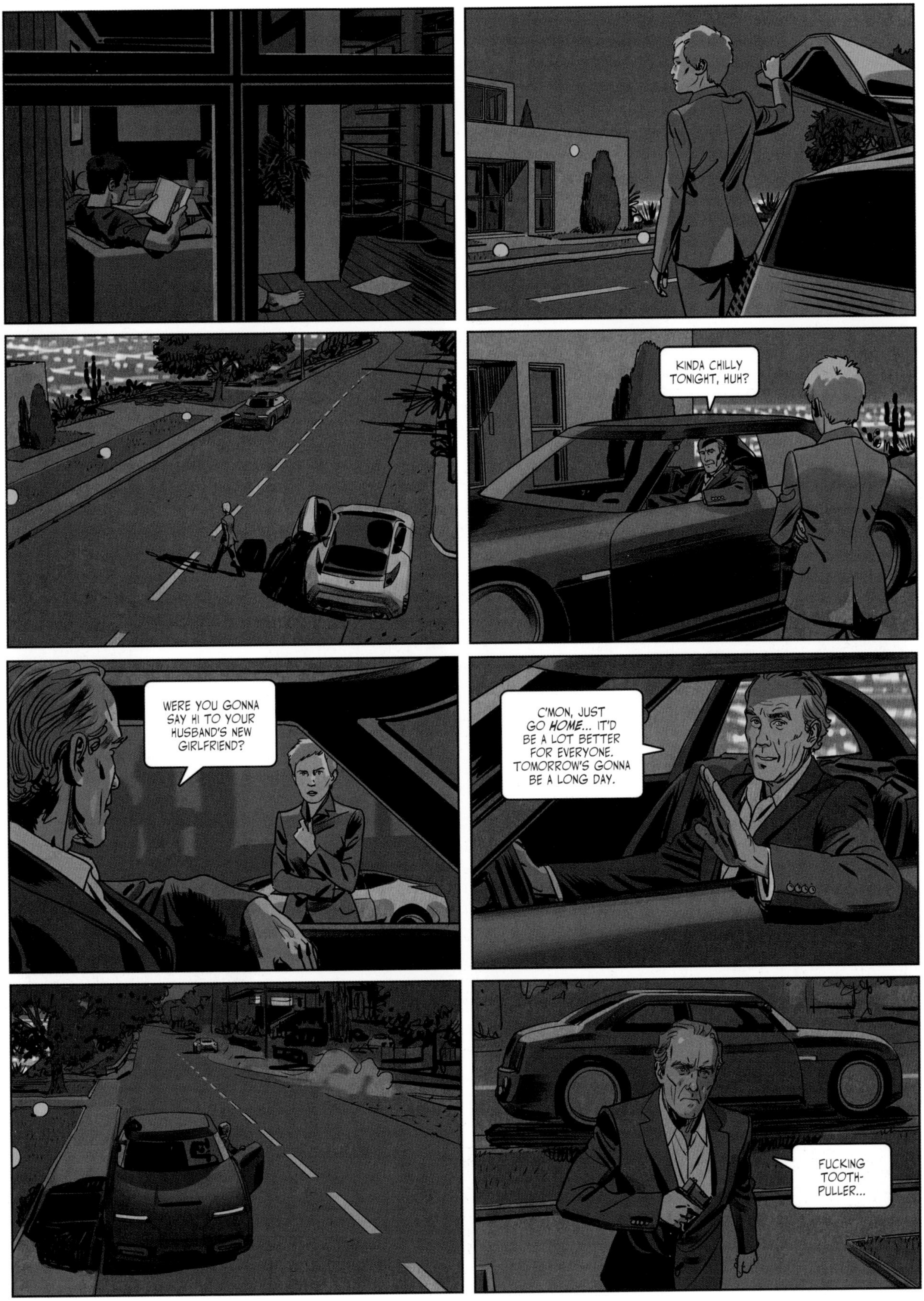
KINDA CHILLY TONIGHT, HUH?
WERE YOU GONNA SAY HI TO YOUR HUSBAND'S NEW GIRLFRIEND?
C'MON, JUST GO *HOME*... IT'D BE A LOT BETTER FOR EVERYONE. TOMORROW'S GONNA BE A LONG DAY.
FUCKING TOOTH-PULLER...

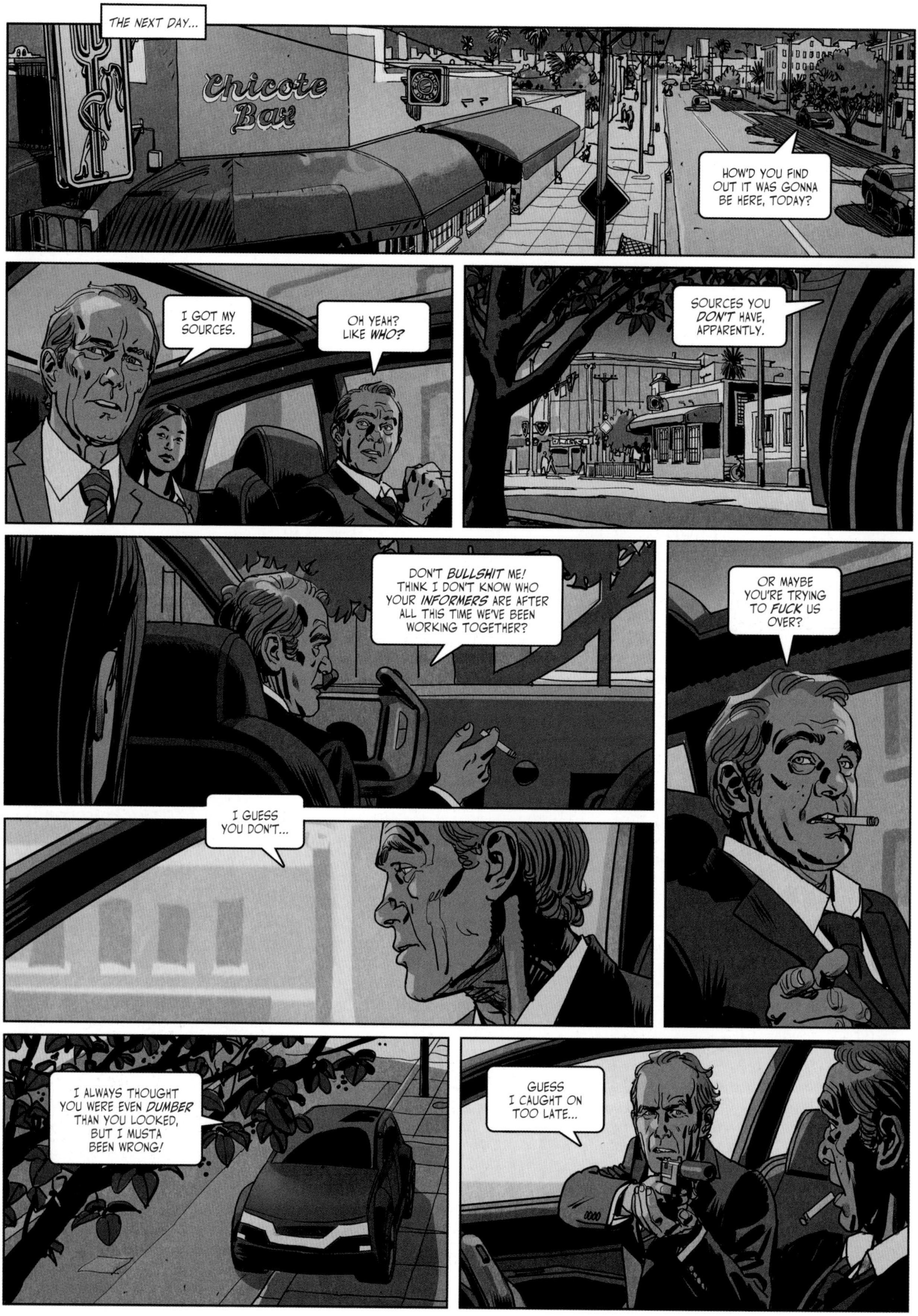
THE NEXT DAY...
Chicote Bar
HOW'D YOU FIND OUT IT WAS GONNA BE HERE, TODAY?
I GOT MY SOURCES.
OH YEAH? LIKE *WHO?*
SOURCES YOU *DON'T* HAVE, APPARENTLY.
DON'T *BULLSHIT* ME! THINK I DON'T KNOW WHO YOUR *INFORMERS* ARE AFTER ALL THIS TIME WE'VE BEEN WORKING TOGETHER?
OR MAYBE YOU'RE TRYING TO *FUCK* US OVER?
I GUESS YOU DON'T...
I ALWAYS THOUGHT YOU WERE EVEN *DUMBER* THAN YOU LOOKED, BUT I MUSTA BEEN WRONG!
GUESS I CAUGHT ON TOO LATE...

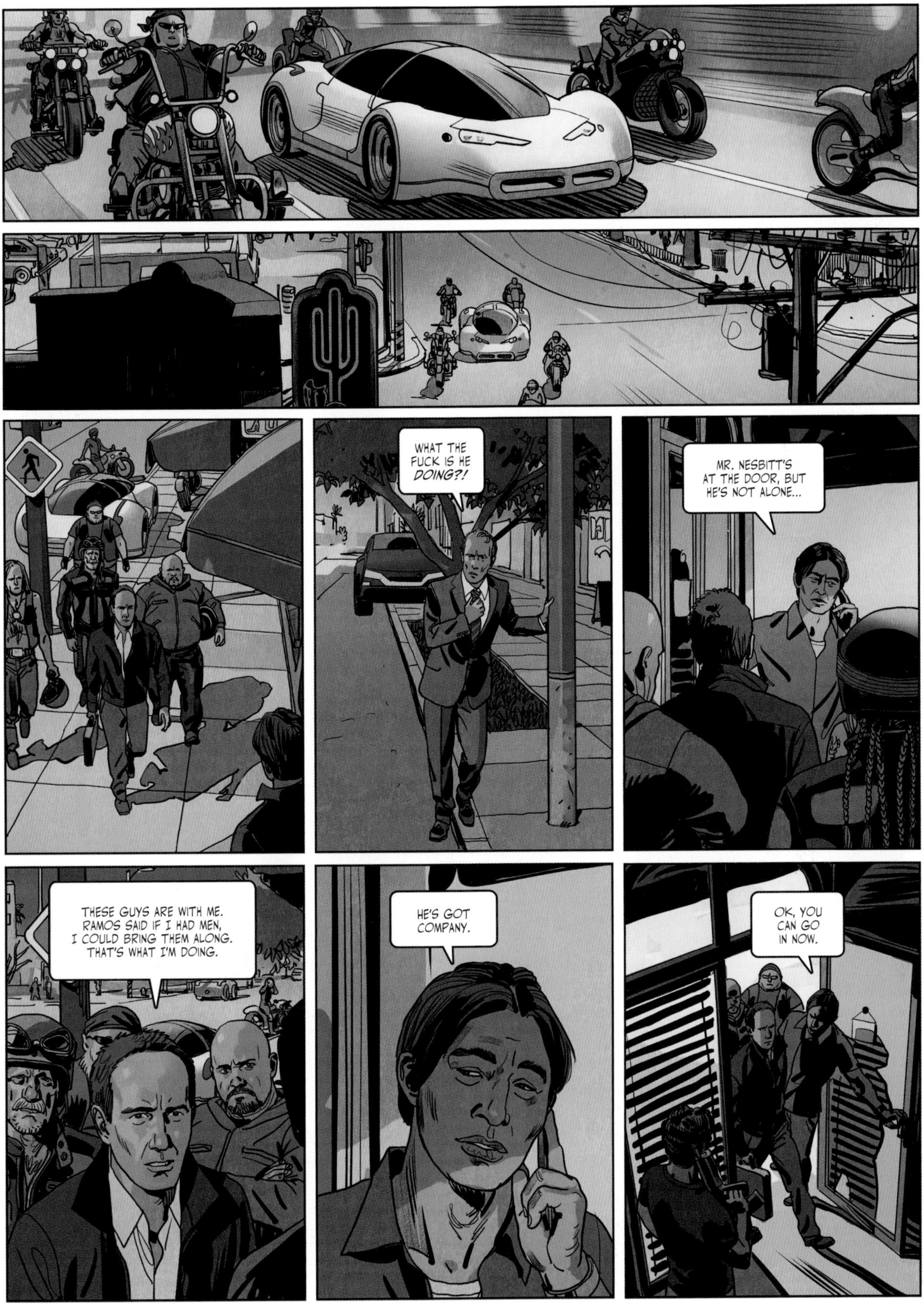
WHAT THE FUCK IS HE DOING?!
MR. NESBITT'S AT THE DOOR, BUT HE'S NOT ALONE...
THESE GUYS ARE WITH ME. RAMOS SAID IF I HAD MEN, I COULD BRING THEM ALONG. THAT'S WHAT I'M DOING.
HE'S GOT COMPANY.
OK, YOU CAN GO IN NOW.

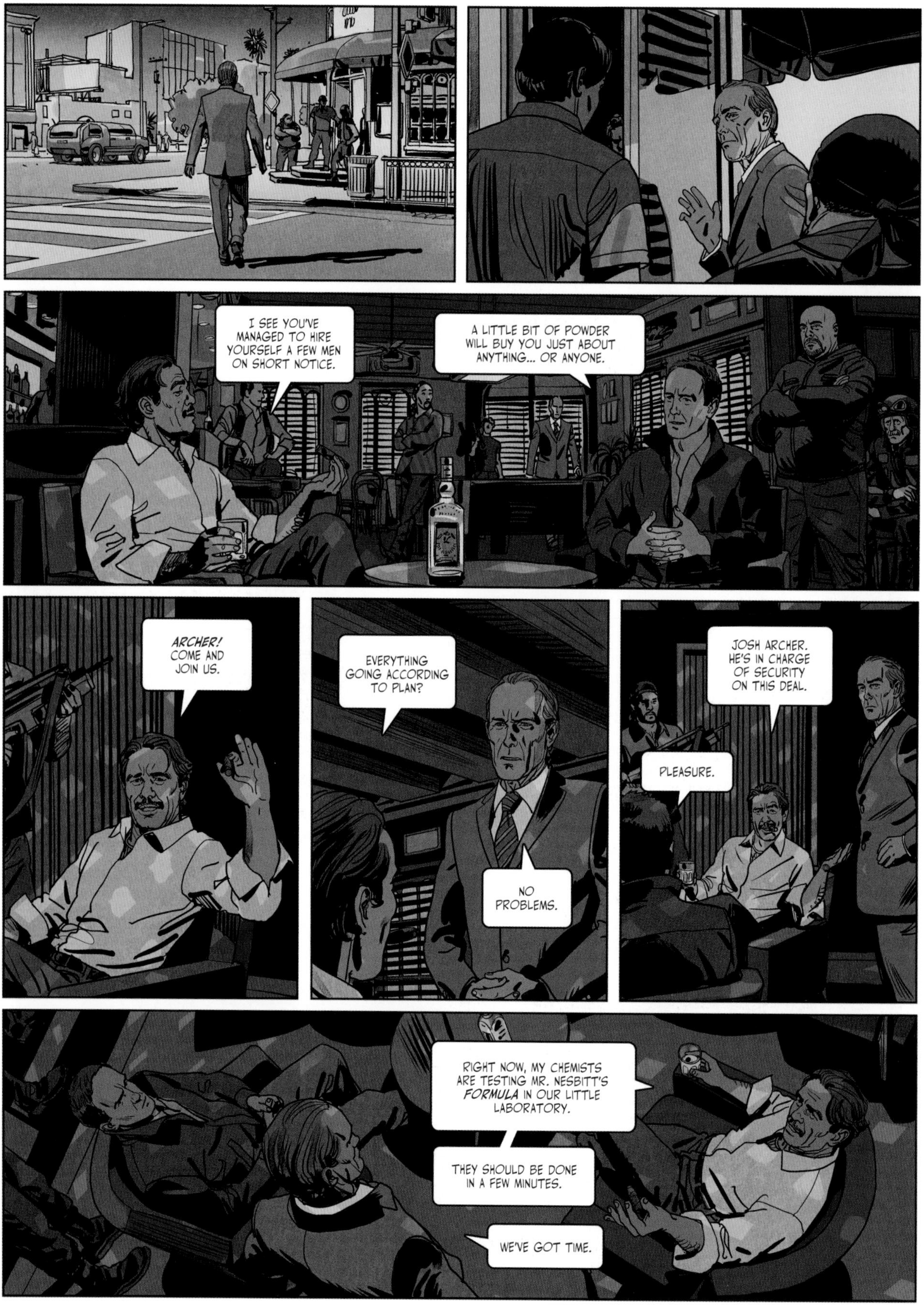
I SEE YOU'VE MANAGED TO HIRE YOURSELF A FEW MEN ON SHORT NOTICE.
A LITTLE BIT OF POWDER WILL BUY YOU JUST ABOUT ANYTHING... OR ANYONE.
ARCHER! COME AND JOIN US.
EVERYTHING GOING ACCORDING TO PLAN?
NO PROBLEMS.
JOSH ARCHER. HE'S IN CHARGE OF SECURITY ON THIS DEAL.
PLEASURE.
RIGHT NOW, MY CHEMISTS ARE TESTING MR. NESBITT'S *FORMULA* IN OUR LITTLE LABORATORY.
THEY SHOULD BE DONE IN A FEW MINUTES.
WE'VE GOT TIME.

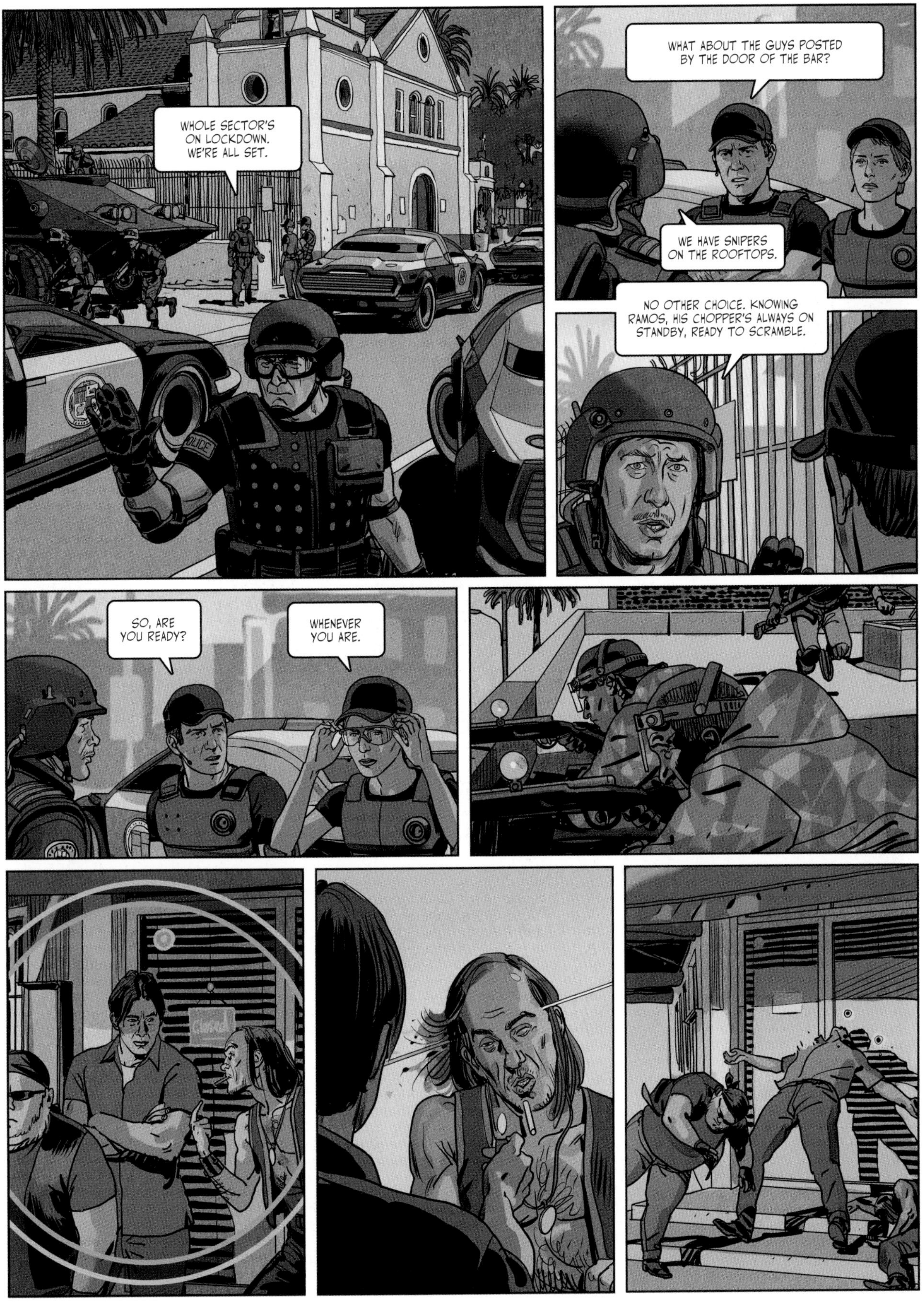
WHOLE SECTOR'S ON LOCKDOWN. WE'RE ALL SET.
WHAT ABOUT THE GUYS POSTED BY THE DOOR OF THE BAR?
WE HAVE SNIPERS ON THE ROOFTOPS.
NO OTHER CHOICE. KNOWING RAMOS, HIS CHOPPER'S ALWAYS ON STANDBY, READY TO SCRAMBLE.
SO, ARE YOU READY?
WHENEVER YOU ARE.
POLICE
Closed

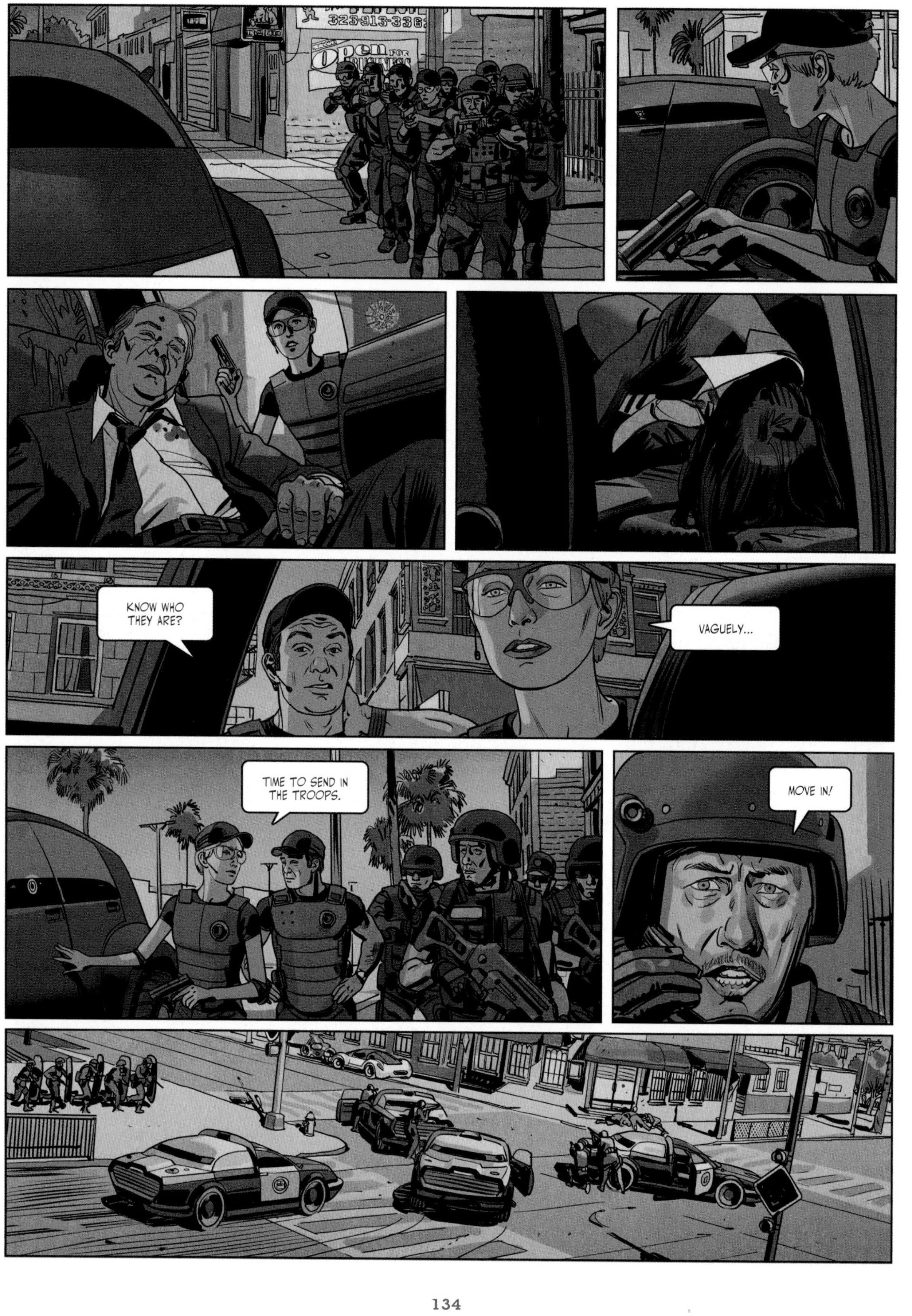
KNOW WHO THEY ARE?
VAGUELY...
TIME TO SEND IN THE TROOPS.
MOVE IN!

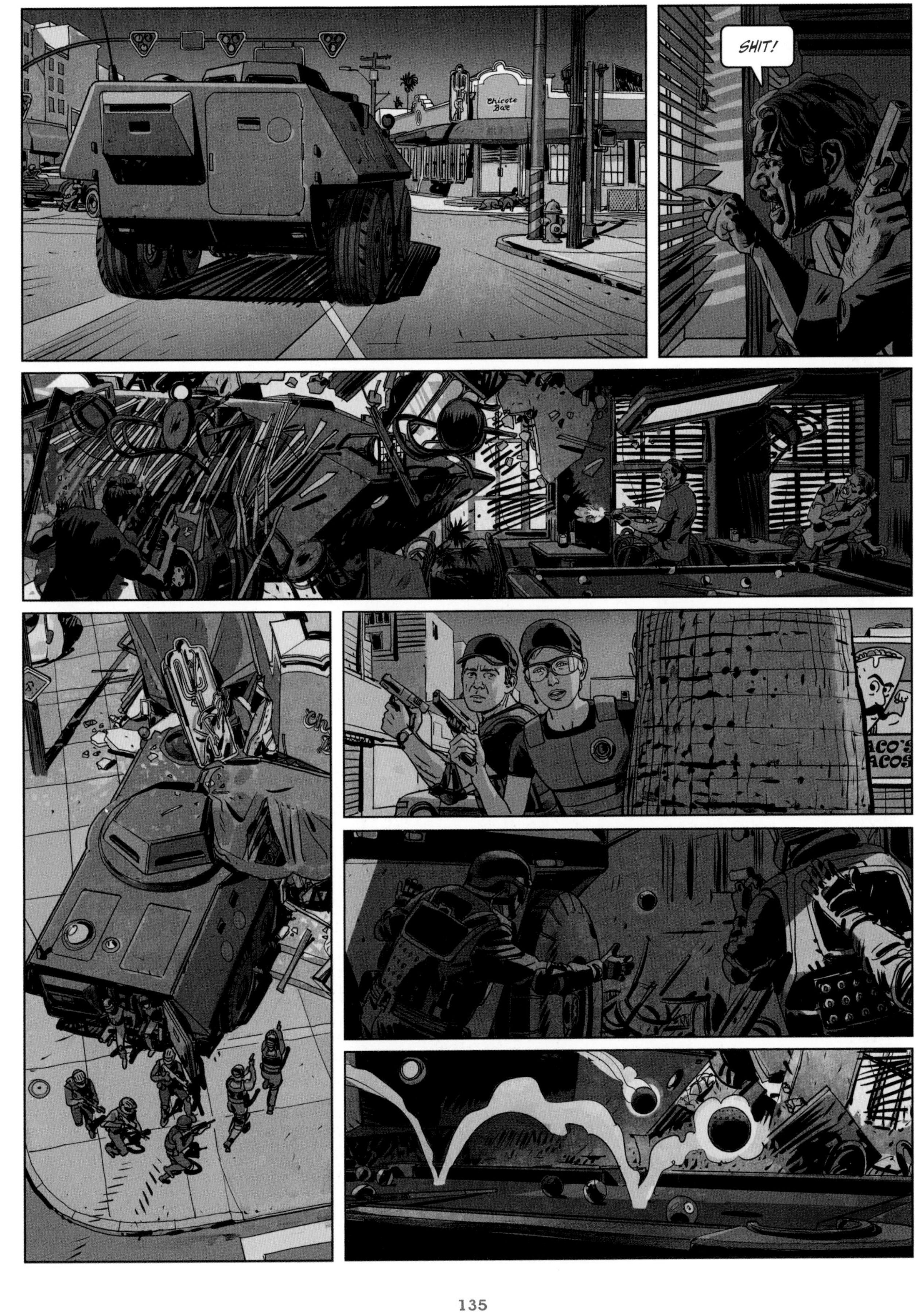
Chicote Bar
SHIT!

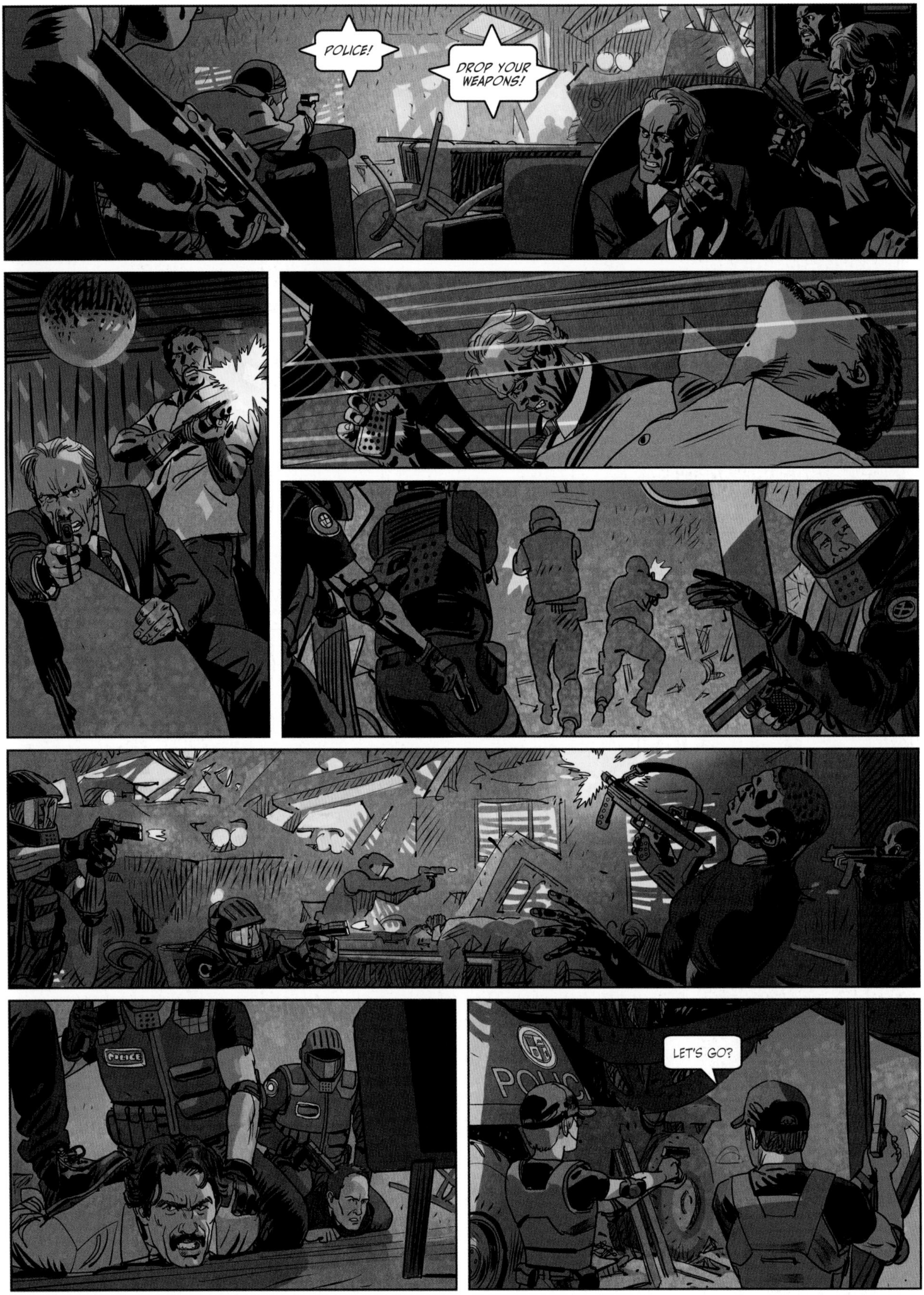
POLICE!
DROP YOUR WEAPONS!
POLICE
POLICE
LET'S GO?

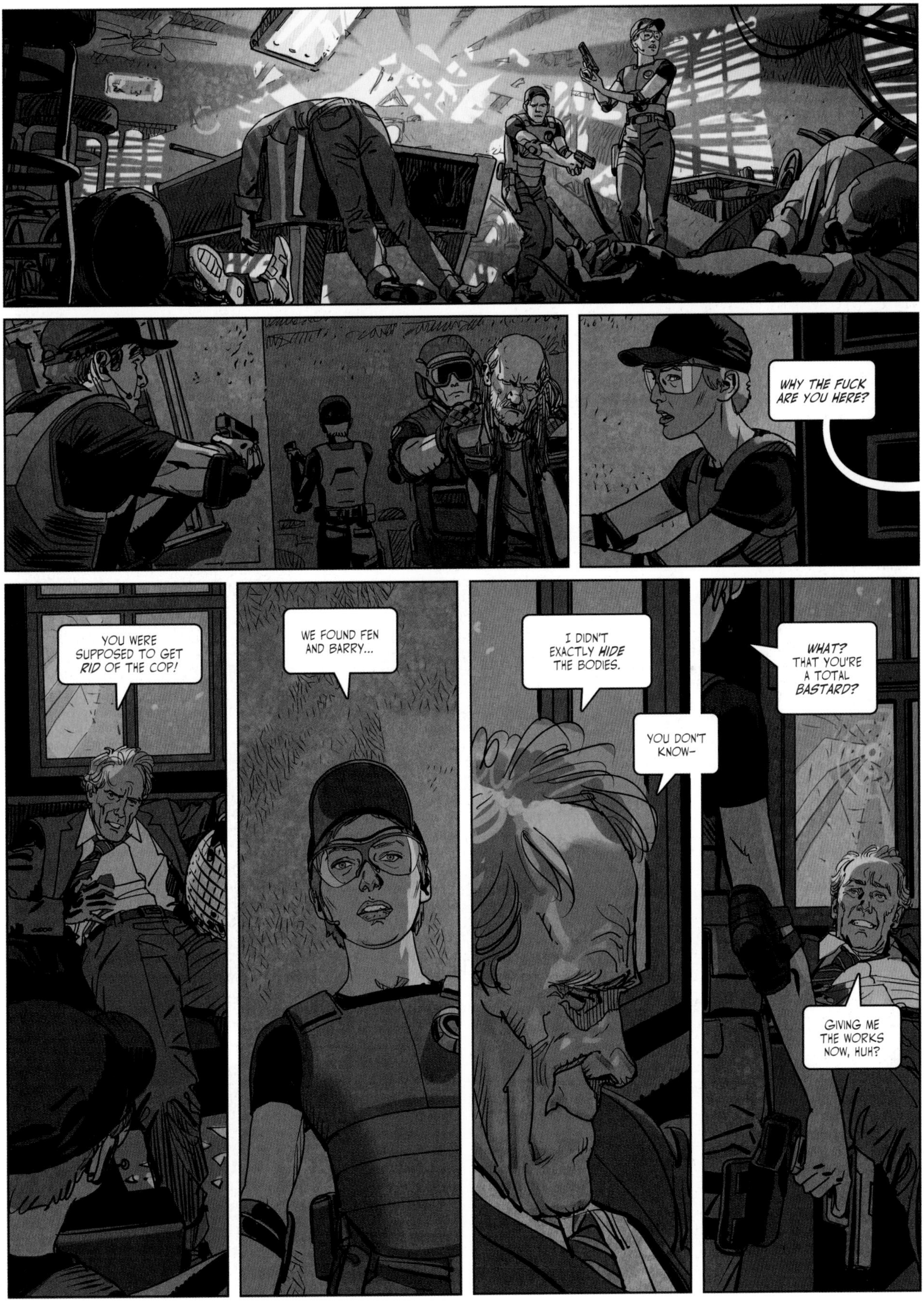

WHY THE FUCK ARE YOU HERE?
YOU WERE SUPPOSED TO GET RID OF THE COP!
WE FOUND FEN AND BARRY...
I DIDN'T EXACTLY HIDE THE BODIES.
YOU DON'T KNOW-
WHAT? THAT YOU'RE A TOTAL BASTARD?
GIVING ME THE WORKS NOW, HUH?

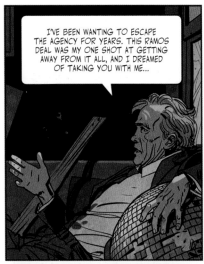

I'VE BEEN WANTING TO ESCAPE THE AGENCY FOR YEARS. THIS RAMOS DEAL WAS MY ONE SHOT AT GETTING AWAY FROM IT ALL, AND I DREAMED OF TAKING YOU WITH ME...

YOU FORGOT ONE MAJOR DETAIL: *ME!* DID YOU REALLY THINK I'D EVER GO *ANYWHERE* WITH YOU?! I DON'T LOVE YOU, JOSH! I'VE NEVER HAD ANY FEELING FOR YOU AT ALL.

YOU ALWAYS STORM AROUND, NEVER GIVING A SHIT ABOUT OTHERS!

LOOK WHERE IT GOT YOU: YOU'RE ALL ALONE...

THAT *BASTARD COP* FUCKED THE WHOLE THING UP... I HAD IT ALL PLANNED OUT PERFECTLY: THEY'D GIVE YOU A NEW FACE, YOU'D GET OVER CHARLIE...

I SHOULDA KILLED HIM SOONER...

WHAT?!

THEN THE TWO OF US COULDA GOT OUTTA HERE TOGETHER...

SHUT THE FUCK UP!

WHAT DID YOU SAY ABOUT CHARLIE?

I'M GONNA CROAK, FLORA. *PLEASE*, GIMME ONE LAST KISS...

WAIT!

THOSE PICS OF CHARLIE...

THEY WERE FAKES...

YOU DON'T WORK FOR THE D.E.A... WHO ARE YOU, THEN?

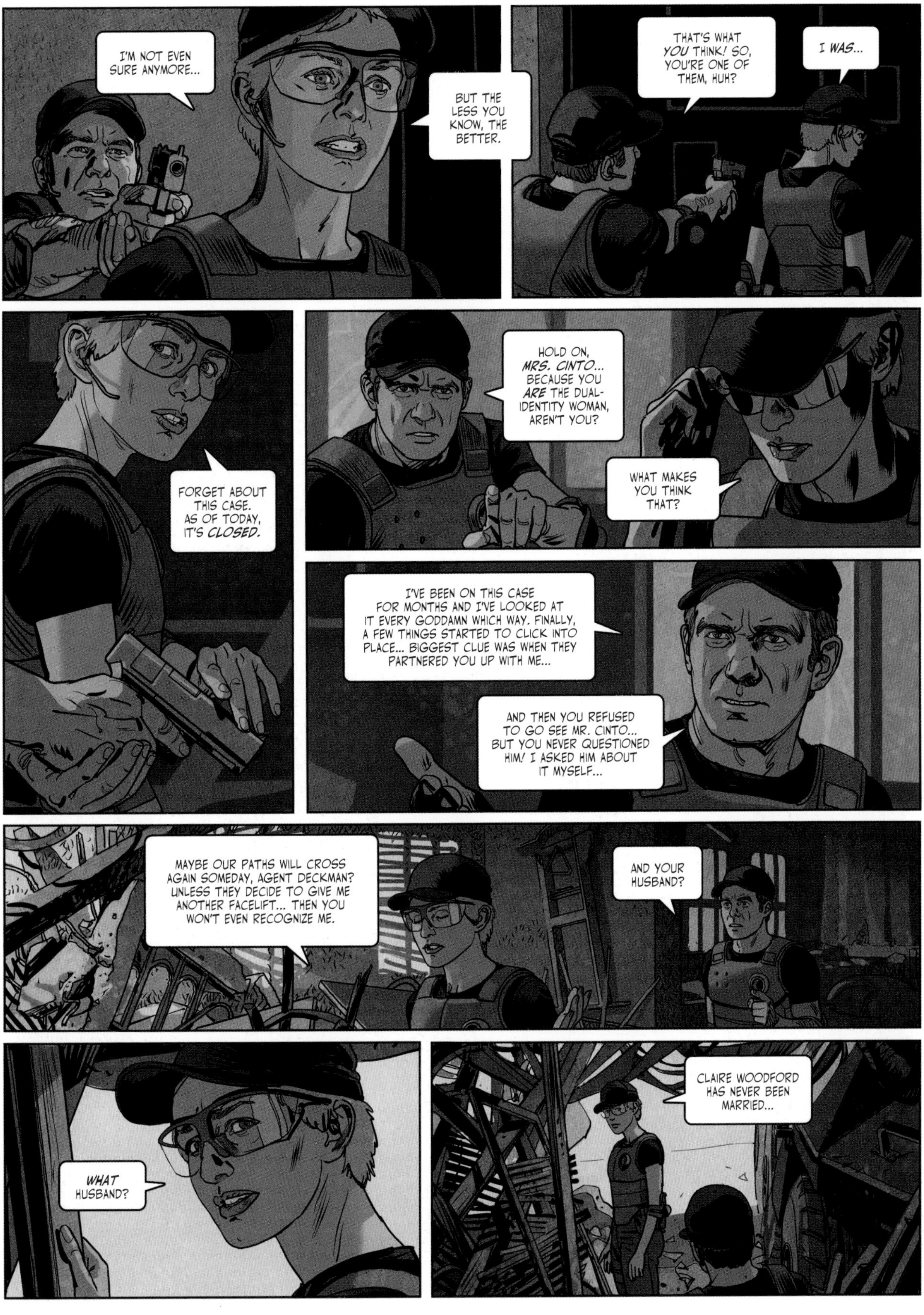
I'M NOT EVEN SURE ANYMORE...
BUT THE LESS YOU KNOW, THE BETTER.
THAT'S WHAT *YOU* THINK! SO, YOU'RE ONE OF THEM, HUH?
I *WAS*...
FORGET ABOUT THIS CASE. AS OF TODAY, IT'S *CLOSED.*
HOLD ON, *MRS. CINTO*... BECAUSE YOU *ARE* THE DUAL-IDENTITY WOMAN, AREN'T YOU?
WHAT MAKES YOU THINK THAT?
I'VE BEEN ON THIS CASE FOR MONTHS AND I'VE LOOKED AT IT EVERY GODDAMN WHICH WAY. FINALLY, A FEW THINGS STARTED TO CLICK INTO PLACE... BIGGEST CLUE WAS WHEN THEY PARTNERED YOU UP WITH ME...
AND THEN YOU REFUSED TO GO SEE MR. CINTO... BUT YOU NEVER QUESTIONED HIM! I ASKED HIM ABOUT IT MYSELF...
MAYBE OUR PATHS WILL CROSS AGAIN SOMEDAY, AGENT DECKMAN? UNLESS THEY DECIDE TO GIVE ME ANOTHER FACELIFT... THEN YOU WON'T EVEN RECOGNIZE ME.
AND YOUR HUSBAND?
WHAT HUSBAND?
CLAIRE WOODFORD HAS NEVER BEEN MARRIED...

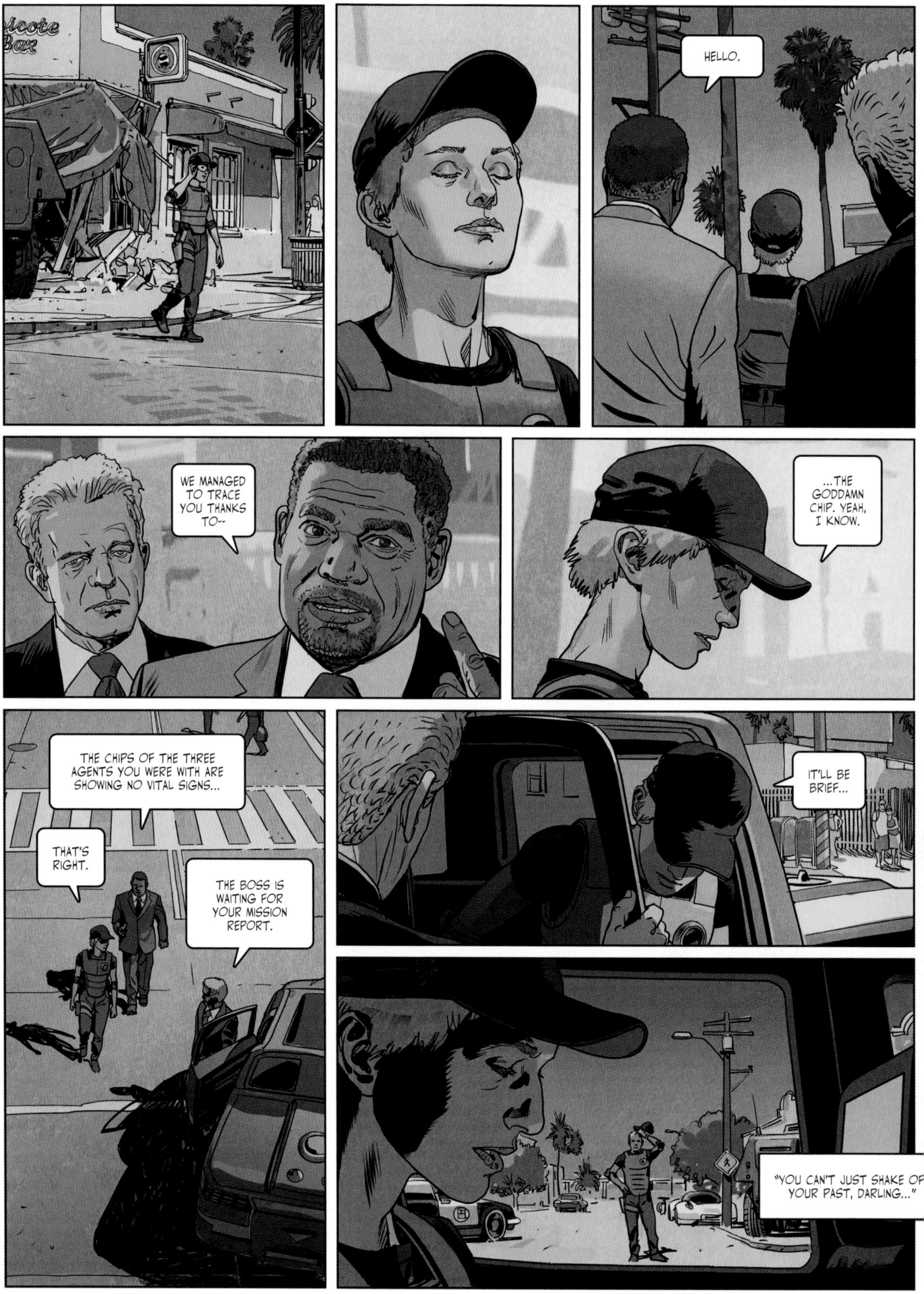
HELLO.
WE MANAGED TO TRACE YOU THANKS TO--
...THE GODDAMN CHIP. YEAH, I KNOW.
THE CHIPS OF THE THREE AGENTS YOU WERE WITH ARE SHOWING NO VITAL SIGNS...
THAT'S RIGHT.
THE BOSS IS WAITING FOR YOUR MISSION REPORT.
IT'LL BE BRIEF...
"YOU CAN'T JUST SHAKE OF
YOUR PAST, DARLING..."

END

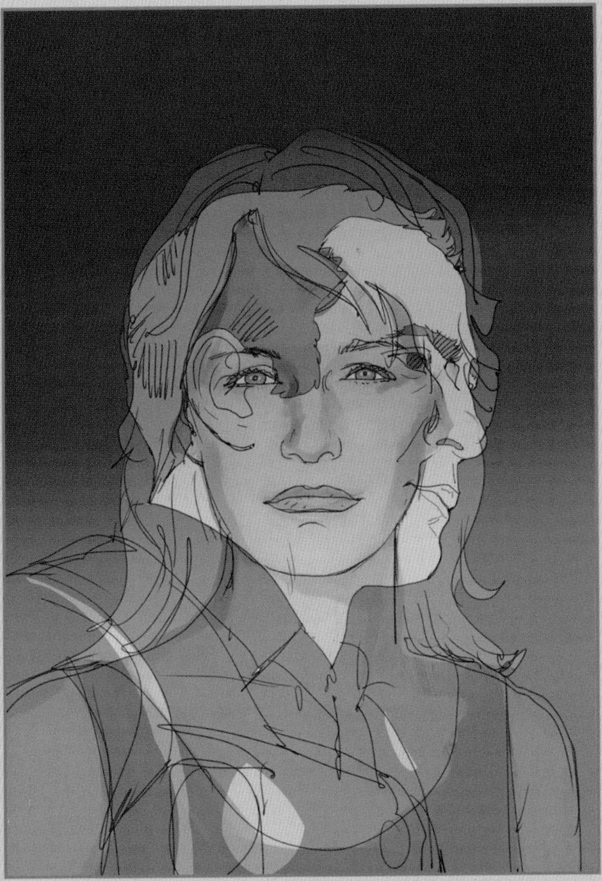

Pencilled cover sketch.

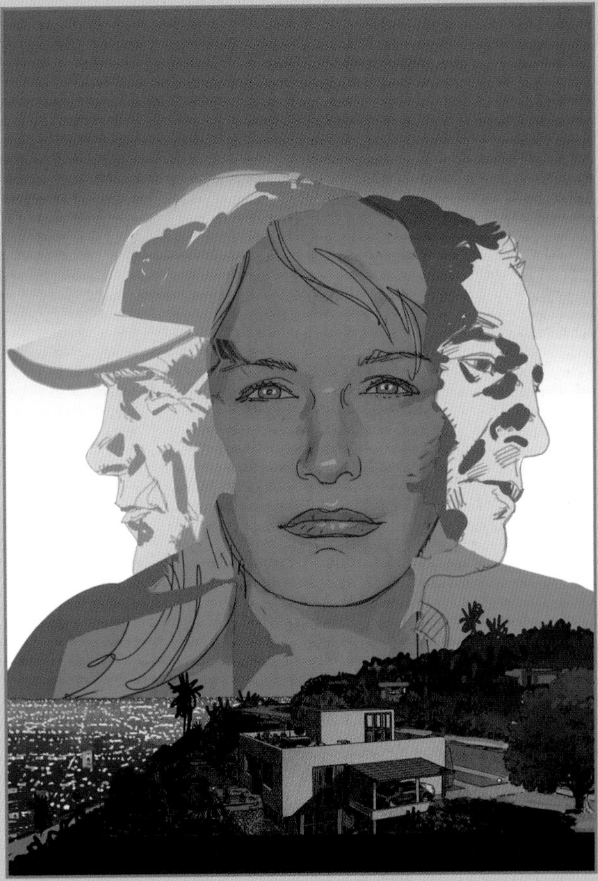

Colored cover sketch.

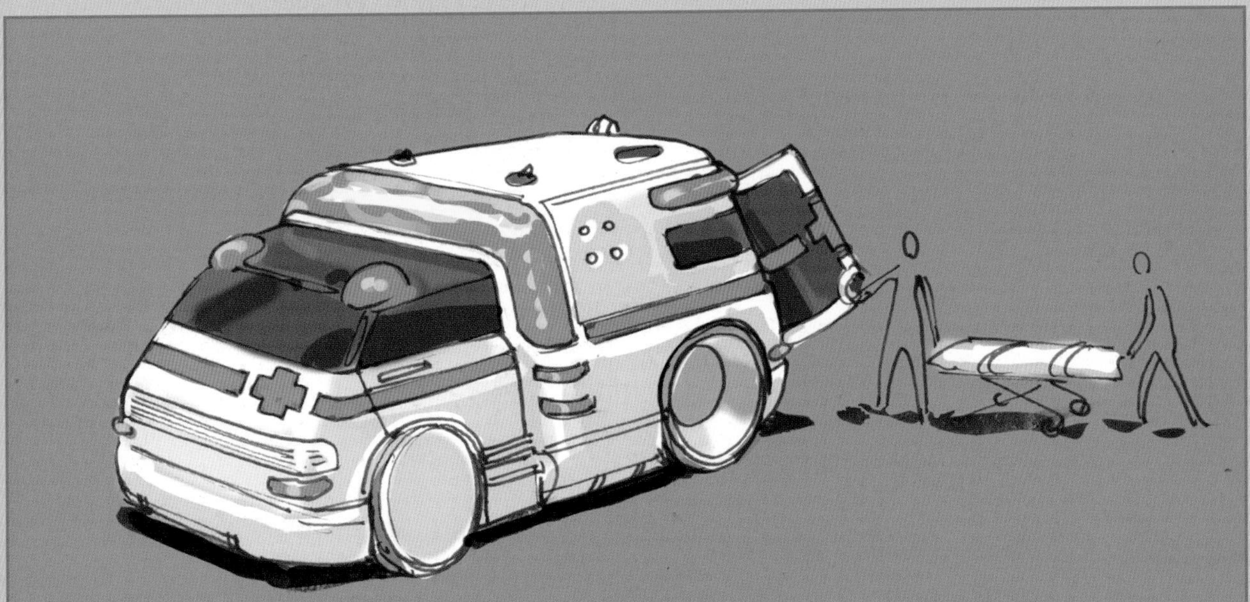

Design for a futuristic ambulance.

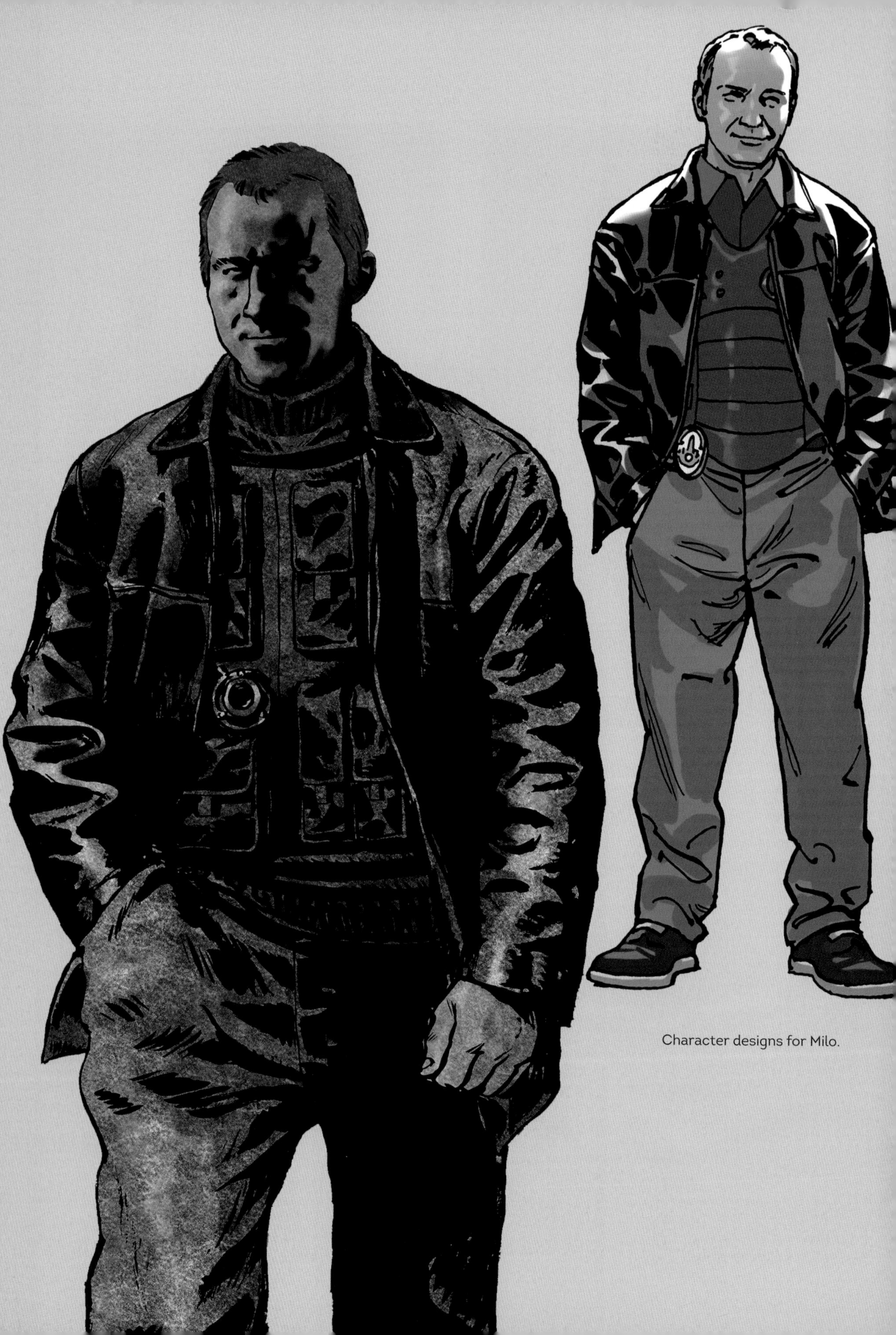

Character designs for Milo.

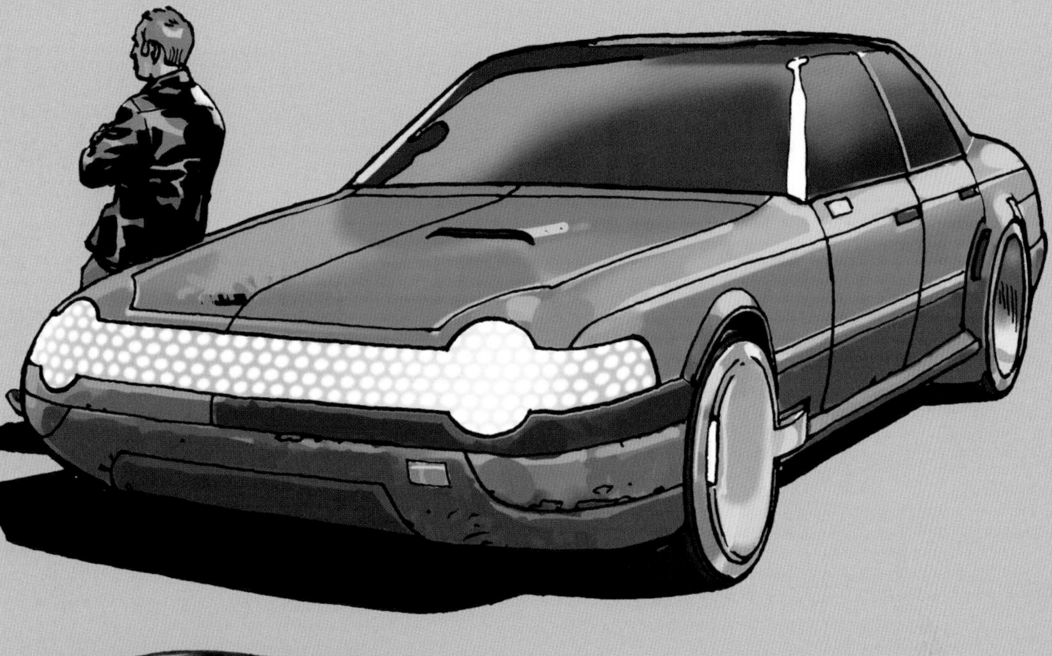

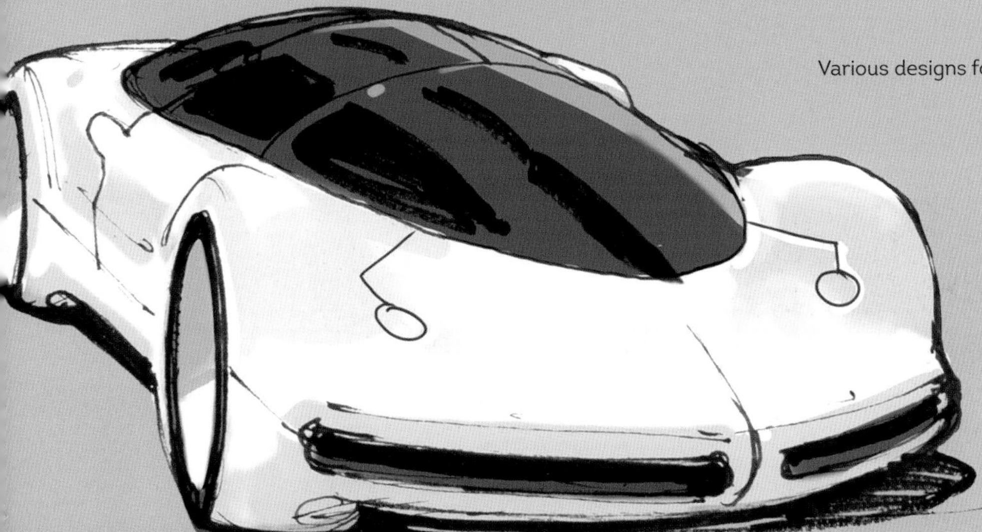

Various designs for futuristic automobiles.

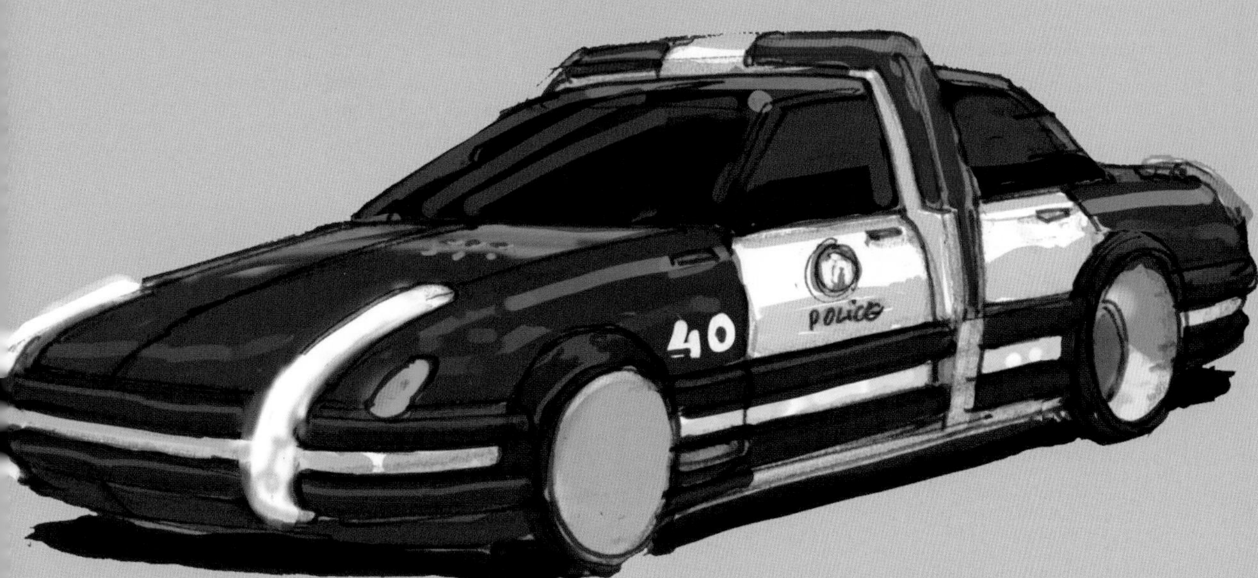
40
POLICE

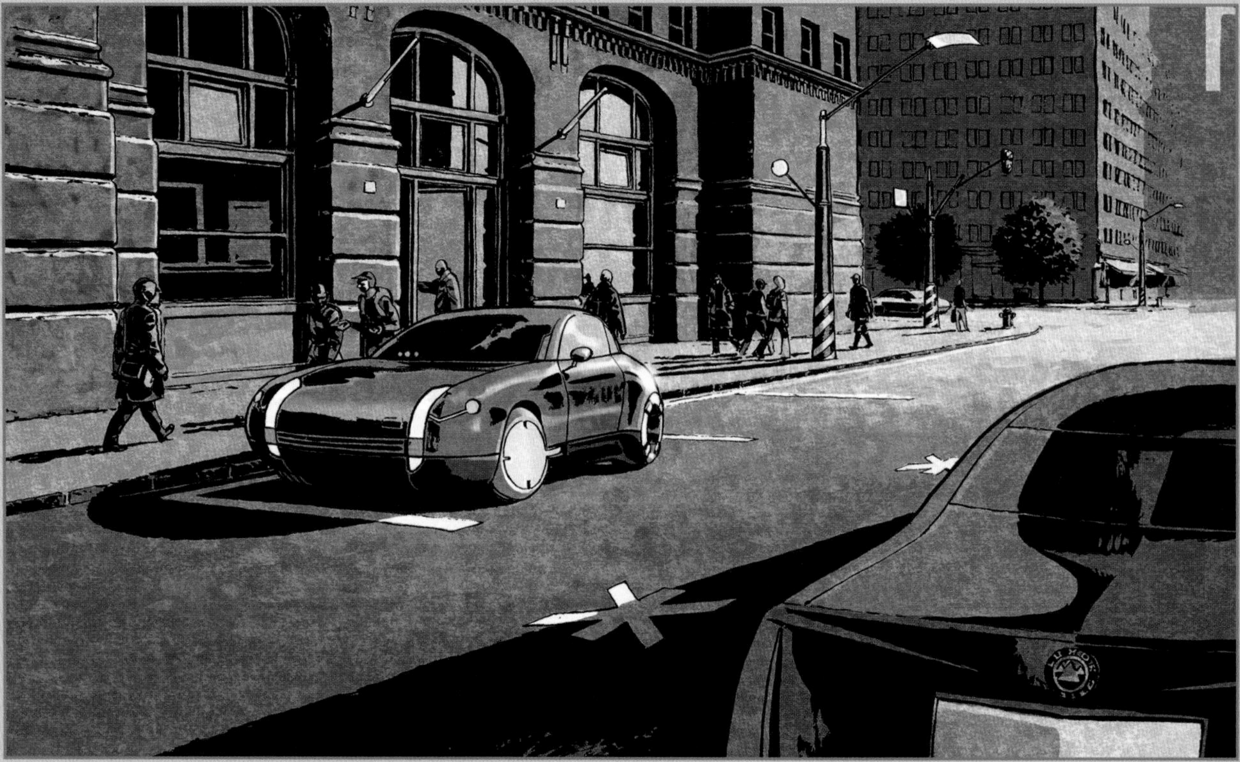

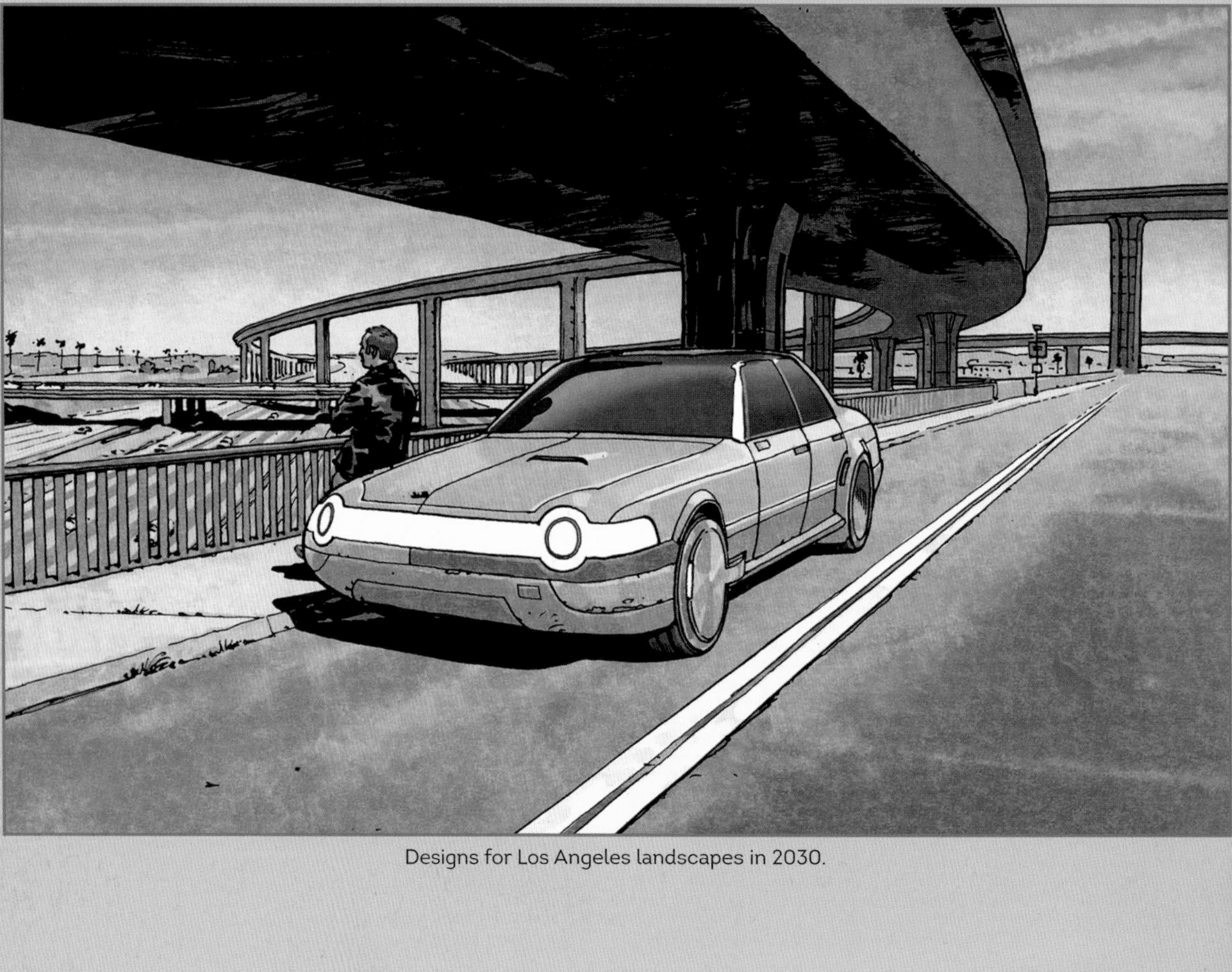

Designs for Los Angeles landscapes in 2030.